C0-AWJ-739

O. HENRY MEMORIAL AWARD PRIZE STORIES

1920

O. HENRY MEMORIAL AWARD

PRIZE STORIES of 1920

CHOSEN BY THE SOCIETY OF ARTS AND SCIENCES

WITH AN INTRODUCTION BY
BLANCHE COLTON WILLIAMS
Author of "A Handbook on Story Writing," "Our Short Story Writers," Etc.
Associate Professor of English, Hunter College of the City of New York
Instructor in Story Writing, Columbia University (Extension Teaching and Summer Session)

GARDEN CITY NEW YORK
DOUBLEDAY, PAGE & COMPANY
1923

PRINTED IN THE UNITED STATES
AT
THE COUNTRY LIFE PRESS, GARDEN CITY, N. Y.

CONTENTS

INTRODUCTION

O. Henry Memorial Award Prize Stories 1919, in its introduction, rendered a brief account of the origin of this monument to O. Henry's genius. Founded in 1918 by the Society of Arts and Sciences, through the initiative of Managing Director John F. Tucker, it took the form of two annual prizes of $500 and $250 for, respectively, the best and second-best stories written by Americans and published in America.

The Committee of Award sifted the periodicals of 1919 and found thirty-two which, in their opinion, were superior specimens of short-story art. The prize-winners, determined in the manner set forth, were Margaret Prescott Montague's "England to America" and Wilbur Daniel Steele's "For They Know Not What They Do." For these stories the authors duly received the awards, on the occasion of the O. Henry Memorial dinner which was given by the Society at the Hotel Astor, June 2, 1920.

Since it appeared to be a fitting extension of the memorial to incorporate in volume form the narratives chosen, they were included, either by title or reprint, in the first book of the series of which this is the second. Thus grouped, they are testimony to unprejudiced selection on the part of the Committee of Award as they are evidence of ability on the part of their authors.

The first volume has met favour from critics and from laymen. For the recognition of tedious, if pleasant, hours necessary to a meticulous survey of twelve months' brief fiction, the Committee of Award are grateful, as they are indebted to the generous coöperation of authors and publishers, but for whom the work would have been impossible of continuation.

The committee express thanks for the approval which affirms that "No more fitting tribute to the genius of William Sidney Porter (O. Henry) could possibly have been devised than that of this 'Memorial Award,'"* which recognizes each

**New York Times*, June 2, 1920.

story as "a definite expression of American life—as O. Henry's was,"* which knows by inescapable logic that a story ranking second with five judges is superior to one ranking first with only one of these. A number of reviewers graciously showed awareness of this fact.

The Committee of Award for 1920 consisted of

BLANCHE COLTON WILLIAMS, Ph. D., Chairman
EDWARD J. WHEELER, Litt. D.
ETHEL WATTS MUMFORD
MERLE ST. CROIX WRIGHT, D.D.
} JUDGES

and JOHN F. TUCKER, Managing Director of the Society, Founder of the O. Henry Memorial.

As in preceding years the Committee held regular meetings at which they weighed the merits of every story-candidate presented. By January, 1921, one hundred and twenty-five remained, among which those rated highest are as follows:†

Babcock, Edwina Stanton, Gargoyle (*Harper's*, Sept.)

Barrett, Richmond Brooks, The Daughter of the Bernsteins (*Smart Set*, July).

"Belden, Jacques," The Duke's Opera (*Munsey's*, October).

Benét, Stephen Vincent, The Funeral of John Bixby (*Munsey's*, July).

Brooks, Jonathan, Bills Playable (*Collier's*, September 18).

Burt, Maxwell Struthers, A Dream or Two (*Harper's*, May); Each in His Generation (*Scribner's*, July).

Cabell, James Branch, The Designs of Miramon (*Century*, August).

Child, Richard Washburn, A Thief Indeed (*Pictorial Review*, June).

Clausen, Carl, The Perfect Crime (*Saturday Evening Post*, Sept. 25).

Cram, Mildred, The Ember (*McCall's*, June); Odell (*Red Book*, May); Wind (*Munsey's*, August).

Dobie, Charles Caldwell, Young China (*Ladies Home Journal*, August).

Edwards, Cleveland, Pride o' Name on Peachtree (*Live Stories*, Feb.).

**Chicago Tribune*, Paris Edition, August 7, 1920.

†Listed alphabetically by authors.

Ferber, Edna, You've Got to Be Selfish (*McClure's*, April).
Fitzgerald, Scott, The Camel's Back (*Saturday Evening Post*, Apr. 24); The Cut-Glass Bowl (*Scribner's*, May); The Off-Shore Pirate (*Saturday Evening Post*, May 29).
Forbes, Esther, Break-Neck Hill (*Grinnell Review*, September).
Gilpatric, Guy, Black Art and Ambrose (*Collier's*, August 21).
Hartman, Lee Foster, The Judgment of Vulcan (*Harper's*, March).
Hergesheimer, Joseph, "Read Them and Weep" (*Century*, January).
Hooker, Brian, Branwen (*Romance*, June).
Hull, Alexander, The Argosies (*Scribner's*, September).
Hume, Wilkie, The Metamorphosis of High Yaller (*Live Stories*, June).
Kahler, Hugh, Fools First (*Saturday Evening Post*, November 20).
Kerr, Sophie, Divine Waste (*Woman's Home Companion*, May).
La Motte, Widows and Orphans (*Century*, September).
Lewis, O. F., Alma Mater (*Red Book*, June). Sparks That Flash in the Night (*Red Book*, October).
Marquis, Don Kale (*Everybody's*, September); Death and Old Man Murtrie (*New Republic*, February 4).
Marshall, Edison, Brother Bill the Elk (*Blue Book*, May).
Means, E. K., The Ten-Share Horse (*Munsey's*, May).
Miller, Alice Duer, Slow Poison (*Saturday Evening Post*, June 12).
Montague, Margaret Prescott, Uncle Sam of Freedom Ridge (*Atlantic Monthly*, June).
*Mumford, Ethel Watts, A Look of the Copperleys (*Ladies Home Journal*, April); Red Gulls (*Pictorial Review*, October).
Newell, Maude Woodruff, Salvage (*Green Book*, July).
Noyes, Frances Newbold, "Contact!"† (*Pictorial Review*, December).

---

*A member of the Committee of Award, this author refused as a matter of course to allow consideration of her stories for republication here or for the prizes. But the other members insist upon their being listed, and upon mention of "Red Gulls" as one of the best stories of 1920.

†Reprinted as by Frances Noyes Hart.

Pelley, William Dudley, The Face in the Window (*Red Book*, May); The Show-Down (*Red Book*, June).
Perry, Lawrence, The Real Game (*Everybody's*, July). A Matter of Loyalty (*Red Book*, July); The Lothario of the Seabird (*Ladies Home Journal*, August); The Rocks of Avalon (*Red Book*, December).
Post, Melville Davisson, The House by the Loch(*Hearst's*, May).
Redington, Sarah, A Certain Rich Woman (*Outlook*, May 5).
Reid, M . F., Doodle Buys a Bull Pup (*Everybody's*, August).
Richardson, Norval, The Bracelet (*McClure's*, July).
Robbins, L. H., "Ain't This the Darnedest World?" (*American*, May); Professor Todd's Used Car (*Everybody's*, July).
"Rutledge, Marice," The Thing They Loved (*Century*, May).
Ryan, Kathryn White, A Man of Cone (*Munsey's*, March).
Scarborough, Dorothy, The Drought (*Century*, May).
"Sidney, Rose," Butterflies (*Pictorial Review*, September).
Smith, Gordon Arthur, No Flowers (*Harper's*, May); The Aristocrat (*Harper's*, November).
Steele, Wilbur Daniel, Both Judge and Jury (*Harper's*, January); God's Mercy (*Pictorial Review*, July); Footfalls (*Pictorial Review*, October).
Synon, Mary, On Scarlet Wings (*Red Book*, July).
Titus, Harold, Aliens (*Ladies Home Journal*, May).
Tuckerman, Arthur, Black Magic, (*Scribner's*, August).
Welles, Harriet, According to Ruskin (*Woman's Home Companion*, June); Distracting Adeline (*Scribner's*, May).
Whitman, Stephen French, The Last Room of All (*Harper's*, June).
Wilkes, Allene Tupper, Toop Goes Skating (*Woman's Home Companion*, November).

From this list were selected seventeen stories which, in the judgment of the Committee, rank highest and which, therefore, are reprinted in this volume.

Since, as will be recalled from the conditions of the award, only American authors were considered, certain familiar foreign names are conspicuously absent. Achmed Abdullah, Stacy Aumonier, F. Britten Austin, Phyllis Bottome, Thomas Burke, Coningsby Dawson, Mrs. Henry Dudeney, Lord

Dunsany, John Galsworthy, Perceval Gibbon, Blasco Ibañez, Maurice Level, A. Neil Lyons, Seumas MacManus, Leonard Merrick, Maria Moravsky, Alfred Noyes, May Sinclair and Hugh Walpole all illustrate recovery from the world war. But with their stories the Committee had nothing to do. The Committee cannot forbear mention, however, of "Under the Tulips" (*Detective Stories*, February 10), one of the two best horror specimens of the year. It is by an Englishwoman, May Edginton.

Half a dozen names from the foreign list just given are synonymous with the best fiction of the period. Yet the short story as practised in its native home continues to excel the short story written in other lands. The English, the Russian, the French, it is being contended in certain quarters, write better literature. They do not, therefore, write better stories. If literature is of a magnificent depth and intricate subtlety in a measure proportionate to its reflection of the vast complexity of a nation that has existed as such for centuries, conceivably it will be facile and clever in a measure proportionate to its reflection of the spirit of the commonwealth which in a few hundred years has acquired a place with age-old empires.

The American short-story is "simple, economical, and brilliantly effective," H. L. Mencken admits.* "Yet the same hollowness that marks the American novel," he continues, "also marks the short story." And of "many current makers of magazine short stories," he asseverates, "such stuff has no imaginable relation to life as men live it in the world." He further comments, "the native author of any genuine force and originality is almost invariably found to be under strong foreign influences, either English or Continental."

With due regard for the justice of this slant—that of a student of Shaw, Ibsen, and Nietzsche—we believe that the best stories written in America to-day reflect life, even life that is sordid and dreary or only commonplace. In the New York *Evening Post*† the present writer observed:

"A backward glance over the short stories of the preceding

*The National Letters, in *Prejudices*, second series, Knopf, N. Y., 1920.

†April 24, 1920.

twelve months discovers two facts. There are many of them, approximately between fifteen hundred and two thousand; there are, comparatively, few of merit.

"You have looked from the rear platform of the limited, across the widening distance, at a town passed a moment ago. A flourishing city, according to the prospectus; a commonplace aggregation of architecture, you say; respectable middle-class homes; time-serving cottages built on the same plan; a heaven-seeking spire; perhaps a work of art in library or townhall. You are rather glad that you have left it behind; rather certain that soon you will have rolled through another, its counterpart.

"But there may be hope, here, of sorts. For a typical American town represents twentieth century life and development, just as current short stories reflect conditions. If the writer failed to represent his age, to reflect its peculiar images, he would not serve it truly."

It is significant that these words preceded by only a few months the publication of Sinclair Lewis's "Main Street," which illustrates in a big and popular way the point in question. Work of satire that it is, it cannot but hold out a solution of the problem presented: in the sweep of the land to the Rockies lies a "dominion which will rise to unexampled greatness when other empires have grown senile."

America is young; its writers are young. But they are reflecting the many-coloured, multiform life of America, in journalism and in art. Quite naturally, they profit by all that has preceded them in other literatures. Since their work stands rooted in romanticism it may legitimately heighten the effects and lights of everyday life.

A glance at the stories republished by the O. Henry Memorial Award Committee for 1920 will reveal their varied nature. The *genus Africanus* is represented by "Black Art and Ambrose," which has a close second in another on the list, "The Metamorphosis of High Yaller," and a third in "The Ten-Share Horse" of E. K. Means. The tabulation reveals a number of cosmic types—Jewish, Chinese, English, French, Irish, Italian, American. The Chinese character is even more ubiquitous than in 1919, but the tales wherein he figures appear to the Committee to be the last drops in the bucket. Two exceptions occur: "Young China," by Charles Caldwell

Dobie, and "Widows and Orphans," by Ellen La Motte. The former knows San Francisco Chinatown, the latter is acquainted with the Oriental at home. One of the Committee regards "The Daughter of the Bernsteins" as the best story of Jewish character. Another sees in it a certain crudeness. Its companions in the year were the tales of Bruno Lessing, Montague Glass, and—in particular—a story by Leon Kelley entitled "Speeches Ain't Business" (*Pictorial Review*, July).

But this note on the list is a digression. With regard to the stories reprinted, "The Last Room of All" illustrates old-world influence, surely, in its recountal of events in an age long past, the time of the Second Emperor Frederick of Swabia. In its revival of old forms, old customs, it is a masquerade. But behold that it is a gorgeous blood-coloured masquerade and that Cercamorte is a distinct portrait of the swash-buckler hero of those times.

The young Americans in "The Camel's Back" support a critical thesis made for their author that he is evolving an idiom. It is the idiom of young America. If you are over thirty, read one of this prodigy's ten-thousand word narratives and discover for the first time that you are separated by a hopeless chasm from the infant world.

"Professor Todd's Used Car" and "Alma Mater" are two of the numerous stories published in 1920 which take up the cudgels for the undertrodden college professor. Incidentally, it is interesting to read from a letter of Mr. Lewis: "The brevity—and the twist in the plot at the end—were consciously patterned on O. Henry's methods."

Without further enumeration of the human types, it is a matter of observation that they exist in many moods and ages as they exist in real life. A revenant who lived one hundred years ago might pick up this volume and secure a fairly accurate idea of society to-day. A visitor from another country might find it a guide to national intelligence and feeling.

A few stories appealed to the Committee for their poetry. "The Funeral of John Bixby," by Stephen Vincent Benét, and "The Duke's Opera," by "Jacques Belden" (the first an allegorical fantasy and the second a poetic-romance) are at the head of this division. With these should be included Don Marquis's "Death and Old Man Murtrie," for its sardonic allegory, and "The Designs of Miramon," by James

Branch Cabell, for its social satire. Individual members of the Committee would have liked to include these—different members preferring different ones of the four—but the Committee as a whole saw the allegory or satire or poetry predominant over story values.

The mysterious and the tragic are found in the work of Mildred Cram and Wilbur Daniel Steele. "Odell" and "Wind" illustrate Miss Cram's particular genius in this direction: but "The Ember," it is voted, ranks first of her publications. Mr. Steele's "Both Judge and Jury" and "God's Mercy" are exotic, perhaps, but the atmosphere he creates is beguiling in comparison with that of mere everyday. "Footfalls" was selected out of an embarrassment of riches offered by this author. The best horror story of the year is Rose Sidney's "Butterflies." It is a Greek tragedy, unrelieved, to be taken or left without palliation.

Athletics, no one will deny, constitutes a definite phase of American life. The sport-struggle is best illustrated in the fiction of Lawrence Perry, whether it be that of a polo match, tennis game, or crew race. "A Matter of Loyalty" is representative of this contest, and in the combined judgment of the Committee the highest ranking of all Mr. Perry's stories. "Bills Playable," by Jonathan Brooks, conceives athletics in a more humorous spirit.

Animal stories fill page upon page of 1920 magazines. Edison Marshall, represented in the 1919 volume, by "The Elephant Remembers," has delivered the epic of "Brother Bill the Elk." In spite of its length, some fifteen thousand words, the Committee were mightily tempted to request it for republication. Its Western author knows the animals in their native lairs. "Break-Neck Hill," for which a member of the Committee suggests the more poignant "Heart-Break Hill" as title, expresses sympathy for the horse in a way the Committee believe hitherto unexploited. "Aliens" received more votes as the best dog story of the year.

Among a number of sea-tales are those by Richard Matthews Hallet, wherein Big Captain Hat appears. The woman sea-captain is by way of being, for the moment, a novel figure.

Anecdotal stories and very brief tales appear to have received editorial sanction in 1920. "No Flowers" is of the former *genre*, and whereas certain of the Committe see in the same author's "The Aristocrat" a larger story, they agree with the majority that the scintillance of this well-polished gem should give it setting here.

Variety of setting and diversity of emotion the reader will find in greater measure, perhaps, than in the first volume of this series. "Butterflies," for example, spells unrelieved horror; "The Face in the Window" demands sympathetic admiration for its heroine; to read "Contact!" means to suffer the familiar Aristotelian purging of the emotions through tears. And their locales are as widely dissimilar as are their emotional appeals. With these, all of which are reprinted herein, the reader will do well to compare Dorothy Scarborough's "Drought," for the pathos of a situation brought about by the elements of nature in Texas.

The Committee could not agree upon the first and second prize stories. The leaders were: "Each in His Generation," "Contact!" "The Thing They Loved," "The Last Room of All," "Slow Poison," "God's Mercy" and "Alma Mater." No story headed more than one list. The point system, to which resort was made, resulted in the first prize falling to "Each in His Generation," by Maxwell Struthers Burt, and the second to "Contact!", by Frances Newbold Noyes (now Frances Noyes Hart).

Mr. Burt's story of Henry McCain and his nephew Adrian compresses within legitimate story limits the antagonism between successive generations. Each representative, bound by traditions and customs of the particular age to which he belongs, is bound also by the chain of inheritance. One interested in the outcome of the struggle between the inexorable thrall of "period" and the inevitable bond of race will find the solution of the problem satisfactory, as will the reader who enjoys the individual situation and wishes most to find out whether Uncle Henry left his money to Adrian or rejected that choice for marriage with the marvellous lady of his own era.

"Contact!" is the first story by the author of "My A.E.F." and in its every line testifies to the vital interest Miss Noyes had and has in the boys who won the war—whether American, French or English. So much one would know from a single rapid reading. A critic might guess that it would have been impossible as a first story if the author had not lived much abroad, as she has done since she was very much of a child. At Oxford, or in the home of Gaston Paris, or travelling around the globe, she received the foundation for the understanding sympathy which endeared her as "Petite" to her soldier boys. A critic might also aver that the steady moving forward of the action, joined to the backward progress, yet both done so surely, could not have been achieved without years of training. And in this respect the narrative is little short of being a *tour de force*. But, as a matter of fact, Miss Noyes dreamed the whole thing! Her antecedent experience proved greater than mere technique.

The Committee wish to comment upon the irregularity of the output of fiction from month to month. May brought forth the greatest number of good stories, as November reaped the fewest. They wish, also, to register notice of the continued flexibility of the short story form. "The Judgment of Vulcan," at one extreme, in some thirteen thousand words none the less relates a short story; "Alma Mater," at the other, accomplishes the same end in two thousand. It is a matter of record that the Committee discovered a number of excellent examples containing not more than two thirds this latter number, a fact that argues against the merging of the short story and the novel. Finally, the Committee believe the fiction of the year 1920 superior to that of 1919.

BLANCHE COLTON WILLIAMS.

NEW YORK CITY,
March 3, 1921.

O. HENRY MEMORIAL AWARD PRIZE STORIES 1920

EACH IN HIS GENERATION

By MAXWELL STRUTHERS BURT

From *Scribner's Magazine*

EVERY afternoon at four o'clock, except when the weather was very bad—autumn, winter, and spring—old Mr. Henry McCain drove up to the small, discreet, polished front door, in the small, discreet, fashionable street in which lived fairly old Mrs. Thomas Denby; got out, went up the white marble steps, rang the bell, and was admitted into the narrow but charming hall—dim turquoise-blue velvet panelled into the walls, an etching or two: Whistler, Brangwyn—by a trim parlour-maid. Ten generations, at least, of trim parlour-maids had opened the door for Mr. McCain. They had seen the sparkling victoria change, not too quickly, to a plum-coloured limousine; they had seen Mr. McCain become perhaps a trifle thinner, the colour in his cheeks become a trifle more confined and fixed, his white hair grow somewhat sparser, but beyond that they had seen very little indeed, although, when they had left Mr. McCain in the drawing-room with the announcement that Mrs. Denby would be down immediately, and were once again seeking the back of the house, no doubt their eyebrows, blonde, brunette, or red, apexed to a questioning angle.

In the manner of youth the parlour-maids had come, worked, fallen in love and departed, but Mr. McCain, in the manner of increasing age, had if anything grown more faithful and exact to the moment. If he were late the fraction of five minutes, one suspected that he regretted it, that it came near to spoiling his entire afternoon. He was not articulate, but occasionally he expressed an idea and the most common was that he "liked his things as he liked them"; his eggs, in other words, boiled just so long, no more —after sixty years of inner debate on the subject he had apparently arrived at the conclusion that boiled eggs were the only kind of eggs permissible —his life punctual and serene. The smallest manifestation of unexpectedness disturbed him. Obviously that was one reason why, after a youth not altogether constant, he had become so utterly constant where Mrs. Denby was concerned. She had a quality of perenniality, charming and assuring, even to each strand of her delicate brown hair. Grayness should have been creeping upon her, but it was not. It was doubtful if Mr. McCain permitted himself, even secretly, to wonder why. Effects, fastidious and constant, were all he demanded from life.

This had been going on for twenty years—this afternoon call; this slow drive afterward in the park; this return by dusk to the shining small house in the shining small street; the good-by, reticently ardent, as if it were not fully Mr. McCain's intention to return again in the evening. Mr. McCain would kiss Mrs. Denby's hand—slim, lovely, with a single gorgeous sapphire upon the third finger. "Good-by, my dear," he would say, "you have given me the most delightful afternoon of my life." For a moment Mrs. Denby's hand would linger on the bowed head; then Mr. McCain would straighten up, smile, square his shoulders in their smart, young-looking coat, and depart to his club, or the large, softly lit house where he dwelt alone. At dinner he would drink two glasses of champagne. Before he drained the last sip of the second pouring he would hold the glass up to the fire, so that the bronze coruscations at the heart of the wine glowed like fireflies in a gold dusk. One imagined him saying to himself: "A perfect woman! A perfect woman—God bless her!" Saying "God bless" any one, mind you, with a distinct warming of the heart, but a thoroughly late-Victorian disbelief in any god to bless. . . . At least, you thought as much.

And, of course, one had not the slightest notion whether he —old Mr. Henry McCain—was aware that this twenty years of devotion on his part to Mrs. Denby was the point upon which had come to focus the not inconsiderable contempt and hatred for him of his nephew Adrian.

It was an obvious convergence, this devotion of all the traits which composed, so Adrian imagined, the despicable soul that lay beneath his uncle's unangled exterior: undeviating self-indulgence; secrecy; utter selfishness—he was selfish even to the woman he was supposed to love; that is, if he was capable of loving any one but himself—a bland hypocrisy; an unthinking conformation to the dictates of an unthinking world. The list could be multiplied. But to sum it up, here was epitomized, beautifully, concretely, the main and minor vices of a generation for which Adrian found little pity in his heart; a generation brittle as ice; a generation of secret diplomacy; a generation that in its youth had covered a lack of bathing by a vast amount of perfume. That was it—! That expressed it perfectly! The just summation! Camellias, and double intentions in speech, and unnecessary reticences, and refusals to meet the truth, and a deliberate hiding of uglinesses!

Most of the time Adrian was too busy to think about his uncle at all—he was a very busy man with his writing: journalistic writing; essays, political reviews, propaganda—and because he was busy he was usually well-content, and not uncharitable, except professionally; but once a month it was his duty to dine with his uncle, and then, for the rest of the night, he was disturbed, and awoke the next morning with the dusty feeling in his head of a man who has been slightly drunk. Old wounds were recalled, old scars inflamed; a childhood in which his uncle's figure had represented to him the terrors of sarcasm and repression; a youth in which, as his guardian, his uncle had deprecated all first fine hot-bloodednesses and enthusiasms; a young manhood in which he had been told cynically that the ways of society were good ways, and that the object of life was material advancement; advice which had been followed by the stimulus of an utter refusal to assist financially except where absolutely necessary. There had been willingness, you understand, to provide a gentleman's education, but no willingness to provide beyond that any of a gentleman's perquisites. That much of his early success had been due to this heroic upbringing, Adrian was too honest not to admit, but then—by God, it had been hard! All the colour of youth! No time to dream—except sorely! Some warping, some perversion! A gasping, heart-breaking knowledge that you could not possibly keep up with the people with whom, paradoxically enough, you were supposed to spend your leisure hours. Here was the making of a radical. And yet, despite all this, Adrian dined with his uncle once a month.

The mere fact that this was so, that it could be so, enraged him. It seemed a renunciation of all he affirmed; an implicit falsehood. He would have liked very much to have got to his feet, standing firmly on his two long, well-made legs, and have once and for all delivered himself of a final philippic. The philippic would have ended something like this:

"And this, sir, is the last time I sacrifice any of my good hours to you. Not because you are old, and therefore think you are wise, when you are not; not because you are blind and besotted and damned—a trunk of a tree filled with dry rot that presently a clean wind will blow away; not because your opinions, and the opinions of all like you, have long ago been proven the lies and idiocies that they are; not even because you haven't one single real right left to live—I haven't come to tell you these things, although they are true; for you are past hope and there is no use wasting words upon you; I have come to tell you that you bore me inexpressibly. (That would be the most dreadful revenge of all. He could see his uncle's face!) That you have a genius for taking the wrong side of every question, and I can no longer endure it. I dissipate my time. Good-night!"

He wouldn't have said it in quite so stately a way, possibly, the sentences would not have been quite so rounded, but the context would have been the same.

Glorious; but it wasn't said. Instead, once a month, he got into his dinner-jacket, brushed his hair very sleekly, walked six blocks, said good-evening to his uncle's butler, and went on back to the library, where, in a room rich with costly bindings, and smelling pleasantly of leather, and warmly yellow with the light of two shaded lamps, he would find his uncle reading before a crackling wood fire. What followed was almost a formula, an exquisite presentation of stately manners, an exquisite avoidance of any topic which might cause a real discussion. The dinner was invariably gentle, persuasive, a thoughtful gastronomic achievement. Heaven might become confused about its weather, and about wars, and things like that, but Mr. McCain never became confused about his menus. He had a habit of commending wine. "Try this claret, my dear fellow, I want your opinion. . . . A drop of this Napoleonic brandy won't hurt you a bit." He even sniffed the bouquet before each sip; passed, that is, the glass under his nose and then drank. But Adrian, with a preconceived image of the personality back of this, and the memory of too many offences busy in his mind, saw nothing quaint or amusing. His gorge rose. Damn his uncle's wines, and his mushrooms, and his soft-footed servants, and his house of nuances and evasions, and his white grapes, large and outwardly perfect, and inwardly sentimental as the generation whose especial fruit they were. As for himself, he had a recollection of ten years of poverty after leaving college; a recollection of sweat and indignities; he had also a recollection of some poor people whom he had known.

Afterward, when the dinner was over, Adrian would go home and awake his wife, Cecil, who, with the brutal honesty of an honest woman, also some of the ungenerosity, had early in her married life flatly refused any share in the ceremonies described. Cecil would lie in her small white bed, the white of her boudoir-cap losing itself in the white of the pillow, a little sleepy and a little angrily perplexed at the perpetual jesuitical philosophy of the male. "If you feel that way," she would ask, "why do you go there, then? Why don't you banish your uncle utterly?" She asked this not without malice, her long, violet, Slavic eyes widely open, and her red mouth, a trifle too large, perhaps, a trifle cruel, fascinatingly interrogative over her white teeth. She loved Adrian and had at times, therefore, the right and desire to torture him. She knew perfectly well why he went. He was his uncle's heir, and until such time as money and other anachronisms of the present social system were done away with, there was no use throwing a fortune into the gutter, even if by your own efforts you were making an income just sufficiently large to keep up with the increased cost of living.

Sooner or later Adrian's mind reverted to Mrs. Denby. This was usually after he had been in bed and had been thinking for a while in the darkness. He could not understand Mrs. Denby. She affronted his modern habit of thought.

"The whole thing is so silly and adventitious!"

"What thing?"

Adrian was aware that his wife knew exactly of what he was talking, but he had come to expect the question. "Mrs. Denby and my uncle." He would grow rather gently cross. "It has always reminded me of those present-day sword-and-cloak romances fat business men used to write about ten years ago and sell so enormously—there's an atmosphere of unnecessary intrigue. What's it all about? Here's the point! Why, if she felt this way about things, didn't she divorce that gentle drunkard of a husband of hers years ago and marry my uncle outright and honestly? Or why, if she couldn't get a divorce—which she could—didn't she leave her husband and go with my uncle? Anything in the open! Make a break—have some courage of her opinions! Smash things; build them up again! Thank God nowadays, at least, we have come to believe in the cleanness of surgery rather than the concealing palliatives of medicine. We're no longer—we modern people—afraid of the world; and the world can never hurt for any length of time any one who will stand up to it and tell it courageously to go to hell. No! It comes back and licks hands.

"I'll tell you why. My uncle and Mrs. Denby are the typical moral cowards of their generation. There's selfishness, too. What a travesty of love! Of course there's scandal, a perpetual scandal; but it's a hidden, sniggering scandal they don't have to meet face to face; and that's all they ask of life, they, and people like them—never to have to meet anything face to face. So long as they can bury their heads like ostriches! . . . Faugh!" There would be a moment's silence; then Adrian would complete his thought. "In my uncle's case," he would grumble in the darkness, "one phase of the selfishness is obvious. He couldn't even get himself originally, I suppose, to face the inevitable matter-of-fact moments of marriage. It began when he was middle-aged, a bachelor—I suppose he wants the sort of Don Juan, eighteen-eighty, perpetual sort of romance that doesn't exist outside the brains of himself and his like. . . . Camellias!"

Usually he tried to stir up argument with his wife, who in these matters agreed with him utterly; even more than agreed with him, since she was the escaped daughter of rich and stodgy people, and had insisted upon earning her own living by portrait-painting. Theoretically, therefore, she was, of course, an anarchist. But at moments like the present her silent assent and the aura of slight weariness over an ancient subject which emanated from her in the dusk, affronted Adrian as much as positive opposition.

"Why don't you try to understand me?"

"I do, dearest!"—a pathetic attempt at eager agreement.

"Well, then, if you do, why is the tone of your voice like that? You know by now what I think. I'm not talking convention; I believe there are no laws higher than the love of a man for a woman. It should seek expression as a seed seeks sunlight. I'm talking about honesty; bravery; a willingness to accept the consequences of one's acts and come through; about the intention to sacrifice for love just what has to be sacrificed. What's the use of it otherwise? That's one real advance the modern mind has made, anyhow, despite all the rest of the welter and uncertainty."

"Of course, dearest."

He would go on. After a while Cecil would awake guiltily and inject a fresh, almost gay interest into her sleepy voice. She was not so unfettered as not to dread the wounded esteem of the unlistened-to male. She would lean over and kiss Adrian.

"Do go to sleep, darling! What's the sense? Pretty soon your uncle will be dead—wretched old man! Then you'll never have to think of him again." Being a childless woman, her red, a trifle cruel mouth would twist itself in the darkness into a small, secretive, maternal smile.

But old Mr. Henry McCain didn't die; instead he seemed to be caught up in the condition of static good health which frequently companions entire selfishness and a careful interest in oneself. His butler died, which was very annoying. Mr. McCain seemed to consider it the breaking of a promise made fifteen or so years before. It was endlessly a trouble instructing a new man, and then, of course, there was Adlington's family to be looked after, and taxes had gone up, and Mrs. Adlington was a stout woman who, despite the fact that Adlington, while alive, had frequently interrupted Mr. McCain's breakfast newspaper reading by asserting that she was a person of no character, now insisted upon weeping noisily every time Mr. McCain granted her an interview. Also, and this was equally unexpected, since one rather thought he would go on living forever, like one of the damper sort of fungi, Mr. Denby came home from the club one rainy spring night with a slight cold and died, three days later, with extraordinary gentleness.

"My uncle," said Adrian, "is one by one losing his accessories. After a while it will be his teeth."

Cecil was perplexed. "I don't know exactly what to do," she complained. "I don't know whether to treat Mrs. Denby as a bereaved aunt, a non-existent family skeleton, or a released menace. I dare say now, pretty soon, she and your uncle will be married. Meanwhile, I suppose it is rather silly of me not to call and see if I can help her in any way. After all, we do know her intimately, whether we want to or not, don't we? We meet her about all the time, even if she wasn't motoring over to your uncle's place in the summer when we stop there."

So she went, being fundamentally kindly and fundamentally curious. She spoke of the expedition as "a descent upon Fair Rosamund's tower."

The small, yellow-panelled drawing-room, where she awaited Mrs. Denby's coming, was lit by a single silver vase-lamp under an orange shade and by a fire of thin logs, for the April evening was damp with a hesitant rain. On the table, near the lamp, was a silver vase with three yellow tulips in it, and Cecil, wandering about, came upon a double photograph frame, back of the vase, that made her gasp. She picked it up and stared at it. Between the alligator edgings, facing each other obliquely, but with the greatest amity, were Mr. Thomas Denby in the fashion of ten years before, very handsome, very well-groomed, with the startled expression which any definite withdrawal from his potational pursuits was likely to produce upon his countenance, and her uncle-in-law, Mr. Henry McCain, also in the fashion of ten years back. She was holding the photographs up to the light, her lips still apart, when she heard a sound behind her, and, putting the frame back guiltily, turned about. Mrs. Denby was advancing toward her. She seemed entirely unaware of Cecil's malfeasance; she was smiling faintly; her hand was cordial, grateful.

"You are very good," she murmured. "Sit here by the fire. We will have some tea directly."

Cecil could not but admit that she was very lovely; particularly lovely in the black of her mourning, with her slim neck, rising up from its string of pearls, to a head small and like a delicate white-and-gold flower. An extraordinarily well-bred woman, a sort of misty Du Maurier woman, of a type that had become almost non-existent, if ever it had existed in its perfection at all. And, curiously enough, a woman whose beauty seemed to have been sharpened by many fine-drawn renunciations. Now she looked at her hands as if expecting Cecil to say something.

"I think such calls as this are always very useless, but then——"

"Exactly—but then! They mean more than anything else in the world, don't they? When one reaches fifty-five one is not always used to kindness. . . . You are very kind. . . ." She raised her eyes.

Cecil experienced a sudden impulsive warmth. "After all, what did she or any one else know about other peoples' lives? Poor souls! What a base thing life often was!"

"I want you to understand that we are always so glad, both Adrian and myself. . . . Any time we can help in any way, you know——"

"Yes, I think you would. You—I have watched you both. You don't mind, do you? I think you're both rather great people—at least, my idea of greatness."

Cecil's eyes shone just a little; then she sat back and drew together her eager, rather childish mouth. This wouldn't do! She had not come here to encourage sentimentalization. With a determined effort she lifted her mind outside the circle of commiseration which threatened to surround it. She deliberately reset the conversation to impersonal limits. She was sure that Mrs. Denby was aware of her intention, adroitly concealed as it was. This made her uncomfortable, ashamed. And yet she was irritated with herself. Why should she particularly care what this woman thought in ways as subtle as this? Obvious kindness was her intention, not mental charity pursued into tortuous by-paths. And, besides, her frank, boyish cynicism, its wariness, revolted, even while she felt herself flattered at the prospect of the confidences that seemed to tremble on Mrs. Denby's lips. It wouldn't do to "let herself in for anything"; to "give herself away." No! She adopted a manner of cool, entirely reflective kindliness. But all along she was not sure that she was thoroughly successful. There was a lingering impression that Mrs. Denby was penetrating the surface to the unwilling interest beneath. Cecil suspected that this woman was trained in discriminations and half-lights to which she and her generation had joyfully made themselves blind. She felt uncomfortably young; a little bit smiled at in the most kindly of hidden ways. Just as she was leaving, the subversive softness came close to her again, like a wave of too much perfume as you open a church-door; as if some one were trying to embrace her against her will.

"You will understand," said Mrs. Denby, "that you have done the very nicest thing in the world. I am horribly lonely. I have few women friends. Perhaps it is too much to ask—but if you could call again sometime. Yes . . . I would appreciate it so greatly."

She let go of Cecil's hand and walked to the door, and stood with one long arm raised against the curtain, her face turned toward the hall.

"There is no use," she said, "in attempting to hide my husband's life, for every one knows what it was, but then—yes, I think you will understand. I am a childless woman, you see; he was infinitely pathetic."

Cecil felt that she must run away, instantly. "I do—" she said brusquely. "I understand more than other women. Perfectly! Good-by!"

She found herself brushing past the latest trim parlour-maid, and out once more in the keen, sweet, young dampness. She strode briskly down the deserted street. Her fine bronze eyebrows were drawn down to where they met. "Good Lord! Damn!"—Cecil swore very prettily and modernly—"What rotten taste! Not frankness, whatever it might seem outwardly; not frankness, but devious excuses! Some more of Adrian's hated past-generation stuff! And yet—no! The woman was sincere—perfectly! She had meant it—that about her husband. And she *was* lovely—and she was fine, too! It was impossible to deny it. But—a childless woman! About that drunken tailor's model of a husband! And then—Uncle Henry! . . ." Cecil threw back her head; her eyes gleamed in the wet radiance of a corner lamp; she laughed without making a sound, and entirely without amusement.

But it is not true that good health is static, no matter how carefully looked after. And, despite the present revolt against the Greek spirit, Time persists in being bigotedly Greek. The tragedy—provided one lives long enough—is always played out to its logical conclusion. For every hour you have spent, no matter how quietly or beautifully or wisely, Nemesis takes toll in the end. You peter out; the engine dulls; the shining coin wears thin. If it's only that it is all right; you are fortunate if you don't become greasy, too, or blurred, or scarred. And Mr. McCain had not spent all his hours wisely or beautifully, or even quietly, underneath the surface. He suddenly developed what he called "acute indigestion." "Odd!" he complained, "and exceedingly tiresome! I've been able to eat like an ostrich all my life." Adrian smiled covertly at the simile, but his uncle was unaware that it was because in Adrian's mind the simile applied to his uncle's conscience, not his stomach.

It *was* an odd disease, that "acute indigestion." It manifested itself by an abrupt tragic stare in Mr. McCain's eyes, a whiteness of cheek, a clutching at the left side of the breast; it resulted also in his beginning to walk very slowly indeed. One day Adrian met Carron, his uncle's physician, as he was leaving a club after luncheon. Carron stopped him. "Look here, Adrian," he said, "is that new man of your uncle's—that valet, or whatever he is—a good man?"

Adrian smiled. "I didn't hire him," he answered, "and I couldn't discharge him if I wanted—in fact, any suggestion of that kind on my part, would lead to his employment for life. Why?"

"Because," said Carron, "he impresses me as being rather young and flighty, and some day your uncle is going to die suddenly. He may last five years; he may snuff out to-morrow. It's his heart." His lips twisted pityingly. "He prefers to call it by some other name," he added, "and he would never send for me again if he knew I had told you, but you ought to know. He's a game old cock, isn't he?"

"Oh, very!" agreed Adrian. "Yes, game! Very, indeed!"

He walked slowly down the sunlit courtway on which the back door of the club opened, swinging his stick and meditating. Spring was approaching its zenith. In the warm May afternoon pigeons tumbled about near-by church spires which cut brown inlays into the soft blue sky. There was a feeling of open windows; a sense of unseen tulips and hyacinths; of people playing pianos. . . . Too bad, an old man dying that way, his hand furtively seeking his heart, when all this spring was about! Terror in possession of him, too! People like that hated to die; they couldn't see anything ahead. Well, Adrian reflected, the real tragedy of it hadn't been his fault. He had always been ready at the slightest signal to forget almost everything—yes, almost everything. Even that time when, as a sweating newspaper reporter, he had, one dusk, watched in the park his uncle and Mrs. Denby drive past in the cool seclusion of a shining victoria. Curious! In itself the incident was small, but it had stuck in his memory more than others far more serious, as concrete instances are likely to do. . . . No, he wasn't sorry; not a bit! He was glad, despite the hesitation he experienced in saying to himself the final word. He had done his best, and this would mean his own release and Cecil's. It would mean at last the blessed feeling that he could actually afford a holiday, and a little unthinking laughter, and, at thirty-nine, the dreams for which, at twenty-five, he had never had full time. He walked on down the courtway more briskly.

That Saturday night was the night he dined with his uncle. It had turned very warm; unusually warm for the time of year. When he had dressed and had sought out Cecil to say good-by to her he found her by the big studio window on the top floor of the apartment where they lived. She was sitting in the window-seat, her chin cupped in her hand, looking out over the city, in the dark pool of which lights were beginning to open like yellow water-lilies. Her white arm gleamed in the gathering dusk, and she was dressed in some diaphanous blue stuff that enhanced the bronze of her hair. Adrian took his place silently beside her and leaned out. The air was very soft and hot and embracing, and up here it was very quiet, as if one floated above the lower clouds of perpetual sound.

Cecil spoke at last. "It's lovely, isn't it?" she said. "I should have come to find you, but I couldn't. These first warm nights! You really understand why people live, after all, don't you? It's like a pulse coming back to a hand you love." She was silent a moment. "Kiss me," she said, finally. "I—I'm so glad I love you, and we're young."

He stooped down and put his arms about her. He could feel her tremble. How fragrant she was, and queer, and mysterious, even if he had lived with her now for almost fifteen years! He was infinitely glad at the moment for his entire life. He kissed her again, kissed her eyes, and she went down the stairs with him to the hall-door. She was to stop for him at his uncle's, after a dinner to which she was going.

Adrian lit a cigarette and walked instead of taking the elevator. It was appropriate to his mood that on the second floor some one with a golden Italian voice should be singing "Louise." He paused for a moment. He was reminded of a night long ago in Verona, when there had been an open window and moonlight in the street. Then he looked at his watch. He was late; he would have to hurry. It amused him that at his age he should still fear the silent rebuke with which his uncle punished unpunctuality.

He arrived at his destination as a near-by church clock struck the half-hour. The new butler admitted him and led him back to where his uncle was sitting by an open window; the curtains stirred in the languid breeze, the suave room was a little penetrated by the night, as if some sly, disorderly spirit was investigating uninvited. It was far too hot for the wood fire—that part of the formula had been omitted, but otherwise each detail was the same. "The two hundredth time!" Adrian thought to himself. "The two hundredth time, at least! It will go on forever!" And then the formula was altered again, for his uncle got to his feet, laying aside the evening paper with his usual precise care. "My dear fellow," he began, "so good of you! On the minute, too! I——" and then he stumbled and put out his hand. "My glasses!" he said.

Adrian caught him and held him upright. He swayed a little. "I—— Lately I have had to use them sometimes, even when not reading," he murmured. "Thank you! Thank you!"

Adrian went back to the chair where his uncle had been sitting. He found the glasses—gold pince-nez—but they were broken neatly in the middle, lying on the floor, as if they had dropped from someone's hand. He looked at them for a moment, puzzled, before he gave them back to his uncle.

"Here they are, sir," he said. "But—it's very curious. They're broken in such an odd way."

His uncle peered down at them. He hesitated and cleared his throat. "Yes," he began; then he stood up straight, with an unexpected twist of his shoulders. "I was turning them between my fingers," he said, "just before you came in. I had no idea—no, no idea! Shall we go in? I think dinner has been announced."

There was the sherry in the little, deeply cut glasses, and the clear soup, with a dash of lemon in it, and the fish, and afterward the roast chicken, with vegetables discreetly limited and designed not to detract from the main dish; and there was a pint of champagne for Adrian and a mild white wine for his uncle. The latter twisted his mouth in a dry smile. "One finds it difficult to get old," he said. "I have always been very fond of champagne. More aesthetically I think than the actual taste. It seems to sum up so well the evening mood—dinner and laughter and forgetting the day. But now——" he flicked contemptuously the stem of his glass—"I am only allowed this uninspired stuff." He stopped suddenly and his face twisted into the slight grimace which Adrian in the last few weeks had been permitted occasionally to see. His hand began to wander vaguely over the white expanse of his shirt.

Adrian pushed back his chair. "Let me—!" he began, but his uncle waved a deprecating hand. "Sit down!" he managed to say. "Please!" Adrian sank back again. The colour returned to his uncle's cheeks and the staring question left his eyes. He took a sip of wine.

"I cannot tell you," he observed with elaborate indifference, "how humiliating this thing is becoming to me. I have always had a theory that invalids and people when they begin to get old and infirm, should be put away some place where they can undergo the unpleasant struggle alone. It's purely selfish—there's something about the sanctity of the individual. Dogs have it right—you know the way they creep off? But I suppose I won't. Pride fails when the body weakens, doesn't it, no matter what the will may be?" He lifted his wine-glass. "I am afraid I am giving you a very dull evening, my dear fellow," he apologized. "Forgive me! We will talk of more pleasant things. I drink wine with you! How is Cecil? Doing well with her painting?"

Adrian attempted to relax his own inner grimness. He responded to his uncle's toast. But he wished this old man, so very near the mysterious crisis of his affairs, would begin to forego to some extent the habit of a lifetime, become a little more human. This ridiculous "façade"! The dinner progressed.

Through an open window the night, full of soft, distant sound, made itself felt once more. The candles, under their red shades, flickered at intervals. The noiseless butler came and went. How old his uncle was getting to look, Adrian reflected. There was a grayness about his cheeks; fine, wire-like lines about his mouth. And he was falling into that sure sign of age, a vacant absent-mindedness. Half the time he was not listening to what he, Adrian, was saying; instead, his eyes sought constantly the shadows over the carved sideboard across the table from him. What did he see there? What question was he asking? Adrian wondered. Only once was his uncle very much interested, and that was when Adrian had spoken of the war and the psychology left in its train. Adrian himself had not long before been released from a weary round of training-camps, where, in Texas dust, or the unpleasant resinous summer of the South, he had gone through a repetition that in the end had threatened to render him an imbecile. He was not illusioned. As separate personalities, men had lost much of their glamour for him; there had been too much sweat, too much crowding, too much invasion of dignity, of everything for which the world claimed it had been struggling and praying. But alongside of this revolt on his part had grown up an immense pity and belief in humanity as a mass—struggling, worm-like, aspiring, idiotic, heroic. The thought of it made him uncomfortable and at the same time elate.

His uncle shook a dissenting head. On this subject he permitted himself mild discussion, but his voice was still that of an old, wearied man, annoyed and bewildered. "Oh, no!" he said. "That's the very feature of it that seems to me most dreadful; the vermicular aspect; the massed uprising; the massed death. About professional armies there was something decent—about professional killing. It was cold-blooded and keen, anyway. But this modern war, and this modern craze for self-revelation! Naked! Why, these books—the young men kept their fingers on the pulses of their reactions. It isn't clean; it makes the individual cheap. War is a dreadful thing; it should be as hidden as murder." He sat back, smiled. "We seem to have a persistent tendency to become serious to-night," he remarked.

Serious! Adrian saw a vision of the drill-grounds, and

smiled sardonically; then he raised his head in surprise, for the new butler had broken all the rules of the household and was summoning his uncle to the telephone in the midst of dessert. He awaited the expected rebuke, but it did not come. Instead, his uncle paused in the middle of a sentence stared, and looked up. "Ah, yes!" he said, and arose from his chair. "Forgive me, Adrian, I will be back shortly." He walked with a new, just noticeable, infirmness toward the door. Once there he seemed to think an apology necessary, for he turned and spoke with absent-minded courtesy.

"You may not have heard," he said, "but Mrs. Denby is seriously ill. Her nurse gives me constant bulletins over the telephone."

Adrian started to his feet, then sat down again. "But—" he stuttered—"but —is it as bad as all that?"

"I am afraid," said his uncle gently, " it could not be worse." The curtain fell behind him.

Adrian picked up his fork and began to stir gently the melting ice on the plate before him, but his eyes were fixed on the wall opposite, where, across the shining table, from a mellow gold frame, a portrait of his grandfather smiled with a benignity, utterly belying his traditional character, into the shadows above the candles. But Adrian was not thinking of his grandfather just then, he was thinking of his uncle—and Mrs. Denby. What in the world——! Dangerously ill, and yet here had been his uncle able to go through with—not entirely calmly, to be sure; Adrian remembered the lack of attention, the broken eye-glasses; and yet, still able to go through with, not obviously shaken, this monthly farce; this dinner that in reality mocked all the real meaning of blood-relationship. Good Lord! To Adrian's modern mind, impatient and courageous, the situation was preposterous, grotesque. He himself would have broken through to the woman he loved, were she seriously ill, if all the city was cordoned to keep him back. What could it mean? Entire selfishness on his uncle's part? Surely not that! That was too inhuman! Adrian was willing to grant his uncle exceptional expertness in the art of self-protection, but there was a limit even to self-protection. There must be some other reason. Discretion? More likely, and yet how absurd! Had Mr. Denby been alive, a meticulous, a fantastic delicacy might have intervened, but Mr. Denby was dead. Who were there to wound, or who left for the telling of tales? A doctor and the servants. This was not altogether reasonable, despite what he knew of his uncle. Here was some oddity of psychology he could not follow. He heard the curtains stir as his uncle reëntered. He looked up, attentive and curious, but his uncle's face was the mask to which he was accustomed.

"How is Mrs. Denby?" he asked.

Mr. McCain hesitated for the fraction of a second. "I am afraid, very ill," he said. "Very ill, indeed! It is pneumonia. I—the doctor thinks it is only a question of a little time, but—well, I shall continue to hope for the best." There was a metallic harshness to his concluding words. "Shall we go into the library?" he continued. "I think the coffee will be pleasanter there."

They talked again of the war; of revolution; of the dark forces at large in the world.

Through that hour or two Adrian had a nakedness of perception unusual even to his sensitive mind. It seemed to him three spirits were abroad in the quiet, softly-lit, book-lined room; three intentions that crept up to him like the waves of the sea, receded, crept back again; or were they currents of air? or hesitant, unheard feet that advanced and withdrew? In at the open windows poured at times the warm, enveloping scent of the spring; pervading, easily overlooked, lawless, persistent, inevitable. Adrian found himself thinking it was like the presence of a woman. And then, overlapping this, would come the careful, dry, sardonic tones of his uncle's voice, as if insisting that the world was an ordinary world, and that nothing, not even love or death, could lay disrespectful fingers upon or hurry for a moment the trained haughtiness of the will. Yet even this compelling arrogance was at times overtaken, submerged, by a third presence, stronger even than the other two; a presence that entered upon the heels of the night; the ceaseless murmur of the streets; the purring of rubber tires upon asphalt; a girl's laugh, high, careless, reckless. Life went on. Never for a moment did it stop.

"I am not sorry that I am getting old," said Mr. McCain. "I think nowadays is an excellent time to die. Perhaps for the very young, the strong—but for me, things are too busy, too hurried. I have always liked my life like potpourri. I liked to keep it in a china jar and occasionally take off the lid. Otherwise one's sense of perfume becomes satiated. Take your young girls; they remain faithful to a love that is not worth being faithful to—all noise, and flushed laughter, and open doors." Quite unexpectedly he began to talk in a way he had never talked before. He held his cigar in his hand until the ash turned cold; his fingers trembled just a little.

"You have been very good to me," he said. Adrian raised startled eyes. "Very good. I am quite aware that you dislike me"—he hesitated and the ghost of a smile hovered about his lips—"and I have always disliked you. Please!" He raised a silencing hand. "You don't mind my saying so? No. Very well, then, there is something I want to tell you. Afterward I will never mention it again. I dare say our mutual dislike is due to the inevitable misunderstanding that exists between the generations. But it is not important. The point is that we have always been well-bred toward each other. Yes, that is the point. You have always been a gentleman, very considerate, very courteous, I cannot but admire you. And I think you will find I have done the best I could. I am not a rich man, as such things go nowadays, but I will hand you on the money that will be yours quite unimpaired, possibly added to. I feel very strongly on that subject. I am old-fashioned enough to consider the family the most important thing in life. After all, we are the only two McCains left." He hesitated again, and twisted for a moment his bloodless hands in his lap, then he raised his eyes and spoke with a curious hurried embarrassment. "I have sacrificed a great deal for that," he said. "Yes, a great deal."

The soft-footed butler stood at his elbow, like an actor in comedy suddenly cast for the rôle of a portentous messenger.

"Miss Niles is calling you again, sir," he said.

"On, yes!—ah—Adrian, I am very sorry, my dear fellow. I will finish the conversation when I come back."

This time the telephone was within earshot; in the hall outside. Adrian heard his uncle's slow steps end in the creaking of a chair as he sat down; then the picking up of the receiver. The message was a long one, for his uncle did not speak for fully a minute; finally his voice drifted in through the curtained doorway.

"You think . . . only a few minutes?"

". . . Ah, yes! Conscious? Yes. Well, will you tell her, Miss Niles?—yes, please listen very carefully—tell her this. That I am not there because I dared not come. Yes; on her account. She will understand. My heart—it's my heart. She will understand. I did not dare. For her sake, not mine. Tell her that. She will understand. Please be very careful in repeating the message, Miss Niles. Tell her I dared not come because of my heart. . . . Yes; thank you. That's it. . . . What? Yes, I will wait, Miss Niles."

Adrian, sitting in the library, suddenly got to his feet and crossed to the empty fireplace and stood with his back to it, enlightenment and a puzzled frown struggling for possession of his face. His uncle's heart! Ah, he understood, then! It was discretion, after all, but not the kind he thought—a much more forgiveable discretion. And, yet, what possible difference could it make should his uncle die suddenly in Mrs. Denby's house? Fall dead across her bed, or die kneeling beside it? Poor, twisted old fool, afraid even at the end that death might catch him out; afraid of a final undignified gesture.

A motor blew its horn for the street crossing. Another girl laughed; a young, thin, excited girl, to judge by her laughter. The curtains stirred and again there was that underlying scent of tulips and hyacinths; and then, from the hall outside, came the muffled thud of a receiver falling to the floor. Adrian waited. The receiver was not picked up. He strode to the door. Crumpled up over the telephone was old Mr. McCain.

Cecil came later. She was very quick and helpful, and jealously solicitous on Adrian's account, but in the taxicab going home she said the one thing Adrian had hoped she wouldn't say, and yet was sure she would. She belonged to a sex which, if it is honest at all, is never reticently so. She believed that between the man she loved and herself there were no possible mental withdrawals. "It is very tragic," she said. "but much better—you know it is better. He belonged to the cumberers of the earth. Yes, so much better; and this way, too!"

In the darkness her hand sought his. Adrian took it, but in his heart was the same choked feeling, the same knowledge that something was gone that could not be found again, that, as a little boy, he had had when they sold, at his father's death, the country place where he had spent his summers. Often he had lain awake at night, restless with the memory of heliotrope, and phlox, and mignonette, and afternoons quiet except for the sound of bees.

"CONTACT!"

By FRANCES NOYES HART*

From *The Pictorial Review*

THE first time she heard it was in the silk-hung and flower-scented peace of the little drawing-room in Curzon Street. His sister Rosemary had wanted to come up to London to get some clothes—Victory clothes they called them in those first joyous months after the armistice, and decked their bodies in scarlet and silver, even when their poor hearts went in black—and Janet had been urged to leave her own drab boarding-house room to stay with the forlorn small butterfly. They had struggled through dinner somehow, and Janet had finished her coffee and turned the great chair so that she could watch the dancing fire (it was cool for May), her cloudy brown head tilted back against the rose-red cushion, shadowy eyes half closed, idle hands linked across her knees. She looked every one of her thirty years—and mortally tired—and careless of both facts. But she managed an encouraging smile at the sound of Rosemary's shy, friendly voice at her elbow. "Janet, these are yours, aren't they? Mummy found them with some things last week, and I thought that you might like to have them."

She drew a quick breath at the sight of the shabby packet.

"Why, yes," she said evenly. "That's good of you, Rosemary. Thanks a lot."

"That's all right," murmured Rosemary diffidently. "Wouldn't you like something to read? There's a most frightfully exciting Western novel——"

The smile took on a slightly ironical edge. "Don't bother about me, my dear. You see, I come from that frightfully exciting West, and I know all about the pet rattlesnakes and

*Frances Newbold Noyes, in *Pictorial Review* for December, 1920.

the wildly Bohemian cowboys. Run along and play with your book—I'll be off to bed in a few minutes."

Rosemary retired obediently to the deep chair in the corner, and with the smile gone but the irony still hovering, she slipped the cord off the packet. A meager and sorry enough array—words had never been for her the swift, docile servitors that most people found them. But the thin gray sheet in her fingers started out gallantly enough—"Beloved." Beloved! She leaned far forward, dropping it with deft precision into the glowing pocket of embers. What next? This was more like—it began "Dear Captain Langdon" in the small, contained, even writing that was her pride, and it went on soberly enough, "I shall be glad to have tea with you next Friday—not Thursday, because I must be at the hut then. It was stupid of me to have forgotten you—next time I will try to do better." Well, she had done better the next time. She had not forgotten him again—never, never again. That had been her first letter; how absurd of Jerry, the magnificently careless, to have treasured it all that time, the miserable, stilted little thing! She touched it with curious fingers. Surely, surely he must have cared, to have cared so much for that!

It seemed incredible that she hadn't remembered him at once when he came into the hut that second time. Of course she had only seen him for a moment and six months had passed—but he was so absurdly vivid, every inch of him, from the top of his shining, dark head to the heels of his shining, dark boots—and there were a great many inches! How could she have forgotten, even for a minute, those eyes dancing like blue fire in the brown young face, the swift, disarming charm of his smile, and, above all, his voice—how, in the name of absurdity could any one who had once heard it ever forget Jeremy Langdon's voice? Even now she had only to close her eyes, and it rang out again, with its clipped, British accent and its caressing magic, as un-English as any Provençal troubadour's! And yet she had forgotten—he had had to speak twice before she had even lifted her head.

"Miss America—oh, I say, she's forgotten me, and I thought that I'd made such an everlasting impression!" The delighted amazement reached even her tired ears, and she had smiled wanly as she pushed the pile of coppers nearer to him.

"Have you been in before? It's stupid of me, but there are

such hundreds of thousands of you, and you are gone in a minute, you see. That's your change, I think."

"Hundreds of thousands of me, hey?" He had leaned across the counter, his face alight with mirth. "I wish to the Lord my angel mother could hear you—it's what I'm forever tellin' her, though just between us, it's stuff and nonsense. I've got a well-founded suspicion that I'm absolutely unique. You wait and see!"

And she had waited—and she had seen! She stirred a little, dropped the note into the flames, and turned to the next, the quiet, mocking mouth suddenly tortured and rebellious.

"No, you must be mad," it ran, the trim writing strangely shaken. "How often have you seen me—five times? Do you know how old I am. How hard and tired and useless? No—no a thousand times. In a little while we will wake up and find that we were dreaming."

That had brought him to her swifter than Fate, triumphant mischief in every line of his exultant face. "Just let those damned old cups slip from your palsied fingers, will you? I'm goin' to take your honourable age for a little country air—it may keep you out of the grave for a few days longer. Never can tell! No use your scowlin' like that—the car's outside, and the big chief says to be off with you. Says you have no more colour than a banshee, and not half the life—can't grasp the fact that it's just chronic antiquity. Fasten the collar about your throat—no, higher! Darlin', darlin', think of havin' a whole rippin' day to ourselves. You're glad, too, aren't you, my little stubborn saint?"

Oh, that joyous and heart-breaking voice, running on and on—it made all the other voices that she had ever heard seem colourless and unreal——

"Darlin' idiot, what do I care how old you are? Thirty, hey? Almost old enough to be an ancestor! Look at me—no, look at me! Dare you to say that you aren't mad about me!"

Mad about him—mad, mad! She lifted her hands to her ears, but she could no more shut out the exultant voice now than she could on that windy afternoon.

"Other fellow got tired of you, did he? Good luck for us, what? You're a fearfully tiresome person, darlin'. It's goin' to take me nine-tenths of eternity to tell you how tiresome you are. Give a chap a chance, won't you? The tiresomest thing about you is the way you leash up that dimple of yours. No, by George, there it is! Janie, look at me——"

She touched the place where the leashed dimple had hidden with a delicate and wondering finger—of all Jerry's gifts to her the most miraculous had been that small fugitive. Exiled now, forever and forever.

"Are you comin' down to White Orchards next week-end? I'm off for France on the twelfth and you've simply got to meet my people. You'll be insane about 'em—Rosemary's the most beguilin' flibbertigibbet, and I can't wait to see you bein' a kind of an elderly grandmother to her. What a bewitchin' little grandmother you're goin' to be one of these days——"

Oh, Jerry! Oh, Jerry, Jerry! She twisted in her chair, her face suddenly a small mask of incredulous terror. No, no, it wasn't true, it wasn't true—never—never—never! And then, for the first time, she heard it. Far off but clear, a fine and vibrant humming, the distant music of wings! The faint, steady pulsing was drawing nearer and nearer—nearer still—it must be flying quite high. The hateful letters scattered about her as she sprang to the open window—no, it was too high to see, and too dark, though the sky was powdered with stars—but she could hear it clearly, hovering and throbbing like some gigantic bird. It must be almost directly over her head, if she could only see it.

"It sounds—it sounds the way a humming-bird would look through a telescope," she said half aloud, and Rosemary murmured sleepily but courteously, "What, Janet?"

"Just an airplane—no, gone now. It sounded like a bird. Didn't you hear it?"

"No," replied Rosemary drowsily. "We get so used to the old things that we don't even notice them any more. Queer time to be flying!"

"It sounded rather—beautiful," said Janet, her face still turned to the stars. "Far off, but so clear and sure. I wonder—I wonder whether it will be coming back?"

Well, it came back. She went down to White Orchards with Rosemary for the following week-end, and after she had smoothed her hair and given a scornful glance at the pale face in the mirror, with its shadowy eyes and defiant mouth, she slipped out to the lower terrace for a breath of the soft country air. Halfway down the flight of steps she stumbled and caught at the balustrade, and stood shaking for a moment, her face pressed against its rough surface. Once before—once before she had stumbled on those steps, but it was not the balustrade that had saved her. She could feel his arms about her now, holding her up, holding her close and safe. The magical voice was in her ears. "Let you go? I'll never let you go! Poor little feet, stumblin' in the dark, what would you do without Jerry? Time's comin', you cheeky little devils, when you'll come runnin' to him when he whistles! No use tryin' to get away—you belong to him."

Oh, whistle to them now, Jerry—they would run to you across the stars!

"How'd you like to marry me before I go back to-morrow? No? No accountin' for tastes, Miss Abbott—lots of people would simply jump at it! All right—April, then. Birds and flowers and all that kind o' thing—pretty intoxicatin', what? No, keep still, darlin' goose. What feller taught you to wear a dress that looks like roses and smells like roses and feels like roses? This feller? Lord help us, what a lovely liar!"

And suddenly she found herself weeping helplessly, desperately, like an exhausted child, shaken to the heart at the memory of the rose-coloured dress.

"You like me just a bit, don't you, funny, quiet little thing? But you'd never lift a finger to hold me—that's the wonder of you—that's why I'll never leave you. No, not for heaven. You can't lose me—no use tryin'."

But she had lost you, Jerry—you had left her, for all your promises, to terrified weeping in the hushed loveliness of the terrace, where your voice had turned her still heart to a dancing star, where your fingers had touched her quiet blood to flowers and flames and butterflies. She had believed you then—what would she ever believe again? And then she caught back the despairing sobs swiftly, for once more she heard, far off, the rushing of wings. Nearer—nearer—humming and singing and hovering in the quiet dusk. Why, it was over the garden! She flung back her head, suddenly eager to see it; it was a friendly and thrilling sound in all that stillness. Oh, it was coming lower—lower still—she could hear the throb of the propellers clearly. Where *was* it? Behind those trees, perhaps? She raced up the flight of steps, dashing the treacherous tears from her eyes, straining up on impatient tiptoes. Surely she could see it now! But already it was growing fainter—drifting steadily away, the distant hum growing lighter and lighter—lighter still——

"Janet!" called Mrs. Langdon's pretty, patient voice. "Dinner-time, dear! Is there any one with you?"

"No one at all, Mrs. Langdon. I was just listening to an airplane."

"An *airplane?* Oh, no, dear—they never pass this way any more. The last one was in October, I think——"

The soft, plaintive voice trailed off in the direction of the dining-room and Janet followed it, a small, secure smile touching her lips. The last one had not passed in October. It had passed a few minutes before, over the lower garden.

She quite forgot it by the next week—she was becoming an adept at forgetting. That was all that was left for her to do! Day after day and night after night she had raised the drawbridge between her heart and memory, leaving the lonely thoughts to shiver desolately on the other side of the moat. She was weary to the bone of suffering, and they were enemies, for all their dear and friendly guise; they would tear her to pieces if she ever let them in. No, no, she was done with them. She would forget, as Jerry had forgotten. She would destroy every link between herself and the past—and pack the neat little steamer trunk neatly—and bid these kind and gentle people good-by—and take herself and her bitterness and her dullness back to the class-room in the Western university town—back to the Romance languages. The Romance languages!

She would finish it all that night, and leave as soon as possible. There were some trinkets to destroy, and his letters from France to burn—she would give Rosemary the rose-coloured dress—foolish, lovely little Rosemary, whom he had loved, and who was lying now fast asleep in the next room curled up like a kitten in the middle of the great bed, her honey-coloured hair falling about her in a shining mist. She swept back her own cloud of hair resolutely, frowning at the candle-lit reflection in the mirror. Two desolate pools in the small, pale oval of her face stared back at her—two pools with something drowned in their lonely depths. Well, she would drown it deeper!

The letters first; how lucky that they still used candle-light! It would make the task much simpler—the funeral pyre already lighted. She moved one of the tall candelabra to the desk, sitting for a long time quite still, her chin cupped in her hands, staring down at the bits of paper. She could smell the wall-flowers under the window as though they were in the room—drenched in dew and moonlight, they were reckless of their fragrance. All this peace and cleanliness and orderly beauty—what a ghastly trick for God to have played—to have taught her to adore them, and then to snatch them away! All about her, warm with candle-light, lay the gracious loveliness of the little room with its dark waxed furniture, its bright glazed chintz, its narrow bed with the cool linen sheets smelling of lavender, and its straight, patterned curtains—oh, that hateful, mustard-coloured den at home, with its golden-oak day-bed!

She wrung her hands suddenly in a little hunted gesture. How could he have left her to that, he who had sworn that he would never leave her? In every one of those letters beneath her linked fingers he had sworn it—in every one perjured—false half a hundred times. Pick up any one of them at random——

"Janie, you darling stick, is 'dear Jerry' the best that you can do? You ought to learn French! I took a perfectly ripping French kid out to dinner last night—name's Liane, from the Varietés—and she was calling me '*mon grand cheri*' before the salad, and '*mon p'tit amour*' before the green mint. Maybe *that'll* buck you up! And I'd have you know that she's so pretty that it's ridiculous, with black velvet hair that she wears like a little Oriental turban, and eyes like golden pansies, and a mouth between a kiss and a prayer—and a nice affable nature into the bargain. But I'm a ghastly jackass—I didn't get any fun out of it at all—because I really didn't even see her. Under the pink shaded candles to my blind eyes it seemed that there was seated the coolest, quietest, whitest little thing, with eyes that were as indifferent as my velvety Liane's were kind, and mockery in her smile. Oh, little masquerader! If I could get my arms about you even for a minute—if I could kiss so much as the tips of your lashes—would you be cool and quiet and mocking then? Janie, Janie, rosy-red as flowers on the terrace and sweeter—sweeter—they're about you now—they'll be about you always!"

Burn it fast, candle—faster, faster. Here's another for you.

"So the other fellow cured you of using pretty names, did he—you don't care much for dear and darling any more? Bit hard on me, but fortunately for you, Janie Janet, I'm rather a dab at languages—'specially when it comes to what the late lamented Boche referred to as 'cosy names.' *Querida mi alma, douchka, Herzliebchen, carissima;* and *bien, bien-aimée,* I'll not run out of salutations for you this side of heaven—no—nor t'other. I adore the serene grace with which you ignore the ravishing Liane. Haven't you any curiosity at all, my Sphinx? No? Well, then, just to punish you, I'll tell you all about it. She's married to the best fellow in the world—a *liaison* officer working with our squadron—and she worships the ground that he walks on and the air that he occasionally flies in. So whenever I run up to the City of Light, *en permission,* I look her up, and take her the latest news—and for an hour, over the candles, we pretend that I am Philippe, and that she is Janie. Only she says that I don't pretend very well—and it's just possible that she's right.

"*Mon petit cœur et grand trésor,* I wish that I could take you flying with me this evening. You'd be daft about it! Lots of it's a rotten bore, of course, but there's something in me that doesn't live at all when I'm on this too, too solid earth. Something that lies there, crouched and dormant, waiting until I've climbed up into the seat, and buckled the strap about me and laid my hands on the 'stick.' It's waiting—waiting for a word—and so am I. And I lean far forward, watching the figure toiling out beyond till the call comes back to me, clear and confident, 'Contact, sir?' And I shout back, as restless and exultant as the first time that I answered it—'Contact!'

"And I'm off—and I'm alive—and I'm free! Ho, Janie! That's simpler than Abracadabra or Open Sesame, isn't it? But it opens doors more magical than ever they swung wide, and something in me bounds through, more swift and eager than any Aladdin. Free! I'm a crazy sort of a beggar, my little love—that same thing in me hungers and thirsts and aches for freedom. I go half mad when people or events try to hold me—you, wise beyond wisdom, never will. Somehow, between us, we've struck the spark that turns a mere piece of machinery into a wonder with wings—somehow, you are forever setting me free. It is your voice—your voice of silver and peace—that's eternally whispering 'Contact!' to me—and I am released, heart, soul, and body! And because you speed me on my way, Janie, I'll never fly so far, I'll never fly so long, I'll never fly so high that I'll not return to you. You hold me fast, forever and forever."

You had flown high and far indeed, Jerry—and you had not returned. Forever and forever! Burn faster, flame!

"My blessed child, who's been frightening you? Airplanes are by all odds safer than taxis—and no end safer than the infernal duffer who's been chaffing you would be if I could once get my hands on him. Damn fool! Don't care if you do hate swearing—damn fools are damn fools, and there's an end to it. All those statistics are sheer melodramatic rot—the chap who fired 'em at you probably has all his money invested in submarines, and is fairly delirious with jealousy. Peg (did I ever formally introduce you to Pegasus, the best pursuit-plane in the R. F. C.—or out of it?)—Peg's about as likely to let me down as you are! We'd do a good deal for each other, she and I—nobody else can really fly her, the darling! But she'd go to the stars for me—and farther still. Never you fear—we have charmed lives, Peg and I—we belong to Janie.

"I think that people make an idiotic row about dying, anyway. It's probably jolly good fun—and I can't see what difference a few years here would make if you're going to have all eternity to play with. Of course you're a ghastly little heathen, and I can see you wagging a mournful head over this already—but every time that I remember what a shocking sell the After Life (exquisite phrase!) is going to be for you, darling, I do a bit of head-wagging myself—and it's not precisely mournful! I can't wait to see your blank consternation—and you needn't expect any sympathy from *me*. My very first words will be, 'I told you so!' Maybe I'll rap them out to you with a table-leg!

"What do you think of all this Ouija Planchette rumpus,

anyway? I can't for the life of me see why any one with a whole new world to explore should hang around chattering with this one. I know that I'd be half mad with excitement to get at the new job, and that I'd find re-assuring the loved ones (exquisite phrase number two) a hideous bore. Still, I can see that it would be nice from their selfish point of view! Well, I'm no ghost yet, thank God—nor yet are you—but if ever I am one, I'll show you what devotion really is. I'll come all the way back from heaven to play with foolish Janie, who doesn't believe that there is one to come from. To foolish, foolish Janie, who still will be dearer than the prettiest angel of them all, no matter how alluringly her halo may be tilted or her wings ruffled. To Janie who, Heaven forgive him, will be all that one poor ghost has ever loved!"

Had there come to him, the radiant and the confident, a moment of terrible and shattering surprise—a moment when he realized that there were no pretty angels with shining wings waiting to greet him—a moment when he saw before him only the overwhelming darkness, blacker and deeper than the night would be, when she blew out the little hungry flame that was eating up the sheet that held his laughter? Oh, gladly would she have died a thousand deaths to have spared him that moment!

"My little Greatheart, did you think that I did not know how brave you are? You are the truest soldier of us all, and I, who am not much given to worship, am on my knees before that shy gallantry of yours, which makes what courage we poor duffers have seem a vain and boastful thing. When I see you as I saw you last, small and white and clear and brave, I can't think of anything but the first crocuses at White Orchards, shining out, demure and valiant, fearless of wind and storm and cold—fearless of Fear itself. You see, you're so very, very brave that you make me ashamed to be afraid of poetry and sentiment and pretty words—things of which I have a good, thumping Anglo-Saxon terror, I can tell you! It's because I know what a heavenly brick you are that I could have killed that statistical jackass for bothering you; but I'll forgive him, since you say that it's all right. And so ghosts are the only things in the world that frighten you—even though you know that there aren't any. You and Madame de Staël, hey? 'I do not believe in ghosts, but I fear them!' It's pretty painful to learn that the mere sight of one would turn you into a gibbering lunatic. Nice sell for an enthusiastic spirit who'd romped clear back from heaven to give you a pleasant surprise—I *don't* think! Well, no fear, young Janie—I'll find some way if I'm put to it—some nice, safe, pretty way that wouldn't scare a neurasthenic baby, let alone the dauntless Miss Abbott. I'll find——"

Oh, no more of that—no more! She crushed the sheet in her hands fiercely, crumpling it into a little ball—the candle-flame was too slow. No, she couldn't stand it—she couldn't—she couldn't, and there was an end to it. She would go raving mad—she would kill herself—she would—— She lifted her head, wrenched suddenly back from that chaos of despair, alert and intent. There it was again, coming swiftly nearer and nearer from some immeasurable distance—down—down—nearer still—the very room was humming and throbbing with it—she could almost hear the singing in the wires. She swung far out over the window edge, searching the moon-drenched garden with eager eyes—surely, surely it would never fly so low unless it were about to land! Engine trouble, perhaps—though she could detect no break in the huge, rhythmic pulsing that was shaking the night. Still——

"Rosemary!" she called urgently. "Rosemary—listen—is there a place where it can land?"

"Where what can land?" asked a drowsy voice.

"An airplane. It's flying so low that it must be in some kind of trouble—do come and see!"

Rosemary came pattering obediently toward her, a small, docile figure, dark eyes misted with dreams, wide with amazement.

"I must be nine-tenths asleep," she murmured gently. "Because I don't hear a single thing, Janet. Perhaps——"

"Hush—listen!" begged Janet, raising an imperative hand—and then her own eyes widened. "Why—it's *gone!*" There was a note of flat incredulity in her voice. "Heavens, how those things must eat up space! Not a minute ago it was fairly shaking this room, and now——"

Rosemary stifled a small pink yawn and smiled ingratiatingly.

"Perhaps you were asleep too," she suggested humbly.

"I don't believe that airplanes ever fly this way any more. Or it might have been that fat Hodges boy on his motorcycle —he does make the most dreadful racket. Oh, Janet, what a perfectly *ripping* night—do see!"

They leaned together on the window-sill, silenced by the white and shining beauty that had turned the pleasant garden into a place of magic and enchantment. The corners of Janet's mouth lifted suddenly. How absurd people were! The fat Hodges boy and his motorcycle! Did they all regard her as an amiable lunatic—even little, lovely, friendly Rosemary, wavering sleepily at her side? It really was maddening. But she felt, amazingly enough, suddenly quiet and joyous and indifferent—and passionately glad that the wanderer from the skies had won safely through and was speeding home. Home! Oh, it was a crying pity that it need ever land—anything so fleet and strong and sure should fly forever! But if they must rest, those beating wings—the old R. F. C. toast went singing through her head and she flung it out into the moonlight, smiling—"Happy landings! Happy landings, you!"

The next day was the one that brought to White Orchards what was to be known for many moons as "the Big Storm." It had been gathering all afternoon, and by evening the heat had grown appalling and incredible, even to Janet's American and exigent standards. The smouldering copper sky looked as though it had caught fire from the world and would burn forever; there was not so much as a whisper of air to break the stillness—it seemed as though the whole tortured earth were holding its breath, waiting to see what would happen next. Every one had struggled through the day assuring one another that when evening came it would be all right—dangling the alluring thought of the cool darkness before each other's hot and weary eyes; but the night proved even more outrageous than the day. To the little group seated on the terrace, dispiritedly playing with their coffee, it seemed almost a personal affront. The darkness closed in on them, smothering, heavy, intolerable; they could feel its weight, as though it were some hateful and tangible thing.

"Like—like black cotton wool," explained Rosemary, stirred to unwonted resentment. She had spent the day curled up in the largest Indian chair on the terrace, round-eyed with fatigue and incredulity.

"I honestly think that we must be dreaming," she murmured to her feverish audience; "I do, honestly. Why, it's only *May*, and we never, never—there was that day in August about five years ago that was almost as bad, though. D'you remember, Mummy?"

"It's hardly the kind of thing that one is likely to forget, love. Do you think that it is necessary for us to talk? I feel somehow that I could bear it much more easily if we kept quite quiet."

Janet stirred a little, uneasily. She hated silence—that terrible, empty space waiting to be filled up with your thoughts—why, the idlest chatter spared you that. She hated the terrace, too—she closed her eyes to shut out the ugly darkness that was pressing against her; behind the shelter of her lids it was cooler and stiller, but open-eyed or closed, she could not shut out memory. The very touch of the bricks beneath her feet brought back that late October day. She had been sitting curled up on the steps in the warm sunlight, with the keen, sweet air stirring her hair and sending the beech-leaves dancing down the flagged path—there had been a heavenly smell of burning from the far meadow, and she was sniffing it luxuriously, feeling warm and joyous and protected in Jerry's great tweed coat—watching the tall figure swinging across from the lodge gate with idle, happy eyes—not even curious. It was not until he had almost reached the steps that she had noticed that he was wearing a foreign uniform—and even then she had promptly placed him as one of Rosemary's innumerable conquests, bestowing on him a friendly and inquiring smile.

"Were you looking for Miss Langdon?" Even now she could see the courteous, grave young face soften as he turned quickly toward her, baring his dark head with that swift foreign grace that turns our perfunctory habits into something like a ritual.

"But no," he had said gently, "I was looking for you, Miss Abbott."

"Now will you please tell me how in the world you knew that I was Miss Abbott?"

And he had smiled—with his lips, not his eyes.

"I should be dull indeed if that I did not know. I am Philippe Laurent, Miss Abbott."

And "Oh," she had cried joyously, "Liane's Philippe!"

"But yes—Liane's Philippe. They are not here, the others? Madame Langdon, the little Miss Rosemary?"

"No, they've gone to some parish fair, and I've been wicked and stayed home. Won't you sit down and talk to me? Please!"

"Miss Abbott, it is not to you that I must talk. What I have to say is indeed most difficult, and it is to Jeremy's Janie that I would say it. May I, then?"

It had seemed to Jeremy's Janie that the voice in which she answered him came from a great distance, but she never took her eyes from the grave and vivid face.

"Yes. And quickly, please."

So he had told her—quickly—in his exquisitely careful English, and she had listened as attentively and politely, huddled up on the brick steps in the sunlight, as though he were running over the details of the last drive, instead of tearing her life to pieces with every word. She remembered now that it hadn't seemed real at all—if it had been to Jerry that these horrors had happened could she have sat there so quietly, feeling the colour bright in her cheeks, and the wind stirring in her hair, and the sunlight warm on her hands? Why, for less than this people screamed, and fainted, and went raving mad!

"You say—that his back is broken?"

"But yes, my dear," Liane's Philippe had told her, and she had seen the tears shining in his gray eyes.

"And he is badly burned?"

"My brave Janie, these questions are not good to ask—not good, not good to answer. This I will tell you. He lives, our Jerry—and so dearly does he love you that he will drag back that poor body from hell itself—because it is yours, not his. This he has sent me to tell you, most lucky lady ever loved."

"You mean—that he isn't going to die?"

"I tell you that into those small hands of yours he has given his life. Hold it fast."

"Will he—will he get well?"

"He will not walk again; but have you not swift feet to run for him?"

And there had come to her, sitting on the terrace in the sunshine, an overwhelming flood of joy, reckless and cruel and triumphant. Now he was hers forever, the restless wanderer —delivered to her bound and helpless, never to stray again. Hers to worship and serve and slave for, his troth to Freedom broken—hers at last!

"I'm coming," she had told the tall young Frenchman breathlessly. "Take me to him—please let's hurry."

"*Ma pauvre petite*, this is war. One does not come and go at will. God knows by what miracle enough red tape unwound to let me through to you, to bring my message and to take one back."

"What message, Philippe?"

"That is for you to say, little Janie. He told me, 'Say to her that she has my heart—if she needs my body, I will live. Say to her that it is an ugly, broken, and useless thing; still, hers. She must use it as she sees fit. Say to her—no, say nothing more. She is my Janie, and has no need of words. Tell her to send me only one, and I will be content.' For that one word, Janie, I have come many miles. What shall it be?"

And she had cried out exultantly, "Why, tell him that I say——" But the word had died in her throat. Her treacherous lips had mutinied, and she had sat there, feeling the blood drain back out of her face—out of her heart—feeling her eyes turn back with sheer terror, while she fought with those stiffened rebels. Such a little word "Live!"—surely they could say that. Was it not what he was waiting for, lying far away and still—schooled at last to patience, the reckless and the restless! Oh, Jerry, Jerry, live! Even now she could feel her mind, like some frantic little wild thing, racing, racing to escape Memory. What had he said to her? "You, wise beyond wisdom, will never hold me—you will never hold me—you will never——"

And suddenly she had dropped her twisted hands in her lap and lifted her eyes to Jerry's ambassador.

"Will you please tell him—will you please tell him that I say—'Contact'?"

"Contact?" He had stood smiling down at her, ironical and tender. "Ah, what a race! That is the prettiest word that you can find for Jerry? But then it means to come very close, to touch, that poor harsh word—there he must find what comfort he can. We, too, in aviation use that word—it is the signal that says—'Now, you can fly!' You do not know our vocabulary, perhaps?"

"I know very little."

"That is all then? No other message? He will understand, our Jerry?"

And Janie had smiled—rather a terrible small smile.

"Oh, yes," she told him. "He will understand. It is the word that he is waiting for, you see."

"I see." But there had been a grave wonder in his voice.

"Would it——" she had framed the words as carefully as though it were a strange tongue that she was speaking—"would it be possible to buy his machine? He wouldn't want any one else to fly it."

"Little Janie, never fear. The man does not live who shall fly poor Peg again. Smashed to kindling-wood and burned to ashes, she has taken her last flight to the heaven for good and brave birds of war. Not enough was left of her to hold in your two hands."

"I'm glad. Then that's all—isn't it? And thank you for coming."

"It is I who thank you. What was hard as death you have made easy. I had thought the lady to whom Jeremy Langdon gave his heart the luckiest creature ever born—now I think him that luckiest one." The grave grace with which he had bent to kiss her hand made of the formal salutation an accolade—"My homage to you, Jerry's Janie!" A quick salute, and he had turned on his heel, swinging off down the flagged path with that swift, easy stride—past the sun-dial—past the lily-pond—past the beech-trees—gone! For hours and hours after he had passed out of sight she had sat staring after him, her hands lying quite still in her lap—staring, staring—they had found her there when they came back, sitting where Rosemary was seated now. Why, there, on those same steps, a bare six months ago—Something snapped in her head, and she stumbled to her feet, clinging to the arm of her chair.

"I can't *stand* it!" she gasped. "No, no, it's no use—I can't, I tell you. I——"

Rosemary's arm was about her—Mrs. Langdon's soft voice in her ears—a deeper note from Rosemary's engineer.

"Oh, I say, poor girl! What is it, dear child—what's the matter? Is it the heat, Janie?"

"The heat!" She could hear herself laughing—frantic, hateful, jangling laughter that wouldn't stop. "Oh, Jerry! Oh-h, Jerry, Jerry, Jerry!"

"It's this ghastly day. Let me get her some water, Mrs. Langdon. Don't cry so, Janie—please, please don't, darling."

"I c-can't help it—I c-can't——" She paused, listening intently, her hand closing sharply over Rosemary's wrist. "Oh, listen, listen—there it comes again—I told you so!"

"Thank Heaven," murmured Mrs. Langdon devoutly, "I thought that it never was going to rise this evening. It's from the south, too, so I suppose that it means rain."

"Rain?" repeated Janet vaguely. "Why in the world should it mean rain?" Her small, pale face looked suddenly brilliant and enchanted, tilted up to meet the thunderous music that was swinging nearer and nearer. "Oh, do listen, you people! This time it's surely going to land!"

Rosemary stared at her blankly. "Land? What *are* you talking about, Janie?"

"My airplane—the one that you said was the fat Hodges boy on a motorcycle! Is there any place near here that it can make a landing?"

"Darling child——" Mrs. Langdon's gentle voice was gentler than ever—"darling child, it's this wretched heat. There isn't any airplane, dear—it's just the wind rising in the beeches."

"The wind?" Janet laughed aloud—they really were too absurd. "Why, Mrs. Langdon, you can hear the *engines*, if you'll only listen! You can hear them, can't you, Mr. Bain?"

The young engineer shook his head. "No plane would risk flying with this storm coming, Miss Abbott. There's been thunder for the last hour or so, and it's getting nearer, too. It's only the wind, I think."

"Oh, you're laughing at me—of course, of course you hear it. Why, it's as clear as—as clear as——"

Her voice trailed off into silence. Quite suddenly, without any transition or warning, she knew. She could feel her heart stand perfectly still for a minute, and then plunge forward in mad flight, racing, racing—oh, it knew, too, that eager heart! She took her hand from the arm of the chair, releasing Rosemary's wrist very gently.

"Yes, of course, it's the heat," she said quietly. She must be careful not to frighten them, these kind ones. "If you don't mind, Mrs. Langdon, I think that I'll go down to the gate to watch the storm burst. No, please, don't any of you come—I'll promise to change everything if I get caught—yes, everything! I won't be long; don't wait for me."

She walked sedately enough until she came to the turn in the path, but after that she ran, only pausing for a minute to listen breathlessly. Oh, yes—following, following, that gigantic music! How he must be laughing at her now—blind, deaf, incredulous little fool that she had been, to doubt that Jerry would find a way! But where could he land? Not in the garden—not at the gates—oh, now she had it—the far meadow. She turned sharply; it was dark, but the path must be here. Yes, this was the wicket gate; her groping fingers were quite steady—they found the latch—released it—the gate swung to behind her flying footsteps. "Oh, Jerry, Jerry!" sang her heart. Why hadn't she worn the rose-coloured frock? It was she who would be a ghost in that trailing white thing. To the right here—yes, there was the hawthorn hedge—only a few steps more—oh, now! She stood as still as a small statue, not moving, not breathing, her hands at her heart, her face turned to the black and torn sky. Nearer, nearer, circling and darting and swooping—the gigantic humming grew louder—louder still—it swept about her thunderously, so close that she clapped her hands over her ears, but she stood her ground, exultant and undaunted. Oh, louder still—and then suddenly the storm broke. All the winds and the rains of the world were unleashed, and fell howling and shrieking upon her; she staggered under their onslaught, drenched to the bone, her dress whipping frantically about her, blinded and deafened by that tumultuous clamour. She had only one weapon against it—laughter—and she laughed now—straight into its teeth. And as though hell itself must yield to mirth, the fury wavered—

failed—sank to muttering. But Janie, beaten to her knees and laughing, never even heard it die.

"Jerry?" she whispered into the darkness, "Jerry?"

Oh, more wonderful than wonder, he was there! She could feel him stir, even if she could not hear him—so close, so close was he that if she even reached out her hand, she could touch him. She stretched it out eagerly, but there was nothing there—only a small, remote sound of withdrawal, as though some one had moved a little.

"You're afraid that I'll be frightened, aren't you?" she asked wistfully. "I wouldn't be—I wouldn't—please come back!"

He was laughing at her, she knew, tender and mocking and caressing; she smiled back, tremulously.

"You're thinking, 'I told you so!' Have you come far to say it to me?"

Only that little stir—the wind was rising again.

"Jerry, come close—come closer still. What are you waiting for, dear and dearest?"

This time there was not even a stir to answer her; she felt suddenly cold to the heart. What had he always waited for?

"You aren't waiting—you aren't waiting to go?" She fought to keep the terror out of her voice, but it had her by the throat. "Oh, no, no—you can't—not again! Jerry, Jerry, don't go away and leave me—truly and truly I can't stand it—truly!"

She wrung her hands together desperately; she was on her knees to him—did he wish her to go lower still? Oh, she had never learned to beg!

"I can't send you away again—I can't. When I sent you to France I killed my heart—when I let you go to death, I crucified my soul. I haven't anything left but my pride—you can have that, too. I can't send you back to your heaven. Stay with me—stay with me, Jerry!"

Not a sound—not a stir—but well she knew that he was standing there, waiting. She rose slowly to her feet.

"Very well—you've won," she said hardly. "Go back to your saints and seraphs and angels; I'm beaten. I was mad to think that you ever cared—go back!" She turned, stumbling, the sobs tearing at her throat; she had gone several steps before she realized that he was following her—and all the hardness and bitterness and despair fell from her like a cloak.

"Oh, Jerry," she whispered, "Jerry, darling, I'm so sorry. And you've come so far—just to find this! What is it that you want; can't you tell me?"

She stood tense and still, straining eyes and ears for her answer—but it was not to eyes or ears that it came.

"Oh, of course!" she cried clearly. "Of course, my wanderer! Ready?"

She stood poised for a second, head thrown back, arms flung wide—a small figure of Victory, caught in the flying wind.

And, "Contact, Jerry!" she called joyously into the darkness. "Contact!"

There was a mighty whirring, a thunder and a roaring above the storm. She stood listening breathlessly to it rise and swell—and then grow fainter—fainter still—dying, dying—dying——

But Janie, her small white face turned to the storm-swept sky behind which shone the stars, was smiling radiantly. For she had sped her wanderer on his way—she had not failed him!

THE CAMEL'S BACK

By F. SCOTT FITZGERALD

From *The Saturday Evening Post*

THE restless, wearied eye of the tired magazine reader resting for a critical second on the above title will judge it to be merely metaphorical. Stories about the cup and the lip and the bad penny and the new broom rarely have anything to do with cups and lips and pennies and brooms. This story is the great exception. It has to do with an actual, material, visible and large-as-life camel's back.

Starting from the neck we shall work tailward. Meet Mr. Perry Parkhurst, twenty-eight, lawyer, native of Toledo. Perry has nice teeth, a Harvard education, and parts his hair in the middle. You have met him before—in Cleveland, Portland, St. Paul, Indianapolis, Kansas City and elsewhere. Baker Brothers, New York, pause on their semi-annual trip through the West to clothe him; Montmorency & Co., dispatch a young man posthaste every three months to see that he has the correct number of little punctures on his shoes. He has a domestic roadster now, will have a French roadster if he lives long enough, and doubtless a Chinese one if it comes into fashion. He looks like the advertisement of the young man rubbing his sunset-coloured chest with liniment, goes East every year to the Harvard reunion—does everything—smokes a little too much—— Oh, you've seen him.

Meet his girl. Her name is Betty Medill, and she would take well in the movies. Her father gives her two hundred a month to dress on and she has tawny eyes and hair, and feather fans of three colours. Meet her father, Cyrus Medill. Though he is to all appearances flesh and blood he is, strange to say, commonly known in Toledo as the Aluminum Man. But when he sits in his club window with two or three Iron Men and the White Pine Man and the Brass Man they look very much as you and I do, only more so, if you know what I mean.

Meet the camel's back—or no—don't meet the camel's back yet. Meet the story.

During the Christmas holidays of 1919, the first real Christmas holidays since the war, there took place in Toledo, counting only the people with the italicized *the*, forty-one dinner parties, sixteen dances, six luncheons male and female, eleven luncheons female, twelve teas, four stag dinners, two weddings and thirteen bridge parties. It was the cumulative effect of all this that moved Perry Parkhurst on the twenty-ninth day of December to a desperate decision.

Betty Medill would marry him and she wouldn't marry him. She was having such a good time that she hated to take such a definite step. Meanwhile, their secret engagement had got so long that it seemed as if any day it might break off of its own weight. A little man named Warburton, who knew it all, persuaded Perry to superman her, to get a marriage license and go up to the Medill house and tell her she'd have to marry him at once or call it off forever. This is some stunt—but Perry tried it on December the twenty-ninth. He presented self, heart, license, and ultimatum, and within five minutes they were in the midst of a violent quarrel, a burst of sporadic open fighting such as occurs near the end of all long wars and engagements. It brought about one of those ghastly lapses in which two people who are in love pull up sharp, look at each other coolly and think it's all been a mistake. Afterward they usually kiss wholesomely and assure the other person it was all their fault. Say it all was my fault! Say it was! I want to hear you say it!

But while reconciliation was trembling in the air, while each was, in a measure, stalling it off, so that they might the more voluptuously and sentimentally enjoy it when it came, they were permanently interrupted by a twenty-minute phone call for Betty from a garrulous aunt who lived in the country. At the end of eighteen minutes Perry Parkhurst, torn by pride and suspicion and urged on by injured dignity, put on his long fur coat, picked up his light brown soft hat and stalked out the door.

"It's all over," he muttered brokenly as he tried to jam his car into first. "It's all over—if I have to choke you for an hour, darn you!" This last to the car, which had been standing some time and was quite cold.

He drove downtown—that is, he got into a snow rut that led him downtown.

He sat slouched down very low in his seat, much too dispirited to care where he went. He was living over the next twenty years without Betty.

In front of the Clarendon Hotel he was hailed from the sidewalk by a bad man named Baily, who had big huge teeth and lived at the hotel and had never been in love.

"Perry," said the bad man softly when the roadster drew up beside him at the curb, "I've got six quarts of the doggonedest champagne you ever tasted. A third of it's yours, Perry, if you'll come upstairs and help Martin Macy and me drink it."

"Baily," said Perry tensely. "I'll drink your champagne. "I'll drink every drop of it. I don't care if it kills me. I don't care if it's fifty-proof wood alcohol."

"Shut up, you nut!" said the bad man gently. "They don't put wood alcohol in champagne. This is the stuff that proves the world is more than six thousand years old. It's so ancient that the cork is petrified. You have to pull it with a stone drill."

"Take me upstairs," said Perry moodily. "If that cork sees my heart it'll fall out from pure mortification."

The room upstairs was full of those innocent hotel pictures of little girls eating apples and sitting in swings and talking to dogs. The other decorations were neckties and a pink man reading a pink paper devoted to ladies in pink tights.

"When you have to go into the highways and byways——" said the pink man, looking reproachfully at Baily and Perry.

"Hello, Martin Macy," said Perry shortly, "where's this stone-age champagne?"

"What's the rush? This isn't an operation, understand. This is a party."

Perry sat down dully and looked disapprovingly at all the neckties.

Baily leisurely opened the door of a wardrobe and brought out six wicked-looking bottles and three glasses.

"Take off that darn fur coat!" said Martin Macy to Perry. "Or maybe you'd like to have us open all the windows."

"Give me champagne," said Perry.

"Going to the Townsends' circus ball to-night?"

"Am not!"

"'Vited?"

"Uh-huh."

"Why not go?"

"Oh, I'm sick of parties," exclaimed Perry, "I'm sick of 'em. I've been to so many that I'm sick of 'em."

"Maybe you're going to the Howard Tates' party?"

"No, I tell you; I'm sick of 'em."

"Well," said Macy consolingly, "the Tates' is just for college kids anyway."

"I tell you——"

"I thought you'd be going to one of 'em anyways. I see by the papers you haven't missed a one this Christmas."

"Hm," grunted Perry morosely.

He would never go to any more parties. Classical phrases played in his mind—that side of his life was closed, closed. Now when a man says "closed, closed" like that, you can be pretty sure that some woman has double-closed him, so to speak. Perry was also thinking that other classical thought, about how cowardly suicide is. A noble thought that one—warm and uplifting. Think of all the fine men we should lose if suicide were not so cowardly!

An hour later was six o'clock, and Perry had lost all resemblance to the young man in the liniment advertisement. He looked like a rough draft for a riotous cartoon. They were singing—an impromptu song of Baily's improvisation:

One Lump Perry, the parlour snake,
Famous through the city for the way he drinks his tea;
Plays with it, toys with it,
Makes no noise with it,
Balanced on a napkin on his well-trained knee.

"Trouble is," said Perry ,who had just banged his hair with Bailey's comb and was tying an orange tie round it to get the effect of Julius Cæsar, "that you fellas can't sing worth a damn. Soon's I leave th' air an' start singin' tenor you start singin' tenor too."

"'M a natural tenor," said Macy gravely. "Voice lacks cultivation, tha's all. Gotta natural voice, m'aunt used say. Naturally good singer."

"Singers, singers, all good singers," remarked Baily, who was at the telephone. "No, not the cabaret; I want night clerk. I mean refreshment clerk or some dog-gone clerk 'at's got food—food! I want——"

"Julius Cæsar," announced Perry, turning round from the mirror. "Man of iron will and stern 'termination."

"Shut up!" yelled Baily. "Say, iss Mr. Baily. Sen' up enormous supper. Use y'own judgment. Right away."

He connected the receiver and the hook with some difficulty and then with his lips closed and an air of solemn intensity in his eyes went to the lower drawer of his dresser and pulled it open.

"Lookit!" he commanded. In his hands he held a truncated garment of pink gingham.

"Pants," he explained gravely. "Lookit!" This was a pink blouse, a red tie and a Buster Brown collar.

"Lookit!" he repeated. "Costume for the Townsends' circus ball. I'm li'l' boy carries water for the elephants."

Perry was impressed in spite of himself.

"I'm going to be Julius Cæsar," he announced after a moment of concentration.

"Thought you weren't going!" said Macy.

"Me? Sure, I'm goin'. Never miss a party. Good for the nerves—like celery."

"Cæsar!" scoffed Baily. "Can't be Cæsar! He's not about a circus. Cæsar's Shakespeare. Go as a clown."

Perry shook his head.

"Nope; Cæsar."

"Cæsar?"

"Sure. Chariot."

Light dawned on Baily.

"That's right. Good idea."

Perry looked round the room searchingly.

"You lend me a bathrobe and this tie," he said finally.

Baily considered.

"No good."

"Sure, tha's all I need. Cæsar was a savage. They can't kick if I come as Cæsar if he was a savage."

"No," said Baily, shaking his head slowly. "Get a costume over at a costumer's. Over at Nolak's."

"Closed up."

"Find out."

After a puzzling five minutes at the phone a small, weary voice managed to convince Perry that it was Mr. Nolak speaking, and that they would remain open until eight because of the Townsends' ball. Thus assured, Perry ate a great amount of filet mignon and drank his third of the last bottle of champagne. At eight-fifteen the man in the tall hat who stands in front of the Clarendon found him trying to start his roadster.

"Froze up," said Perry wisely. "The cold froze it. The cold air."

"Froze, eh?"

"Yes. Cold air froze it."

"Can't start it?"

"Nope. Let it stand here till summer. One those hot ole August days'll thaw it out awright."

"Goin' let it stand?"

"Sure. Let 'er stand. Take a hot thief to steal it. Gemme taxi."

The man in the tall hat summoned a taxi.

"Where to, mister?"

"Go to Nolak's—costume fella."

II

Mrs. Nolak was short and ineffectual looking, and on the cessation of the world war had belonged for a while to one of the new nationalities. Owing to the unsettled European conditions she had never since been quite sure what she was. The shop in which she and her husband performed their daily stint was dim and ghostly and peopled with suits of armour and Chinese mandarins and enormous papier-mâché birds suspended from the ceiling. In a vague background many rows of masks glared eyelessly at the visitor, and there were glass cases full of crowns and scepters and jewels and enormous stomachers and paints and powders and crape hair and face creams and wigs of all colours.

When Perry ambled into the shop Mrs. Nolak was folding up the last troubles of a strenuous day, so she thought, in a drawer full of pink silk stockings.

"Something for you?" she queried pessimistically.

"Want costume of Julius Hur, the charioteer."

Mrs. Nolak was sorry, but every stitch of charioteer had been rented long ago. Was it for the Townsends' circus ball?

It was.

"Sorry," she said, "but I don't think there's anything left that's really circus."

This was an obstacle.

"Hm," said Perry. An idea struck him suddenly. "If you've got a piece of canvas I could go's a tent."

"Sorry, but we haven't anything like that. A hardware store is where you'd have to go to. We have some very nice Confederate soldiers."

"No, no soldiers."

"And I have a very handsome king."

He shook his head.

"Several of the gentlemen," she continued hopefully, "are wearing stovepipe hats and swallow-tail coats and going as ringmasters—but we're all out of tall hats. I can let you have some crape hair for a moustache."

"Want somep'm 'stinctive."

"Something—let's see. Well, we have a lion's head, and a goose, and a camel——"

"Camel?" The idea seized Perry's imagination, gripped it fiercely.

"Yes, but it needs two people."

"Camel. That's an idea. Lemme see it."

The camel was produced from his resting place on a top shelf. At first glance he appeared to consist entirely of a very gaunt, cadaverous head and a sizable hump, but on being spread out he was found to possess a dark brown, unwholesome-looking body made of thick, cottony cloth.

"You see it takes two people," explained Mrs. Nolak, holding the camel up in frank admiration. "If you have a friend he could be part of it. You see there's sorta pants for two people. One pair is for the fella in front and the other pair for the fella in back. The fella in front does the lookin' out through these here eyes an' the fella in back he's just gotta stoop over an' folla the front fella round."

"Put it on," commanded Perry.

Obediently Mrs. Nolak put her tabby-cat face inside the camel's head and turned it from side to side ferociously.

Perry was fascinated.

"What noise does a camel make?"

"What?" asked Mrs. Nolak as her face emerged, somewhat smudgy. "Oh, what noise? Why, he sorta brays."

"Lemme see it in a mirror."

Before a wide mirror Perry tried on the head and turned from side to side appraisingly. In the dim light the effect was distinctly pleasing. The camel's face was a study in pessimism, decorated with numerous abrasions, and it must be admitted that his coat was in that state of general negligence peculiar to camels—in fact, he needed to be cleaned and pressed—but distinctive he certainly was. He was majestic. He would have attracted attention in any gathering if only by his melancholy cast of feature and the look of pensive hunger lurking round his shadowy eyes.

"You see you have to have two people," said Mrs. Nolak again.

Perry tentatively gathered up the body and legs and wrapped them about him, tying the hind legs as a girdle round his waist. The effect on the whole was bad. It was even irreverent—like one of those medieval pictures of a monk changed into a beast by the ministrations of Satan. At the very best the ensemble resembled a humpbacked cow sitting on her haunches among blankets.

"Don't look like anything at all," objected Perry gloomily.

"No," said Mrs. Nolak; "you see you got to have two people."

A solution flashed upon Perry.

"You got a date to-night?"

"Oh, I couldn't possibly——"

"Oh, come on," said Perry encouragingly. "Sure you can! Here! Be a good sport and climb into these hind legs."

With difficulty he located them and extended their yawning depths ingratiatingly. But Mrs. Nolak seemed loath. She backed perversely away.

"Oh, no——"

"C'm on! Why, you can be the front if you want to. Or we'll flip a coin."

"Oh, no——"

"Make it worth your while."

Mrs. Nolak set her lips firmly together.

"Now you just stop!" she said with no coyness implied. "None of the gentlemen ever acted up this way before. My husband——"

"You got a husband?" demanded Perry. "Where is he?"

"He's home."

"Wha's telephone number?"

After considerable parley he obtained the telephone number pertaining to the Nolak penates and got into communication with that small, weary voice he had heard once before that day. But Mr. Nolak, though taken off his guard and somewhat confused by Perry's brilliant flow of logic, stuck staunchly to his point. He refused firmly but with dignity to help out Mr. Parkhurst in the capacity of back part of a camel.

Having rung off, or rather having been rung off on, Perry sat down on a three-legged stool to think it over. He named over to himself those friends on whom he might call, and then his mind paused as Betty Medill's name hazily and sorrowfully occurred to him. He had a sentimental thought. He would ask her. Their love affair was over, but she could not refuse this last request. Surely it was not much to ask—to help him keep up his end of social obligation for one short night. And if she insisted she could be the front part of the camel and he would go as the back. His magnanimity pleased him. His mind even turned to rosy-coloured dreams of a tender reconciliation inside the camel—there hidden away from all the world.

"Now you'd better decide right off."

The bourgeois voice of Mrs. Nolak broke in upon his mellow fancies and roused him to action. He went to the phone and called up the Medill house. Miss Betty was out; had gone out to dinner.

Then, when all seemed lost, the camel's back wandered curiously into the store. He was a dilapidated individual with a cold in his head and a general trend about him of downwardness. His cap was pulled down low on his head, and his chin was pulled down low on his chest, his coat hung down to his shoes, he looked run-down, down at the heels, and—Salvation Army to the contrary—down and out. He said that he was the taxicab driver that the gentleman had hired at the Clarendon Hotel. He had been instructed to wait outside, but he had waited some time and a suspicion had grown upon him that the gentleman had gone out the back way with purpose to defraud him—gentlemen sometimes did—so he had come in. He sank down on to the three-legged stool.

"Wanta go to a party?" demanded Perry sternly.

"I gotta work," answered the taxi driver lugubriously. "I gotta keep my job."

"It's a very good party."

"'S a very good job."

"Come on!" urged Perry. "Be a good fella. See—it's pretty!" He held the camel up and the taxi driver looked at it cynically.

"Huh!"

Perry searched feverishly among the folds of the cloth.

"See!" he cried enthusiastically, holding up a selection of folds. "This is your part. You don't even have to talk. All you have to do is to walk—and sit down occasionally. You do all the sitting down. Think of it. I'm on my feet all the time and you can sit down some of the time. The only time I can sit down is when we're lying down, and you can sit down when—oh, any time. See?"

"What's 'at thing?" demanded the individual dubiously "A shroud?"

"Not at all," said Perry hurriedly. "It's a camel."

"Huh?"

Then Perry mentioned a sum of money, and the conversation left the land of grunts and assumed a practical tinge. Perry and the taxi driver tried on the camel in front of the mirror.

"You can't see it," explained Perry, peering anxiously out through the eyeholes, "but honestly, ole man, you look sim'ly great! Honestly!"

A grunt from the hump acknowledged this somewhat dubious compliment.

"Honestly, you look great!" repeated Perry enthusiastically. "Move round a little."

The hing legs moved forward, giving the effect of a huge cat-camel hunching his back preparatory to a spring.

"No; move sideways."

The camel's hips went neatly out of joint; a hula dancer would have writhed in envy.

"Good, isn't it?" demanded Perry, turning to Mrs. Nolak for approval.

"It looks lovely," agreed Mrs. Nolak.

"We'll take it," said Perry.

The bundle was safely stowed under Perry's arm and they left the shop.

"Go to the party!" he commanded as he took his seat in the back.

"What party?"

"Fanzy-dress party."

"Where 'bouts is it?"

This presented a new problem. Perry tried to remember, but the names of all those who had given parties during the holidays danced confusedly before his eyes. He could ask Mrs. Nolak, but on looking out the window he saw that the shop was dark. Mrs. Nolak had already faded out, a little black smudge far down the snowy street.

"Drive uptown," directed Perry with fine confidence. "If you see a party, stop. Otherwise I'll tell you when we get there."

He fell into a hazy daydream and his thoughts wandered again to Betty—he imagined vaguely that they had had a disagreement because she refused to go to the party as the back part of the camel. He was just slipping off into a chilly doze when he was wakened by the taxi driver opening the door and shaking him by the arm.

"Here we are, maybe."

Perry looked out sleepily. A striped awning led from the curb up to a spreading gray stone house, from inside which issued the low drummy whine of expensive jazz. He recognized the Howard Tate house.

"Sure," he said emphatically; "'at's it! Tate's party tonight. Sure, everybody's goin'."

"Say," said the individual anxiously after another look at the awning, "you sure these people ain't gonna romp on me for comin' here?"

Perry drew himself up with dignity.

"'F anybody says anything to you, just tell 'em you're part of my costume."

The visualization of himself as a thing rather than a person seemed to reassure the individual.

"All right," he said reluctantly.

Perry stepped out under the shelter of the awning and began unrolling the camel.

"Let's go," he commanded.

Several minutes later a melancholy, hungry-looking camel, emitting clouds of smoke from his mouth and from the tip of his noble hump, might have been seen crossing the threshold of the Howard Tate residence, passing a startled footman without so much as a snort, and leading directly for the main stairs that led up to the ballroom. The beast walked with a peculiar gait which varied between an uncertain lockstep and a stampede—but can best be described by the word "halting." The camel had a halting gait—and as he walked he alternately elongated and contracted like a gigantic concertina.

III

The Howard Tates are, as everyone who lives in Toledo knows, the most formidable people in town. Mrs. Howard Tate was a Chicago Todd before she became a Toledo Tate, and the family generally affect that conscious simplicity which has begun to be the earmark of American aristocracy. The Tates have reached the stage where they talk about pigs and farms and look at you icy-eyed if you are not amused. They have begun to prefer retainers rather than friends as dinner guests, spend a lot of money in a quiet way and, having lost all sense of competition, are in process of growing quite dull.

The dance this evening was for little Millicent Tate, and though there was a scattering of people of all ages present the dancers were mostly from school and college—the younger married crowd was at the Townsends' circus ball up at the Tallyho Club. Mrs. Tate was standing just inside the ballroom, following Millicent round with her eyes and beaming whenever she caught her eye. Beside her were two middle-aged sycophants who were saying what a perfectly exquisite child Millicent was. It was at this moment that Mrs. Tate was grasped firmly by the skirt and her youngest daughter, Emily, aged eleven, hurled herself with an "Oof—!" into her mother's arms.

"Why, Emily, what's the trouble?"

"Mamma," said Emily, wild-eyed but voluble, "there's something out on the stairs."

"What?"

"There's a thing out on the stairs, mamma. I think it's a big dog, mamma, but it doesn't look like a dog."

"What do you mean, Emily?"

The sycophants waved their heads and hemmed sympathetically.

"Mamma, it looks like a—like a camel."

Mrs. Tate laughed.

"You saw a mean old shadow, dear, that's all."

"No, I didn't. No, it was some kind of thing, mamma—big. I was downstairs going to see if there were any more people and this dog or something, he was coming upstairs. Kinda funny, mamma, like he was lame. And then he saw me and gave a sort of growl and then he slipped at the top of the landing and I ran."

Mrs. Tate's laugh faded.

"The child must have seen something," she said.

The sycophants agreed that the child must have seen something—and suddenly all three women took an instinctive step away from the door as the sounds of muffled footsteps were audible just outside.

And then three startled gasps rang out as a dark brown form rounded the corner and they saw what was apparently a huge beast looking down at them hungrily.

"Oof!" cried Mrs. Tate.

"O-o-oh!" cried the ladies in a chorus.

The camel suddenly humped his back, and the gasps turned to shrieks.

"Oh—look!"

"What is it?"

The dancing stopped, but the dancers hurrying over got quite a different impression of the invader from that of the ladies by the door; in fact, the young people immediately suspected that it was a stunt, a hired entertainer come to amuse the party. The boys in long trousers looked at it rather disdainfully and sauntered over with their hands in their pockets, feeling that their intelligence was being insulted. But the girls ran over with much handclapping and many little shouts of glee.

"It's a camel!"

"Well, if he isn't the funniest!"

The camel stood there uncertainly, swaying slightly from side to side and seeming to take in the room in a careful, appraising glance; then as if he had come to an abrupt decision he turned and ambled swiftly out the door.

Mr. Howard Tate had just come out of his den on the lower floor and was standing chatting with a good-looking young man in the hall. Suddenly they heard the noise of shouting upstairs and almost immediately a succession of bumping sounds, followed by the precipitous appearance at the foot of the stairway of a large brown beast who seemed to be going somewhere in a great hurry.

"Now what the devil!" said Mr. Tate, starting.

The beast picked itself up with some dignity and affecting an air of extreme nonchalance, as if he had just remembered an important engagement, started at a mixed gait toward the front door. In fact, his front legs began casually to run.

"See here now," said Mr. Tate sternly. "Here! Grab it, Butterfield! Grab it!"

The young man enveloped the rear of the camel in a pair of brawny arms, and evidently realizing that further locomotion was quite impossible the front end submitted to capture and stood resignedly in a state of some agitation. By this time a flood of young people was pouring downstairs, and Mr. Tate, suspecting everything from an ingenious burglar to an escaped lunatic, gave crisp directions to the good-looking young man:

"Hold him! Lead him in here; we'll soon see."

The camel consented to be led into the den, and Mr. Tate, after locking the door, took a revolver from a table drawer and instructed the young man to take the thing's head off. Then he gasped and returned the revolver to its hiding place.

"Well, Perry Parkhurst!" he exclaimed in amazement.

"'M in the wrong pew," said Perry sheepishly. "Got the wrong party, Mr. Tate. Hope I didn't scare you."

"Well—you gave us a thrill, Perry." Realization dawned on him. "Why, of course; you're bound for the Townsends' circus ball."

"That's the general idea."

"Let me introduce Mr. Butterfield, Mr. Parkhurst. Parkhurst is our most famous young bachelor here." Then turning to Perry: "Butterfield is staying with us for a few days."

"I got a little mixed up," mumbled Perry. "I'm very sorry."

"Heavens, it's perfectly all right; most natural mistake in the world. I've got a clown costume and I'm going down there myself after a while. Silly idea for a man of my age." He turned to Butterfield. "Better change your mind and come down with us."

The good-looking young man demurred. He was going to bed.

"Have a drink, Perry?" suggested Mr. Tate.

"Thanks, I will."

"And, say," continued Tate quickly, "I'd forgotten all about your—friend here." He indicated the rear part of the camel. "I didn't mean to seem discourteous. Is it any one I know? Bring him out."

"It's not a friend," explained Perry hurriedly. "I just rented him."

"Does he drink?"

"Do you?" demanded Perry, twisting himself tortuously round.

There was a faint sound of assent.

"Sure he does!" said Mr. Tate heartily. "A really efficient camel ought to be able to drink enough so it'd last him three days."

"Tell you, sir," said Perry anxiously, "he isn't exactly dressed up enough to come out. If you give me the bottle I can hand it back to him and he can take his inside."

From under the cloth was audible the enthusiastic smacking sound inspired by this suggestion. When a butler had appeared with bottles, glasses, and siphon one of the bottles was handed back, and thereafter the silent partner could be heard imbibing long potations at frequent intervals.

Thus passed a peaceful hour. At ten o'clock Mr. Tate decided that they'd better be starting. He donned his clown's costume; Perry replaced the camel's head with a sigh; side by side they progressed on foot the single block between the Tate house and the Tallyho Club.

The circus ball was in full swing. A great tent fly had been put up inside the ballroom and round the walls had been built rows of booths representing the various attractions of a circus side show, but these were now vacated and on the floor swarmed a shouting, laughing medley of youth and colour—clowns, bearded ladies, acrobats, bareback riders, ringmasters, tattooed men and charioteers. The Townsends had determined to assure their party of success, so a great quantity of liquor had been surreptitiously brought over from their house in automobiles and it was flowing freely. A green ribbon ran along the wall completely round the ballroom, with pointing arrows alongside of it and signs which instructed the uninitiated to "Follow the green line!" The green line led down to the bar, where waited pure punch and wicked punch and plain dark-green bottles.

On the wall above the bar was another arrow, red and very wavy, and under it the slogan: "Now follow this!"

But even amid the luxury of costume and high spirits represented there the entrance of the camel created something of a stir, and Perry was immediately surrounded by a curious, laughing crowd who were anxious to penetrate the identity of this beast who stood by the wide doorway eyeing the dancers with his hungry, melancholy gaze.

And then Perry saw Betty. She was standing in front of a booth talking to a group of clowns, comic policemen and ringmasters. She was dressed in the costume of an Egyptian snake charmer, a costume carried out to the smallest detail. Her tawny hair was braided and drawn through brass rings, the effect crowned with a glittering Oriental tiara. Her fair face was stained to a warm olive glow and on her bare arms and the half moon of her back writhed painted serpents with single eyes of venomous green. Her feet were in sandals and her skirt was slit to the knees, so that when she walked one caught a glimpse of other slim serpents painted just above her bare ankles. Wound about her neck was a huge, glittering, cotton-stuffed cobra, and her bracelets were in the form of tiny garter snakes. Altogether a very charming and beautiful costume—one that made the more nervous among the older women shrink away from her when she passed, and the more troublesome ones to make great talk about "shouldn't be allowed" and "perfectly disgraceful."

But Perry, peering through the uncertain eyes of the camel, saw only her face, radiant, animated and glowing with excitement, and her arms and shoulders, whose mobile, expressive gestures made her always the outstanding figure in any gathering. He was fascinated and his fascination exercised a strangely sobering effect on him. With a growing clarity the events of the day came back—he had lost forever this shimmering princess in emerald green and black. Rage rose within him, and with a half-formed intention of taking her away from the crowd he started toward her—or rather he elongated slightly, for he had neglected to issue the preparatory command necessary to locomotion.

But at this point fickle Kismet, who for a day had played with him bitterly and sardonically, decided to reward him in full for the amusement he had afforded her. Kismet turned the tawny eyes of the snake charmer to the camel. Kismet led her to lean toward the man beside her and say, "Who's that? That camel?"

They all gazed.

"Darned if I know."

But a little man named Warburton, who knew it all, found it necessary to hazard an opinion:

"It came in with Mr. Tate. I think it's probably Warren Butterfield, the architect, who's visiting the Tates."

Something stirred in Betty Medill—that age-old interest of the provincial girl in the visiting man.

"Oh," she said casually after a slight pause.

At the end of the next dance Betty and her partner finished up within a few feet of the camel. With the informal audacity that was the keynote of the evening she reached out and gently rubbed the camel's nose.

"Hello, old camel."

The camel stirred uneasily.

"You 'fraid of me?" said Betty, lifting her eyebrows in mock reproof. "Don't be. You see I'm a snake charmer, but I'm pretty good at camels too."

The camel bowed very low and the groups round laughed and made the obvious remark about the beauty and the beast.

Mrs. Townsend came bustling up.

"Well, Mr. Butterfield," she beamed, "I wouldn't have recognized you."

Perry bowed again and smiled gleefully behind his mask.

"And who is this with you?" she inquired.

"Oh," said Perry in a disguised voice, muffled by the thick

cloth and quite unrecognizable, "he isn't a fellow, Mrs. Townsend. He's just part of my costume."

This seemed to get by, for Mrs. Townsend laughed and bustled away. Perry turned again to Betty.

"So," he thought, "this is how much she cares! On the very day of our final rupture she starts a flirtation with another man—an absolute stranger."

On an impulse he gave her a soft nudge with his shoulder and waved his head suggestively toward the hall, making it clear that he desired her to leave her partner and accompany him. Betty seemed quite willing.

"By-by, Bobby," she called laughingly to her partner. "This old camel's got me. Where are we going, Prince of Beasts?"

The noble animal made no rejoinder, but stalked gravely along in the direction of a secluded nook on the side stairs.

There Betty seated herself, and the camel, after some seconds of confusion which included gruff orders and sounds of a heated dispute going on in his interior, placed himself beside her, his hind legs stretching out uncomfortably across two steps.

"Well, camel," said Betty cheerfully, "how do you like our happy party?"

The camel indicated that he liked it by rolling his head ecstatically and executing a gleeful kick with his hoofs.

"This is the first time that I ever had a tête-à-tête with a man's valet round"—she pointed to the hind legs—"or whatever that is."

"Oh," said Perry, "he's deaf and blind. Forget about him."

"That sure is some costume! But I should think you'd feel rather handicapped—you can't very well shimmy, even if you want to."

The camel hung his head lugubriously.

"I wish you'd say something," continued Betty sweetly. "Say you like me, camel. Say you think I'm pretty. Say you'd like to belong to a pretty snake charmer."

The camel would.

"Will you dance with me, camel?"

The camel would try.

Betty devoted half an hour to the camel. She devoted at

least half an hour to all visiting men. It was usually sufficient. When she approached a new man the current débutantes were accustomed to scatter right and left like a close column deploying before a machine gun. And so to Perry Parkhurst was awarded the unique privilege of seeing his love as others saw her. He was flirted with violently!

IV

This paradise of frail foundation was broken into by the sound of a general ingress to the ballroom; the cotillion was beginning. Betty and the camel joined the crowd, her brown hand resting lightly on his shoulder, defiantly symbolizing her complete adoption of him.

When they entered, the couples were already seating themselves at tables round the walls, and Mrs. Townsend, resplendent as a super bareback rider with rather too rotund calves, was standing in the centre with the ringmaster who was in charge of arrangements. At a signal to the band everyone rose and began to dance.

"Isn't it just slick!" breathed Betty.

"You bet!" said the camel.

"Do you think you can possibly dance?"

Perry nodded enthusiastically. He felt suddenly exuberant. After all, he was here incognito talking to his girl—he felt like winking patronizingly at the world.

"I think it's the best idea," cried Betty, "to give a party like this! I don't see how they ever thought of it. Come on, let's dance!"

So Perry danced the cotillion. I say danced, but that is stretching the word far beyond the wildest dreams of the jazziest terpsichorean. He suffered his partner to put her hands on his helpless shoulders and pull him here and there gently over the floor while he hung his huge head docilely over her shoulder and made futile dummy motions with his feet. His hind legs danced in a manner all their own, chiefly by hopping first on one foot and then on the other. Never being sure whether dancing was going on or not, the hind legs played safe by going through a series of steps whenever the music started playing. So the spectacle was frequently presented of the front part of the camel standing at ease and the rear keeping up a constant energetic motion calculated to rouse a sympathetic perspiration in any soft-hearted observer.

He was frequently favoured. He danced first with a tall lady covered with straw who announced jovially that she was a bale of hay and coyly begged him not to eat her.

"I'd like to; you're so sweet," said the camel gallantly.

Each time the ringmaster shouted his call of "Men up!" he lumbered ferociously for Betty with the cardboard wienerwurst or the photograph of the bearded lady or whatever the favour chanced to be. Sometimes he reached her first, but usually his rushes were unsuccessful and resulted in intense interior arguments.

"For heaven's sake," Perry would snarl fiercely between his clenched teeth, "get a little pep! I could have gotten her that time if you'd picked your feet up."

"Well, gimme a little warnin'!"

"I did, darn you."

"I can't see a dog-gone thing in here."

"All you have to do is follow me. It's just like dragging a load of sand round to walk with you."

"Maybe you wanta try back here."

"You shut up! If these people found you in this room they'd give you the worst beating you ever had. They'd take your taxi license away from you!"

Perry surprised himself by the ease with which he made this monstrous threat, but it seemed to have a soporific influence on his companion, for he muttered an "aw gwan" and subsided into abashed silence.

The ringmaster mounted to the top of the piano and waved his hand for silence.

"Prizes!" he cried. "Gather round!"

"Yea! Prizes!"

Self-consciously the circle swayed forward. The rather pretty girl who had mustered the nerve to come as a bearded lady trembled with excitement, hoping to be rewarded for an evening's hideousness. The man who had spent the afternoon having tattoo marks painted on him by a sign painter skulked on the edge of the crowd, blushing furiously when any one told him he was sure to get it.

"Lady and gent performers of the circus," announced the ringmaster jovially, "I am sure we will all agree that a good time has been had by all. We will now bestow honour where honour is due by bestowing the prizes. Mrs. Townsend has asked me to bestow the prizes. Now, fellow performers, the first prize is for that lady who has displayed this evening the most striking, becoming"—at this point the bearded lady sighed resignedly—"and original costume." Here the bale of hay pricked up her ears. "Now I am sure that the decision which has been decided upon will be unanimous with all here present. The first prize goes to Miss Betty Medill, the charming Egyptian snake charmer."

There was a great burst of applause, chiefly masculine, and Miss Betty Medill, blushing beautifully through her olive paint, was passed up to receive her award. With a tender glance the ringmaster handed down to her a huge bouquet of orchids.

"And now," he continued, looking round him, "the other prize is for that man who has the most amusing and original costume. This prize goes without dispute to a guest in our midst, a gentleman who is visiting here but whose stay we will hope will be long and merry—in short to the noble camel who has entertained us all by his hungry look and his brilliant dancing throughout the evening."

He ceased and there was a hearty burst of applause, for it was a popular choice. The prize, a huge box of cigars, was put aside for the camel, as he was anatomically unable to accept it in person.

"And now," continued the ringmaster, "we will wind up the cotillion with the marriage of Mirth to Folly!

"Form for the grand wedding march, the beautiful snake charmer and the noble camel in front!"

Betty skipped forward cheerily and wound an olive arm round the camel's neck. Behind them formed the procession of little boys, little girls, country jakes, policemen, fat ladies, thin men, sword swallowers, wild men of Borneo, armless wonders and charioteers, some of them well in their cups, all of them excited and happy and dazzled by the flow of light and colour round them and by the familiar faces strangely unfamiliar under bizarre wigs and barbaric paint. The voluminous chords of the wedding march done in mad syncopation issued in a delirious blend from the saxophones and trombones—and the march began.

"Aren't you glad, camel?" demanded Betty sweetly as

they stepped off. "Aren't you glad we're going to be married and you're going to belong to the nice snake charmer ever afterward?"

The camel's front legs pranced, expressing exceeding joy.

"Minister, minister! Where's the minister?" cried voices out of the revel. "Who's going to be the cler-gy-man?"

The head of Jumbo, rotund negro waiter at the Tallyho Club for many years, appeared rashly through a half-opened pantry door.

"Oh, Jumbo!"

"Get old Jumbo. He's the fella!"

"Come on, Jumbo. How 'bout marrying us a couple?"

"Yea!"

Jumbo despite his protestations was seized by four brawny clowns, stripped of his apron and escorted to a raised dais at the head of the ball. There his collar was removed and replaced back side forward to give him a sanctimonious effect. He stood there grinning from ear to ear, evidently not a little pleased, while the parade separated into two lines leaving an aisle for the bride and groom.

"Lawdy, man," chuckled Jumbo, "Ah got ole Bible 'n' ev'ythin', sho nuff."

He produced a battered Bible from a mysterious interior pocket.

"Yea. Old Jumbo's got a Bible!"

"Razor, too, I'll bet!"

"Marry 'em off, Jumbo!"

Together the snake charmer and the camel ascended the cheering aisle and stopped in front of Jumbo, who adopted a grave pontifical air.

"Where's your license, camel?"

"Make it legal, camel."

A man near by prodded Perry.

"Give him a piece of paper, camel. Anything'll do."

Perry fumbled confusedly in his pocket, found a folded paper and pushed it out through the camel's mouth. Holding it upside down Jumbo pretended to scan it earnestly.

"Dis yeah's a special camel's license," he said. "Get you ring ready, camel."

Inside the camel Perry turned round and addressed his worse half.

"Gimme a ring, for Pete's sake!"

"I ain't got none," protested a weary voice.

"You have. I saw it."

"I ain't goin' to take it offen my hand."

"If you don't I'll kill you."

There was a gasp and Perry felt a huge affair of rhinestone and brass inserted into his hand.

Again he was nudged from the outside.

"Speak up!"

"I do!" cried Perry quickly.

He heard Betty's responses given in a laughing debonair tone, and the sound of them even in this burlesque thrilled him.

If it was only real! he thought. If it only was!

Then he had pushed the rhinestone through a tear in the camel's coat and was slipping it on her finger, muttering ancient and historic words after Jumbo. He didn't want any one to know about this ever. His one idea was to slip away without having to disclose his identity, for Mr. Tate had so far kept his secret well. A dignified young man, Perry—and this might injure his infant law practice.

"Kiss her, camel!"

"Embrace the bride!"

"Unmask, camel, and kiss her!"

Instinctively his heart beat high as Betty turned to him laughingly and began playfully to stroke the cardboard muzzle. He felt his self-control giving away, he longed to seize her in his arms and declare his identity and kiss those scarlet lips that smiled teasingly at him from only a foot away—when suddenly the laughter and applause round them died away and a curious hush fell over the hall. Perry and Betty looked up in surprise. Jumbo had given vent to a huge "Hello!" in such a startled and amazed voice that all eyes were bent on him.

"Hello!" he said again. He had turned round the camel's marriage license, which he had been holding upside down, produced spectacles and was studying it intently.

"Why," he exclaimed, and in the pervading silence his words were heard plainly by everyone in the room, "this yeah's a sho-nuff marriage permit."

"What?"

"Huh?"

"Say it again, Jumbo!"

"Sure you can read?"

Jumbo waved them to silence and Perry's blood burned to fire in his veins as he realized the break he had made.

"Yassuh!" repeated Jumbo. "This yeah's a sho-nuff license, and the pa'ties concerned one of 'em is dis yeah young lady, Miz Betty Medill, and th' other's Mistah Perry Pa'k-hurst."

There was a general gasp, and a low rumble broke out as all eyes fell on the camel. Betty shrank away from him quickly, her tawny eyes giving out sparks of fury.

"Is you Mistah Pa'khurst, you camel?"

Perry made no answer. The crowd pressed up closer and stared at him as he stood frozen rigid with embarrassment, his cardboard face still hungry and sardonic. regarding the ominous Jumbo.

"You-all bettah speak up!" said Jumbo slowly, "this yeah's a mighty serous mattah. Outside mah duties at this club ah happens to be a sho-nuff minister in the Firs' Cullud Baptis' Church. It done look to me as though you-all is gone an' got married."

V

The scene that followed will go down forever in the annals of the Tallyho Club. Stout matrons fainted, strong men swore, wild-eyed débutantes babbled in lightning groups instantly formed and instantly dissolved, and a great buzz of chatter, virulent yet oddly subdued, hummed through the chaotic ballroom. Feverish youths swore they would kill Perry or Jumbo or themselves or someone and the Baptis' preacheh was besieged by a tempestuous covey of clamorous amateur lawyers, asking questions, making threats, demanding precedents, ordering the bonds annulled, and especially trying to ferret out any hint or suspicion of prearrangement in what had occurred.

On the corner Mrs. Townsend was crying softly on the shoulder of Mr. Howard Tate, who was trying vainly to comfort her; they were exchanging "all my fault's" volubly and voluminously. Outside on a snow covered walk Mr. Cyrus Medill, the Aluminum Man, was being paced slowly up and down between two brawny charioteers, giving vent now to a grunt, now to a string of unrepeatables, now to wild pleadings that they'd just let him get at Jumbo. He was facetiously attired for the evening as a wild man of Borneo, and the most exacting stage manager after one look at his face would have acknowledged that any improvement in casting the part would have been quite impossible.

Meanwhile the two principals held the real centre of the stage. Betty Medill—or was it Betty Parkhurst?—weeping furiously, was surrounded by the plainer girls—the prettier ones were too busy talking about her to pay much attention to her—and over on the other side of the hall stood the camel, still intact except for his head-piece, which dangled pathetically on his chest. Perry was earnestly engaged in making protestations of his innocence to a ring of angry, puzzled men. Every few minutes just as he had apparently proved his case someone would mention the marriage certificate, and the inquisition would begin again.

A girl named Marion Cloud, considered the second best belle of Toledo, changed the gist of the situation by a remark she made to Betty.

"Well," she said maliciously, "it'll all blow over, dear. The courts will annul it without question."

Betty's tears dried miraculously in her eyes, her lips shut tightly together, and she flashed a withering glance at Marion. Then she rose and scattering her sympathizers right and left walked directly across the room to Perry, who also rose and stood looking at her in terror. Again silence crept down upon the room.

"Will you have the decency," she said, "to grant me five minutes' conversation—or wasn't that included in your plans?"

He nodded, his mouth unable to form words.

Indicating coldly that he was to follow her she walked out into the hall with her chin uptilted and headed for the privacy of one of the little card rooms.

Perry started after her, but was brought to a jerky halt by the failure of his hind legs to function.

"You stay here!" he commanded savagely.

"I can't," whined a voice from the hump, "unless you get out first and let me get out."

Perry hesitated, but the curious crowd was unbearable, and unable any longer to tolerate eyes he muttered a command and with as much dignity as possible the camel moved carefully out on its four legs.

Betty was waiting for him.

"Well," she began furiously, "you see what you've done! You and that crazy license! I told you you shouldn't have gotten it! I told you!"

"My dear girl, I——"

"Don't dear-girl me! Save that for your real wife if you ever get one after this disgraceful performance."

"I——"

"And don't try to pretend it wasn't all arranged. You know you gave that coloured waiter money! You know you did! Do you mean to say you didn't try to marry me?"

"No—I mean, yes—of course——"

"Yes, you'd better admit it! You tried it, and now what are you going to do? Do you know my father's nearly crazy? It'll serve you right if he tries to kill you. He'll take his gun and put some cold steel in you. O-o-oh! Even if this marr—this thing can be annulled it'll hang over me all the rest of my life!"

Perry could not resist quoting softly: "'Oh, camel, wouldn't you like to belong to the pretty snake charmer for all your——'"

"Shut up!" cried Betty.

There was a pause.

"Betty," said Perry finally with a very faint hopefulness, "there's only one thing to do that will really get us out clear. That's for you to marry me."

"Marry you!"

"Yes. Really it's the only——"

"You shut up! I wouldn't marry you if—if——"

"I know. If I were the last man on earth. But if you care anything about your reputation——"

"Reputation!" she cried. "You're a nice one to think about my reputation *now*. Why didn't you think about my reputation before you hired that horrible Jumbo to—to——"

Perry tossed up his hands hopelessly.

"Very well. I'll do anything you want. Lord knows I renounce all claims!"

"But," said a new voice, "I don't."

Perry and Betty started, and she put her hand to her heart. "For heaven's sake, what was that?"

"It's me," said the camel's back.

In a minute Perry had whipped off the camel's skin, and a lax, limp object, his clothes hanging on him damply, his hand clenched tightly on an almost empty bottle, stood defiantly before them.

"Oh," cried Betty, tears starting again to her eyes, "you brought that object in here to frighten me! You told me he was deaf—that awful person!"

The ex-camel's back sat down on a chair with a sigh of satisfaction.

"Don't talk 'at way about me, lady. I ain't no person. I'm your husband."

"Husband!"

The cry was wrung simultaneously from Betty and Perry.

"Why, sure. I'm as much your husband as that gink is. The smoke didn't marry you to the camel's front. He married you to the whole camel. Why, that's my ring you got on your finger!"

With a little cry she snatched the ring from her finger and flung it passionately at the floor.

"What's all this?" demanded Perry dazedly.

"Jes' that you better fix me an' fix me right. If you don't I'm a-gonna have the same claim you got to bein' married to her!"

"That's bigamy," said Perry, turning gravely to Betty.

Then came the supreme moment of Perry's early life, the ultimate chance on which he risked his fortunes. He rose and looked first at Betty, where she sat weakly, her face aghast at this new complication, and then at the individual who swayed from side to side on his chair, uncertainly yet menacingly.

"Very well," said Perry slowly to the individual, "you can have her. Betty, I'm going to prove to you that as far as I'm concerned our marriage was entirely accidental. I'm going to renounce utterly my rights to have you as my wife, and give you to—to the man whose ring you wear—your lawful husband."

There was a pause and four horror-stricken eyes were turned on him.

"Good-by, Betty," he said brokenly. "Don't forget me in your new-found happiness. I'm going to leave for the Far West on the morning train. Think of me kindly, Betty."

With a last glance at them he turned on his heel and his head bowed on his chest as his hand touched the door knob.

"Good-by," he repeated. He turned the door knob.

But at these words a flying bundle of snakes and silk and tawny hair hurled itself at him.

"Oh, Perry, don't leave me! I can't face it alone! Perry, Perry, take me with you!"

Her tears rained down in a torrent and flowed damply on his neck. Calmly he folded his arms about her.

"I don't care," she cried tearfully. "I love you and if you can wake up a minister at this hour and have it done over again I'll go West with you."

Over her shoulder the front part of the camel looked at the back part of the camel—and they exchanged a particularly subtle, esoteric sort of wink that only true camels can understand.

BREAK-NECK HILL

By ESTHER FORBES

From *The Grinnell Review*

DOWN Holly Street the tide had set in for church. It was a proper, dilatory tide. Every silk-hat glistened, every shoe was blacked, the flowers on the women's hats were as fresh as the daffodils against the house fronts. Few met face to face, now and then a faster walker would catch up with acquaintances and join them or, with a flash of raised hat, bow, and pass on down the stream.

Then the current met an obstacle. A man, young and graceful and very much preoccupied, walked through the church-goers, faced in the opposite direction. His riding breeches and boots showed in spite of the loose overcoat worn to cover them. He bowed continually, like royalty from a landau, almost as mechanically, and answered the remarks that greeted him.

"Hello, Geth."

"Hello."

"Good morning, Mr. Gething. Not going to church this morning." This from a friend of his mother.

"Good morning. No, not this morning." He met a chum.

"Good riding day, eh?"

"Great."

"Well, Geth, don't break your neck."

"You bet not."

"I'll put a P. S. on the prayer for you," said the wag.

"Thanks a lot." The wag was always late—even to church on Easter morning. So Gething knew the tail of the deluge was reached and past. He had the street almost to himself. It was noticeable that the man had not once called an acquaintance by name or made the first remark. His answers had been as reflex as his walking. Geth was thinking, and in the sombre eyes was the dumb look of a pain that would not be told—perhaps he considered it too slight.

He left Holly Street and turned into Holly Park. Here from the grass that bristled so freshly, so ferociously green, the tree trunks rose black and damp. Brown pools of water reflected a blue radiant sky through blossoming branches. Gething subsided on a bench well removed from the children and nurse maids. First he glanced at the corner of Holly Street and the Boulevard where a man from his father's racing stable would meet him with his horse. His face, his figure, his alert bearing, even his clothes promised a horse-man. The way his stirrups had worn his boots would class him as a rider. He rode with his foot "through" as the hunter, steeple chaser, and polo-player do—not on the ball of his foot in park fashion.

He pulled off his hat and ran his hand over his close-cropped head. Evidently he was still thinking. Across his face the look of pain ebbed and returned, then he grew impatient. His wrist-watch showed him his horse was late and he was in a hurry to be started, for what must be done had best be done quickly. Done quickly and forgotten, then he could give his attention to the other horses. There was Happiness—an hysterical child, and Goblin, who needed training over water jumps, and Sans Souci, whose lame leg should be cocained to locate the trouble—all of his father's stable of great thoroughbreds needed something except Cuddy, who waited only for the bullet. Gething's square brown hand went to his breeches pocket, settled on something that was cold as ice and drew it out—the revolver. The horse he had raced so many times at Piping Rock, Brookline, Saratoga had earned the right to die by this hand which had guided him. Cuddy's high-bred face came vividly before his eyes and the white star would be the mark. He thrust the revolver back in his pocket hastily for a child had stopped to look at him, then slowly rose and fell to pacing the gravel walk. A jay screamed overhead, "Jay, jay, jay!"

"You fool," Geth called to him and then muttered to himself. "Fool, fool—oh, Geth——" From the boulevard a voice called him.

"Mr. Gething—if you please, sir——!" It was Willet the trainer.

"All right, Willet." The trainer was mounted holding a lean greyhound of a horse. Gething pulled down the stirrups.

"I meant to tell you to bring Cuddy for me to ride, last time, you know."

"Not that devil. I could never lead him in. Frenchman, here, is well behaved in cities."

Gething swung up. He sat very relaxed upon a horse. There was a lifetime of practice behind that graceful seat and manner with the reins. The horse started a low shuffling gait that would take them rapidly out of the city to the Gething country place and stables.

"You know," Geth broke silence, "Cuddy's got his—going to be shot."

"Not one of us, sir," said Willet, "but will sing Hallelujah! He kicked a hole in Muggins yesterday. None of the boys dare touch him, so he hasn't been groomed proper since your father said he was to go. It's more dangerous wipin' him off than to steeplechase the others." Geth agreed. "I know it isn't right to keep a brute like that."

"No, sir. When he was young and winning stakes it seemed different. I tell you what, we'll all pay a dollar a cake for soap made out 'er old Cuddy."

"There'll be no soap made out of old Cuddy," Gething interrupted him, "I'll ride him out—up to the top of Break-Neck Hill and shoot him there. You'd better begin the trench by noon. When it's dug I'll take him to the top and——"

"But nobody's been on his back since your father said it was useless to try to make him over. Too old for steeple-chasing and too much the racer for anything else, and too much the devil to keep for a suvnor."

"Well, I'll ride him once again."

"But, Mr. Geth, he's just been standing in his box or the paddock for four weeks now. We've been waiting for you to say when he was to be shot. He's in a sweet temper and d' y'er know, I think, I do——"

"What do you think?" Willet blushed purple.

"I think Cuddy's got something in his head, some plan if he gets out. I think he wants to kill some one before he dies. Yes, sir, *kill* him. And you know if he gets the start of you there is no stopping the dirty devil."

"Yes, he does tear a bit," Geth admitted. "But I never

was on a surer jumper. Lord! How the old horse can lift you!" Gething dropped into a disconsolate silence, interrupted before long by Willet.

"Happiness will get Cuddy's box—she's in a stall. Cuddy was always mean to her—used to go out of his way to kick her —and she, sweet as a kitten."

"So you'll give her his box in revenge?"

"Revenge? Oh, no sir. Just common sense." Any thought of a sentimental revenge was distasteful to the trainer, but he was glad that good Happiness should get his box and disappointed about the soap. It would have lent relish to his somewhat perfunctory washings to say to himself, "Doubtless this here bit of soap is a piece of old Cuddy."

"How long will the trench take?"

"A good bit of time, sir. Cuddy isn't no kitten we're laying by. I'll put them gardeners on the job—with your permission—and they know how to shovel. You'll want an old saddle on him?"

"No, no, the one I've raced him in, number twelve, and his old bridle with the chain bit."

"Well, well," said Willet rubbing his veiny nose.

He considered the horse unworthy of any distinction, but in his desire to please Geth, took pains to prepare Cuddy for his death and burial. Gething was still at the big house although it was four o'clock and the men on Break-Neck Hill were busy with their digging. Willet called them the sextons.

"And we, Joey," he addressed a stable boy, "we're the undertakers. Handsome corpse, what?" Cuddy stood in the centre of the barn floor fastened to be groomed. He was handsome, built on the cleanest lines of speed and strength, lean as an anatomical study, perfect for his type. The depth of chest made his legs, neck, and head look fragile. His face was unusually beautiful—the white-starred face which had been before Geth's eyes as he had sat in Holly Park. His pricked ears strained to hear, his eyes to see. The men working over him were beneath his notice.

"Look at him," complained Joey, "he pays no more attention to us than as if we weren't here." Cuddy usually kicked during grooming, but his present indifference was more insulting.

"Huh!" said Willet, "he knows them sextons went to Break-

Neck to dig the grave for him. Don't yer, Devil? Say, Joey, look at him listening like he was counting the number of spadefuls it takes to make a horse's grave. He's thinking, old Cuddy is, and scheming what he'd like to do. I wouldn't ride him from here to Break-Neck, not for a thousand dollars." He began rapidly with the body brush on Cuddy's powerful haunch, then burst out:

"He thinks he'll be good and we'll think he's hit the sawdust trail, or perhaps he wants to look pretty in his coffin. Huh! Give me that curry. You wash off his face a bit." Cuddy turned his aristocratic face away from the wet cloth and blew tremulously. Joey tapped the blazing star on his forehead.

"Right there," he explained to Willet, "but anyhow he's begun to show his age." He pointed the muzzle which had the run forward look of an old horse and to the pits above the eyes. The grooming was finished but neither Gething came to the stable from the big house nor the trench diggers from Break-Neck to say that their work was done.

"Say, Joey," suggested Willet, "I'll do up his mane in red and yellow worsteds, like he was going to be exhibited. Red and yellow look well on a bay. You get to the paddock and see Frenchman hasn't slipped his blanket while I fetch the worsteds from the office."

Cuddy left alone, stopped his listening and began pulling at his halter. It held him firm. From the brown dusk of their box-stalls two lines of expectant horses' faces watched him. The pretty chestnut, Happiness, already had been transferred to his old box, her white striped face was barely visible. Farther down, on the same side, Goblin stood staring stupidly and beyond were the heads of the three brothers, Sans Pareil, Sans Peur and the famous Sans Souci who could clear seven feet of timber (and now was lame.) Opposite stood Bohemia, cold blood in her veins as a certain thickness about the throat testified, and little Martini, the flat racer. On either side of him were Hotspur and Meteor and there were a dozen others as famous. Above each stall was hung the brass plate giving the name and pedigree and above that up to the roof the hay was piled sweet and dusty-smelling. The barn swallows twittered by an open window in the loft. In front of Cuddy the great double doors were open to the fields and pastures, the gray hills and the radiant sky. Cuddy reared abruptly striking out with his front legs, crouched and sprang against his halter again, but it held him fast. Willet, on returning with his worsted, found him as he had left him, motionless as a bronze horse on a black marble clock.

Willet stood on a stool the better to work on the horse's neck. His practised fingers twisted and knotted the mane and worsted, then cut the ends into hard tassels. The horse's withers were reached and the tassels bobbing rakishly gave a hilarious look to the condemned animal.

Four men, very sweaty, carrying spades entered.

"It's done," said the first, nodding, "and it's a big grave. Glad pet horses don't die oftener."

"This ain't a pet," snapped Willet. "He's just that much property and being of no more use is thrown away—just like an old tin can. No more sense in burying one than the other. If I had my way about it I'd——" But Geth entered. With his coat off he gave an impression of greater size, like Cuddy his lines were graceful enough to minimize his weight.

"Hole dug? Well, let's saddle up and start out." He did not go up to Cuddy to speak to him as he usually would have done, but as if trying to avoid him, he fell to patting Happiness's striped face. She was fretful in her new quarters. "Perhaps," thought Willet, "she knows it's old Cuddy and *he's* gone out for good." All the horses seemed nervous and unhappy. It was as if they knew that one of their number was to be taken out to an inglorious death—not the fortune to die on the turf track as a steeple-chaser might wish, but ignominiously, on a hill top, after a soft canter through spring meadows.

Cuddy stood saddled and bridled and then Willet turned in last appeal to his master's son.

"Mr. Geth, I wouldn't ride him—not even if I rode as well as you, which I don't. That horse has grown worse and worse these last months. He wants to kill some one, that's what he wants." Geth shook his head.

"No use, Willet, trying to scare me. I know what I'm doing, eh Cuddy?" He went to the horse and rubbed the base of his ears. The satin head dropped forward on to the man's chest, a rare response from Cuddy. Gething led him out of the stable, Willet held his head as the man mounted.

As he thrust his foot in the stirrup Cuddy lunged at Willet, his savage yellow teeth crushed into his shoulder. The rider pulled him off striking him with his heavy hunting whip. The horse squealed, arched himself in the air and sidled down the driveway. He did not try to run or buck, but seemed intent on twisting himself into curves and figures. The two went past the big house with its gables and numberless chimneys and down to the end of the driveway.

There is a four foot masonry wall around the Gething country-place ("farm" they call it). The horse saw it and began jerking at his bit and dancing, for ever since colt-hood walls had had but one meaning for him.

"Well, at it old man," laughed Gething. At a signal Cuddy flew at it, rose into the air with magnificent strength and landed like thistle-down.

"Cuddy," cried the man, "there never was a jumper like you. Break-Neck will keep, we'll find some more walls first." He crossed the road and entered a rough pasture. It was a day of such abounding life one could pity the worm the robin pulled. For on such a day everything seemed to have the right to live and be happy. The crows sauntered across the sky, care free as hoboes. Under foot the meadow turf oozed water, the shad-bush petals fell like confetti before the rough assault of horse and rider. Gething liked this day of wind and sunshine. In the city there had been the smell of oiled streets to show that spring had come, here was the smell of damp earth, pollen, and burnt brush. Suddenly he realized that Cuddy, too, was pleased and contented for he was going quietly now, occasionally he threw up his head and blew "Heh, heh!" through his nostrils. Strange that Willet had thought Cuddy wanted to kill some one—all he really wanted was a bit of a canter.

A brook was reached. It was wide, marshy, edged with cowslips. It would take a long jump to clear it. Gething felt the back gather beneath him, the tense body flung into the air, the flight through space, then the landing well upon the firm bank.

"Bravo, Cuddy!" the horse plunged and whipped his head between his forelegs, trying to get the reins from the rider's hands. Gething let himself be jerked forward until his face almost rested on the veiny neck.

"Old tricks, Cuddy. I knew *that* one before you wore your first shoes." He still had easy control and began to really let him out. There was a succession of walls and fences and mad racing through fields when the horse plunged in his gait and frightened birds fluttered from the thicket and Gething hissed between his teeth as he always did when he felt a horse going strong beneath him.

Then they came to a hill that rose out of green meadows. It was covered with dingy pine trees except the top that was bared like a tonsure. A trail ran through the woods; a trail singularly morose and unattractive. The pines looked shabby and black in comparison to the sun on the spring meadows. This was Break-Neck Hill. Perhaps Cuddy felt his rider stiffen in the saddle for he refused passionately to take the path. He set his will against Gething's and fought, bucking and rearing. When a horse is capable of a six foot jump into the air his great strength and agility make his bucking terrible. The broncho is a child in size and strength compared to Cuddy's race of super-horse. Twice Geth went loose in his flat saddle and once Cuddy almost threw himself. The chain bit had torn the edges of his mouth and blood coloured his froth. Suddenly he acquiesced and quiet again, he took the sombre path. Geth thrust his right hand into his pocket, the revolver was still there. His hand left it and rested on the bobbing, tasseled mane.

"Old man," he addressed the horse, "I know you don't know where you're going and I know you don't remember much, but you must remember Saratoga and how we beat them all. And Cuddy, you'd understand—if you could—how it's all over now and why I want to do it for you myself."

The woods were cleared. It was good to leave their muffled dampness for the pure sunshine of the crest. On the very top of the hill clean-cut against the sky stood a great wind-misshaped pine. At the foot of this pine was a bank of fresh earth and Gething knew that beyond the bank was the trench. He bent in his saddle and pressed his forehead against the warm neck. Before his eyes was the past they had been together, the sweep of the turf course, the grandstand a-flutter, grooms with blankets, jockeys and gentlemen in silk, owners' wives with cameras, then the race that always seemed so short—a rush of horses, the stretching over the jumps, and the purse or not, it did not matter.

He straightened up with a grim set to his jaw and gathered the loosened reins. Cuddy went into a canter and so approached the earth bank. Suddenly he refused to advance and again the two wills fought, but not so furiously. Cuddy was shaking with fear. The bank was a strange thing, a fearsome thing, and the trench beyond, ghastly. His neck stretched forward. "Heh, heh!" he blew through his nostrils.

"Six steps nearer, Cuddy." Geth struck him lightly with his spurs. The horse paused by the bank and began rocking slightly.

"Sist! be quiet," for they were on the spot Gething wished. The horse gathered himself, started to rear, then sprang into the air, cleared earth-mound and trench and bounded down the hill. The tremendous buck-jump he had so unexpectedly taken, combined with his frantic descent, gave Gething no chance to get control until the level was reached. Then, with the first pull on the bridle, he realized it was too late. For a while at least Cuddy was in command. Gething tried all his tricks with the reins, the horse dashed on like a furious gust of wind, he whirled through the valley, across a ploughed field, over a fence and into more pastures. Gething, never cooler, fought for the control. The froth blown back against his white shirt was rosy with blood. Cuddy was beyond realizing his bit. Then Gething relaxed a little and let him go. He could guide him to a certain extent. Stop him he could not.

The horse was now running flatly and rapidly. He made no attempt to throw his rider. What jumps were in his way he took precisely. Unlike the crazed runaway of the city streets Cuddy never took better care of himself. It seemed that he was running for some purpose and Gething thought of Willet's often repeated remark, "Look at 'im—old Cuddy, he's thinking." Two miles had been covered and the gait had become business-like. Gething, guiding always to the left, was turning him in a huge circle. The horse reeked with sweat. "Now," thought Gething, "he's had enough," but at the first pressure on the bit Cuddy increased his speed. His breath caught in his throat. There was another mile and the wonderful run grew slower. The man felt the great horse trip and recover himself. He was tired out. Again the fight between master and horse began. Cuddy resisted weakly, then threw up his beautiful, white-starred face as if in entreaty.

"Oh, I'm——" muttered Gething and let the reins lie loose on his neck, "your own way, Cuddy. Your way is better than mine. Old friend, I'll not try to stop you again." For he knew if he tried he could now gain control. The early dusk of spring had begun to settle on the surface of the fields in a hazy radiance, a marvelous light that seemed to breathe out from the earth and stream through the sky. A mile to the east upon a hill was a farm house. The orange light from the sunset found every window, blinded them and left them blank oblongs of orange. The horse and rider passed closer to this farm. Two collies rushed forward, then stopped to bark and jump. The light enveloped them and gave each a golden halo.

Again Gething turned still keeping toward the left. A hill began to rise before them and up it the horse sped, his breath whirring and rattling in his throat, but his strength still unspent. To the very top he made his way and paused dazed. "Oh, Cuddy," cried Gething, "this is Break-Neck." For there was the wind-warped pine, the bank of earth, the trench. The horse came to a shivering standstill. The bank looked strange to him. He stood sobbing, his body rocking slightly, rocking gently, then with a sigh, came slowly down on to the turf. Gething was on his feet, his hand on the dripping neck.

"You always were a bad horse and I always loved you," he whispered, "and that was a great ride, and now——" He rose abruptly and turned away as he realized himself alone in the soft twilight. The horse was dead. Then he returned to the tense body, so strangely thin and wet, and removed saddle and bridle. With these hung on his arm he took the sombre path through the pines for home.

BLACK ART AND AMBROSE

By GUY GILPATRIC

From *Collier's, The National Weekly*

"... *The Naytives of the Seacoast told me many fearsome Tales of these Magycians, or Voodoos, as they called Them. It would seem that the Mystic Powers of these Magycians is hereditary, and that the Spells, Incantacions, and other Secretts of their Profession are passed on One to the Other and holden in great Awe by the People. The Marke of this horride Culte is the Likeness of a great Human Eye, carved in the Fleshe of the Backe, which rises in Ridges as it heals and lasts Forever* ..."

—Extract from "A Truthful Accounte of a Voyage and Journey to the Land of Afrique, Together with Numerous Drawings and Mappes, and a most Humble Petition Regarding the Same." Presented by Roberte Walting, Gent. in London, Anno D. 1651.

A FEW blocks west of the subway, and therefore off the beaten track of the average New Yorker, is San Juan Hill. If you ever happen on San Juan unawares, you will recognize it at once by its clustering family of mammoth gas houses, its streets slanting down into the North River, and the prevailing duskiness of the local complexion. If you chance to stray into San Juan after sundown, you will be relieved to note that policemen are plentiful, and that they walk in pairs. This last observation describes the social status of San Juan or any other neighbourhood better than volumes of detailed episodes could begin to do.

Of late years many of the Fust Famblies of San Juan have migrated northward to the teeming negro districts of Harlem, but enough of the old stock remains to lend the settlement its time-honoured touch of gloom. Occasionally, too, it still makes its way to the public notice by sanguinary affrays and race riots. San Juan Hill is a geographical, racial, and sociological fact, and will remain so until the day when safety razors become a universal institution.

San Juan is a community in itself. It has its churches, its clubs, its theatres, its stores, and—sighs of relief from the police—it *used* to have its saloons. It is a cosmopolitan community, too—as cosmopolitan as it can be and still retain its Senegambian motif.

Negroes from Haiti, Jamaica, Salvador, Cuba; from Morocco and Senegal; blue-black negroes from the Pacific; ebony negroes from the South; brown, tan, yellow, and buff negroes from everywhere inhabit San Juan. Every language from Arabic to Spanish is spoken by these—the cosmopolites of cosmopolitan San Juan.

Pussonally, Mr. Ambrose de Vere Travis spoke only English. Because he hailed from Galveston, Tex., he spoke it with a Gulf intonation at once liquid, rich, and musical. He stood six feet five on his bare soles, so his voice was somewhat reminiscent of the Vatican organ.

Ambrose was twenty-four years old. Our story finds him a New Yorker of three years' standing, all of which he had spent as a dweller on San Juan Hill. Originally the giant Mr. Travis had served as furnace tender in the subterraneous portions of the Swalecliffe Arms apartments, that turreted edifice in the Eighties that frowns across at the Palisades from Riverside Drive. But his size and the size of his smile had won for Ambrose the coveted and uniformed position of doorman, a post at which he served with considerable success and the incidental tips.

The recently wealthy Mr. Braumbauer, for instance, really felt that he *was* somebody, when Ambrose opened the door of his car and bowed him under the portcullis of Swalecliffe. And y'understand me, a feller's willing he should pay a little something for service once in a while. And so, one way and another, Ambrose managed to eke from his job a great deal more than he drew on pay day.

But Mr. Travis's source of income did not stop there—far from it. He had brought from Galveston a genius for rolling sevens—or, if he missed seven the first roll, he could generally make his point within the next three tries. He could hold the dice longer than any man within the San Juan memory, which, in view of the fact that craps is to San Juan what bridge is to Boston, is saying a great deal. Ambrose was simply a demon with the bones, and he was big enough to get away with it.

True, there had been difficulties.

One evening at the Social Club Ambrose held the dice for a straight sixteen passes. He and five other courtiers of fortune were bounding the ivories off the cushion of a billiard table, to the end that the contest be one of chance and not of science. In the midst of Ambrose's stentorian protests that the baby needed footwear, one of the losers forgot his breeding to the extent of claiming that Ambrose had introduced a loaded die. As he seconded his claims with a razor, the game met a temporary lull.

When the furniture had ceased crashing, the members of the club emerged from beneath the pool tables to see Mr. Travis tying up a slashed hand, while he of the razor lay moaning over a broken shoulder and exuding teeth in surprising quantities.

After this little incident no one ever so far forgot himself as to breathe the faintest aspersion on Mr. Travis, his dice, his way of throwing them down or of picking them up.

It was generally conceded that his conduct throughout the fray had been of the best, and the affair did much to raise him in popular esteem—especially as he was able to prove the caviler's charges to be utterly unfounded.

And so, with his physical beauty, his courage, and his wealth, Mr. Ambrose de Vere Travis became something of a figure in San Juan's social circles.

Just when Ambrose fell in love with Miss Aphrodite Tate is not quite clear.

Aphrodite (pronounced just as spelled) was so named because her father thought it had something to do with Africa. She was astoundingly, absolutely, and gratifyingly black, and Ambrose was sure that he had never seen any one quite so beautiful.

Aphrodite lived with her parents, the ancient and revered Fremont-Tates, patroons of San Juan. In the daytime she was engaged as maid by a family that *suttingly* treated her lovely; while in the evening she could usually be found at the St. Benedict Young People's Club. And it was here that Ambrose met her.

True love ran smoothly for a long time. At last, when he felt the time was ripe, Ambrose pleaded urgent business for two evenings and shook down the Social Club dice fanciers for the price of the ring.

Then Mr. Dominique Raffin loomed dark on the horizon. Mr. Raffin did not loom as dark as he might have loomed, however, because he was half white. He hailed from Haiti, and was the son of a French sailor and a transplanted Congo wench. He was slight of build and shifty of eye. His excuse for being was a genius for music. He could play anything, could this pasty Dominique, but of all instruments he was at his tuneful best on the alto saxophone.

"Lawd! *Oh*, Lawd!" his audience would ejaculate, as with closed eyes and heads thrown back they would drink in the sonorous emanations from the brazen tube. "Dat's de horn ob de Angel Gabriel—dat's de heabenly music ob de spears!" And so Dominique's popularity grew among the ladies of San Juan, even if among the gentlemen it did not.

To tell the truth, Dominique was something of a beau. Because he played in an orchestra, he had ample opportunity to study the deportment of people who passed as fashionable. His dress was immaculate; his hair was not so kinky that it couldn't be plastered down with brilliantine, and he perfumed himself copiously. His fingers were heavily laden with rings. Dominique's voice was whining—irritating.

His native tongue was French, but he had learned to speak English in Jamaica. Thus his accent was a curious mixture of French and Cockney, lubricated with oily African.

Altogether, it is not to be wondered that such sturdy sons of Ham as Ambrose disliked the snaky Mr. Raffin. Disliked him the more when his various musical and cultural accomplishments made him a general favourite with the ladies. And then, when he absolutely cut Mr. Travis from the affections of Miss Tate, the wrath of the blacker and more wholesome San Jaun citizens knew no bounds.

As for Ambrose—he sulked. Even his friends, the fur-lined tenants of Swalecliffe Arms, noticed that something worried the swart guardian of their gate. In the evenings Ambrose gave his entire time to frenzied rolling of the bones and was surprised to see that here, at least, luck had not deserted him.

On the few occasions when he forsook the green baize for an evening's dancing at the St. Benedict Young People's Guild, the sight of the coveted Miss Aphrodite whirling in the arms of the hated Raffin almost overcame him.

Finally the lovesick Mr. Travis decided to call upon the lady of his heart and demand an explanation. After some rehearsal of what he wanted to say, Ambrose betook himself to the tenement in which the Tate family dwelt. At sight of her cast-off swain, Miss Aphrodite showed the whites of her eyes and narrowed her lips to a thin straight line—perhaps an inch and a half thin. Evidently she was displeased.

Aphrodite opened the interview by inquiring why she was being pestered and intermediated by a low-down black nigger that didn't have no mo' brains than he had manners. Her feelings was likely to git the better of her at any moment; in which event Mr. Travis had better watch out, that was all—jest watch out.

The astounded Mr. Travis did his best to pacify this Amazon; to explain that he had merely come to inquire the reason for her displeasure; to learn in what respect Mr. Raffin had proved himself so sweetly desirable.

The answer was brief and crushing. It seemed that where Mr. Travis was a big, bulky opener of doors, Mr. Raffin was a sleek and cultured Chesterfield—a musician—an artist. Where Mr. Travis could not dance without stepping on everybody in the room, Mr. Raffin was a veritable Mordkin. Where Mr. Travis hung out with a bunch of no-good crap-shooting black buck niggers, Mr. Raffin's orchestral duties brought him into the most cultured s'ciety. In short, the yellow man from Haiti was a gentleman; the black man from Texas was a boor.

This unexpected tirade made the unhappy Ambrose a trifle weak in the knees. Then pride came to the rescue, and he drew himself to his full and towering six feet five. He held out his mammoth hands before Miss Aphrodite and warned her that with them, at the first provocation, he would jest take and bust Mr. Raffin in two. This done, he would throw the shuddering fragments into the street, and with his feet—Exhibit B—would kick them the entire length and breadth of the neighbourhood.

This threat only aroused new fires of scorn and vituperation, and Miss Tate informed her guest that, should he ever attempt the punitive measures described, Mr. Raffin would cut him up into little pieces. It seemed that Mr. Raffin carried a knife, and that he knew how to use it.

Mr. Travis snorted at this, and stamped out of the Tat apartment.

At his exit, doors closed softly on every floor, because the neighbours had listened to the tête-à-tête with intense interest. Even people in the next house had been able to hear most of it.

Ambrose made his furious way toward the Social Club, his mind set on mortal encounter with the hated Dominique. But—here was an inspiration!—why not win his money away from him first? To win away his last cent—to humble him—to ruin him—and then to break him in two and kick the pieces through the San Juan causeways, as per programme. This would be a revenge indeed!

Ambrose noted with satisfaction that Mr. Raffin was already at play, and crossing the smoke-filled room he threw down some money and took his place in the game.

Now, Mr. Travis was ordinarily a very garrulous and vociferous crap shooter, but to-night he was savagely silent. There was a disturbing, electric *something* in the air that the neutrals felt and feared. There was a look in the Travis eye that boded ill for somebody, and one by one the more prudent gamesters withdrew.

Then suddenly the storm broke.

Later accounts were not clear as to just what started the fray, but start it did.

Dominique's knife appeared from some place, and the table crashed. Then the knife swished through space like a hornet and buried its point harmlessly in a door across the room.

What followed is still a subject of wondering conversation on San Juan Hill.

It seems that Mr. Travis seized Mr. Raffin by the collar of his coat, and swung him round and round and over his head. Mr. Raffin streamed almost straight out, like the imitation airplanes that whirl dizzily about the tower in an amusement park. Suddenly there was a rending of cloth, and Dominique shot through the air to encounter the wall with a soul-satisfying thump.

Ambrose looked bewildered at the torn clothing he held in his hand, and then at the limp form of his late antagonist. Mr. Raffin lay groaning, naked from the waist up.

Ambrose strode across to administer further chastisement,

out was halted by a cry from one of the onlookers. This man stood pointing at Dominique's naked back—pointing, and staring with eyes that rolled with genuine negro terror.

"Look!" gasped the affrighted one. "Look! It's de Voodoo Eye—*dat man's a witch!* Ambrose, fo' de Lawd's sake, git away from hyar!"

"What you-all talkin' about?" scoffed Ambrose, striding closer, and rolling Dominique so that the light shone full on his back. "What you-all talkin'—— *Good Lawd!*"

This last ejaculation from Ambrose was caused by the sight that met his gaze.

There, on the yellow back before him, reaching from shoulder to shoulder, was tattooed the likeness of a great human eye!

Everyone saw it now. To some—the Northern darkies—it meant nothing. But to the old-school Southern negroes it meant mystery—magic—death. *It was the sign of the Voodoo!*

Several of the more superstitious onlookers retreated in poor order, their teeth chattering. Their mammies had told them about the Voodoo Eye. They remembered the tales whispered in the slave quarters about people being prayed to death by these baleful creatures of ill omen! They weren't going to take any chances!

Ambrose, for all his natural courage, was shaken. He remembered old Tom Blue, the Texas Voodoo, who poisoned twenty-one people and came to life after the white men lynched him. And now he had laid rough hands on one of the deadly clan; had brought upon himself the wrath of a man who could simply *wish* him to death!

Trembling, he stooped down and looked at the Devil's Sign. He looked again—closely. Then he broke out into a ringing peal of wholesome darky laughter.

"Git up!" he shouted, as Dominique showed signs of life. "Git up, Mr. Voodoo, befo' Ah gits impatient an' throws you out de window!"

This recklessness—this defiance of the dread power—shocked even the least superstitious of the audience. By this time they were all under the spell of this mysterious mark. Those who hadn't recognized it at once had been quickly enlightened by the others.

Ambrose seized Dominique by the shoulder and dragged

him to his feet. Swaying unsteadily, the mulatto looked around him through eyes closed to snakelike slits.

"Raffin," said Ambrose, "you-all has on yo' back de Eye ob Voodoo. Dese gennlemen hyar thinks yo' *is* a Voodoo. Ah know yo' *ain't!*"

"I *am* a Voodoo! An' you, you *sacré cochon,*" hissed Raffin, "I'll make you wish you had nevaire been born!"

"Well, jes' fo' de present," laughed Ambrose, good humour spreading all over his face, "you-all had better git outa my way, an' stay *out!* Git outa hyar *quick!*"

Dominique, his evil face twitching with fury, picked up the ragged shreds of his coat and walked unsteadily out.

At his exit a dead silence fell upon the remaining members. Then they gathered together in excited groups and discussed the incident in heated undertones. Ambrose, quite unconcerned, took up a pack of cards and commenced a game of solitaire.

He wasn't worrying. He knew that Dominique was no more a Voodoo than he was. Startled at first, he had noticed that the eye had not been carved in Dominique's back, as it should have been, but had been tattooed. This in itself made the thing doubtful. But more than this, the marks were the unmistakably accurate work of an electric tattooing machine.

Ambrose had spent his youth on the Galveston water front, and knew tattooing in all its forms. Electric tattooing on a Voodoo was about as much in keeping with the ancient and awesome dignity of the cult as spangled tights would be on the King of England. No—it was ridiculous. Dominique was not a Voodoo!

Ambrose continued his solitaire, humming as he played. Occasionally he cast an amused eye at the excited groups across the room, and was not surprised when Mr. Behemoth Scott, president of the club, at last came over to him.

"Mistah Travis," began Mr. Scott deferentially, clearing his throat, "would you-all be good enough to jine our little gatherin' while we confabulate on dis hyar recent contabulaneous incident?"

"Suttingly, Mr. Scott, suttingly!" said Ambrose, pushing back his chair, and crossing the room with the quaking official. "What can Ah do fo' you-all?"

"Well, jest this," said Mr. Scott. "You gennlemen kin'ly

correc' me or bear out what Ah say. Leavin' aside all argument whether they *is* sech things as Voodoos, Ah guess any of you gennlemen from the South will remember Aunt Belle Agassiz and Tom Blue. Ah guess yo' mammies all done tole 'bout the African Voodoos, an' how ebery now an' den one of 'em crops up still. An' Ah guess dat we've seen to-night dat we've got a Voodoo among us. Now, Mr. Travis"—here he turned to Ambrose—"we know what Aunt Belle Agassiz done on de Mathis Plantation in Georgia—*you* ought to know what Tom Blue did in Texas. So we wants to warn you, as a fren' an' membah of dis club in good standin', dat you better leave town to-night."

An assenting murmur arose from the crowd, with much rolling of eyes and nodding of heads.

Ambrose held up his hand for silence. A serious expression came over his features, and he towered tall and straight before them.

"Gennlemen," he said, "Ah sho appreciates yo' good sperit in dis hyar unfo'tunate affair. But Ah tells you-all hyar an' now dat Dominique Raffin ain't no mo' Voodoo den Ah is. Now, Ah ain't sayin' dat he *ain't* a Voodoo, an' Ah ain't sayin' dat Ah *am* one. All Ah says is dat Ah's as *much* of a Voodoo as he is—an' Ah'm willin' to prove it!"

"How you-all do dat, Ambrose?" asked somebody.

"Ah'm comin' to dat," replied Ambrose. "If you-all wants to decide dis mattah beyont all doubt, Ah respekf'ly suggests dat we hold a *see*-ance in dis hyar room, under any c'nditions dat you-all kin d'vise. If Ah cain't show yo mo' supernat'ral man'festations dan he can, Ah gives him fifty dollahs. If it's de oder way 'roun', he leaves de city within twenty-fo' hours. Is dat fair?"

"Well, it suttinly soun's puff'cly jest," replied Mr. Scott. "We-all will appint a committee to frame de rules of de *see*-ance, an' make 'em fair fo' both. You's been willin' to prove yo'-se'f, Ambrose, an' yo' couldn't do mo'. If dis m'latter Voodoo don't want to do lak'wise, he can leave dese pahts moughty sudden. Ain't dat so, gennlemen?"

"Yassuh—he'll leave *quick!*" was the threatening reply.

"All right den, Ambrose," continued the spokesman, "we'll 'range fo' dis sperit-summonin' contes' jes' as soon as we kin. We'll have it nex' Satiddy night at lates'. Meanwhile we-all is moughty obleeged to yo' for yo' willin'-ness to do de right thing."

The great night arrived, and San Juan, dressed in its gala finery, wended its chattering way to the Senegambian séance. But beneath the finery and the chatter ran a subtle undercurrent of foreboding, for your negro is superstitious, and, well, *Voodoos are Voodoos!*

Dominique Raffin, dressed in somber black, went to the club alone and unattended save by Miss Aphrodite Tate. San Juan, fearing the Raffin mulatto and his ghostly powers, had held its respectful distance ever since the evening when Ambrose and his rage had revealed them. Familiarity breeding contempt, Miss Aphrodite knew her man, and feared him not.

They found the rooms of the social club full of excited negroes, for never before in San Juan's history had such a momentous event been scheduled. Raffin and Aphrodite were received with a fearsome respect by Behemoth Scott, who had been appointed master of ceremonies.

"Jes' make yo'se'f to home," he greeted them. "Mista Travis ain't come yit; we has ten minutes befo' de contes' styarts."

At last, with a bare minute to spare, Ambrose smilingly entered. He wore his splendid full-dress suit, a wonderful creation of San Juan's leading tailor, who, at Ambrose's tasteful suggestion, had faced the lapels with satin of the most royal purple. Set out by this background of colourful lapel was a huge yellow chrysanthemum, while on the broad red band that diagonally traversed his shining shirt front glittered like a decoration, the insignia from his Swalecliffe uniform cap.

"Good evenin', folks," was his cheerful greeting. "If you-all is quite ready fo' dis *see*-ance, an' provided mah—er—wuthy opponent am ready, Ah'd jes' as soon *pro*ceed."

Miss Aphrodite gazed on the imposing figure of Ambrose with more than a little admiration. Comparing him with the trembling Raffin, she found much in his favour.

All but his footwear. Accustomed as she had become to the glistening patent leathers affected by Raffin, Ambrose's clumsy congress gaiters somewhat marred his gorgeousness. Nevertheless, she felt her affections wavering. Her speculations were interrupted by the voice of the master of ceremonies:

"Ladies an' gennlemen," began Mr. Scott, "we-all has d'cided to form a circle of twelve of our membahs wif dese two Voodoo gennlemen asettin' opp'site each oder in de circle. In o'dah to preclude any poss'bility of either Mista Travis or Mista Raffin from leavin' dere places, we has d'cided to tie dem to dere cheers by ropes passed 'roun' dere bodies an' fastened to de backs of de cheers. De lights will den be distinguished. When he lights is tu'ned out, Mista Raffin will be given fifteen minutes in which to summon de supernat'ral proofs—whatevah dey may be—of his bein' Voodoo. Den Mista Travis will be given his chanct."

Amid the hushed whisperings of the assemblage the committee, six men and six women, Aphrodite included, took their places in the circle. Ambrose and the mulatto were seated opposite each other and were perhaps twelve feet apart. Raffin, nervously licking his lips, sat bolt upright while members of the committee passed ropes around him and the back of his chair, and tied his hands. In direct contrast to his rival, Ambrose slouched down in his seat and joked with the trembling members as they secured him in his place.

Those not on the committee crowded close to the chair backs of the circle in order that nothing should escape them. The excitement was tense, and everyone was breathing hard. When all was ready Mr. Behemoth Scott took his place in the circle. Drawing a long breath and grasping his chair for support, he spoke in a hushed and husky voice: "All raidy, now? Ah asks silence from eve'body. *Turn out de lights!*"

At the fateful words Stygian darkness enveloped the crowded room. The shades had been drawn and not the faintest ray from the dim street lights penetrated the place. It was stifling hot, and the assembled investigators were perspiring freely. . . .

Silence—black, awe-inspired silence! Two hundred pairs of superstitious eyes peered into the horrible gloom—two hundred pairs of ears strained at the tomblike stillness. The suspense was awful, and none dared move. Occasionally some familiar sound came from the world outside: the clang of the Tenth Avenue car or the whistle of a tugboat out in the river, but these sounds were of another existence—they seemed distant and unfamiliar and wholly out of place in the mystery and terror of the Voodoo seance.

The minutes slid by, and nothing happened. The suspense was worse than ever. Something stirred in the circle. Two hundred hearts missed a beat. Then the whining, terror-stricken voice of the mulatto broke the stillness: "Let Travis try," he whispered hoarsely. "My spirits will not come until 'e 'as tried. Let 'im try fo' fifteen minutes, and when 'e 'as failed I will summon the ghost of Bula-Wayo, the king of all the tribes of the Niger. But let Travis try first!" This last almost pleadingly.

A moment more of silence and Ambrose's deep voice boomed forth in the darkness.

"Ah's willin'," he declared. "Anythin' dat now appears will be mah doin'—ten minits is all Ah asks. Am dat sat'sfact'ry?"

"Yaas," replied the voice of Behemoth Scott. "Go ahaid wif yo' sperit-summonin', Mista Travis."

"Ah'll cawncentrate now," replied Ambrose, "an' sho'tly you-all will witness ample proof of mah bein' a genuine Voodoo. *Ah's stahtin'*."

Silence more terrible than ever fell upon the waiting negroes. Then—horror of horrors! a peculiar grating, rustling sound came from the vicinity of Ambrose—a slight creaking—and again silence. The investigators held hands of neighbours who trembled from sheer panic, whose breath came hard and panting from this awful suspense!

Another creaking, as though Ambrose had shifted his weight in his chair. . . .

Then—baleful—in its green, ghastly glow—a dim, indistinct light shone in the centre of the circle! Moving slowly, like a newly awakened spirit, it waved in the very midst of the gasping committee. Back and forth, up and down, it moved—glowing, vaporous, ghostly. Two hundred pairs of bulging eyes saw the horror—and realized that it was an enormous hand, terribly deformed!

Some one moaned with terror—a woman screamed. "De hand ob death!" shrieked a man. "Run—run fo' yo' lives!"

The stampede was spontaneous! Chairs were overturned and tables smashed in this frightful panic in the dark. No one thought of turning on the lights—everyone's sole aim was to leave that appalling shining hand—and get out!

A crashing on the stairway marked where Raffin, chair and all, was making his fear-stricken way to the street. In one brief minute the place was apparently empty save for Ambrose. Still tied to his chair, he inquired: "Is any one hyar?"

For a second there was silence, then the dulcet tones of Miss Aphrodite fell on the big negro's ear: "Ah's hyar, Ambrose," she said.

"Well, den"—recognizing her voice—"would you mine lightin' de gas till Ah can tie mahself loose from dis hyar throne ob glory?"

In a moment a feeble gaslight shone, disclosing Aphrodite—somewhat disarranged by the panic—standing smiling in front of the erstwhile Voodoo. She looked down at his feet. There, sure enough, one huge member was unshod and stockingless; the elastic-slit congress gaiter, lost in the shuffle, lay out of the radius of Ambrose's long leg. Miss Aphrodite picked it up and, stooping, slipped it over his mighty toes, noticing as she did so the thick coating of phosphorescent paint that still covered them.

"Ambrose," she whispered, "Ah wasn't scaired. No ghos' eber was bohn dat had han's de size ob yo' feet!"

An embarrassed silence followed; the gas jet flickered weakly; then Ambrose said: "Untie mah han's, Aphrodite—Ah'd jes' lak to hug you!"

"Oh, Ambrose," she cried coyly. But she untied the rope just the same.

Again came silence, broken only by a certain strange sound. Then Ambrose's voice came softly through the gloom: "Aphrodite," it said, "yo' lips am jes' lak plush!"

THE JUDGMENT OF VULCAN

By LEE FOSTER HARTMAN

From *Harper's Monthly Magazine*

TO DINE on the veranda of the Marine Hotel is the one delightful surprise which Port Charlotte affords the adventurer who has broken from the customary paths of travel in the South Seas. On an eminence above the town, solitary and aloof like a monastery, and deep in its garden of lemon-trees, it commands a wide prospect of sea and sky. By day, the Pacific is a vast stretch of blue, flat like a floor, with a blur of distant islands on the horizon—chief among them Muloa, with its single volcanic cone tapering off into the sky. At night, this smithy of Vulcan becomes a glow of red, throbbing faintly against the darkness, a capricious and sullen beacon immeasurably removed from the path of men. Viewed from the veranda of the Marine Hotel, its vast flare on the horizon seems hardly more than an insignificant spark, like the glowing cigar-end of some guest strolling in the garden after dinner.

It may very likely have been my lighted cigar that guided Eleanor Stanleigh to where I was sitting in the shadows. Her uncle, Major Stanleigh, had left me a few minutes before, and I was glad of the respite from the queer business he had involved me in. The two of us had returned that afternoon from Muloa, where I had taken him in my schooner, the *Sylph*, to seek out Leavitt and make some inquiries—very important inquiries, it seemed, in Miss Stanleigh's behalf.

Three days in Muloa, under the shadow of the grim and flame-throated mountain, while I was forced to listen to Major Stanleigh's persistent questionnaire and Leavitt's erratic and garrulous responses—all this, as I was to discover later, at the instigation of the Major's niece—had made me frankly curious about the girl.

I had seen her only once, and then at a distance across the veranda, one night when I had been dining there with a friend; but that single vision of her remained vivid and unforgetable—a tall girl of a slender shapeliness, crowned by a mass of reddish-gold hair that smoldered above the clear olive pallor of her skin. With that flawless and brilliant colouring she was marked for observation—had doubtless been schooled to a perfect indifference to it, for the slow, almost indolent, grace of her movements was that of a woman coldly unmindful of the gazes lingering upon her. She could not have been more than twenty-six or -seven, but I got an unmistakable impression of weariness or balked purpose emanating from her in spite of her youth and glorious physique. I looked up to see her crossing the veranda to join her uncle and aunt—correct, well-to-do English people that one placed instantly—and my stare was only one of many that followed her as she took her seat and threw aside the light scarf that swathed her bare and gleaming shoulders.

My companion, who happened to be the editor of the local paper, promptly informed me regarding her name and previous residence—the gist of some "social item" which he had already put into print; but these meant nothing, and I could only wonder what had brought her to such an out-of-the-way part of the world as Port Charlotte. She did not seem like a girl who was traveling with her uncle and aunt; one got rather the impression that she was bent on a mission of her own and was dragging her relatives along because the conventions demanded it. I hazarded to my companion the notion that a woman like Miss Stanleigh could have but one of two purposes in this lonely part of the world—she was fleeing from a lover or seeking one.

"In that case," rejoined my friend, with the cynical shrug of the newspaper man, "she has very promptly succeeded. It's whispered that she is going to marry Joyce—of Malduna Island, you know. Only met him a fortnight ago. Quite a romance, I'm told."

I lifted my eyebrows at that, and looked again at Miss Stanleigh. Just at that instant she happened to look up. It was a wholly indifferent gaze; I am confident that she was no more aware of me than if I had been one of the veranda posts which her eyes had chanced to encounter. But in the indescribable sensation of that moment I felt that here was a woman who bore a secret burden, although, as my informing host put it, her heart had romantically found its haven only two weeks ago.

She was endeavouring to get trace of a man named Farquharson, as I was permitted to learn a few days later. Ostensibly, it was Major Stanleigh who was bent on locating this young Englishman—Miss Stanleigh's interest in the quest was guardedly withheld—and the trail had led them a pretty chase around the world until some clue, which I never clearly understood, brought them to Port Charlotte. The major's immediate objective was an eccentric chap named Leavitt who had marooned himself in Muloa. The island offered an ideal retreat for one bent on shunning his own kind, if he did not object to the close proximity of a restive volcano. Clearly, Leavitt did not. He had a scientific interest in the phenomena exhibited by volcanic regions and was versed in geological lore, but the rumours about Leavitt—practically no one ever visited Muloa—did not stop at that. And, as Major Stanleigh and I were to discover, the fellow seemed to have developed a genuine affection for Lakalatcha, as the smoking cone was called by the natives of the adjoining islands. From long association he had come to know its whims and moods as one comes to know those of a petulant woman one lives with. It was a bizarre and preposterous intimacy, in which Leavitt seemed to find a wholly acceptable substitute for human society, and there was something repellant about the man's eccentricity. He had various names for the smoking cone that towered a mile or more above his head: "Old Flame-eater," or "Lava-spitter," he would at times familiarly and irreverently call it; or, again, "The Maiden Who Never Sleeps," or "The Single-breasted Virgin"—these last, however, always in the musical Malay equivalent. He had no end of names—romantic, splenetic, of opprobrium, or outright endearment—to suit, I imagine, Lakalatcha's varying moods. In one respect they puzzled me—they were of conflicting genders, some feminine and some masculine, as if in Leavitt's loose-frayed imagination the mountain that beguiled his days and disturbed his nights were hermaphroditic.

Leavitt as a source of information regarding the missing Farquharson seemed proposterous when one reflected how out of touch with the world he had been, but, to my astonishment, Major Stanleigh's clue was right, for he had at last stumbled upon a man who had known Farquharson well and who was voluminous about him—quite willingly so. With the *Sylph* at anchor, we lay off Muloa for three nights, and Leavitt gave us our fill of Farquharson, along with innumerable digressions about volcanoes, neoplatonism, the Single Tax, and what not. There was no keeping Leavitt to a coherent narrative about the missing Farquharson. He was incapable of it, and Major Stanleigh and myself had simply to wait in patience while Leavitt, delighted to have an audience, dumped out for us the fantastic contents of his mind, odd vagaries, recondite trash, and all. He was always getting away from Farquharson, but, then, he was unfailingly bound to come back to him. We had only to wait and catch the solid grains that now and then fell in the winnowing of that unending stream of chaff. It was a tedious and exasperating process, but it had its compensations. At times Leavitt could be as uncannily brilliant as he was dull and boresome. The conviction grew upon me that he had become a little demented, as if his brain had been tainted by the sulphurous fumes exhaled by the smoking crater above his head. His mind smoked, flickered, and flared like an unsteady lamp, blown upon by choking gases, in which the oil had run low.

But of the wanderer Farquharson he spoke with precision and authority, for he had shared with Farquharson his bungalow there in Muloa—a period of about six months, it seemed—and there Farquharson had contracted a tropic fever and died.

"Well, at last we have got all the facts," Major Stanleigh sighed with satisfaction when the *Sylph* was heading back to Port Charlotte. Muloa, lying astern, we were no longer watching. Leavitt, at the water's edge, had waved us a last good-by and had then abruptly turned back into the forest, very likely to go clambering like a demented goat up the flanks of his beloved volcano and to resume poking about in its steaming fissures—an occupation of which he never tired.

"The evidence is conclusive, don't you think?—the grave, Farquharson's personal effects, those pages of the poor devil's diary."

I nodded assent. In my capacity as owner of the *Sylph* I had merely undertaken to furnish Major Stanleigh with passage to Muloa and back, but the events of the last three days had made me a party to the many conferences, and I was now on terms of something like intimacy with the rather stiff and pompous English gentleman. How far I was from sharing his real confidence I was to discover later when Eleanor Stanleigh gave me hers.

"My wife and niece will be much relieved to hear all this—a family matter, you understand, Mr. Barnaby," he had said to me when we landed. "I should like to present you to them before we leave Port Charlotte for home."

But, as it turned out, it was Eleanor Stanleigh who presented herself, coming upon me quite unexpectedly that night after our return while I sat smoking in the shadowy garden of the Marine Hotel. I had dined with the major, after he had explained that the ladies were worn out by the heat and general developments of the day and had begged to be excused. And I was frankly glad not to have to endure another discussion of the deceased Farquharson, of which I was heartily tired after hearing little else for the last three days. I could not help wondering how the verbose and pompous major had paraphrased and condensed that inchoate mass of biography and reminiscence into an orderly account for his wife and niece. He had doubtless devoted the whole afternoon to it. Sitting under the cool green of the lemon-trees, beneath a sky powdered with stars, I reflected that I, at least, was done with Farquharson forever. But I was not, for just then Eleanor Stanleigh appeared before me.

I was startled to hear her addressing me by name, and then calmly begging me to resume my seat on the bench under the arbor. She sat down also, her flame-coloured hair and bare shoulders gleaming in the darkness. She was the soul of directness and candour, and after a thoughtful, searching look into my face she came to the point at once. She wanted to hear about Farquharson—from me.

"Of course, my uncle has given me a very full account of what he learned from Mr. Leavitt, and yet many things puzzle me—this Mr. Leavitt most of all."

"A queer chap," I epitomized him. "Frankly, I don't quite make him out, Miss Stanleigh—marooning himself on that infernal island and seemingly content to spend his days there."

"Is he so old?" she caught me up quickly.

"No, he isn't," I reflected. "Of course, it's difficult to judge ages out here. The climate, you know. Leavitt's well under forty, I should say. But that's a most unhealthy spot he has chosen to live in."

"Why does he stay there?"

I explained about the volcano. "You can have no idea what an obsession it is with him. There isn't a square foot of its steaming, treacherous surface that he hasn't been over, mapping new fissures, poking into old lava-beds, delving into the crater itself on favourable days——"

"Isn't it dangerous?"

"In a way, yes. The volcano itself is harmless enough. It smokes unpleasantly now and then, splutters and rumbles as if about to obliterate all creation, but for all its bluster it only manages to spill a trickle or two of fresh lava down its sides—just tamely subsides after deluging Leavitt with a shower of cinders and ashes. But Leavitt won't leave it alone. He goes poking into the very crater, half strangling himself in its poisonous fumes, scorching the shoes off his feet, and once, I believe, he lost most of his hair and eyebrows—a narrow squeak. He throws his head back and laughs at any word of caution. To my notion, it's foolhardy to push a scientific curiosity to that extreme."

"Is it, then, just scientific curiosity?" mused Miss Stanleigh.

Something in her tone made me stop short. Her eyes had lifted to mine—almost appealingly, I fancied. Her innocence, her candour, her warm beauty, which was like a pale phosphorescence in the starlit darkness—all had their potent effect upon me in that moment. I felt impelled to a sudden burst of confidence.

"At times I wonder. I've caught a look in his eyes, when he's been down on his hands and knees, staring into some infernal vent-hole—a look that is—well, uncanny, as if he were peering into the bowels of the earth for something quite outside the conceptions of science. You might think that volcano had worked some spell over him, turned his mind. He prattles to it or storms at it as if it were a living creature. Queer, yes; and he's impressive, too, with a sort of magnetic personality that attracts and repels you violently at the same time. He's like a cake of ice dipped in alcohol and set aflame. I can't describe him. When he talks——"

"Does he talk about himself?"

I had to confess that he had told us practically not a word. He had discussed everything under heaven in his brilliant, erratic way, with a fleer of cynicism toward it all, but he had left himself out completely. He had given us Farquharson with relish, and in infinite detail, from the time the poor fellow first turned up in Muloa, put ashore by a native craft. Talking about Farquharson was second only to his delight in talking about volcanoes. And the result for me had been innumerable vivid but confused impressions of the young Englishman who had by chance invaded Leavitt's solitude and had lingered there, held by some attraction, until he sickened and died. It was like a jumbled mosaic put together again by inexpert hands.

"Did you get the impression that the two men had very much in common?"

"Quite the contrary," I answered. "But Major Stanleigh should know——"

"My uncle never met Mr. Farquharson."

I was fairly taken aback at that, and a silence fell between us. It was impossible to divine the drift of her questions. It was as if some profound mistrust weighed upon her and she was not so much seeking to interrogate me as she was groping blindly for some chance word of mine that might illuminate her doubts.

I looked at the girl in silent wonder, yes, and in admiration of her bronze and ivory beauty in the full flower of her glorious youth—and I thought of Joyce. I felt that it was like her to have fallen in love simply but passionately at the mere lifting of the finger of Fate. It was only another demonstration of the unfathomable mystery, or miracle, which love is. Joyce was lucky, indeed favoured of the gods, to have touched the spring in this girl's heart which no other man could reach, and by the rarest of chances—her coming out to this remote corner of the world. Lucky Joyce! I knew him slightly—a straightforward young fellow, very simple and whole-souled, enthusiastically absorbed in developing his rubber lands in Malduna.

Miss Stanleigh remained lost in thought while her fingers

oyed with the pendant of the chain that she wore. In the
arkness I caught the glitter of a small gold cross.

"My. Barnaby," she finally broke the silence, and paused.
I have decided to tell you something. This Mr. Farquhar-
on was my husband."

Again a silence fell, heavy and prolonged, in which I sat as
f drugged by the night air that hung soft and perfumed about
ıs. It seemed incredible that in that fleeting instant she had
poken at all.

"I was young—and very foolish, I suppose."

With that confession, spoken with simple dignity, she broke
ff again. Clearly, some knowledge of the past she deemed
t necessary to impart to me. If she halted over her words,
t was rather to dismiss what was irrelevant to the matter in
ıand, in which she sought my counsel.

"I did not see him for four years—did not wish to. . . .
And he vanished completely. . . . Four years!—just a
velcome blank!"

Her shoulders lifted and a little shiver went over her.

"But even a blank like that can become unendurable. To
e always dragging at a chain, and not knowing where it leads
o. . . ." Her hand slipped from the gold cross on her
reast and fell to the other in her lap, which it clutched tightly.
'Four years. . . . I tried to make myself believe that
e was gone forever—was dead. It was wicked of me."

My murmur of polite dissent led her to repeat her words.

"Yes, and even worse than that. During the past month
I have actually prayed that he might be dead. . . . I
hall be punished for it."

I ventured no rejoinder to these words of self-condem-
ation. Joyce, I reflected, mundanely, had clearly swept
er off her feet in the ardour of their first meeting and in-
tant love.

"It must be a great relief to you," I murmured at length,
'to have it all definitely settled at last."

"If I could only feel that it was!"

I turned in amazement, to see her leaning a little forward,
er hands still tightly clasped in her lap, and her eyes fixed
ıpon the distant horizon where the red spark of Lakalatcha's
tertorous breathing flamed and died away. Her breast rose
nd fell, as if timed to the throbbing of that distant flare,

"I want you to take me to that island—to-morrow."

"Why, surely, Miss Stanleigh," I burst forth, "there can't be any reasonable doubt. Leavitt's mind may be a little flighty—he may have embroidered his story with a few gratuitous details; but Farquharson's books and things—the material evidence of his having lived there——"

"And having died there?"

"Surely Leavitt wouldn't have fabricated that! If you had talked with him——"

"I should not care to talk with Mr. Leavitt," Miss Stanleigh cut me short. "I want only to go and see—if he *is* Mr. Leavitt."

"If he *is* Mr. Leavitt!" For a moment I was mystified, and then in a sudden flash I understood. "But that's preposterous—impossible!"

I tried to conceive of Leavitt in so monstrous a rôle, tried to imagine the missing Farquharson still in the flesh and beguiling Major Stanleigh and myself with so outlandish a story, devising all that ingenious detail to trick us into a belief in his own death. It would indeed have argued a warped mind, guided by some unfathomable purpose.

"I devoutly hope you are right," Miss Stanleigh was saying, with deliberation. "But it is not preposterous, and it is not impossible—if you had known Mr. Farquharson as I have."

It was a discreet confession. She wished me to understand—without the necessity of words. My surmise was that she had met and married Farquharson, whoever he was, under the spell of some momentary infatuation, and that he had proved himself to be an unspeakable brute whom she had speedily abandoned.

"I am determined to go to Muloa, Mr. Barnaby," she announced, with decision. "I want you to make the arrangements, and with as much secrecy as possible. I shall ask my aunt to go with me."

I assured Miss Stanleigh that the *Sylph* was at her service.

Mrs. Stanleigh was a large bland woman, inclined to stoutness and to making confidences, with an intense dislike of the tropics and physical discomforts of any sort. How her niece prevailed upon her to make that surreptitious trip to Muloa, which we set out upon two days later, I have never been able to imagine. The accommodations aboard the schooner were cramped, to say the least, and the good lady had a perfect horror of volcanoes. The fact that Lakalatcha had behind it a record of a century or more of good conduct did not weigh with her in the least. She was convinced that it would blow its head off the moment the *Sylph* got within range. She was fidgety, talkative, and continually concerned over the state of her complexion, inspecting it in the mirror of her bag at frequent intervals and using a powder-puff liberally to mitigate the pernicious effects of the tropic sun. But once having been induced to make the voyage, I must admit she stuck manfully by her decision, ensconcing herself on deck with books and cushions and numerous other necessities to her comfort, and making the best of the sleeping quarters below. As the captain of the *Sylph*, she wanted me to understand that she had intrusted her soul to my charge, declaring that she would not draw an easy breath until we were safe again in Port Charlotte.

"This dreadful business of Eleanor's," was the way she referred to our mission, and she got round quite naturally to telling me of Farquharson while acquainting me with her fears about volcanoes. Some years before, Pompeii and Herculaneum had had a most unsettling effect upon her nerves. Vesuvius was slightly in eruption at the time. She confessed to never having had an easy moment while in Naples. And it was in Naples that her niece and Farquharson had met. It had been, as I surmised, a swift, romantic courtship, in which Farquharson, quite irreproachable in antecedents and manners, had played the part of an impetuous lover. Italian skies had done the rest. There was an immediate marriage, in spite of Mrs. Stanleigh's protests, and the young couple were off on a honeymoon trip by themselves. But when Mrs. Stanleigh rejoined her husband at Nice, and together they returned to their home in Sussex, a surprise was in store for them. Eleanor was already there—alone, crushed, and with lips absolutely sealed. She had divested herself of everything that linked her to Farquharson; she refused to adopt her married name.

"I shall bless every saint in heaven when we have quite done with this dreadful business of Eleanor's," Mrs. Stanleigh confided to me from her deck-chair. "This trip that she insists on making herself seems quite uncalled for. But you needn't think, Captain Barnaby, that I'm going to set foot on that dreadful island—not even for the satisfaction of seeing Mr. Farquharson's grave—and I'm shameless enough to say that it *would* be a satisfaction. If you could imagine the tenth part of what I have had to put up with, all these months we've been traveling about trying to locate the wretch! No, indeed—I shall stay right here on this boat and intrust Eleanor to your care while ashore. And I should not think it ought to take long, now should it?"

I confessed aloud that I did not see how it could. If by any chance the girl's secret conjecture about Leavitt's identity was right, it would be verified in the mere act of coming face to face with him, and in that event it would be just as well to spare the unsuspecting aunt the shock of that discovery.

We reached Muloa just before nightfall, letting go the anchor in placid water under the lee of the shore while the *Sylph* swung to and the sails fluttered and fell. A vast hush lay over the world. From the shore the dark green of the forest confronted us with no sound or sign of life. Above, and at this close distance blotting out half the sky over our heads, towered the huge cone of Lakalatcha with scarred and blackened flanks. It was in one of its querulous moods. The feathery white plume of steam, woven by the wind into soft, fantastic shapes, no longer capped the crater; its place had been usurped by thick, dark fumes of smoke swirling sullenly about. In the fading light I marked the red, malignant glow of a fissure newly broken out in the side of the ragged cone, from which came a thin, white trickle of lava.

There was no sign of Leavitt, although the *Sylph* must have been visible to him for several hours, obviously making for the island. I fancied that he must have been unusually absorbed in the vagaries of his beloved volcano. Otherwise he would have wondered what was bringing us back again and his tall figure in shabby white drill would have greeted us from the shore. Instead, there confronted us only the belt of dark, matted green girdling the huge bulk of Lakalatcha which soared skyward, sinister, mysterious, eternal.

In the brief twilight the shore vanished into dim obscurity. Miss Stanleigh, who for the last hour had been standing by the rail, silently watching the island, at last spoke to me over her shoulder:

"Is it far inland—the place? Will it be difficult to find in the dark?"

Her question staggered me, for she was clearly bent on seeking out Leavitt at once. A strange calmness overlay her. She paid no heed to Lakalatcha's gigantic, smoke-belching cone, but, with fingers gripping the rail, scanned the forbidding and inscrutable forest, behind which lay the answer to her torturing doubt.

I acceded to her wish without protest. Leavitt's bungalow lay a quarter of a mile distant. There would be no difficulty in following the path. I would have a boat put over at once, I announced in a casual way which belied my real feelings, for I was beginning to share some of her own secret tension at this night invasion of Leavitt's haunts.

This feeling deepened within me as we drew near the shore. Leavitt's failure to appear seemed sinister and enigmatic. I began to evolve a fantastic image of him as I recalled his queer ways and his uncanny tricks of speech. It was as if we were seeking out the presiding deity of the island, who had assumed the guise of a Caliban holding unearthly sway over its unnatural processes.

With Williams, the boatswain, carrying a lantern, we pushed into the brush, following the choked trail that led to Leavitt's abode. But the bungalow, when we had reached the clearing and could discern the outlines of the building against the masses of the forest, was dark and deserted. As we mounted the veranda, the loose boards creaked hollowly under our tread; the doorway, from which depended a tattered curtain of coarse burlap, gaped black and empty.

The lantern, lifted high in the boatswain's hand, cleft at a stroke the darkness within. On the writing-table, cluttered with papers and bits of volcanic rock, stood a bottle and half-empty glass. Things lay about in lugubrious disorder, as if the place had been hurriedly ransacked by a thief. Some of the geological specimens had tumbled from the table to the floor, and stray sheets of Leavitt's manuscripts lay under his chair. Leavitt's books, ranged on shelving against the wall, alone seemed undisturbed. Upon the top of the shelving stood two enormous stuffed birds, moldering and decrepit, regarding the sudden illumination with unblinking, bead-like eyes. Between them a small dancing faun in greenish bronze tripped a Bacchic measure with head thrown back in a transport of derisive laughter.

For a long moment the three of us faced the silent, disordered room, in which the little bronze faun alone seemed alive, convulsed with diabolical mirth at our entrance. Somehow it recalled to me Leavitt's own cynical laugh. Suddenly Miss Stanleigh made toward the photographs above the bookshelves.

"This is he," she said, taking up one of the faded prints.

"Yes—Leavitt," I answered.

"*Leavitt?*" Her fingers tightened upon the photograph. Then, abruptly, it fell to the floor. "Yes, yes—of course." Her eyes closed very slowly, as if an extreme weakness had seized her.

In the shock of that moment I reached out to support her, but she checked my hand. Her gray eyes opened again. A shudder visibly went over her, as if the night air had suddenly become chill. From the shelf the two stuffed birds regarded us dolefully, while the dancing faun, with head thrown back in an attitude of immortal art, laughed derisively.

"Where is he? I must speak to him," said Miss Stanleigh.

"One might think he were deliberately hiding," I muttered, for I was at a loss to account for Leavitt's absence.

"Then find him," the girl commanded. I cut short my speculations to direct Williams to search the hut in the rear of the bungalow, where, behind bamboo palings, Leavitt's Malay servant maintained an aloof and mysterious existence. I sat down beside Miss Stanleigh on the veranda steps to find my hands sooty from the touch of the boards. A fine volcanic ash was evidently drifting in the air, and now to my ear, attuned to the profound stillness, the wind bore a faint humming sound.

"Do you hear that?" I whispered. It was like the far-off murmur of a gigantic caldron, softly a-boil—a dull vibration that seemed to reach us through the ground as well as through the air.

The girl listened a moment, and then started up. "I hear voices—somewhere."

"Voices?" I strained my ears for sounds other than the insistent ferment of the great cone above our heads. "Perhaps Leavitt——"

"Why do you still call him Leavitt?"

"Then you're quite certain——" I began, but an involuntary exclamation from her cut me short.

The light of Williams's lantern, emerging from behind the bamboo palings, disclosed the burly form of the boatswain with a shrinking Malay in tow. He was jabbering in his native tongue, with much gesticulation of his thin arms, and going into contortions at every dozen paces in a sort of pantomime to emphasize his words. Williams urged him along unceremoniously to the steps of the veranda.

"Perhaps you can get the straight of this, Mr. Barnaby," said the boatswain. "He swears that the flame-devil in the volcano has swallowed his master alive."

The poor fellow seemed indeed in a state of complete funk. With his thin legs quaking under him, he poured forth in Malay a crazed, distorted tale. According to Wadakimba, Leavitt—or Farquharson, to give him his real name—had awakened the high displeasure of the flame-devil within the mountain. Had we not observed that the cone was smoking furiously? And the dust and heavy taint of sulphur in the air? Surely we could feel the very tremor of the ground under our feet. All that day the enraged monster had been spouting mud and lava down upon the white *tuan* who had remained in the bungalow, drinking heavily and bawling out maledictions upon his enemy. At length, in spite of Wadakimba's efforts to dissuade him, he had set out to climb to the crater, vowing to show the flame-devil who was master. He had compelled the terrified Wadakimba to go with him a part of the way. The white *tuan*—was he really a god, as he declared himself to be?—had gone alone up the tortuous, fissured slopes, at times lost to sight in yellowish clouds of gas and steam, while his screams and threats of vengeance came back to Wadakimba's ears. Overhead, Lakalatcha continued to rumble and quiver and clear his throat with great showers of mud and stones.

Farquharson must have indeed parted with his reason to have attempted that grotesque sally. Listening to Wadakimba's tale, I pictured the crazed man, scorched to tatters, heedless of bruises and burns, scrambling up that difficult and perilous ascent, and hurling his ridiculous blasphemy into the flares of smoke and steam that issued from that vast caldron lit by subterranean fires. At its simmering the whole island trembled. A mere whiff of the monster's breath and he would have been snuffed out, annihilated in an instant. According to Wadakimba, the end had indeed come in that fashion. It was as if the mountain had suddenly given a deep sigh. The blast had carried away solid rock. A sheet of flame had licked the spot where Farquharson had been hurled headlong, and he was not.

Wadakimba, viewing all this from afar, had scuttled off to his hut. Later he had ventured back to the scene of the tragedy. He had picked up Farquharson's scorched helmet, which had been blown off to some distance, and he also exhibited a pair of binoculars washed down by the tide of lava, scarred and twisted by the heat, from which the lenses had melted away.

I translated for Miss Stanleigh briefly, while she stood turning over in her hands the twisted and blackened binoculars, which were still warm. She heard me through without question or comment, and when I proposed that we get back to the *Sylph* at once, mindful of her aunt's distressed nerves, she assented with a nod. She seemed to have lost the power of speech. In a daze she followed as I led the way back through the forest.

Major Stanleigh and his wife deferred their departure for England until their niece should be properly married to Joyce. At Eleanor's wish, it was a very simple affair, and as Joyce's bride she was as eager to be off to his rubber-plantation in Malduna as he was to set her up there as mistress of his household. I had agreed to give them passage on the *Sylph*, since the next saling of the mail-boat would have necessitated a further fortnight's delay.

Mrs. Stanleigh, with visions of seeing England again, and profoundly grateful to a benevolent Providence that had not only brought "this dreadful business of Eleanor's" to a happy termination, but had averted Lakalatcha's baptism of fire from descending upon her own head, thanked me profusely and a little tearfully. It was during the general chorus of farewells at the last moment before the *Sylph* cast off. Her last appeal, cried after us from the wharf where she stood frantically waving a wet handkerchief, was that I should give Muloa a wide berth.

It brought a laugh from Joyce. He had discovered the good lady's extreme perturbation in regard to Lakalatcha, and had promptly declared for spending a day there with his bride. It was an exceptional opportunity to witness the volcano in its active mood. Each time that Joyce had essayed this teasing pleasantry, which never failed to draw Mrs. Stanleigh's protests, I observed that his wife remained silent. I assumed that she had decided to keep her own counsel in regard to the trip she had made there.

"I'm trusting you not to take Eleanor near that dreadful island, Mr. Barnaby," was the admonition shouted across the widening gap of water.

It was a quite unnecessary appeal, for Joyce, who was presently sitting with his wife in a sheltered quarter of the deck, had not the slightest interest in the smoking cone which was as yet a mere smudge upon the horizon. Eleanor, with one hand in Joyce's possession, at times watched it with a seemingly vast apathy until some ardent word from Joyce would draw her eyes back to his and she would lift to him a smile that was like a caress. The look of weariness and balked purpose that had once marked her expression had vanished. In the week since she had married Joyce she seemed to have grown younger and to be again standing on the very threshold of life with girlish eagerness. She hung on Joyce's every word, communing with him hour after hour, utterly content, indifferent to all the world about her.

In the cabin that evening at dinner, when the two of them deigned to take polite cognizance of my existence, I announced to Joyce that I proposed to hug the island pretty close during the night. It would save considerable time.

"Just as you like, Captain," Joyce replied, indifferently.

"We may get a shower of ashes by doing so, if the wind should shift." I looked across the table at Mrs. Joyce.

"But we shall reach Malduna that much sooner?" she queried.

I nodded. "However, if you feel any uneasiness, I'll give the island a wide berth." I didn't like the idea of dragging her—the bride of a week—past that place with its unspeakable memories, if it should really distress her.

Her eyes thanked me silently across the table. "It's very kind of you, but"—she chose her words with significant deliberation—"I haven't a fear in the world, Mr. Barnaby."

Evening had fallen when we came up on deck. Joyce bethought himself of some cigars in his stateroom and went back. For the moment I was alone with his wife by the rail, watching the stars beginning to prick through the darkening sky. The *Sylph* was running smoothly, with the wind almost aft; the scud of water past her bows and the occasional creak of a block aloft were the only sounds audible in the silence that lay like a benediction upon the sea.

"You may think it unfeeling of me," she began, quite abruptly, "but all this past trouble of mine, now that it is ended, I have completely dismissed. Already it begins to seem like a horrid dream. And as for that island"—her eyes looked off toward Muloa now impending upon us and lighting up the heavens with its sullen flare—"it seems incredible that I ever set foot upon it.

"Perhaps you understand," she went on, after a pause, "that I have not told my husband. But I have not deceived him. He knows that I was once married, and that the man is no longer living. He does not wish to know more. Of course he is aware that Uncle Geoffrey came out here to—to see a Mr. Leavitt, a matter which he has no idea concerned me. He thanks the stars for whatever it was that did bring us out here, for otherwise he would not have met me."

"It has turned out most happily," I murmured.

"It was almost disaster. After meeting Mr. Joyce—and I was weak enough to let myself become engaged—to have discovered that I was still chained to a living creature like that. . . . I should have killed myself."

"But surely the courts——"

She shook her head with decision. "My church does not recognize that sort of freedom."

We were drawing steadily nearer to Muloa. The mountain was breathing slowly and heavily—a vast flare that lifted fan-like in the skies and died away. Lightning played fitfully through the dense mass of smoke and choking gases that hung like a pall over the great cone. It was like the night sky that overhangs a city of gigantic blast-furnaces, only infinitely multiplied. The sails of the *Sylph* caught the ruddy tinge like a phantom craft gliding through the black night, its canvas still dyed with the sunset glow. The faces of the crew, turned to watch the spectacle, curiously fixed and inhuman, were picked out of the gloom by the same fantastic light. It was as if the schooner, with masts and riggings etched black against the lurid sky, sailed on into the Day of Judgment.

It was after midnight. The *Sylph* came about, with sails trembling, and lost headway. Suddenly she vibrated from stem to stern, and with a soft grating sound that was unmistakable came to rest. We were aground in what should have been clear water, with the forest-clad shore of Muloa lying close off to port.

The helmsman turned to me with a look of silly fright on his face, as the wheel revolved useless in his hands. We had shelved with scarcely a jar sufficient to disturb those sleeping below, but in a twinkling Jackson, the mate, appeared on deck in his pajamas, and after a swift glance toward the familiar shore turned to me with the same dumfounded look that had frozen upon the face of the steersman.

"What do you make of this?" he exclaimed, as I called for the lead.

"Be quiet about it," I said to the hands that had started into movement. "Look sharp now, and make no noise." Then I turned to the mate, who was perplexedly rubbing one bare foot against the other and measuring with his eye our distance from the shore. The *Sylph* should have turned the point of the island without mishap, as she had done scores of times.

"It's the volcano we have to thank for this," was my conjecture. "Its recent activity has caused some displacement of the sea bottom."

Jackson's head went back in sudden comprehension. "It's a miracle you didn't plow into it under full sail."

We had indeed come about in the very nick of time to avoid disaster. As matters stood I was hopeful. "With any sort of luck we ought to float clear with the tide."

The mate cocked a doubtful eye at Lakalatcha, uncomfortably close above our heads, flaming at intervals and bathing the deck with an angry glare of light. "If she should begin spitting up a little livelier . . ." he speculated with a shrug, and presently took himself off to his bunk after an inspection below had shown that none of the schooner's seams had started. There was nothing to do but to wait for the tide to make and lift the vessel clear. It would be a matter of three or four hours. I dismissed the helmsman; and the watch forward, taking advantage of the respite from duty, were soon recumbent in attitudes of heavy sleep.

The wind had died out and a heavy torpor lay upon the water. It was as if the stars alone held to their slow courses above a world rigid and inanimate. The *Sylph* lay with a slight list, her spars looking inexpressibly helpless against the sky, and, as the minutes dragged, a fine volcanic ash, like some mortal pestilence exhaled by the monster cone, settled down upon the deck, where, forward in the shadow, the watch lay curled like dead men.

Alone, I paced back and forth—countless soft-footed miles, it seemed, through interminable hours, until at length some obscure impulse prompted me to pause before the open skylight over the cabin and thrust my head down. A lamp above the dining-table, left to burn through the night, feebly illuminated the room. A faint snore issued at regular intervals from the half-open door of the mate's stateroom. The door of Joyce's stateroom opposite was also upon the hook for the sake of air.

Suddenly a soft thump against the side of the schooner, followed by a scrambling noise, made me turn round. The dripping, bedraggled figure of a man in a sleeping-suit mounted the rope ladder that hung over the side, and paused, grasping the rail. I had withdrawn my gaze so suddenly from the glow of the light in the cabin that for several moments the intruder from out of the sea was only a blurred form with one leg hung over the rail, where he hung as if spent by his exertions.

Just then the sooty vapours above the edged maw of the volcano were rent by a flare of crimson, and in the fleeting instant of unnatural daylight I beheld Farquharson, barefooted, and dripping with sea-water, confronting me with a sardonic, triumphant smile. The light faded in a twinkling, but in the darkness he swung his other leg over the rail and sat perched there, as if challenging the testimony of my senses.

"Farquharson!" I breathed aloud, utterly dumfounded.

"Did you think I was a ghost?" I could hear him softly laughing to himself in the interval that followed. "You should have witnessed Wadakimba's fright at my coming back from the dead. Well, I'll admit I almost was done for."

Again the volcano breathed in torment. It was like the sudden opening of a gigantic blast-furnace, and in that instant I saw him vividly—his thin, saturnine face, his damp black hair pushed sleekly back, his lips twisted to a cruel smile, his eyes craftily alert, as if to some ambushed danger continually at hand. He was watching me with a sort of malicious relish in the shock he had given me.

"It was not your intention to stop at Muloa," he observed, dryly, for the plight of the schooner was obvious.

"We'll float clear with the tide," I muttered.

"But in the meantime"—there was something almost menacing in his deliberate pause—"I have the pleasure of this little call upon you."

A head lifted from among the inert figures and sleepily regarded us before it dropped back into the shadows. The stranded ship, the recumbent men, the mountain flaming overhead—it was like a phantom world into which had been suddenly thrust this ghastly and incredible reality.

"Whatever possessed you to swim out here in the middle of the night?" I demanded, in a harsh whisper.

He chose to ignore the question, while I waited in a chill of suspense. It was inconceivable that he could be aware of the truth of the situation and deliberately bent on forcing it to its unspeakable, tragic issue.

"Of late, Captain Barnaby, we seem to have taken to visiting each other rather frequently, don't you think?"

It was lightly tossed off, but not without its evil implication; and I felt his eyes intently fixed upon me as he sat hunched up on the rail in his sodden sleeping-suit, like some huge, ill-omened bird of prey.

To get rid of him, to obliterate the horrible fact that he still existed in the flesh, was the instinctive impulse of my staggered brain. But the peril of discovery, the chance that those sleeping below might waken and hear us, held me in a vise of indecision.

"If I could bring myself to reproach you, Captain," he went on, ironically polite, "I might protest that your last visit to this island savoured of a too-inquisitive intrusion. You'll pardon my frankness. I had convinced you and Major Stanleigh that Farquharson was dead. To the world at large that should have sufficed. That I choose to remain alive is my own affair. Your sudden return to Muloa—with a lady—would have upset everything, if Fate and that inspired fool of a Malay had not happily intervened. But now, surely, there can be no doubt that I am dead?"

I nodded assent in a dumb, helpless way.

"And I have a notion that even you, Captain Barnaby, will never dispute that fact."

He threw back his head suddenly—for all the world like the dancing faun—and laughed silently at the stars.

My tongue was dry in my mouth as I tried to make some rejoinder. He baffled me completely, and meanwhile I was in a tingle of fear lest the mate should come up on deck to see what progress the tide had made, or lest the sound of our voices might waken the girl in Joyce's stateroom.

"I can promise you that," I attempted to assure him in weak, sepulchral tones. "And now, if you like, I'll put you ashore in the small boat. You must be getting chilly in that wet sleeping-suit."

"As a matter of fact I am, and I was wondering if you would not offer me something to drink."

"You shall have a bottle to take along," I promised, with alacrity, but he demurred.

"There is no sociability in that. And you seem very lonesome here—stuck for two more hours at least. Come, Captain, fetch your bottle and we will share it together."

He got down from the rail, stretched his arms lazily above his head, and dropped into one of the deck chairs that had been placed aft for the convenience of my two passengers.

"And cigars, too, Captain," he suggested, with a politeness that was almost impertinence. "We'll have a cozy hour or two out of this tedious wait for the tide to lift you off."

I contemplated him helplessly. There was no alternative but to fall in with whatever mad caprice might seize his brain.

If I opposed him, it would lead to high and querulous words; and the hideous fact of his presence there—of his mere existence—I was bound to conceal at all hazards.

"I must ask you to keep quiet," I said, stiffly.

"As a tomb," he agreed, and his eyes twinkled disagreeably in the darkness. "You forget that I am supposed to be in one."

I went stealthily down into the cabin, where I secured a box of cigars and the first couple of bottles that my hands laid hold of in the locker. They proved to contain an old Tokay wine which I had treasured for several years to no particular purpose. The ancient bottles clinked heavily in my grasp as I mounted again to the deck.

"Now this is something like," he purred, watching like a cat my every motion as I set the glasses forth and guardedly drew the cork. He saluted me with a flourish and drank.

To an onlooker that pantomime in the darkness would have seemed utterly grotesque. I tasted the fragrant, heavy wine and waited—waited in an agony of suspense—my ears strained desperately to catch the least sound from below. But a profound silence enveloped the schooner, broken only by the occasional rhythmic snore of the mate.

"You seem rather ill at ease," Farquharson observed from the depths of the deck chair when he had his cigar comfortably aglow. "I trust it isn't this little impromptu call of mine that's disturbing you. After all, life has its unusual moments, and this, I think, is one of them." He sniffed the bouquet of his wine and drank. "It is rare moments like this—bizarre, incredible, what you like—that compensate for the tedium of years."

His disengaged hand had fallen to the side of the chair, and I now observed in dismay that a scarf belonging to Joyce's wife had been left lying in the chair, and that his fingers were absently twisting the silken fringe.

"I wonder that you stick it out, as you do, on this island," I forced myself to observe, seeking safety in the commonplace, while my eyes, as if fascinated, watched his fingers toying with the ends of the scarf. I was forced to accept the innuendo beneath his enigmatic utterances. His utter baseness and depravity, born perhaps of a diseased mind, I could understand. I had led him to bait a trap with the fiction of his own death, but he could not know that it had been already sprung upon his unsuspecting victims.

He seemed to regard me with contemptuous pity. "Naturally, you wonder. A mere skipper like yourself fails to understand—many things. What can you know of life cooped up in this schooner? You touch only the surface of things just as this confounded boat of yours skims only the top of the water. Once in a lifetime you may come to real grips with life—strike bottom, eh?—as your schooner has done now. Then you're aground and quite helpless. What a pity!"

He lifted his glass and drank it off, then thrust it out to be refilled. "Life as the world lives it—bah!" he dismissed it with the scorn of one who counts himself divested of all illusions. "Life would be an infernal bore if it were not for its paradoxes. Now you, Captain Barnaby, would never dream that in becoming dead to the world—in other people's belief—I have become intensely alive. There are opened up infinite possibilities——"

He drank again and eyed me darkly, and then went on in his crack-brained way. "What is life but a challenge to pretense, a constant exercise in duplicity, with so few that come to master it as an art? Every one goes about with something locked deep in his heart. Take yourself, Captain Barnaby. You have your secrets—hidden from me, from all the world—which, if they could be dragged out of you——"

His deep-set eyes bored through the darkness upon me. Hunched up in the deck chair, with his legs crossed under him, he was like an animated Buddha venting a dark philosophy and seeking to undermine my mental balance with his sophistry.

"I'm a plain man of the sea," I rejoined, bluntly. "I take life as it comes."

He smiled derisively, drained his glass, and held it out again. "But you have your secrets, rather clumsily guarded, to be sure——"

"What secrets?" I cried out, goaded almost beyond endurance.

He seemed to deprecate the vigour of my retort and lifted a cautioning hand. "Do you want every one on board to hear this conversation?"

At that moment the smoke-wrapped cone of Lakalatcha was cleft by a sheet of flame, and we confronted each other in a sort of blood-red dawn.

"There is no reason why we should quarrel," he went on, after darkness had enveloped us again. "But there are times which call for plain speaking. Major Stanleigh is probably hardly aware of just what he said to me under a little artful questioning. It seems that a lady who—shall we say, whom we both have the honour of knowing?—is in love. Love, mark you. It is always interesting to see that flower bud twice from the same stalk. However, one naturally defers to a lady, especially when one is very much in her way. *Place aux dames*, eh? Exit poor Farquharson! You must admit that his was an altruistic soul. Well, she has her freedom—if only to barter it for a new bondage. Shall we drink to the happy future of that romance?"

He lifted to me his glass with ironical invitation, while I sat aghast and speechless, my heart pounding against my ribs. This intolerable colloquy could not last forever. I deliberated what I should do if we were surprised. At the sound of a footfall or the soft creak of a plank I felt that I might lose all control and leap up and brain him with the heavy bottle in my grasp. I had an insane desire to spring at his throat and throttle his infamous bravado, tumble him overboard and annihilate the last vestige of his existence.

"Come, Captain," he urged, "you, too, have shared in smoothing the path for these lovers. Shall we not drink to their happy union?"

A feeling of utter loathing went over me. I set my glass down. "It would be a more serviceable compliment to the lady in question if I strangled you on the spot," I muttered, boldly.

"But you are forgetting that I am already dead." He threw his head back as if vastly amused, then lurched forward and held out his glass a little unsteadily to be refilled.

He gave me a quick, evil look. "Besides, the noise might disturb your passengers."

I could feel a cold perspiration suddenly breaking out upon my body. Either the fellow had obtained an inkling of the truth in some incredible way, or was blindly on the track of it, guided by some diabolical scent. Under the spell of his eyes,

I could not manage the outright lie which stuck in my throat.

"What makes you think I have passengers?" I parried, weakly.

With intent or not, he was again fingering the fringe of the scarf that hung over the arm of the chair.

"It is not your usual practice, but you have been carrying them lately."

He drained his glass and sat staring into it, his head drooping a little forward. The heavy wine was beginning to have its effect upon him, but whether it would provoke him to some outright violence or drag him down into a stupor, I could not predict. Suddenly the glass slipped from his fingers and shivered to pieces on the deck. I started violently at the sound, and in the silence that followed I thought I heard a footfall in the cabin below.

He looked up at length from his absorbed contemplation of the bits of broken glass. "We were talking about love, were we not?" he demanded, heavily.

I did not answer. I was straining to catch a repetition of the sound from below. Time was slipping rapidly away, and to sit on meant inevitable discovery. The watch might waken or the mate appear to surprise me in converse with my nocturnal visitor. It would be folly to attempt to conceal his presence and I despaired of getting him back to shore while his present mood held, although I remembered that the small boat, which had been lowered after we went aground, was still moored to the rail amidships.

Refilling my own glass, I offered it to him. He lurched forward to take it, but the fumes of the wine suddenly drifted clear of his brain. "You seem very much distressed," he observed, with ironic concern. "One might think you were actually sheltering these precious love-birds."

Perspiration broke out anew upon my face and neck. "I don't know what you are talking about," I bluntly tried to fend off his implication. I felt as if I were helplessly strapped down and that he was about to probe me mercilessly with some sharp instrument. I strode to turn the direction of his thoughts by saying, "I understand that the Stanleighs are returning to England."

"The Stanleighs—quite so," he nodded agreement, and fixed me with a maudlin stare. Something prompted me to fill his glass again. He drank it off mechanically. Again I poured, and he obediently drank. With an effort he tried to pick up the thread of our conversation:

"What did you say? Oh, the Stanleighs . . . yes, yes, of course." He slowly nodded his head and fell silent. "I was about to say . . ." He broke off again and seemed to ruminate profoundly. . . . "Love-birds——" I caught the word feebly from his lips, spoken as if in a daze. The glass hung dripping in his relaxed grasp.

It was a crucial moment in which his purpose seemed to waver and die in his clouded brain. A great hope sprang up in my heart, which was hammering furiously. If I could divert his fuddled thoughts and get him back to shore while the wine lulled him to forgetfulness.

I leaned forward to take the glass which was all but slipping from his hand, when Lakalatcha flamed with redoubled fury. It was as if the mountain had suddenly bared its fiery heart to the heavens, and a muffled detonation reached my ears.

Farquharson straightened up with a jerk and scanned the smoking peak, from which a new trickle of white-hot lava had broken forth in a threadlike waterfall. He watched its graceful play as if hypnotized, and began babbling to himself in an incoherent prattle. All his faculties seemed suddenly awake, but riveted solely upon the heavy labouring of the mountain. He was chiding it in Malay as if it were a fractious child. When I ventured to urge him back to shore he made no protest, but followed me into the boat. As I pushed off and took up the oars he had eyes for nothing but the flaming cone, as if its leaping fires held for him an Apocalyptic vision.

I strained at the oars as if in a race, with all eternity at stake, blindly urging the boat ahead through water that flashed crimson at every stroke. The mountain now flamed like a beacon, and I rowed for dear life over a sea of blood.

Farquharson sat entranced before the spectacle, chanting to himself a kind of insane ritual, like a Parsee fire-worshipper making obeisance before his god. He was rapt away to some plane of mystic exaltation, to some hinterland of the soul that merged upon madness. When at length the boat crunched upon the sandy shore he got up unsteadily from the stern and pointed to the pharos that flamed in the heavens.

"The fire upon the altar is lit," he addressed me, oracularly, while the fanatic light of a devotee burned in his eyes. "Shall we ascend and prepare the sacrifice?"

I leaned over the oars, panting from my exertions, indifferent to his rhapsody.

"If you'll take my advice, you'll get back at once to your bungalow and strip off that wet sleeping-suit," I bluntly counseled him, but I might as well have argued with a man in a trance.

He leaped over the gunwale and strode up the beach. Again he struck his priest-like attitude and invoked me to follow.

"The fire upon the altar waits," he repeated, solemnly. Suddenly he broke into a shrill laugh and ran like a deer in the direction of the forest that stretched up the slopes of the mountain.

The mate's face, thrust over the rail as I drew alongside the schooner, plainly bespoke his utter bewilderment. He must have thought me bereft of my senses to be paddling about at that hour of the night. The tide had made, and the *Sylph*, righting her listed masts, was standing clear of the shoal. The deck was astir, and when the command was given to hoist the sails it was obeyed with an uneasy alacrity. The men worked frantically in a bright, unnatural day, for Lakalatcha was now continuously aflame and tossing up red-hot rocks to the accompaniment of dull sounds of explosion.

My first glance about the deck had been one of relief to note that Joyce and his wife were not there, although the commotion of getting under sail must have awakened them. A breeze had sprung up which would prove a fair wind as soon as the *Sylph* stood clear of the point. The mate gave a grunt of satisfaction when at length the schooner began to dip her bow and lay over to the task. Leaving him in charge, I started to go below, when suddenly Mrs. Joyce, fully dressed, confronted me. She seemed to have materialized out of the air like a ghost. Her hair glowed like burnished copper in the unnatural illumination which bathed the deck, but her face was ashen, and the challenge of her eyes made my heart stop short.

"You have been awake long?" I ventured to ask.

"Too long," she answered, significantly, with her face

turned away, looking down into the water. She had taken my arm and drawn me toward the rail. Now I felt her fingers tighten convulsively. In the droop of her head and the tense curve of her neck I sensed her mad impulse which the dark water suggested.

"Mrs. Joyce!" I remonstrated, sharply.

She seemed to go limp all over at the words. I drew her along the deck for a faltering step or two, while her eyes continued to brood upon the water rushing past. Suddenly she spoke:

"What other way out is there?"

"Never that," I said, shortly. I urged her forward again. "Is your husband asleep?"

"Thank God, yes!"

"Then you have been awake——"

"For over an hour," she confessed, and I detected the shudder that went over her body.

"The man is mad——"

"But I am married to him." She stopped and caught at the rail like a prisoner gripping at the bars that confine him. "I cannot—cannot endure it! Where are you taking me? Where *can* you take me? Don't you see that there is no escape—from this?"

The *Sylph* rose and sank to the first long roll of the open sea.

"When we reach Malduna——" I began, but the words were only torture.

"I cannot—cannot go on. Take me back!—to that island! Let me live abandoned—or rather die——"

"Mrs. Joyce, I beg of you. . . ."

The schooner rose and dipped again.

For what seemed an interminable time we paced the deck together while Lakalatcha flamed farther and farther astern. Her words came in fitful snatches as if spoken in a delirium, and at times she would pause and grip the rail to stare back, wild-eyed, at the receding island.

Suddenly she started, and in a sort of blinding, noon-day blaze I saw her face blanch with horror. It was as if at that moment the heavens had cracked asunder and the night had fallen away in chaos. Turning, I saw the cone of the mountain lifting skyward in fragments—and saw no more, for the blinding vision remained seared upon the retina of my eyes.

Across the water, slower paced, came the dread concussion of sound.

"Good God! It's carried away the whole island!" I heard the mate's voice bellowing above the cries of the men. The *Sylph* scudded before the approaching storm of fire redescending from the sky. . . .

The first gray of the dawn disclosed Mrs. Joyce still standing by the rail, her hand nestling within the arm of her husband, indifferent to the heavy grayish dust that fell in benediction upon her like a silent shower of snow.

The island of Muloa remains to-day a charred cinder lapped about by the blue Pacific. At times gulls circle over its blackened and desolate surface devoid of every vestige of life. From the squat, truncated mass of Lakalatcha, shorn of half its lordy height, a feeble wisp of smoke still issues to the breeze, as if Vulcan, tired of his forge, had banked its fire before abandoning it.

THE ARGOSIES

By ALEXANDER HULL

From *Scribner's Magazine*

THERE may have been some benevolent force watching over Harber. In any case, that would be a comforting belief. Certainly Harber himself so believed, and I know he had no trouble at all convincing his wife. Yes, the Harbers believed.

But credulity, you may say, was ever the surest part in love's young golden dream: and you, perhaps, not having your eyes befuddled with the rose-fog of romance, will see too clearly to believe. What can I adduce for your conviction? The facts only. After all, that is the single strength of my position.

There was, of course, the strange forehanded, subtle planning of the other girl, of Janet Spencer. Why did she do it? Was it that, feeling her chances in Tawnleytown so few, counting the soil there so barren, driven by an ambition beyond the imagination of staid, stodgy, normal Tawnleytown girls, she felt she must create opportunities where none were? She was very lovely, Harber tells me, in a fiery rose-red of the fairy-tale way; though even without beauty it needn't have been hard for her. Young blood is prone enough to adventure; the merest spark will set it akindle. I should like to have known that girl. She must have been very clever. Because, of course, she couldn't have foreseen, even by the surest instinct, the coincidence that brought Harber and Barton together. Yes, there is a coincidence in it. It's precisely upon that, you see, that Harber hangs his belief.

I wonder, too, how many of those argosies she sent out seeking the golden fleece returned to her? It's a fine point for speculation. If one only knew. . . . ah, but it's pitiful how much one doesn't, and can't, know in this hard and complex world! Or was it merely that she tired of them and wanted to be rid of them? Or again, do I wrong her there, and were there no more than the two of them, and did she simply suffer a solitary revulsion of feeling, as Harber did? But no, I'm sure I'm right in supposing Barton and Harber to have been but two ventures out of many, two arrows out of a full quiver shot in the dark at the bull's-eye of fortune. And, by heaven, it was splendid shooting . . . even if none of the other arrows scored!

Harber tells me he was ripe for the thing without any encouragement to speak of. Tawnleytown was dull plodding for hot youth. Half hidden in the green of fir and oak and maple, slumberous with midsummer heat, it lay when he left it. Thickly powdered with the fine white dust of its own unpaven streets, dust that sent the inhabitants chronically sneezing and weeping and red-eyed about town, or sent them north to the lakes for exemption, dust that hung impalpably suspended in the still air and turned the sunsets to things of glorious rose and red and gold though there wasn't a single cloud or streamer in the sky to catch the light, dust that lay upon lawns and walks and houses in deep gray accumulation . . . precisely as if these were objects put away and never used and not disturbed until they were white with the inevitable powdery accretion that accompanies disuse. Indeed, he felt that way about Tawnleytown, as if it were a closed room of the world, a room of long ago, unused now, unimportant, forgotten.

So unquestionably he was ready enough to go. He had all the fine and far-flung dreams of surging youth. He peopled the world with his fancies, built castles on every high hill. He felt the urge of ambition fiercely stirring within him, latent power pulsing through him. What would you? Wasn't he young and in love?

For there had been, you must know, a good deal between them. What does one do in these deadly dull little towns for amusement, when one is young and fain and restless? Harber tells me they walked the streets and shaded lanes in the dim green coolness of evening, lounged in the orchard hammock, drifted down the little river, past still pools, reed-bordered, under vaulting sycamores, over hurrying reaches fretted with pebbles, forgot everything except one another and their fancies and made, as youth must, love. That was the programme complete, except for the talk, the fascinating, never-ending talk. Volumes on volumes of it—whole libraries of it.

So, under her veiled fostering, the feeling that he must leave Tawnleytown kept growing upon Harber until one evening it crystallized in decision.

It was on a Sunday. They had taken a lunch and climbed Bald Knob, a thousand feet above the town, late in the afternoon. The dying sun and the trees had given them a splendid symphony in black and gold, and had silenced them for a little. They sat looking down over the valley in which the well-known landmarks slowly grew dark and indistinguishable and dim lights blossomed one after another. The sound of church bells rose faintly through the still air. The pale last light faded in the sky.

Harber and Janet sat in the long grass, their hearts stirring with the same urgent, inarticulate thoughts, their hands clasped together.

"Let's wait for Eighty-seven," she said.

Harber pressed her hand for reply.

In the mind of each of them Eighty-seven was the symbol of release from Tawnleytown, of freedom, of romance.

Presently a shifting light appeared in the east, a faint rumble became perceptible and increased. The swaying shaft of light intensified and a moment later the long-drawn poignancy of a chime-whistle blowing for the river-road crossing, exquisitely softened by distance, echoingly penetrated the still valley.

A streak of thunderous light swam into view and passed them, plunging into a gap in the west. The fire-box in the locomotive opened and flung a flood of light upon a swirling cloud of smoke. A sharp turn in the track, a weak blast of the whistle at the bridge-head, and the "Limited," disdaining contemptible Tawnleytown, had swept out of sight—into the world—at a mile to the minute.

"If I were on it," said Harber slowly.

Janet caught her breath sharply. "You're a man!" she said fiercely. "You could be—so easily!"

Harber was startled for a moment. Her kindling of his

flame of adventure had been very subtle until now. Perhaps she hadn't been sure before to-day of her standing. But this afternoon, upon the still isolation of Bald Knob, there had been many kisses exchanged, and brave vows of undying love. And no doubt she felt certain of him now.

With Harber, however, the pathway had seemed leading otherwhere. He wasn't the sort of youth to kiss and ride away. And, discounting their adventurous talk, he had tacitly supposed that his course the last few weeks spelled the confinement of the four walls of a Tawnleytown cottage, the fetters of an early marriage. He had been fighting his mounting fever for the great world, and thinking, as the train sped by, that after all "home was best." It would be. It must be. So, if his fine dreams were the price he must pay for Janet, still he would pay them! And he was startled by her tone.

Her slim fingers tightened upon his.

"Why do you stay?" she cried passionately. "Why don't you go?"

"There's you," he began.

"Yes!" she exclaimed. "Oh, I'm selfish, maybe! I don't know! But it's as much for me as for you that I say it!"

Her words poured out tumultuously.

"Where are all our wonderful dreams—if you stay here? Gone aglimmering! Gone! I can't see them all go—I can't! Can you?"

Was he to have, then, both Janet and his dreams? His heart quickened. He leaned impulsively toward her.

She pushed his face away with her free hand.

"No—no! Wait till I'm through! We've always known we weren't like other Tawnleytown folk, haven't we, dear? We've always said that we wanted more out of life than they —that we wouldn't be content with half a loaf—that we wanted the bravest adventures, the yellowest gold, the finest emotions, the greater power! And if now . . .

"See those lights down there—so few—and so faint. We can't live our lives there. Seventy-five dollars a month in the bank for you—and dull, deadly monotony for both of us —no dreams—no adventures—nothing big and fine! We can't be content with that! Why don't you go, John?

"Don't mind me—don't let me keep you—for as soon as

you've won, you can come back to me—and then—we'll see the world together!"

"Janet—Janet!" said Harber, with pounding heart. "How do you know—that I'll win?"

"Ah," she said strangely, "I know! You can't fail—*I won't let you fail!*"

Harber caught her suddenly in his arms and kissed her as if it were to be his last token of her.

"I'm going then!" he whispered. "I'm going!"

"When?"

"There's no time to be lost!" he said, thinking fast. "If I had known that you were willing, that you would wait—if . . . Janet, I'm going to-morrow!"

Her arms tightened about him convulsively. "Promise me—promise me!" she demanded tensely, "that you'll never, never forget me—that you'll come back to me!"

Harber laughed in her face. "Janet," he said solemnly, "I'll never forget you. I'll come back to you. I'll come back—'though 'twere ten thousand mile!'"

And they walked home slowly, wrapt once more in their fascinating talk, fanning the flames of one another's desires, painting for their future the rich landscapes of paradise. Youth! Brave, hot youth!

The next day Harber contemptuously threw over his job in the bank and fared forth into the wide world that was calling.

Well, he went south, then east, then west, and west, and farther west. So far that presently, after three years, he found himself not west at all, but east—far east. There were between him and Janet Spencer now thousands on thousands of miles of vast heaving seas, and snow-capped mountain ranges, and limitless grassy plains.

Three years of drifting! You'd say, perhaps, knowing the frailty of vows, that the connection might have been lost. But it hadn't. Harber was but twenty-three. Faithfulness, too, comes easier then than later in life, when one has seen more of the world, when the fine patina of illusion has worn off. Besides, there was, I'm sure, a touch of genius about that girl, so that one wouldn't forget her easily, certainly not in three years. And then, you know, Harber had had her letters. Not many of them. Perhaps a dozen to the year.

Pitifully few, but they were filled with a wonderful fascination against which the realities of his wandering life had been powerless to contend. Like a slender cable they bound him—they held him!

Well, he was in Sydney now, standing on the water-front, beneath a bright-blue Australian sky, watching the crinkling water in the Circular Quay as it lifted and fell mightily but easily, and seeing the black ships . . . ah, the ships! Those masterful, much more than human, entities that slipped about the great world nosing out, up dark-green tropical rivers in black, fir-bound fjords, through the white ice-flows of the Arctics, all its romance, all its gold! Three years hadn't dulled the keen edge of his appetite for all that; rather had whetted it.

Nevertheless, as he stood there, he was thinking to himself that he must have done with wandering; the old saw that a rolling stone gathered no moss was cropping up sharply, warningly, in his mind. He had in the three years, however—and this is rather remarkable—accumulated about three thousand dollars. Three thousand dollars! Why, in this quarter of the world, three thousand dollars should be like three thousand of the scriptural mustard-seed—they should grow a veritable forest!

What was puzzling him, however, was where to plant the seed. He was to meet here a man who had a plan for planting in the islands. There were wild rumours afloat of the fortunes that could be made in rubber and vanilla out in the Papuan "Back Beyond." Harber was only half inclined to believe them, perhaps; but half persuaded is well along the way.

He heard his name called, and, turning, he saw a man coming toward him with the rolling gait of the seaman. As he came closer, Harber observed the tawny beard, the sea-blue eyes surrounded by the fine wrinkles of humour, the neat black clothing, the polished boots, and, above all, the gold earrings that marked the man in his mind as Farringdon, the sea-captain who had been anxious to meet him.

Harber answered the captain's gleam of teeth with one of his own, and they turned their backs upon the water and went to Harber's room, where they could have their fill of talk undisturbed. Harber says they talked all that afternoon and evening, and well into the next morning, enthusiastically finding one another the veritable salt of the earth, honourable, level-headed, congenial, temperamentally fitted for exactly what they had in mind—partnership.

"How much can you put in?" asked Harber finally.

"Five hundred pounds," said the captain.

"I can match you," said Harber.

"Man, but that's fine!" cried the captain. "I've been looking for you—you, you know—*just you*—for the last two years! And when Pierson told me about you . . . why, it's luck, I say!"

It was luck for Harber, too. Farringdon, you see, knew precisely where he wanted to go, and he had his schooner, and he knew that part of the world, as we say, like a man knows his own buttons. Harber, then, was to manage the plantation; they were going to set out rubber, both Para and native, and try hemp and maybe coffee while they waited for the Haevia and the Ficus to yield. And Farringdon was ready to put the earnings from his schooner against Harber's wage as manager. The arrangement, you see, was ideal.

Skip seven years with me, please. Consider the plantation affair launched, carried, and consummated. Farringdon and Harber have sold the rubber-trees as they neared bearing, and have sold them well. They're out of that now. In all likelihood, Harber thinks, permanently. For that seven years has seen other projects blossom. Harber, says Farringdon, has "the golden touch." There has been trading in the islands, and a short and fortunate little campaign on the stock-market through Sydney brokers, and there has been, more profitable than anything else, the salvaging of the Brent Interisland Company's steamer *Pailula* by Farringdon's schooner, in which Harber had purchased a half-interest; so the partners are, on the whole, rather well fixed. Harber might be rated at, perhaps, some forty thousand pounds, not counting his interest in the schooner.

One of Janet Spencer's argosies, then, its cargo laden, is ready to set sail for the hills of home. In short, Harber is now in one of the island ports of call, waiting for the steamer from Fiji. In six weeks he will be in Tawnleytown if all goes well.

It isn't, and yet it is, the same Harber. He's thirty now, lean and bronzed and very fit. He can turn a hundred tricks now where then he could turn one. The tropics have agreed with him. There seems to have been some subtle affinity between them, and he almost wishes that he weren't leaving them. He certainly wouldn't be, if it were not for Janet.

Yes, that slender thread has held him. Through ten years it has kept him faithful. He has eyed askance, ignored, even rebuffed, women. The letters, that still come, have turned the trick, perhaps, or some clinging to a faith that is inherent in him. Or sheer obstinacy? Forgive the cynicism. A little of each, no doubt. And then he hadn't often seen the right sort of women. I say that deliberately, because:

The night before the steamer was due there was a ball—yes, poor island exiles, they called it that!—and Harber, one of some thirty "Europeans" there, went to it, and on the very eve of safety . . .

The glare and the oily smell of the lanterns, the odour of jasmine, frangipanni, vanilla, and human beings sickeningly mingled in the heat, the jangling, out-of-tune music, the wearisome island gossip and chatter, drove him at length out into the night, down a black-shadowed pathway to the sea. The beach lay before him presently, gleaming like silver in the soft blue radiance of the jewelled night. As he stood there, lost in far memories, the mellow, lemon-coloured lights from the commissioner's residence shone beautifully from the fronded palms and the faint wave of the waltzes of yesteryear became poignant and lovely, and the light trade-wind, clean here from the reek of lamps and clothing and human beings, vaguely tanged with the sea, blew upon him with a light, insistent pressure. Half dreaming, he heard the sharp sputter of a launch—bearing belated comers to the ball, no doubt—but he paid no attention to it. He may have been on the beach an hour before he turned to ascend to the town.

And just at the top of the slope he came upon a girl.

She hadn't perceived him, and she stood there, slim and graceful, the moonlight bright upon her rapt face, with her arms outstretched and her head flung back, in an attitude of utter abandonment. Harber felt his heart stir swiftly. He knew what she was feeling, as she looked out over the shimmering half-moon of harbour, across the moaning white feather of reef, out to the illimitable sea, and drank in the essence of the beauty of the night. Just so, at first, had it clutched him with the pain of ecstasy, and he had never forgotten it. There would be no voicing that feeling; it must ever remain inarticulate. Nor was the girl trying to voice it. Her exquisite pantomime alone spelled her delight in it and her surrender to it.

He saw at a glance that he didn't know her. She was "new" to the islands. Her clothes were evidence enough for that. There was a certain verve to them that spoke of a more sophisticated land. She might have been twenty-five though she seemed younger. She was in filmy white from slipper to throat, and over her slender shoulders there drifted a gossamer banner of scarf, fluttering in the soft trade-wind. Harber was very close to see this, and still she hadn't observed him.

"Don't let me startle you, please!" he said, as he stepped from the shadow of the trumpet-flower bush that had hitherto concealed him.

Her arms came down slowly, her chin lowered; her pose, if you will, melted away. Her voice when she spoke was low and round and thrilled, and it sent an answering thrill through Harber.

"I'm mad!" she said. "Moon-mad—or tropic-mad. I didn't hear you. I was worshipping the night!"

"As I have been," said Harber, feeling a sudden pagan kinship with her mood.

She smiled, and her smile seemed the most precious thing in the world. "You, too? But it isn't new to you . . . and when the newness is gone every one—here at least—seems dead to it!"

"Sometimes I think it's always new," replied Harber. "And yet I've had years of it . . . but how did you know?"

"You're Mr. Harber, aren't you?"

"Yes. But——"

"Only that I knew you were here, having heard of you from the Tretheways, and I'd accounted for every one else. I couldn't stay inside because it seemed to me that it was wicked when I had come so far for just this, to be inside stuffily dancing. One can dance all the rest of one's life in Michigan, you know! So——"

"It's the better place to be—out here," said Harber abruptly. "Need we go in?"

"I don't know," she said doubtfully. "Maybe you can tell me. You see, I've promised some dances. What's the usage here? Dare I run away from them?"

"Oh, it might prove a three-day scandal if you did," said Harber. "But I know a bench off to the right, where it isn't likely you'll be found by any questing partner, and you needn't confess to having had a companion. Will you come and talk to me?"

"I'm a bird of passage," she answered, smiling, "and I've only to unfold my wings and fly away from the smoke of scandal. Yes, I'll come—if you won't talk—too much. You see, after all, I won't flatter you. It's the night I want, not talk . . . the wonderful night!"

But, of course, they did talk. She was an American girl, she told him, and had studied art a little, but would never be much of a painter. She had been teaching classes in a city high school in the Middle West, when suddenly life there seemed to have gone humdrum and stale. She had a little money saved, not much, but enough if she managed well, and she'd boldly resigned and determined, once at least before she was too old, to follow spring around the world. She had almost given up the idea of painting now, but thought presently she might go in for writing, where, after all, perhaps, her real talent lay. She had gotten a letter of introduction in Suva to the Tretheways and she would be here until the next steamer after the morrow's.

These were the bare facts. Harber gave a good many more than he got, he told me, upon the theory that nothing so provoked confidence as giving it. He was a little mad himself that night, he admits, or else very, very sane. As you will about that. But, from the moment she began to talk, the thought started running through his head that there was fate in this meeting.

There was a sort of passionate fineness about her that caught and answered some instinct in Harber . . . and I'm afraid they talked more warmly than the length of their acquaintance justified, that they made one another half-promises, not definite, perhaps, but implied; promises that. . . .

"I *must* go in," she said at last, reluctantly.

He knew that she must, and he made no attempt to gainsay her.

"You are going to America," she went on. "If you should——"

And just at that moment, Harber says, anything seemed possible to him, and he said eagerly: "Yes—if you will—I should like——"

How well they understood one another is evident from that. Neither had said it definitely, but each knew.

"Have you a piece of paper?" she asked.

Harber produced a pencil, and groped for something to write upon. All that his pockets yielded was a sealed envelope. He gave it to her.

She looked at it closely, and saw in the brilliant moonshine that it was sealed and stamped and addressed.

"I'll spoil it for mailing," she said.

"It doesn't matter," Harber told her ineptly. "Or you can write it lightly, and I'll erase it later."

There was a little silence. Then suddenly she laughed softly, and there was a tiny catch in the voice. "So that you can forget?" she said bravely. "No! I'll write it fast and hard . . . so that you can . . . never . . . forget!"

And she gave him first his pencil and envelope, and afterward her hand, which Harber held for a moment that seemed like an eternity and then let go. She went into the house, but Harber didn't follow her. He went off to his so-called hotel.

In his room, by the light of the kerosene-lamp, he took out the envelope and read what she had written. It was:

Vanessa Simola, Claridon, Michigan.

He turned over the envelope and looked at the address on the other side, in his own handwriting:

Miss Janet Spencer, Tawnleytown. . . .

And the envelope dropped from his nerveless fingers to the table.

Who shall say how love goes or comes? Its ways are a sacred, insoluble mystery, no less. But it had gone for Harber: and just as surely, though so suddenly, had it come! Yes, life had bitterly tricked him at last. She had sent him this girl . . . too late! The letter in the envelope was written to tell Janet Spencer that within six weeks he would be in Tawnleytown to claim her in marriage.

One must be single-minded like Harber to appreciate his terrible distress of mind. The facile infidelity of your ordinary mortal wasn't for Harber. No, he had sterner stuff in him.

Vanessa! The name seemed so beautiful . . . like the girl herself, like the things she had said. It was an Italian name. She had told him her people had come from Venice, though she was herself thoroughly a product of America. "So that you can never forget," she had said. Ah, it was the warm blood of Italy in her veins that had prompted that! An American girl wouldn't have said that!

He slit the envelope, letting the letter fall to the table, and put it in his pocket.

Yet why should he save it? He could never see her again, he knew. Vain had been those half-promises, those wholly lies, that his eyes and lips had given her. For there was Janet, with her prior promises. Ten years Janet had waited for him . . . ten years . . . and suddenly, aghast, he realized how long and how terrible the years are, how they can efface memories and hopes and desires, and how cruelly they had dealt with him, though he had not realized it until this moment. Janet . . . why, actually, Janet was a stranger, he didn't know Janet any more! She was nothing but a frail phantom of recollection: the years had erased her! But this girl—warm, alluring, immediate. . . .

No—no! It couldn't be.

So much will the force of an idea do for a man, you see. Because, of course, it could have been. He had only to destroy the letter that lay there before him, to wait on until the next sailing, to make continued love to Vanessa, and never to go to Tawnleytown again. There was little probability that Janet would come here for him. Ten years and ten thousand miles . . . despite all that he had vowed on Bald Knob that Sunday so long ago, wouldn't you have said that was barrier enough?

Why, so should I! But it wasn't.

For Harber took the letter and put it in a fresh envelope, and in the morning he went aboard the steamer without seeing the girl again . . . unless that bit of white standing near the top of the slope, as the ship churned the green harbour water heading out to sea, were she, waving.

But he kept the address she had written.

Why? He never could use it. Well, perhaps he didn't want to forget too soon, though it hurt him to remember. How many of us, after all, have some little memory like that, some intimate communion with romance, which we don't tell, but cling to? And perhaps the memory is better than the reality would have been. We imagine . . . but that again is cynical. Harber will never be that now. Let me tell you why.

It's because he hadn't been aboard ship on his crossing to Victoria twenty-four hours before he met Clay Barton.

Barton was rolled up in rugs, lying in a deck-chair, biting his teeth hard together to keep them from chattering, though the temperature was in the eighties, and most of the passengers in white. Barton appeared to be a man of forty, whereas he turned out to be in his early twenties. He was emaciated to an alarming degree and his complexion was of the pale, yellow-green that spoke of many recurrences of malaria. The signs were familiar to Harber.

He sat down beside Barton, and, as the other looked at him half a dozen times tentatively, he presently spoke to him.

"You've had a bad time of it, haven't you?"

"Terrible," said Barton frankly. "They say I'm convalescent now. I don't know. Look at me. What would you say?"

Harber shook his head.

Barton laughed bitterly. "Yes, I'm pretty bad," he agreed readily. And then, as he talked that day and the two following, he told Harber a good many things.

"I tell you, Harber," he said, "we'll do anything for money. Here I am—and I knew damned well it was killing me, too. And yet I stuck it out six months after I'd any earthly business to—just for a few extra hundreds."

"Where were you? What were you doing?" asked Harber.

"Trading-post up a river in the Straits Settlements," said Barton. "A crazy business from the beginning—and yet I made money. Made it lots faster than I could have back home. Back there you're hedged about with too many rules. And competition's too keen. You go into some big corporation office at seventy-five a month, maybe, and unless you have luck you're years getting near anything worth having. And you've got to play politics, bootlick your boss—all that. So I got out.

"Went to California first, and got a place in an exporting firm in San Francisco. They sent me to Sydney and then to Fiji. After I'd been out for a while and got the hang of things, I cut loose from them.

"Then I got this last chance, and it looked mighty good—and I expect I've done for myself by it. Five years or a little better. That's how long I've lasted. Back home I'd have been good for thirty-five. A short life and a merry one, they say. Merry. Good God!"

He shook his head ironically.

"The root of all evil," he resumed after a little. "Well, but you've got to have it—can't get along without it in *this* world. You've done well, you say?"

Harber nodded.

"Well, so should I have, if the cursed fever had let me alone. In another year or so I'd have been raking in the coin. And now here I am—busted—done—*fini*, as the French say. I burned the candle at both ends—and got just what was coming to me, I suppose. But how *could* I let go, just when everything was coming my way?"

"I know," said Harber. "But unless you can use it——"

"You're right there. Not much in it for me now. Still, the medicos say a cold winter back home will . . . I don't know. Sometimes I don't think I'll last to . . .

"Where's the use, you ask, Harber? You ask me right now, and I can't tell you. But if you'd asked me before I got like this, I could have told you quick enough. With some men, I suppose, it's just an acquisitive nature. With me, that didn't cut any figure. With me, it was a girl. I wanted to make the most I could for her in the shortest time. A girl . . . well . . ."

Harber nodded. "I understand. I came out for precisely the same reason myself," he remarked.

"You did?" said Barton, looking at him sadly. "Well, luck was with you, then. You look so—so damned fit! You can go back to her . . . while I . . . ain't it hell? Ain't it?" he demanded fiercely.

"Yes," admitted Harber, "it is. But at the same time, I'm not sure that anything's ever really lost. If she's worth while——"

Barton made a vehement sign of affirmation.

"Why, she'll be terribly sorry for you, but she won't *care*," concluded Harber. "I mean, she'll be waiting for you, and glad to have you coming home, so glad that . . ."

"Ah . . . yes. That's what . . . I haven't mentioned the fever in writing to her, you see. It will be a shock."

Harber, looking at him, thought that it would, indeed.

"I had a letter from her just before we sailed," went on the other, more cheerfully. "I'd like awfully, some time, to have you meet her. She's a wonderful girl—wonderful. She's clever. She's much cleverer than I am, really . . . about most things. When we get to Victoria, you must let me give you my address."

"Thanks," said Harber. "I'll be glad to have it."

That was the last Harber saw of him for five days. The weather had turned rough, and he supposed the poor fellow was seasick, and thought of him sympathetically, but let it rest there. Then, one evening after dinner, the steward came for him and said that Mr. Clay Barton wanted to see him. Harber followed to Barton's stateroom, which the sick man was occupying alone. In the passageway near the door, he met the ship's doctor.

"Mr. Harber?" said the doctor. "Your friend in there—I'm sorry to say—is——"

"I suspected as much," said Harber. "He knows it himself, I think."

"Does he?" said the doctor, obviously relieved. "Well, I hope that he'll live till we get him ashore. There's just a chance, of course, though his fever is very high now. He's quite lucid just now, and has been insisting upon seeing you. Later he mayn't be conscious. So——"

Harber nodded. "I'll go in."

Barton lay in his berth, still, terribly thin, and there were two pink patches of fever burning upon his cheek-bones. He opened his eyes with an infinite weariness as Harber entered the room, and achieved a smile.

"Hard luck, old fellow," said Harber, crossing to him.

"'S all *up!*" said Barton, grinning gamely. "I'm through. Asked 'em to send you in. Do something for me, Harber—tha's right, ain't it—Harber's your name?"

"Yes. What is it, Barton?"

Barton closed his eyes, then opened them again.

"Doggone memory—playin' tricks," he apologized faintly. "This, Harber. Black-leather case inside leather grip there—by the wall. Money in it—and letters. Everything goes—to the girl. Nobody else. I know you're straight. Take 'em to her?"

"Yes," said Harber.

"Good," said Barton. "All right, then! Been expecting this. All ready for it. Name—address—papers—all there. She'll have no trouble—getting money. Thanks, Harber." And after a pause, he added: "Better take it now—save trouble, you know."

Harber got the leather case from the grip and took it at once to his own stateroom.

When he returned, Barton seemed for the moment, with the commission off his mind, a little brighter.

"No end obliged, Harber," he murmured.

"All right," said Harber, "but ought you to talk?"

"Won't matter now," said Barton grimly. "Feel like talking now. To-morrow may be—too late!" And after another pause, he went on: "The fine dreams of youth—odd where they end, isn't it?

"This—and me—so different. So different! Failure. She was wise—but she didn't know everything. The world was too big—too hard for me. 'You can't fail,' she said, '*I won't let you fail!*' But you see——"

Harber's mind, slipping back down the years, with Barton, to his own parting, stopped with a jerk.

"What!" he exclaimed.

Barton seemed drifting, half conscious, half unconscious of what he was saying. He did not appear to have heard Harber's exclamation over the phrase so like that Janet had given him.

"We weren't like the rest," droned Barton. "No—we wanted more out of life than they did. We couldn't be content—with half a loaf. We wanted—the bravest adventures—the yellowest gold—the . . ."

Picture that scene, if you will. What would *you* have said? Harber saw leaping up before him, with terrible clarity, as if it were etched upon his mind, that night in Tawnleytown ten years before. It was as if Barton, in his semidelirium, were reading the words from *his* past!

"I won't let you fail! . . . half a loaf . . . the bravest adventures . . . the yellowest gold."

Incredible thing! That Barton and *his* girl should have stumbled upon so many of the phrases, the exact phrases! And suddenly full knowledge blinded Harber. . . . No! No! He spurned it. It couldn't be. And yet, he felt that if Barton were to utter one more phrase of those that Janet had said and, many, many times since, written to *him*, the impossible, the unbelievable, would be stark, unassailable fact.

He put his hand upon Barton's arm and gently pressed it.

"Barton," he said, "tell me—Janet—Tawnleytown?"

Barton stared with glassy, unseeing eyes for a moment; then his eyelids fell.

"The bravest adventures—the yellowest gold," he murmured. Then, so faintly as almost to baffle hearing: "Where —all—our—dreams? Gone—aglimmering. Gone."

That was all.

Impossible? No, just very, very improbable. But how, by its very improbability, it does take on the semblance of design! See how by slender a thread the thing hung, how every corner of the plan fitted. Just one slip Janet Spencer made; she let her thoughts and her words slip into a groove; she repeated herself. And how unerringly life had put her finger upon that clew! So reasoned Harber.

Well, if the indictment were true, there was proof to be had in Barton's leather case!

Harber, having called the doctor, went to his stateroom.

He opened the leather case. Inside a cover of yellow oiled silk he found first a certificate of deposit for three thousand pounds, and beneath it a packet of letters.

He unwrapped them.

And, though somehow he had known it without the proof, at the sight of them something caught at his heart with a clutch that made it seem to have stopped beating for a long time. For the sprawling script upon the letters was almost as familiar to him as his own. Slowly he reached down and took

up the topmost letter, drew the thin shiny sheets from th
envelope, fluttered them, dazed, and stared at the signatur

Yours, my dearest lover,

JANET.

Just so had she signed *his* letters. It *was* Janet Spencer
Two of her argosies, each one laden with gold for her, had me
in their courses, had sailed for a little together.

The first reasonable thought that came to Harber, when h
was convinced of the authenticity of the miracle, was that h
was free—free to go after the girl he loved, after Vanessa
Simola. I think that if he could have done it, he'd have
turned the steamer back to the Orient in that moment. The
thought that the ship was plunging eastward through a waste
of smashing heavy seas was maddening, no less!

He didn't want to see Janet or Tawnleytown, again. He
did have, he told me, a fleeting desire to know just how many
other ships Janet might have launched, but it wasn't strong
enough to take him to see her. He sent her the papers and
letters by registered mail under an assumed name.

And then he went to Claridon, Michigan, to learn of her
people when Vanessa might be expected home. They told
him she was on her way. So, fearing to miss her if he went
seeking, he settled down there and stayed until she came.
It was seven months of waiting he had . . . but it was
worth it in the end.

And that was Harber's romance. Just an incredible coincidence, you say. I know it. I told Harber that. And Mrs. Harber.

And *she* said nothing at all, but looked at me inscrutably, with a flicker of scorn in her sea-gray eyes.

Harber smiled lazily and serenely, and leaned back in his chair, and replied in a superior tone: "My dear Sterne, things that are made in heaven—like my marriage—don't just happen. Can't you see that your stand simply brands you an unbeliever?"

And, of course, I *can* see it. And Harber may be right. I don't know. Does any one, I wonder?

ALMA MATER

BY O. F. LEWIS

From *The Red Book*

PROFESSOR HORACE IRVING had taught Latin for nearly forty years at Huntington College. Then he had come back to Stuyvesant Square, in New York. Now he lived in a little hall bedroom, four flights up, overlooking the Square.

Habitually he walked from the Square westward to Fourth Avenue, in the afternoon, when the weather permitted. He had been born only three doors from where he now lived. The house of his birth had gone. It was sixty years since he had been a boy and played in this Square. Now he would pause at the corner of Fourth Avenue in his walks, and remember the Goelet's cow and the big garden and the high iron fence at Nineteenth Street and Broadway. Great buildings now towered there.

South along Fourth Avenue he would walk, a little man, scarcely five feet four in height, even with the silk hat and the Prince Albert coat. His white hair grew long over his collar, and people would notice that almost more than anything else about him. He may have weighed between ninety and a hundred pounds. The coat was worn and shiny, but immaculate. The tall hat was of a certain type and year, but carefully smoothed and still glossy.

He would pause often, between Nineteenth Street and Eighteenth Street, peopling the skyscrapers with ghosts of a former day, when houses and green gardens lined the streets. The passers-by watched him casually, perhaps as much as any one notices any one else in New York. He was, in the Fourteenth Street district, a rarer specimen than Hindus or Mexican medicine-men. Through the ten years since he had come, pensioned, from Huntington College, he had become walking landmark in this region.

He always walked down on the east side of the street, cross ing at Fourteenth Street. He was carefully piloted, an saluted, by the traffic policeman. It was a bad crossing Below Fourteenth Street things looked much more as they ha looked when he was young.

The bookstores were an unceasing hobby to the old man The secondhand dealers never made any objection to hi reading books upon the shelves. His purchases were perhap two books a week, at ten or even five cents each. Now an again he would find one of his own "Irving's Latin Prose Composition" texts in the five-cent pile. Opening the book, he usually would discover strange pencilled pictures drawn scrawlingly over many of the pages. His "Latin Composition" wasn't published after 1882, the year the firm failed. It might have been different for him, with a different publisher.

Late one afternoon in April, Professor Irving stood in his customary niche at the corner of Fourth Avenue and Ninth Street, watching the traffic from a sheltered spot against the wall of the building. He was becoming exceedingly anxious about the approaching storm. It had come up since he left Stuyvesant Square, and he had no umbrella. He must not get his silk hat wet. His thin overcoat was protecting him but feebly from the wind, which with the disappearance of the sun had grown sharp and biting. It was rapidly becoming dark. Lights were flashing in the windows up and down the Avenue.

The Professor decided to stand in a doorway till the shower had passed over. The chimes in the Metropolitan Tower struck the first quarter after four, the sounds welling in gusts to the old man's ears. A little man came to stand in the doorway beside the Professor. The latter saw that the little man had a big umbrella. Silk hats were so fearfully expensive in these days!

The heavy drops beat against the pavement in torrents. The first flash of lightning of the year was followed by a deep roll of thunder.

"I got to go!" said the little man. "Keep the umbrella! I got another where I work. I'm only fifty-five. You're

lder than me, a lot. You better start home. You'll get
oaked, standing here!" And the little man was gone before
he Professor could reply.

"An exceedingly kindly, simple man," thought the old
'rofessor. He had planned, while standing with his unknown
enefactor, that he would go into some store and wait. But
ow he would chance it, and cross the street. He saw a lull
n the traffic. He started and was nearly swept off his feet.
Ie got to the middle of the street. The umbrella grew
nwieldy, swinging this way and that, as if tugged by unseen
ands. It turned inside out. Blaring noises from the pass-
ng cars confused the Professor.

The shaft of the umbrella swung violently around and
knocked the silk hat from Professor Irving's head. His white
hair was caught by the wind. Lashed in another direction,
the shaft now struck the Professor's glasses, and they flew
away. Now he could see little or nothing. He became bewildered.

Great glaring headlights broke upon him, passed him, and
then immediately other glaring lights flared up toward him
out of the sheets of water. He couldn't see because of his
lost glasses and because of the stinging rain. He rushed between two cars. He slipped. . . .

The chimes on the Metropolitan Tower rang out, in wails of
wild sound, the half-hour after four.

The attendance that evening at the annual banquet of the
New York alumni of Huntington College exceeded all previous
records. The drive for two million five hundred thousand
dollars was on. It was a small college, but as Daniel Webster
said of Dartmouth, there were those who loved it.

The east ballroom of the hotel was well filled with diners.
Recollections of college days were shouted across tables and
over intervening aisles. There was a million still to raise:
but old Huntington would put it across! They'd gotten out
more of the older men, the men with money, than had ever
been seen before at an alumni dinner.

The income on one million would go into better salaries for
the professors and other teachers. They'd been shamefully
underpaid—men who'd been on the faculty twenty to thirty
years getting two thousand! Well, Huntington College had

now a new president, one of the boys of twenty years ago. Yes sir, things were different. It was in the air.

In the midst of the dinner course, the toastmaster rapped loudly with the gavel for attention. It was hard to obtain quiet.

"Men," said the toastmaster, and there was a curious note in his voice, "I ask your absolute silence. Middleton, whom you all know is one of the editorial staff of the *Sphere*, has just come in. He can stay only a few minutes. He came especially to tell you something."

A man standing behind the toastmaster stepped into the toastmaster's place. He was in business clothes, a sharp contrast to the rest of the diners. He was loudly applauded. He raised his right hand and shook his head.

"Boys," he said, "I've got a tragic piece of news for you—for those of you who were in college any time up to ten years ago." He paused and looked the diners over.

"Four fifths of you men who are here to-night knew old Hoddy Irving, our 'prof' in Latin. He served old Huntington College for forty years, the longest term any professor ever served. He made no demands—ever. He took us freshmen under his wing. I used to walk now and then with him, miles around the college, when it wasn't so built up as it now is. He loved the fields and the animals and the trees. He taught me a lot of things besides Latin. Don't you remember the funny little walk he had, sort of a hop forward? Don't you remember the way he'd come up to the college dormitories nights, sometimes, from his house down on the Row, and knock timidly at our doors, and come in and visit? Don't you remember that we used to clear some of those tables mighty quickly, of the chips and the bottles?"

There were titters, and some one shouted: "You said it!"

"And then, don't you remember, that some ten years ago they turned the old man off, with a pension—so-called—of half his salary. But what was his salary? Two thousand dollars—two thousand dollars at the end of forty years!! You and I, and old Huntington College, turned old Hoddy out to pasture, this pasture, on a thousand a year! And to-night, right now, he's lying in Bellevue, both legs broken, skull fractured, and not a damn cent in the world except in-

rance enough to bury him. And to-morrow he'll be ours
bury, boys—old Hoddy Irving!"

A confusion of voices rose in the room, and over them all a
No!" from some one who seemed to cry out in pain.

"Yes!" said Middleton as the murmurs ceased. "Our
d Hoddy, starving, loaded up with debt, alone, down in a
iserable hall bedroom in Stuyvesant Square. How did I
ome to know about it? One of our reporters, who covers
ellevue, dug up the story in his day's work. They brought
this old, disheveled, unconscious man—and in his pocket
as his name. Kenyon, the reporter, went over to the house
n the Square and found there another old fellow that old
oddy chummed some with, and who knew all the circum-
tances.

"It seems Hoddy had an invalid old sister—and they hadn't
ny money except this pension. How the two old souls got
long no one will never know. But she died awhile ago, and
hat put Hoddy into a lot more debt. And this miserable
ittle eighty dollars a month has had to carry him and his
ebts. And not a whimper that old man utters. Always
indly, Hoddy was, always telling stories from the forty years
t Huntington—and we fellows here, a lot of us rotten with
noney, and not knowing that the old fellow——"

Middleton's voice broke. It was some time before he
roceeded.

"This afternoon, at the corner of Fourth Avenue and Ninth
treet, just as that tornado broke, he tried to cross the street.
He got in a jam of cars, and of course the windshields were all
nussed up with rain, and the chauffeurs couldn't see anything
head—and they don't know whose car it was. The police
ay it was just four thirty-one when they picked him up.

"Well, that's all, except that—I'm going down to Bellevue,
nd if one or two of you want to come—perhaps old Hoddy
will know us—even this late."

Middleton had finished. From various parts of the room
came the words: "I'll go! Let me go!" Men were frankly
wiping their eyes.

At a distant table arose Martin Delano. He was reputed
to be the wealthiest alumnus of Huntington. He was said
to have made almost fabulous millions during the war. In the
Street he was known as "Merciless Martin." They were

planning to strike him this evening for at least a hundre
thousand.

Martin Delano stood holding the edge of the table with on
hand, the other fingering a spoon on the table. He stoo
there long. Several times he opened his lips as though t
speak. He took out his handkerchief and wiped his cheek
and forehead. Evidently he was deeply moved.

"Mr. Toastmaster, may I ask the privilege of going dow
to Bellevue with Mr. Middleton? I would ask that I be al
lowed to insist on going down. I have sinned, grievousl
sinned, in forgetting old Hoddy. Now, when it's too late——
Thirty years ago, and more, when I was a green, frightene
freshman from Vermont, he took me to his heart. He wa
known as the Freshman's Friend. That's what Hoddy alway
did—take the green and frightened freshman to his heart
Probably, if he hadn't done that to me, I'd have gone bacl
home in my lonesomeness. And then——

"Yes, I have sinned—and it might have been so different
I want to go down there! And I'm coming back here, befor
you men are through to-night, and I'll tell you more."

At about half-past ten Martin Delano came back. H
walked into the room just as one of the speakers had finished
The toastmaster caught his eye and beckoned to him to com
to the speaker's table. Delano stood in front of the crowd
He had walked forward, seeing no one on his way.

"Hoddy—Hoddy has gone, boys!"

Then quickly, silently, the three hundred men arose and
stood. After a time they heard Delano say: "Sit down,
boys!"

He waited till they were seated. "There's a lot that I
might tell, men—terrible things—that I won't tell, for it's all
over. Just this—and I suppose you're about through now
and breaking up. It was the poor old Prof of ours—shattered,
deathly white, a lot older. But will you believe it, the same
dear old smile, or almost a smile, on his face! Unconscious,
but babbling. And about what? The college—Alma Mater!
Those were just the words—Alma Mater! The college that
gave him the half pay and forgot him on the very night when
we are trying to raise a miserable two million, that things like
this sha'n't happen again!

"And boys, when we bent over him and whispered our

names, he seemed after a while to understand that we were there—but in the classroom, the old Number 3 in Holmes Hall! And fellows, he called on—on me to recite——"

Merciless Martin Delano couldn't go on. Finally he spoke.

"And so, Mr. President, I wish, sir, as a slight token of my appreciation of what that simple great man has done for Huntington College to give to our Alma Mater—our Alma Mater, sir—the sum of two hundred and fifty thousand dollars to be used for the erection of a suitable building, for whatever purpose is most necessary, and that building to be called after Horace Irving.

"And sir, I also desire to give to the fund for properly providing for the salaries of our professors and other teachers, the sum of two hundred and fifty thousand dollars—those men who teach in our Alma Mater.

"And I ask one word more: I have arranged that Professor Irving is to be buried from my house. If you will permit me, I will leave now."

The alumni of Huntington College were silent. There was no sound, save the occasional pushing of a chair, or the click of a plate or a glass upon the table, as Martin Delano passed from the room.

It was after one o'clock. Martin Delano was in his library, his arms flung across the table, his face between them.

In the opaque blur of swirling rain, his car had passed the corner of Fourth Avenue and Ninth Street at precisely half-past four that afternoon. He had happened to take out his watch at the moment the Metropolitan clock struck the second quarter.

He would never know whether it had been his car or another!

SLOW POISON

By ALICE DUER MILLER

From *The Saturday Evening Post*

THE Chelmsford divorce had been accomplished with the utmost decorum, not only outwardly in the newspapers, but inwardly among a group of intimate friends. They were a homogeneous couple—were liked by the same people, enjoyed the same things, and held many friends in common. These were able to say with some approach to certainty that everyone had behaved splendidly, even the infant of twenty-three with whom Julian had fallen in love.

Of course there will always be the question—and we used to argue it often in those days—how well a man can behave who, after fifteen perfectly satisfactory years of married life, admits that he has fallen in love with another woman. But if you believe in the clap-of-thunder theory, as I do, why, then, for a man nearing forty, taken off his feet by a blond-headed girl, Julian, too, behaved admirably.

As for Mrs. Julian, there was never any doubt as to her conduct. I used to think her—and I was not alone in the opinion—the most perfect combination of gentleness and power, and charity and humour, that I had ever seen. She was a year or so older than Julian—though she did not look it—and a good deal wiser, especially in the ways of the world; and, oddly enough, one of the features that worried us most in the whole situation was how he was ever going to get on, in the worldly sense, without her. He was to suffer not only from the loss of her counsel but from the lack of her indorsement. There are certain women who are a form of insurance to a man; and Anne gave a poise and solidity to Julian's presentation of himself which his own flibbertigibbet manner made particularly necessary.

I think this view of the matter disturbed Anne herself, though she was too clever to say so; or perhaps too numbed by the utter wreck of her own life to see as clearly as usual the rocks ahead of Julian. It was she, I believe, who first mentioned, who first thought of divorce, and certainly she who arranged the details. Julian, still in the more ideal stage of his emotion, had hardly wakened to the fact that his new love was marriageable. But Mrs. Julian, with the practical eye of her sex, saw in a flash all it might mean to him, at his age, to begin life again with a young beauty who adored him.

She saw this, at least, as soon as she saw anything; for Julian, like most of us when the occasion rises, developed a very pretty power of concealment. He had for a month been seeing Miss Littell every day before any of us knew that he went to see her at all. Certainly Anne, unsuspicious by nature, was unprepared for the revelation.

It took place in the utterly futile, unnecessary way such revelations always do take place. The two poor innocent dears had allowed themselves a single indiscretion; they had gone out together, a few days before Christmas, to buy some small gifts for each other. They had had an adventure with a beggar, an old man wise enough to take advantage of the holiday season, and the no less obvious holiday in the hearts of this pair. He had forced them to listen to some quaint variant of the old story, and they had between them given him all the small change they had left—sixty-seven cents, I think it was.

That evening at dinner Julian, ever so slightly afraid of the long pause, had told Anne the story as if it had happened to him alone. A few days afterward the girl, whom she happened to meet somewhere or other, displaying perhaps a similar nervousness, told the same story. Even the number of cents agreed.

I spoke a moment ago of the extraordinary power of concealment which we all possess; but I should have said the negative power to avoid exciting suspicion. Before that moment, before the finger points at us, the fool can deceive the sage; and afterward not even the sage can deceive the veriest fool.

Julian had no desire to lie to his wife. Indeed, he told me he had felt from the first that she would be his fittest confidante. He immediately told her everything—a dream rather than a narrative.

Nowhere did Anne show her magnanimity more than in accepting the rather extravagant financial arrangements which Julian insisted on making for her. He was not a rich man, and she the better economist of the two. We knew she saw that in popular esteem Julian would pay the price of her pride if she refused, and that in this ticklish moment of his life the least she could do was to let him have the full credit for his generosity.

"And after all," as she said to me, "young love can afford to go without a good many things necessary to old age."

It was the nearest I heard her come to a complaint.

As soon as everything was settled she sailed for Florence, where she had friends and where, she intimated, she meant to spend most of her time.

I said good-by to her with real emotion, and the phrase I used as to my wish to serve her was anything but a convention.

Nor did she take it so.

"Help Julian through this next year," she said. "People will take it harder than he knows. He'll need you all." And she was kind enough to add something about my tact. Poor lady! She must have mentally withdrawn her little compliment before we met many times again.

II

Perhaps the only fault in Anne's education of her husband had been her inability to cling. In his new ménage this error was rectified, and the effect on him was conspicuously good; in fact, I think Rose's confidence in his greatness pulled them through the difficult time.

For there was no denying that it was difficult. Many people looked coldly on them. and I know there was even some talk of asking him to resign from the firm of architects of which he was a member. The other men were all older, and very conservative. Julian represented to them everything that was modern and dangerous. Granger, the leading spirit, was in the habit of describing himself as holding old-fashioned views, by which he meant that he had all the virtues of the

Pilgrim Fathers and none of their defects. I never liked him, but I could not help respecting him. The worst you could say of him was that his high standards were always successful. You felt that so fanatical a sense of duty ought to have required some sacrifices.

To such a man Julian's conduct appeared not only immoral but inadvisable, and unfitting in a young man, especially without consulting his senior partners.

We used to say among ourselves that Granger's reason for wanting to get rid of Julian was not any real affection for the dim old moral code, but rather his acute realization that without Anne his junior partner was a less valuable asset.

Things were still hanging fire when I paid her the first of my annual visits. She was dreadfully distressed at my account of the situation. She had the manner one sometimes sees in dismissed nurses who meet their former little charges unwashed or uncared for. She could hardly believe it was no longer her business to put the whole matter right.

"Can't she do something for him?" she said. "Make her bring him a great building. That would save him."

It was this message that I carried home to Rose; at least I suggested the idea to her as if it were my own. I had my doubts of her being able to carry it out.

Out of loyalty to Julian, or perhaps I ought to say out of loyalty to Anne, we had all accepted Rose, but we should soon have loved her in any case. She was extraordinarily sweet and docile, and gave us, those at least who were not parents, our first window to the east, our first link with the next generation, just at the moment when we were relinquishing the title ourselves. I am afraid that some of the males among us envied Julian more than perhaps in the old days we had ever envied him Anne.

But we hardly expected her to further his career as Anne had done, and yet, oddly enough, that was exactly what she did. Her methods had all the effectiveness of youth and complete conviction. She forced Julian on her friends and relations, not so much on his account as on theirs. She wanted them to be sure of the best. The result was that orders flowed in. Things took a turn for the better and continued to improve, as I was able to report to Anne when I went to see her at Florence or at Paris. She was always well lodged, well served, and surrounded by the pleasantest people; yet each time I saw her she had a look exiled and circumscribed, a look I can only describe as that of a spirit in reduced circumstances.

She was always avid for details of Julian and all that concerned him; and as times improved I was stupid enough to suppose I pleased her by giving them from the most favourable angle. It seemed to me quite obvious, as I saw how utterly she had ruined her own life, that she ought at least to have the comfort of knowing that she had not sacrificed it in vain. And so I allowed myself, not an exaggeration but a candour more unrestrained than would be usual in the circumstances.

Led on by her burning interest I told her many things I might much better have kept to myself; not only accounts of his work and his household and any new friends in our old circle, but we had all been amazed to see a sense of responsibility develop in Julian in answer to his new wife's dependence on him. With this had come a certain thoughtfulness in small attentions, which, I saw too late, Anne must always have missed in him. She was so much more competent in the smaller achievements of life than he that it had been wisdom to leave them to her; and Anne had often traveled alone and attended to the luggage, when now Rose was personally conducted like a young empress. The explanation was simple enough: Anne had the ability to do it, and the other had not. Even if I had stopped to think, I might fairly have supposed that Anne would find some flattery in the contrast. I should have been wrong.

Almost the first thing she asked me was whether he came home to luncheon. In old times, though his house was only a few blocks from his office, he had always insisted that it took too much time. Anne had never gained her point with him, though she put some force into the effort. Now I had to confess he did.

"It's much better for him," she said with pleasure, and quite deceived me; herself, too, perhaps.

Yet even I, for all my blindness, felt some uneasiness the year Rose's son was born. I do not think the desire for offspring had ever taken up a great deal of room in Julian's consciousness, but of course Anne had wanted children, and I felt very cruel, sitting in her little apartment in Paris, describing the baby who ought to have been hers. How different her position would have been now if she had some thin-legged little girl to educate or some raw-boned boy to worry over; and there was that overblessed woman at home, necessary not only to Julian but to Julian's son.

It was this same year, but at a later visit, that I first became aware of a change in Anne. At first the charm of her surroundings, her pretty clothes, even to the bright little buckles on her shoes, blinded me to the fact that she herself was changed. I do not mean that she was aged. One of the delightful things about her was that she was obviously going to make an admirable old lady; the delicate boniness of her face and the clearness of her skin assured that. This was a change more fundamental. Even in her most distracted days Anne had always maintained a certain steadiness of head. She had trodden thorny paths, but she had always known where she was going. I had seen her eyelids red, but I had never failed to find in the eyes themselves the promise of a purpose. But now it was gone. I felt as if I were looking into a little pool which had been troubled by a stone, and I waiting vainly for the reflection to re-form itself.

So painful was the impression that before I sailed for home I tried to convey to her the dangers of her mood.

"I think you are advising me to be happy," she said.

"I am advising no such thing," I answered. "I am merely pointing out that you run the risk of being more unhappy than you are. My visits—or rather the news I bring you—are too important to you. You make me feel as if it were the only event of the year—to you who have always had such an interesting life of your own."

"I have not had a life of my own since I was twenty," she returned. It was at twenty she had married.

"Then think of Julian," I said, annoyed not only at my own clumsiness but at the absence of anything of Anne's old heroic spirit. "For his sake, at least, you must keep your head. Why, my dear woman, one look at your face, grown as desperate as it sometimes appears now, would ruin Julian with the whole world. Even I, knowing the whole story, would find it hard to forgive him if you should fail to continue to be the splendid triumphant creature whom we know you were designed to be."

She gave me a long queer look, which meant something tremendous. Evidently my words had made an impression. They had, but not just the one I intended.

III

One of the first people I always saw on returning was Julian. How often he thought of Anne I do not know, but he spoke of her with the greatest effort. He invariably took care to assure himself that she was physically well, but beyond this it would have been a brave person who dared to go. He did not want to hear the details of her life and appearance.

It was with some trepidation, therefore, that a few months after this I came to tell him that Anne was about to return to America. Why she was coming, or for how long, her letter did not say. I only knew that the second Saturday in December would see her among us again. It seemed fair to assume that her stay would not be long. Julian evidently thought so for he arranged to be in the West for three or four weeks.

I went to meet her. The day was cold and rainy, and as soon as I saw her I made up my mind that the crossing had been a bad one, and I was glad no one else had come to the wharf with me. She was standing by the rail, wrapped in a voluminous fur coat—the fashions were slim in the extreme—and her hat was tied on by a blue veil.

I may as well admit that from the moment I heard of her projected return I feared that her real motive for coming, conscious or unconscious, was to see Julian again. So when I told her of his absence I was immensely relieved that she took it as a matter of course.

"I suppose we might have met," she observed. "As it is, I can go about without any fear of an awkward encounter." I say I was relieved, but I was also excessively puzzled. Why had Anne come home?

It was a question I was to hear answered in a variety of ways during the next few months, by many of Anne's friends and partisans; for, as I think I have said, Anne had inspired great attachment since her earliest days. Why had she come home? they exclaimed. Why not, pray? Had she done anything criminal that she was to be exiled? Did I think it pleasant to live abroad on a small income? Even if she could get on without her friends, could they do without her?

The tone of these questions annoyed me not a little when I heard them, which was not for some time. Soon after Anne's arrival I, too, was called away, and it was not until February that I returned and was met by the carefully set piece—Anne the Victim.

With that ill-advised self-confidence of which I have already made mention, I at once set about demolishing this picture. I told Anne's friends, who were also mine, that she would thank them very little for their attitude. I found myself painting her life abroad as a delirium of intellect and luxury. I even found myself betraying professional secrets and arguing with total strangers as to the amount of her income.

Even in Montreal faint echoes of this state of things had reached me, but not until I went to see Anne on my return did I get any idea of their cause. She had taken a furnished apartment from a friend, in a dreary building in one of the West Forties. Only a jutting front of limestone and an elevator man in uniform saved it, or so it seemed to me, from being an old-fashioned boarding house. Its windows, small, as if designed for an African sun, looked northward upon a darkened street. Anne's apartment was on the second floor, and the requirements of some caryatids on the outside rendered her fenestration particularly meager. Her friend, if indeed it were a friend, had not treated her generously in the matter of furniture. She had left nothing superfluous but two green glass jugs on the mantelpiece, and had covered the chairs with a chintz, the groundwork of which was mustard colour.

Another man who was there when I came in, who evidently had known Anne in different surroundings, expressed the most hopeful view possible when he said that doubtless it would all look charming when she had arranged her own belongings.

Anne made a little gesture. "I haven't any belongings," she said.

I didn't know what she meant, perhaps merely a protest against the tyranny of things, but I saw the effect her speech produced on her auditor. Perhaps she saw it. too, for presently she added: "Oh, yes! I have one."

And she went away, and came back carrying a beautiful old silver loving cup. I knew it well.

It came from Julian's forebears. Anne had always loved it, and I was delighted that she should have it now. She set it on a table before a mirror, and here it did a double share to make the room possible.

When we were alone I expressed my opinion of her choice of lodgings.

"This sunless cavern!" I said. "This parlour-car furniture!"

She looked a little hurt. "You don't like it?" she said.

"Do you?" I snapped back.

After a time I had recourse to the old argument that it didn't look well; that it wasn't fair to Julian. But she had been expecting this.

"My dear Walter," she answered, "you must try to be more consistent. In Paris you told me that I must cease to regulate my life by Julian. You were quite right. This place pleases me, and I don't intend to go to a hotel, which I hate, or to take a house, which is a bother, in order to soothe Julian's feelings. I have begun to lead my life to suit myself."

The worst of it was, I could think of no answer.

A few evenings afterward we dined at the same house. Anne arrived with a scarf on her head, under the escort of a maid. She had come in a trolley car. Nobody's business but her own, perhaps, if she would have allowed it to remain so, but when she got up to go, and other people were talking of their motors' being late, Anne had to say: "Mine is never late; it goes past the corner every minute."

I could almost hear a sigh, "Poor angel!" go round the room.

The next thing that happened was that Julian sent for me. He was in what we used to call in the nursery "a state."

"What's this I hear about Anne's being hard up?" he said. "Living in a nasty flat, and going out to dinner in the cars?" And he wouldn't listen to an explanation. "She must take more; she must be made to take more."

I had one of my most unfortunate inspirations. I thought I saw an opportunity for Julian to make an impression.

"I don't think she would listen to me," I said. "Why don't you get Mr. Granger to speak to her?"

The idea appealed to Julian. He admired Mr. Granger, and remembered that he and Anne had been friends. Whereas I thought, of course, that Mr. Granger would thus be made to see that the fault, if there were a fault, was not of Julian's generosity. Stupidly enough I failed to see that if Julian's offer was graceful Anne's gesture of refusal would be upon a splendid scale.

And it must have been very large, indeed, to stir old Granger as it did. He told me there had been tears in his eyes while she spoke of her husband's kindness. Kindness! He could not but compare her surroundings with the little house, all geraniums and muslin curtains, in which the new Mrs. Chelmsford was lodged. Anne had refused, of course. In the circumstances she could not accept. She said she had quite enough for a single woman. The phrase struck Granger as almost unbearably pathetic.

One day I noticed the loving cup—which was always on Anne's table, which was admired by everyone who came to the apartment, and was said to recall her, herself, so pure and graceful and perfect—one day the loving cup was gone.

I was so surprised when my eye fell on its vacant place that I blurted out: "Goodness, Anne, where's your cup?"

The next moment I could have bitten out my tongue. Anne stood still in the middle of the room, twisting her hands a little, and everyone—there were three or four of us there—stopped talking.

"Oh," she said. "oh, Walter, I know you'll scold me for being officious and wrong-headed, but I have sent the cup back to Julian's son. I think he ought to have it."

Everyone else thought the deed extremely noble. I took my hat and went to Rose. Rose was not very enthusiastic. A beautiful letter had accompanied the cup. We discussed the advisability of sending it back; but of course that would have done no good. The devilish part of a favour is that to accept or reject it is often equally incriminating. Anne held the situation in the hollow of her hand. Besides, as Rose pointed out, we couldn't very well return it without asking Julian, and we had both agreed that for the present Julian had better remain in ignorance of the incident. He would have thought it mean-spirited to allow any instance of Anne's generosity to remain concealed from the public. Rose and I were willing to allow it to drop.

I was sorry, therefore, when I found, soon after, not only that everyone knew of the gift but that phrases of the beautiful letter itself were current, with marks of authenticity upon them. It was not hard to trace them to Anne's intimates.

I have no idea to this day whether Anne was deliberately trying to ruin the man for whom she had sacrificed so much; or whether one of those large, unconscious, self-indulgent movements of our natures was carrying her along the line of least resistance. There are some people, I know, who can behave well only so long as they have the centre of the stage, and are driven by a necessity almost moral to regain such a place at any cost, so that they may once again begin the exercise of their virtues.

Anne's performance was too perfect, I thought, for conscious art, and she was not a genius. She was that most dangerous of all engines, a good person behaving wickedly. All her past of high-mindedness and kindness protected her now like an armour from the smallest suspicion. All the grandeur of her conduct at the time of the divorce was remembered as a proof that she at least had a noble soul. Who could doubt that she wished him well?

If so, she soon appeared to be the only person who did. For, as we all know, pity is one of the most dangerous passions to unloose. It demands a victim. We rise to pathos, only over the dead bodies of our nearest and dearest.

Every phrase, every gesture of Anne's stirred one profoundly, and it was inevitable, I suppose, that Julian should be selected as the sacrifice. I noticed that people began to speak of him in the past, though he was still moving among us—"As Julian used to say."

He and Anne fortunately never met, but she and the new Mrs. Julian had one encounter in public. If even then Anne would have shown the slightest venom all might still have been well. But, no, the worn, elderly woman, face to face with the young beauty who had possessed herself of everything in the world, showed nothing but a tenderness so perfect that every heart was wrung. I heard Rose criticized for not receiving her in the same spirit.

The next day Julian was blackballed at a philanthropic club at which he had allowed himself to be proposed merely from a sense of civic duty.

Over the incident I know Anne wept. I heard her tears.

"Oh, if I could have spared him that!" she said.

My eyes were cold, but those of Mr. Granger, who came in while her eyelids were still red, were full of fire.

She spent a week with the Grangers that summer. The whole family—wife, sons and daughters—had all yielded to the great illusion.

It must not be supposed that I had failed to warn Julian. The supineness of his attitude was one of the most irritating features of the case. He answered me as if I were violating the dead; asked me if by any chance I didn't see he deserved all he was getting.

No one was surprised when in the autumn he resigned from his firm. There had been friction between the partners for some time. Soon afterward he and Rose sailed for Italy, where they have lived ever since. He had scarcely any income except that which he made in his profession; his capital had gone to Anne. He probably thought that what he had would go further abroad.

I do not know just how Anne took his departure, except that I am sure she was wonderful about it. I had ceased to see her. She has, however, any number of new friends, whose fresh interest in her story keeps it continually alive. She has given up her ugly flat and taken a nice little house, and in summer I notice she has red geraniums in the window boxes. I often see a nice little motor standing before her door—the result doubtless of a year's economy.

Whenever her friends congratulate her on the improvement in her finances she says she owes it all to me—I am such an excellent man of business.

"I admire Walter so much," I am told she says, "though I'm afraid I have lost him as a friend. But then, in the last few years I have lost so much." And she smiles that brave sad smile of hers.

THE FACE IN THE WINDOW

By WILLIAM DUDLEY PELLEY

From *The Red Book*

AT NINE O'CLOCK this morning Sheriff Crumpett entered our New England town post-office for his mail. From his box he extracted his monthly Grand Army paper and a letter in a long yellow envelope. This envelope bore the return-stamp of a prominent Boston lumber-company. The old man crossed the lobby to the writing-shelf under the Western Union clock, hooked black-rimmed glasses on a big nose and tore a generous inch from the end of the envelope.

The first inclosure which met his eyes was a check. It was heavy and pink and crisp, and was attached to the single sheet of letter-paper with a clip. Impressed into the fabric of the safety-paper were the indelible figures of a protector: *Not over Five Thousand* ($5000) *Dollars.*

The sheriff read the name of the person to whom it was payable and gulped. His gnarled old hand trembled with excitement as he glanced over the clipped letter and then went through it again.

November 10, 1919.

MY DEAR SHERIFF:

Enclosed please find my personal check for five thousand dollars. It is made out to Mrs. McBride. Never having known the lady personally, and because you have evidently represented her with the authorities, I am sending it to you for proper delivery. I feel, from your enthusiastic account of her recent experience, that it will give you pleasure to present it to her.

Under the circumstances I do not begrudge the money. When first advised of Ruggam's escape, it was hot-headed impulse which prompted me to offer a reward so large. The old clan-blood of the Wileys must have made me murder-mad that Ruggam should regain his freedom permanently after the hellish thing he did to my brother. The newspapers heard of it, and then I could not retract.

That, however, is a thing of the past. I always did detest a welcher;

and if this money is going to a woman to whom it will be manna from heaven—to use your words—I am satisfied. Convey to her my personal congratulations, gratitude and best wishes.

Cordially yours,
C. V. D. WILEY.

"Good old Chris!" muttered the sheriff. "He's rich because he's white." He thrust both check and letter back into the long envelope and headed for the office of our local daily paper at a smart pace.

The earning of five thousand dollars reward-money by Cora McBride made an epochal news-item, and in that night's paper we headlined it accordingly—not omitting proper mention of the sheriff and giving him appropriate credit.

Having so started the announcement permeating through the community, the old man employed the office phone and called the local livery-stable. He ordered a rig in which he might drive at once to the McBride house in the northern part of town.

"But half that money ought to be yourn!" protested the proprietor of the stable as the sheriff helped him "gear up the horse" a few minutes later.

"Under the circumstances, Joseph, can you see me takin' it? No; it ain't in me to horn in for no rake-off on one o' the Lord's miracles."

The old man climbed into the sleigh, took the reins from the liveryman and started the horse from the livery yard.

Two weeks ago—on Monday, the twenty-seventh of the past October—the telephone-bell rang sharply in our newspaper-office a few moments before the paper went to press. Now, the telephone-bell often rings in our newspaper-office a few moments before going to press. The confusion on this particular Monday afternoon, however, resulted from Albany calling on the long-distance. Albany—meaning the nearest office of the international press-association of which our paper is a member—called just so, out of a clear sky, on the day McKinley was assassinated, on the day the *Titanic* foundered and on the day Austria declared war on Serbia.

The connection was made, and over the wire came the voice of young Stewart, crisp as lettuce.

"Special dispatch . . . . Wyndgate, Vermont, October 27th. . . . Ready?"

The editor of our paper answered in the affirmative. The rest of us grouped anxiously around his chair. Stewart proceeded:

"'Hapwell Ruggam, serving a life-sentence for the murder of Deputy Sheriff Martin Wiley at a Lost Nation kitchen-dance two years ago, killed Jacob Lambwell, his guard, and escaped from prison at noon to-day.

"'Ruggam had been given some repair work to do near the outer prison-gate. It was opened to admit a tradesman's automobile. As Guard Lambwell turned to close the gate, Ruggam felled him with his shovel. He escaped to the adjacent railroad-yards, stole a corduroy coat and pair of blue overalls hanging in a switchman's shanty and caught the twelve-forty freight up Green River.'"

Stewart had paused. The editor scribbled frantically. In a few words aside he explained to us what Stewart was sending. Then he ordered the latter to proceed.

"'Freight Number Eight was stopped by telegraph near Norwall. The fugitive, assuming correctly that it was slowing down for search, was seen by a brakeman fleeing across a pasture between the tracks and the eastern edge of Haystack Mountain. Several posses have already started after him, and sheriffs all through northern New England are being notified.

"'Christopher Wiley, lumber magnate and brother of Ruggam's former victim, on being told of the escape, has offered a reward of five thousand dollars for Ruggam's capture, dead or alive. Guard Lambwell was removed to a hospital, where he died at one-thirty'. . . . *All right?*"

The connection was broken, and the editor removed the headpiece. He began giving orders. We were twenty minutes behind usual time with the papers, but we made all the trains.

When the big Duplex was grinding out newsprint with a roar that shook the building, the boys and girls gathered around to discuss the thing which had happened.

The Higgins boy, saucer-eyed over the experience of being "on the inside" during the handling of the first sizable news-story since he had become our local reporter, voiced the interrogation on the faces of other office newcomers.

"Ruggam," the editor explained, "is a poor unfortunate who should have been sent to an asylum instead of the penitentiary. He killed Mart Wiley, a deputy sheriff, at a Lost Nation kitchen-dance two years ago."

"Where's the Lost Nation?"

"It's a term applied to most of the town of Partridgeville in the northern part of the county—an inaccessible district back in the mountains peopled with gone-to-seed stock and half-civilized illiterates who only get into the news when they load up with squirrel whisky and start a programme of progressive hell. Ruggam was the local blacksmith."

"What's a kitchen-dance?"

"Ordinarily a kitchen-dance is harmless enough. But the Lost Nation folks use it as an excuse for a debauch. They gather in some sizable shack, set the stove out into the yard, soak themselves in aromatic spirits of deviltry and dance from Saturday night until Monday noon——"

"And this Ruggam killed a sheriff at one of them?"

"He got into a brawl with another chap about his wife. Someone passing saw the fight and sent for an officer. Mart Wiley was deputy, afraid of neither man, God nor devil. Martin had grown disgusted over the petty crime at these kitchen-dances and started out to clean up this one right. Hap Ruggam killed him. He must have had help, because he first got Mart tied to a tree in the yard. Most of the crowd was pie-eyed by this time, anyhow, and would fight at the drop of a hat. After tying him securely, Ruggam caught up a billet of wood and—and killed him with that."

"Why didn't they electrocute him?" demanded young Higgins.

"Well, the murder wasn't exactly premeditated. Hap wasn't himself; he was drunk—not even able to run away when Sheriff Crumpett arrived in the neighbourhood to take him into custody. Then there was Hap's bringing up. All these made extenuating circumstances."

"There was something about Sheriff Wiley's pompadour," suggested our little lady proofreader.

"Yes," returned the editor. "Mart had a queer head of hair. It was dark and stiff, and he brushed it straight back in a pompadour. When he was angry or excited, it actually rose on his scalp like wire. Hap's counsel made a great fuss over Mart's pompadour and the part it sort of played in egging Hap on. The sight of it, stiffening and rising the way it did maddened Ruggam so that he beat it down hysterically in retaliation for the many grudges he fancied he owed the officer. No, it was all right to make the sentence life-imprisonment, only it should have been an asylum. Hap's not right. You'd know it without being told. I guess it's his eyes. They aren't mates. They light up weirdly when he's drunk or excited, and if you know what's healthy, you get out of the way."

By eight o'clock that evening most of the valley's deer-hunters, all of the local adventurers who could buy, borrow or beg a rifle, and the usual quota of high-school sons of thoughtless parents were off on the man-hunt in the eastern mountains.

Among them was Sheriff Crumpett's party. On reaching the timber-line they separated. It was agreed that if any of them found signs of Ruggam, the signal for assistance was five shots in quick succession "and keep shooting at intervals until the rest come up."

We newspaper folk awaited the capture with professional interest and pardonable excitement. . . .

In the northern part of our town, a mile out on the Wickford road, is the McBride place. It is a small white house with a red barn in the rear and a neat rail fence inclosing the whole. Six years ago Cora McBride was bookkeeper in the local garage. Her maiden name was Allen. The town called her "Tomboy Allen." She was the only daughter of old Zeb Allen, for many years our county game-warden. Cora, as we had always known—and called—her, was a full-blown, red-blooded, athletic girl who often drove cars for her employer in the days when steering-wheels manipulated by women were offered as clinching proof that society was headed for the dogs.

Duncan McBride was chief mechanic in the garage repair-shop. He was an affable, sober, steady chap, popularly known as "Dunk the Dauntless" because of an uncanny ability to cope successfully with the ailments of 90 per cent. of the internal-combustion hay-balers and refractory tin-Lizzies in the county when other mechanics had given them up in disgust.

When he married his employer's bookkeeper, Cora's folks gave her a wedding that carried old Zeb within half an hour of insolvency and ran to four columns in the local daily. Duncan and the Allen girl motored to Washington in a demonstration-car, and while Dunk was absent, the yard of the garage resembled the premises about a junkshop. On their return they bought the Johnson place, and Cora quickly demonstrated the same furious enthusiasm for homemaking and motherhood that she had for athletics and carburetors.

Three years passed, and two small boys crept about the yard behind the white rail fence. Then—when Duncan and his wife were "making a great go of matrimony" in typical Yankee fashion—came the tragedy that took all the vim out of Cora, stole the ruddy glow from her girlish features and made her middle-aged in a twelvemonth. In the infantile-paralysis epidemic which passed over New England three years ago the McBrides suffered the supreme sorrow—twice. Those small boys died within two weeks of each other.

Duncan of course kept on with his work at the garage. He was quieter and steadier than ever. But when we drove into the place to have a carburetor adjusted or a rattle tightened, we saw only too plainly that on his heart was a wound the scars of which would never heal. As for Cora, she was rarely seen in the village.

Troubles rarely come singly. One afternoon this past August, Duncan completed repairs on Doc Potter's runabout. Cranking the machine to run it from the workshop, the "dog" on the safety-clutch failed to hold. The acceleration of the engine threw the machine into high. Dunk was pinned in front while the roadster leaped ahead and rammed the delivery truck of the Red Front Grocery.

Duncan was taken to our memorial hospital with internal injuries and dislocation of his spine. He remained there many weeks. In fact, he had been home only a couple of days when the evening stage left in the McBride letter-box the daily paper containing the story of Ruggam's "break" and of the reward offered for his capture.

Cora returned to the kitchen after obtaining the paper and sank wearily into a wooden chair beside the table with the red cloth. Spreading out the paper, she sought the usual mental distraction in the three- and four-line bits which make up our local columns.

As the headlines caught her eye, she picked up the paper

and entered the bedroom where Duncan lay. There were telltale traces of tears on his unshaven face, and an ache in his discouraged heart that would not be assuaged; for it was becoming rumoured about the village that Dunk the Dauntless might never operate on the vitals of an ailing tin-Lizzie again.

"Dunnie," cried his wife, "Hap Ruggam's escaped!" Sinking down beside the bedroom lamp, she read him the article aloud.

Her husband's name was mentioned therein; for when the sheriff had commandeered an automobile from the local garage to convey him and his posse to Lost Nation and secure Ruggam, Duncan had been called forth to preside at the steering-wheel. He had thus assisted in the capture and later had been a witness at the trial.

The reading ended, the man rolled his head.

"If I wasn't held here, I might go!" he said. "I might try for that five thousand myself!"

Cora was sympathetic enough, of course, but she was fast approaching the stage where she needed sympathy herself.

"We caught him over on the Purcell farm," mused Duncan. "Something ailed Ruggam. He was drunk and couldn't run. But that wasn't all. He had had some kind of crazy-spell during or after the killing and wasn't quite over it. We tied him and lifted him into the auto. His face was a sight. His eyes aren't mates, anyhow, and they were wild and unnatural. He kept shrieking something about a head of hair—black hair—sticks up like wire. He must have had an awful impression of Mart's face and that hair of his."

"I remember about Aunt Mary Crumpett's telling me of the trouble her husband had with his prisoner in the days before the trial," his wife replied. "He had those crazy-spells often, nights. He kept yelling that he saw Martin Wiley's head with its peculiar hair, and his face peering in at him through the cell window. Sometimes he became so bad that Sheriff Crumpett thought he'd have apoplexy. Finally he had to call Dr. Johnson to attend him."

"Five thousand dollars!" muttered Duncan. "Gawd! I'd hunt the devil *for nothing* if I only had a chance of getting out of this bed."

Cora smoothed her husband's rumpled bed, comforted him and laid her own tired head down beside his hand. When he had dozed off, she arose and left the room.

In the kitchen she resumed her former place beside the table with the cheap red cloth; and there, with her face in her hands, she stared into endless distance.

"Five thousand dollars! Five thousand dollars!" Over and over she whispered the words, with no one to hear.

The green-birch fire snapped merrily in the range. The draft sang in the flue. Outside, a soft, feathery snow was falling, for winter came early in the uplands of Vermont this past year. To Cora McBride, however, the winter meant only hardship. Within another week she must go into town and secure work. Not that she minded the labour nor the trips through the vicious weather! The anguish was leaving Duncan through those monotonous days before he should be up and around. Those dreary winter days! What might they not do to him—alone.

Five thousand dollars! Like many others in the valley that night she pictured with fluttering heart what it would mean to possess such a sum of money; but not once in her pitiful flight of fancy did she disregard the task which must be performed to gain that wealth.

It meant traveling upward in the great snowbound reaches of Vermont mountain-country and tracking down a murderer who had killed a second time to gain his freedom and would stop at nothing again.

And yet—*five thousand dollars!*

How much will a person do, how far will a normal human being travel, to earn five thousand dollars—if the need is sufficiently provocative?

As Cora McBride sat there in the homely little farmhouse kitchen and thought of the debts still existent, contracted to save the already stricken lives of two little lads forgotten now by all but herself and Duncan and God, of the chances of losing their home if Duncan could work no more and pay up the balance of their mortgage, of the days when Duncan must lie in the south bedroom alone and count the figures on the wall-paper—as she sat there and contemplated these things, into Cora McBride's heart crept determination.

At first it was only a faint challenge to her courage. As the minutes passed, however, her imagination ran riot, with five thousand dollars to help them in their predicament. The challenge grew. Multitudes of women down all the years had attempted wilder ventures for those who were dear to them. Legion in number had been those who set their hands and hearts to greater tasks, made more improbable sacrifices, taken greater chances. Multitudes of them, too, had won—on little else than the courage of ignorance and the strength of desperation.

She had no fear of the great outdoors, for she had lived close to the mountains from childhood and much of her old physical resiliency and youthful daredeviltry remained. And the need was terrible; no one anywhere in the valley, not even her own people, knew how terrible.

Cora McBride, alone by her table in the kitchen, that night made her decision.

She took the kitchen lamp and went upstairs. Lifting the top of a leather trunk, she found her husband's revolver. With it was a belt and holster, the former filled with cartridges. In the storeroom over the back kitchen she unhooked Duncan's mackinaw and found her own toboggan-cap. From a corner behind some fishing-rods she salvaged a pair of summer-dried snowshoes; they had facilitated many a previous hike in the winter woods with her man of a thousand adventures. She searched until she found the old army-haversack Duncan used as a game-bag. Its shoulder-straps were broken but a length of rope sufficed to bind it about her shoulders, after she had filled it with provisions.

With this equipment she returned below-stairs. She drew on heavy woollen stockings and buckled on arctics. She entered the cold pantry and packed the knapsack with what supplies she could find at the hour. She did not forget a drinking-cup, a hunting-knife or matches. In her blouse she slipped a household flash-lamp.

Dressed finally for the adventure, from the kitchen she called softly to her husband. He did not answer. She was overwhelmed by a desire to go into the south bedroom and kiss him, so much might happen before she saw him again. But she restrained herself. She must not waken him.

She blew out the kerosene lamp, gave a last glance about

her familiar kitchen and went out through the shed door, closing it softly behind her.

It was one of those close, quiet nights when the bark of a distant dog or whinny of a horse sounds very near at hand. The snow was falling feathery.

An hour later found her far to the eastward, following an old side road that led up to the Harrison lumber-job. She had meantime paid Dave Sheldon, a neighbour's boy, encountered by his gate, to stay with Duncan during her absence which she explained with a white lie. But her conscience did not bother. Her conscience might be called upon to smother much more before the adventure was ended.

Off in the depths of the snowing night she strode along, a weird figure against the eerie whiteness that illumined the winter world. She felt a strange wild thrill in the infinite out-of-doors. The woodsman's blood of her father was having its little hour.

And she knew the woods. Intuitively she felt that if Ruggam was on Haystack Mountain making his way toward Lost Nation, he would strike for the shacks of the Green Mountain Club or the deserted logging-camps along the trail, secreting himself in them during his pauses for rest, for he had no food, and provisions were often left in these structures by hunters and mountain hikers. Her plan was simple. She would investigate each group of buildings. She had the advantage of starting on the northwest side of Haystack. She would be working toward Ruggam, while the rest of the posses were trailing him.

Mile after mile she covered. She decided it must be midnight when she reached the ghostly buildings of the Harrison tract, lying white and silent under the thickening snow. It was useless to search these cabins; they were too near civilization. Besides, if Ruggam had left the freight at Norwall on the eastern side of Haystack at noon, he had thirty miles to travel before reaching the territory from which she was starting. So she skirted the abandoned quiet of the clearing, laid the snowshoes properly down before her and bound the thongs securely about her ankles.

She had plenty of time to think of Ruggam as she padded along. He had no snowshoes to aid him, unless he had managed to secure a pair by burglary, which was improbable. So it was not difficult to calculate about where she should begin watching for him. She believed he would keep just off the main trail to avoid detection, yet take its general direction in order to secure shelter and possible food from the mountain buildings. When she reached the country in which she might hope to encounter him, she would zigzag across that main trail in order to pick up his foot-tracks if he had passed her undetected. In that event she would turn and follow. She knew that the snow was falling too heavily to continue in such volume indefinitely; it would stop as suddenly as it had started.

The hours of the night piled up. The silent, muffling snowfall continued. And Cora McBride began to sense an alarming weariness. It finally dawned upon her that her old-time vigour was missing. The strength of youth was hers no longer. Two experiences of motherhood and no more exercise than was afforded by the tasks of her household, had softened her muscles. Their limitations were now disclosed.

The realization of those limitations was accompanied by panic. She was still many miles even from Blind Brook Cabin, and her limbs were afire from the unaccustomed effort. This would never do. After pauses for breath that were coming closer and closer together, she set her lips each time grimly. "Tomboy Allen" had not counted on succumbing to physical fatigue before she had climbed as far as Blind Brook. If she were weakening already, what of those many miles on the other side?

Tuesday the twenty-eighth of October passed with no tidings of Ruggam's capture. The Holmes boy was fatally shot by a rattleheaded searcher near Five-Mile Pond, and distraught parents began to take thought of their own lads missing from school. Adam MacQuarry broke his leg near the Hell Hollow schoolhouse and was sent back by friends on a borrowed bobsled. Several ne'er-do-wells, long on impulse and short on stickability, drifted back to more comfortable quarters during the day, contending that if Hap were captured, the officers would claim the reward anyhow—so what was the use bucking the System?

The snowfall stopped in the early morning. Sunrise disclosed the world trimmed from horizon to horizon in fairy fluff. Householders jocosely shoveled their walks; small children resurrected attic sleds; here and there a farmer appeared on Main Street during the forenoon in a pung-sleigh or cutter with jingling bells. The sun soared higher, and the day grew warmer. Eaves began dripping during the noon hour, to stop when the sun sank about four o'clock behind Bancroft's hill.

After the sunset came a perfect evening. The starlight was magic. Many people called in at the newspaper-office, after the movies, to learn if the man hunt had brought results.

Between ten and eleven o'clock the lights on the valley floor blinked out; the town had gone to bed—that is, the lights blinked out in all homes excepting those on the eastern outskirts, where nervous people worried over the possibilities of a hungry, hunted convict's burglarizing their premises, or drawn-faced mothers lived mentally through a score of calamities befalling red-blooded sons who had now been absent twenty-four hours.

Sometime between nine o'clock and midnight—she had no way of telling accurately—Cora McBride stumbled into the Lyons clearing. No one would have recognized in the staggering, bedraggled apparition that emerged from the silhouette of the timber the figure that had started so confidently from the Harrison tract the previous evening.

For over an hour she had hobbled blindly. It was wholly by accident that she had stumbled into the clearing. And the capture of Ruggam had diminished in importance. Warm food, water that would not tear her raw throat, a place to lie and recoup her strength after the chilling winter night—these were the only things that counted now. Though she knew it not, in her eyes burned the faint light of fever. When a snag caught her snowshoe and tripped her, there was hysteria in her cry of resentment.

As she moved across from the timber-line her hair was revealed fallen down; she had lost a glove, and one hand and wrist were cruelly red where she had plunged them several times into the snow to save herself from falling upon her face. She made but a few yards before the icy thong of her right snowshoe snapped. She did not bother to repair it. Carrying it beneath her arm, she hobbled brokenly toward the shelter of the buildings.

Her failure at the other cabins, the lack, thus far, of all signs of the fugitive, the vastness of the hunting-ground magnified by the loneliness of winter, had convinced her finally that her quest was futile. It was all a venture of madness. The idea that a woman, alone and single-handed, with no weapon but a revolver, could track down and subdue a desperate murderer in winter mountains where hardly a wild thing stirred, and make him return with her to the certain penalty—this proved how much mental mischief had again been caused by the lure of money. The glittering seduction of gold had deranged her. She realized it now, her mind normal in an exhausted body. So she gained the walls of the buildings and stumbled around them, thoughtless of any possible signs of the fugitive.

The stars were out in myriads. The Milky Way was a spectacle to recall vividly the sentiment of the Nineteenth Psalm. The log-buildings of the clearing, every tree-trunk and bough in the woods beyond, the distant skyline of stump and hollow, all stood out sharply against the peculiar radiance of the snow. The night was as still as the spaces between the planets.

Like some wild creature of those winter woods the woman clumped and stumbled around the main shack, seeking the door.

Finding it, she stopped; the snowshoe slipped from beneath her arm; one numb hand groped for the log door-casing in support; the other fumbled for the revolver.

Tracks led into that cabin!

A paralysis of fright gripped Cora McBride. Something told her intuitively that she stood face to face at last with what she had traveled all this mountain wilderness to find. Yet with sinking heart it also came to her that if Hap Ruggam had made these tracks and were still within, she must face him in her exhausted condition and at once make that tortuous return trip to civilization. There would be no one to help her.

She realized in that moment that she was facing the primal. And she was not primal. She was a normal woman, weakened to near-prostration by the trek of the past twenty-four hours. Was it not better to turn away while there was time?

She stood debating thus, the eternal silence blanketing forest-world and clearing. But she was allowed to make no decision.

A living body sprang suddenly upon her. Before she could cry out, she was borne down precipitously from behind.

She tried to turn the revolver against the Thing upon her, but the gun was twisted from her raw, red fingers. The snow into which she had been precipitated blinded her. She smeared an arm across her eyes, but before clear sight was regained, talon fingers had gripped her shoulders. She was half lifted, half dragged through the doorway, and there she was dropped on the plank flooring. Her assailant, turning, made to close and bar the door.

When she could see clearly, she perceived a weak illumination in the cabin. On the rough bench-table, shaded by two slabs of bark, burned the stub of a tallow candle probably left by some hunting-party.

The windows were curtained with rotting blankets. Some rough furniture lay about; rusted cooking-utensils littered the tables, and at one end was a sheet-iron stove. The place had been equipped after a fashion by deer-hunters or mountain hikers, who brought additional furnishings to the place each year and left mouldy provisions and unconsumed firewood behind.

The man succeeded finally in closing the door. He turned upon her.

He was short and stocky. The stolen corduroy coat covered blacksmith's muscles now made doubly powerful by dementia. His hair was lifeless black and clipped close, prison-fashion. His low forehead hung over burning, mismated eyes. From her helplessness on the floor Cora McBride stared up at him.

He came closer.

"Get up!" he ordered. "Take that chair. And don't start no rough-house; whether you're a woman or not, I'll drill you!"

She groped to the indicated chair and raised herself, the single snowshoe still dragging from one foot. Again the man surveyed her. She saw his eyes and gave another inarticulate cry.

"Shut your mouth and keep it shut! You hear me?"

She obeyed.

The greenish light burned brighter in his mismated eyes, which gazed intently at the top of her head as though it held something unearthly.

"Take off your hat!" was his next command.

She pulled off the toque. Her hair fell in a mass on her snow-blotched shoulders. Her captor advanced upon her. He reached out and satisfied himself by touch that something was not there which he dreaded. In hypnotic fear she suffered that touch. It reassured him.

"Your hair now," he demanded; "it don't stand up, does it? No, o' course it don't. You ain't *him;* you're a woman. But if your hair comes up, I'll kill you—understand? If your hair comes up, *I'll kill you!*"

She understood. She understood only too well. She was not only housed with a murderer; she was housed with a maniac. She sensed, also, why he had come to this mountain shack so boldly. In his dementia he knew no better. And she was alone with him, unarmed now.

"I'll keep it down," she whispered, watching his face out of fear-distended eyes.

The wind blew one of the rotten blankets inward. Thereby she knew that the window-aperture on the south wall contained no sash. He must have removed it to provide means of escape in case he were attacked from the east door. He must have climbed out that window when she came around the shack; that is how he had felled her from behind.

He stepped backward now until he felt the edge of the bench touch his calves. Then he sank down, one arm stretched along the table's rim, the hand clutching the revolver.

"Who are you?" he demanded.

"I'm Cora McB——" She stopped—she recalled in a flash the part her husband had played in his former capture and trial. "I'm Cora Allen," she corrected. Then she waited, her wits in chaos. She was fighting desperately to bring order out of that chaos.

"What you doin' up here?"

"I started for Millington, over the mountain. I lost my way."

"Why didn't you go by the road?"

"It's further."

"That's a lie! It ain't. And don't lie to me, or I'll kill you!"

"Who are you?" she heard herself asking. "And why are you acting this way with me?"

The man leaned suddenly forward.

"You mean to tell me you don't know?"

"A lumberjack, maybe, who's lost his way like myself?"

His expression changed abruptly.

"What you luggin' *this* for?" He indicated the revolver.

"For protection."

"From what?"

"Wild things."

"There ain't no wild things in these mountains this time o' year; they're snowed up, and you know it."

"I just felt safer to have it along."

"To protect you from men-folks, maybe?"

"There are no men in these mountains I'm afraid of!" She made the declaration with pathetic bravado.

His eyes narrowed.

"I think I better kill you," he decided. "You've seen me; you'll tell you seen me. Why shouldn't I kill you? You'd only tell."

"Why? What have I done to you?" she managed to stammer. "Why should you object to being seen?"

It was an unfortunate demand. He sprang up with a snarl. Pointing the revolver from his hip, he drew back the hammer.

"*Don't!*" she shrieked. "Are you crazy? Don't you know how to treat a woman—in distress?"

"Distress, *hell!* You know who I be. And I don't care whether you're a woman or not, I ain't goin' to be took—you understand?"

"Certainly I understand."

She said it in such a way that he eased the hammer back into place and lowered the gun. For the moment again she was safe. In response to her terrible need, some of her latent Yankee courage came now to aid her. "I don't see what you're making all this rumpus about," she told him in as indifferent a voice as she could command. "I don't see why you should want to kill a friend who might help you—if you're really in need of help."

"I want to get to Partridgeville," he muttered after a moment.

"You're not far from there. How long have you been on the road?"

"None of your business."

"Have you had any food?"

"No."

"If you'll put up that gun and let me get off this snowshoe and pack, I'll share with you some of the food I have."

"Never you mind what I do with this gun. Go ahead and fix your foot, and let's see what you got for grub." The man resumed his seat.

She twisted up her tangled hair, replaced her toque and untied the dangling snowshoe.

Outside a tree cracked in the frost. He started in hair-trigger fright. Creeping to the window, he peeped cautiously between casing and blanket. Convinced that it was nothing, he returned to his seat by the table.

"It's too bad we couldn't have a fire," suggested the woman then. "I'd make us something hot." The stove was there, rusted but still serviceable; available wood was scattered around. But the man shook his bullet head.

After a trying time unfastening the frosted knots of the ropes that had bound the knapsack upon her back, she emptied it on to the table. She kept her eye, however, on the gun. He had disposed of it by thrusting it into his belt. Plainly she would never recover it without a struggle. And she was in no condition for physical conflict.

"You're welcome to anything I have," she told him.

"Little you got to say about it! If you hadn't given it up, I'd took it away from you. So what's the difference?"

She shrugged her shoulders. She started around behind him but he sprang toward her.

"Don't try no monkey-shines with me!" he snarled. "You stay here in front where I can see you."

She obeyed, watching him make what poor meal he could from the contents of her bag.

She tried to reason out what the dénouement of the situation was to be. He would not send her away peacefully, for she knew he dared not risk the story she would tell regardless of any promises of secrecy she might give him. If he left her bound in the cabin, she would freeze before help came—if it ever arrived.

No, either they were going to leave the place and journey forth together—the Lord only knew where or with what outcome—or the life of one of them was to end in this tragic place within the coming few minutes. For she realized she must use that gun with deadly effect if it were to come again into her possession.

The silence was broken only by the noises of his lips as he ate ravenously. Outside, not a thing stirred in that snow-bound world. Not a sound of civilization reached them. They were a man and woman in the primal, in civilization and yet a million miles from it.

"The candle's going out," she announced. "Is there another?"

"There'll be light enough for what I got to do," he growled.

Despite her effort to appear indifferent, her great fear showed plainly in her eyes.

"Are we going to stay here all night?" she asked with a pathetic attempt at lightness.

"That's my business."

"Don't you want me to help you?"

"You've helped me all you can with the gun and food."

"If you're going to Partridgeville, I'd go along and show you the way."

He leaped up.

"*Now I know you been lyin'!*" he bellowed. "You said you was headed for Millington. And you ain't at all. You're watchin' your chance to get the drop on me and have me took—that's what you're doin'!"

"Wait!" she pleaded desperately. "I *was* going to Millington. But I'd turn back and show you the way to Partridgeville to help you."

"What's it to you?" He had drawn the gun from his belt and now was fingering it nervously.

"You're lost up here in the mountains, aren't you?" she said. "I couldn't let you stay lost if it was possible for me to direct you on your way."

"You said you was lost yourself."

"I was lost—until I stumbled into this clearing. That gave me my location."

"Smart, ain't you? Damn' smart, but not too smart for me, you woman!" The flare flamed up again in his crooked eyes. "You know who I be, all right. You know what I'm aimin' to do. And you're stallin' for time till you can put one over. But you can't—see? I'll have this business done with. I'll end this business!"

She felt herself sinking to her knees. He advanced and gripped her left wrist. The crunch of his iron fingers sent an arrow of pain through her arm. It bore her down.

"For God's sake—*don't!*" she whispered hoarsely, overwhelmed with horror. For the cold, sharp nose of the revolver suddenly punched her neck.

"I ain't leavin' no traces behind. Might as well be hung for a sheep as a lamb. Never mind if I do——"

"Look!" she cried wildly. "Look, look, *look!*" And with her free hand she pointed behind him.

It was an old trick. There was nothing behind him. But in that instant of desperation instinct had guided her.

Involuntarily he turned.

With a scream of pain she twisted from his grasp and blotted out the candle.

A long, livid pencil of orange flame spurted from the gunpoint. She sensed the powder-flare in her face. He had missed.

She scrambled for shelter beneath the table. The cabin was now in inky blackness. Across that black four more threads of scarlet light were laced. The man stumbled about seeking her, cursing with blood-curdling blasphemy.

Suddenly he tripped and went sprawling. The gun clattered from his bruised fingers; it struck the woman's knee.

Swiftly her hand closed upon it. The hot barrel burned her palm.

She was on her feet in an instant. Her left hand fumbled in her blouse, and she found what had been there all along—the flash-lamp.

With her back against the door, she pulled it forth. With the gun thrust forward for action she pressed the button.

"I've got the gun—*get up!*" she ordered. "Don't come too near me or I'll shoot. Back up against that wall."

The bull's-eye of radiance blinded him. When his eyes

became accustomed to the light, he saw its reflection on the barrel of the revolver. He obeyed.

"Put up your hands. Put 'em up *high!*"

"Suppose I won't?"

"I'll kill you."

"What'll you gain by that?"

"Five thousand dollars."

"Then you know who I be?"

"Yes."

"And was aimin' to take me in?"

"Yes."

"How you goin' to do that if I won't go?"

"You're goin' to find out."

"You won't get no money shootin' me."

"Yes, I will—just as much—dead as alive."

With his hands raised a little way above the level of his shoulders, he stood rigidly at bay in the circle of light.

"Well," he croaked at last, "go ahead and shoot. I ain't aimin' to be took—not by no woman. Shoot, damn you, and have it done with. I'm waitin'!"

"Keep up those hands!"

"I won't!" He lowered them defiantly. "I w-wanted to m-make Partridgeville and see the old lady. She'd 'a' helped me. But anything's better'n goin' back to that hell where I been the last two years. Go on! Why don't you shoot?"

"You wanted to make Partridgeville and see—*who?*"

"My mother—and my wife."

"Have you got a mother? Have you got a—wife?"

"Yes, and three kids. Why don't you shoot?"

It seemed an eon that they stood so. The McBride woman was trying to find the nerve to fire. She could not. In that instant she made a discovery that many luckless souls make too late: *to kill a man* is easy to talk about, easy to write about. But to stand deliberately face to face with a fellow-human—alive, pulsing, breathing, fearing, hoping, loving, living,—point a weapon at him that would take his life, blot him from the earth, negate twenty or thirty years of childhood, youth, maturity, and make of him in an instant—nothing!—that is quite another matter.

He was helpless before her now. Perhaps the expression on his face had something to do with the sudden revulsion that halted her finger. Facing certain death, some of the evil in those crooked eyes seemed to die out, and the terrible personality of the man to fade. Regardless of her danger, regardless of what he would have done to her if luck had not turned the tables, Cora McBride saw before her only a lone man with all society's hand against him, realizing he had played a bad game to the limit and lost, two big tears creeping down his unshaved face, waiting for the end.

"Three children!" she whispered faintly.

"Yes."

"You're going back to see them?"

"Yes, and my mother. Mother'd help me get to Canada—somehow."

Cora McBride had forgotten all about the five thousand dollars. She was stunned by the announcement that this man had relatives—a mother, a wife, *three* babies. The human factor had not before occurred to her. Murderers! They have no license to let their eyes well with tears, to have wives and babies, to possess mothers who will help them get to Canada regardless of what their earthly indiscretions may have been.

At this revelation the gun-point wavered. The sight of those tears on his face sapped her will-power even as a wound in her breast might have drained her life-blood.

Her great moment had been given her. She was letting it slip away. She had her reward in her hand for the mere pulling of a trigger and no incrimination for the result. For a bit of human sentiment she was bungling the situation unpardonably, fatally.

Why did she not shoot? Because she was a woman. Because it is the God-given purpose of womanhood to give life, not take it.

The gun sank, sank—down out of the light, down out of sight.

And the next instant he was upon her.

The flash-lamp was knocked from her hand and blinked out. It struck the stove and she heard the tinkle of the broken lens. The woman's hand caught at the sacking before the window at her left shoulder. Gripping it wildly to save herself from that onslaught, she tore it away. For the second time the revolver was twisted from her raw fingers.

The man reared upward, over her.

"Where are you?" he roared again and again. "I'll show you! Lemme at you!"

Outside the great yellow moon of early winter, arising late, was coming up over the silhouetted line of purple mountains to the eastward. It illumined the cabin with a faint radiance, disclosing the woman crouching beneath the table.

The man saw her, pointed his weapon point-blank at her face and fired.

To Cora McBride, prostrate there in her terror, the impact of the bullet felt like the blow of a stick upon her cheek-bone rocking her head. Her cheek felt warmly numb. She pressed a quick hand involuntarily against it, and drew it away sticky with blood.

Click! Click! Click!

Three times the revolver mechanism was worked to accomplish her destruction. But there was no further report. The cylinder was empty.

"Oh, God!" the woman moaned. "I fed you and offered to help you. I refused to shoot you because of your mother—your wife—your babies. And yet you——"

"Where's your cartridges?" he cried wildly. "You got more; gimme that belt!"

She felt his touch upon her. His crazy fingers tried to unbutton the clasp of the belt and holster. But he could secure neither while she fought him. He pinioned her at length with his knee. His fingers secured a fistful of the cylinders from her girdle, and he opened the chamber of the revolver.

She realized the end was but a matter of moments. Nothing but a miracle could save her now.

Convulsively she groped about for something with which to strike. Nothing lay within reach of her bleeding fingers, however, but a little piece of dried sapling. She tried to struggle loose, but the lunatic held her mercilessly. He continued the mechanical loading of the revolver.

The semi-darkness of the hut, the outline of the moon afar through the uncurtained window—these swam before her. . . . Suddenly her eyes riveted on that curtainless window and she uttered a terrifying cry.

Ruggam turned.

Outlined in the window aperture against the low-hung moon *Martin Wiley, the murdered deputy, was staring into the cabin!*

From the fugitive's throat came a gurgle. Some of the cartridges he held spilled to the flooring. Above her his figure became rigid. There was no mistaking the identity of the apparition. They saw the man's hatless head and some of his neck. They saw his dark pompadour and the outline of his skull. As that horrible silhouette remained there, Wiley's pompadour lifted slightly as it had done in life.

The cry in the convict's throat broke forth into words.

"Mart Wiley!" he cried, "Mart Wiley! *Mart—Wiley!*"

Clear, sharp, distinct was the shape of that never-to-be-forgotten pompadour against the disk of the winter moon. His features could not be discerned, for the source of light was behind him, but the silhouette was sufficient. It was Martin Wiley; he was alive. His head and his wirelike hair were moving—rising, falling.

Ruggam, his eyes riveted upon the phantom, recoiled mechanically to the western wall. He finished loading the revolver by the sense of touch. Then:

Spurt after spurt of fire lanced the darkness, directed at the Thing in the window. While the air of the hut reeked with the acrid smoke, the echo of the volley sounded through the silent forest-world miles away.

But the silhouette in the window remained.

Once or twice it moved slightly as though in surprise; that was all. The pompadour rose in bellicose retaliation—the gesture that had always ensued when Wiley was angered or excited. But to bullets fired from an earthly gun the silhouette of the murdered deputy's ghost, arisen in these winter woods to prevent another slaughter, was impervious.

Ruggam saw; he shrieked. He broke the gun and spilled out the empty shells. He fumbled in more cartridges, locked the barrel and fired again and again, until once more it was empty.

Still the apparition remained.

The man in his dementia hurled the weapon; it struck the sash and caromed off, hitting the stove. Then Hap Ruggam collapsed upon the floor.

The woman sprang up. She found the rope thongs which

had bound her pack to her shoulders. With steel-taut nerves, she rolled the insensible Ruggam over.

She tied his hands; she tied his ankles. With her last bit of rope she connected the two bindings tightly behind him so that if he recovered, he would be at her mercy. Her task accomplished, on her knees beside his prone figure, she thought to glance up at the window.

Wiley's ghost had disappeared.

Sheriff Crumpett and his party broke into the Lyons clearing within an hour. They had arrived in answer to five successive shots given a few moments apart, the signal agreed upon. The mystery to them, however, was that those five shots had been fired by some one not of their party.

The sheriff and his men found the McBride woman, her clothing half torn from her body, her features powder-marked and blood-stained; but she was game to the last, woman-fashion weeping only now that all was over. They found, too, the man they had combed the country to find—struggling fruitlessly in his bonds, her prisoner.

And they likewise found the miracle.

On the snow outside under the window they came upon a black porcupine about the size of a man's head which, scenting food within the cabin, had climbed to the sill, and after the habit of these little animals whose number is legion all over the Green Mountains, had required fifteen bullets pumped into its carcass before it would release its hold.

Even in death its quills were raised in uncanny duplication of Mart Wiley's pompadour.

A MATTER OF LOYALTY

By LAWRENCE PERRY

From *The Red Book*

STANDING in the bow of the launch, Dr. Nicholls, coach of the Baliol crew, leaned upon his megaphone, his eyes fixed upon two eight-oared crews resting upon their oars a hundred feet away. From his hand dangled a stop-watch. The two crews had just completed a four-mile race against the watch.

A grim light came into the deeply set gray eyes of Jim Deacon as the coach put the watch into his pocket. Deacon was the stroke of the second varsity, an outfit which in aquatics bears the same relation to a university eight as the scrub team does to a varsity football eleven. But in the race just completed the second varsity had been much of a factor—surprisingly, dishearteningly so. Nip and tuck it had been, the varsity straining to drop the rival boat astern, but unable to do so. At the finish not a quarter of a length, not fifteen feet, had separated the two prows; a poor showing for the varsity to have made with the great rowing classic of the season coming on apace—a poor showing, that is, assuming the time consumed in the four-mile trip was not especially low.

Only the coach could really know whether the time was satisfactory or not. But Jim Deacon suspected that it was poor, his idea being based upon knowledge he had concerning the capabilities of his own crew; in other words, he knew it was only an average second varsity outfit. The coach knew it too. That was the reason his jaws were set, his eyes vacant. At length he shook his head.

"Not good, boys—not good." His voice was gentle, though usually he was a rip-roaring mentor. "Varsity, you weren't rowing. That's the answer—not rowing together. What's the matter, eh?"

"I thought, Dr. Nicholls, that the rhythm was very good——"

The coach interrupted Rollins, the captain, with a gesture.

"Oh, rhythm! Yes, you row prettily enough. You look well. I should hope so, at this time of the season. But you're not shoving the boat fast; you don't pick up and get her moving. You're leaking power somewhere; as a matter of fact, I suspect you're not putting the power in. I know you're not. Ashburton, didn't that lowering of your seat fix you? Well, then,"—as the young man nodded affirmatively—"how about your stretcher, Innis? Does it suit you now?"

As Innis nodded, signifying that it did, Deacon saw the coach's eyes turn to Doane, who sat at stroke of the varsity.

"Now," muttered the stroke of the second varsity, his eyes gleaming, "we'll hear something."

"Doane, is there anything the trouble with you? You're feeling well, aren't you?"

"Yes sir. Sure!" The boy flushed. Tall, straight, handsome he sat in the boat, fingering the oar-handle nervously. In appearance he was the ideal oarsman. And yet——

Deacon, watching the coach, could almost see his mind working. Now the time had come, the issue clearly defined. Another stroke must be tried and found not wanting, else the annual eight-oared rowing classic between those ancient universities Baliol and Shelburne would be decided before it was rowed.

Deacon flushed as the coach's glittering eyeglasses turned toward him. It was the big moment of the senior's four years at college. Four years! And six months of each of those years a galley-slave—on the machines in the rowing-room of the gymnasium, on the ice-infested river with the cutting winds of March sweeping free; then the more genial months with the voice of coach or assistant coach lashing him. Four years of dogged, unremitting toil with never the reward of a varsity seat, and now with the great regatta less than a week away, the big moment, the crown of all he had done.

Words seemed on the verge of the coach's lips. Deacon's eyes strained upon them as he sat stiffly in his seat. But no words came; the coach turned away.

"All right," he said spiritlessly. "Paddle back to the float.

The coxswains barked their orders; sixteen oars rattled in their locks; the glistening shells moved slowly homeward.

Tingling from his plunge in the river, Jim Deacon walked up the bluff from the boathouse to the group of cottages which constituted Baliol's rowing-quarters. Some of the freshman crew were playing indoor baseball on the lawn under the gnarled trees, and their shouts and laughter echoed over the river. Deacon stood watching them. His face was of the roughhewn type; in his two upper-class years his heavy frame had taken on a vast amount of brawn and muscle. Now his neck was meet for his head and for his chest and shoulders; long, slightly bowed limbs filled out a picture of perfect physique.

No one had known him really well in college. He was working his way through. Besides, he was a student in one of the highly scientific engineering courses which demanded a great deal of steady application. With no great aptitude for football—he was a bit slow-footed—with little time or inclination for social activities, he had concentrated upon rowing, not only as a diversion from his arduous studies, an ordered outlet for physical energy, but with the idea of going out into the world with that hallmark of a Baliol varsity oar which he had heard and believed was likely to stand him in stead in life. Baliol alumni, which include so many men of wealth and power, had a habit of not overlooking young graduates who have brought fame to their alma mater.

As Deacon stood watching the freshmen at play, Dick Rollins, the crew captain, came up.

"They sent down the time-trial results from the Shelburne quarters, Deacon."

Never in his life had one of the great men of the university spoken that many words, or half as many, to Jim Deacon, who stared at the speaker.

"The time—oh, yes; I see."

"They did twenty minutes, thirty seconds."

Deacon whistled.

"Well," he said at length, "you didn't get the boat moving much to-day." He wanted to say more, but could think of nothing. Words came rather hard with him.

"You nearly lugged the second shell ahead of us to-day, hang you."

"No use letting a patient die because he doesn't know he's sick."

Rollins grimaced.

"Yes, we were sick. Doc Nicholls knows a sick crew when he sees one. He—he thinks you're the needed tonic, Deacon."

"Eh?"

"He told me you were to sit in at stroke in Junior Doane's place to-morrow. I'd been pulling for the change the past few days. Now he sees it."

"You were pulling—— But you're Doane's roommate."

"Yes, it's tough. But Baliol first, you know."

Deacon stared at the man. He wanted to say something but couldn't. The captain smiled.

"Look here, Deacon; let's walk over toward the railroad a bit. I want to talk to you." Linking his arm through Deacon's, he set out through the yard toward the quaint old road with its little cluster of farm cottages and rolling stone-walled meadow-land bathed in the light of the setting sun.

"Jim, old boy, you're a queer sort of a chap, and—and—the fact is, the situation will be a bit ticklish. You know what it means for a fellow to be thrown out of his seat just before a race upon which he has been counting heart and soul."

"I don't know. I can imagine."

"You see, it's Doane. You know about his father——"

"I know all about his father," was the reply.

"Eh?" Rollins stared at him, then smiled. "I suppose every rowing man at Baliol does. But you don't know as much as I do. On the quiet, he's the man who gave us the new boathouse last year. He's our best spender. He was an old varsity oar himself."

"Sure, I know."

"That's the reason the situation is delicate. Frankly, Jim, Doc Nicholls and the rest of us would have liked to see Junior Doane come through. I think you get what I mean. He's a senior; he's my best friend."

"He stroked the boat last year."

"Yes, and Shelburne beat us. Naturally he wants to get back at that crowd."

"But he can't—not if he strokes the boat, Rollins. If you don't know it, I'm telling you. If I thought different, I'd say so." Deacon abruptly paused after so long a speech.

"You don't have to tell me. I know it. We're not throwing a race to Shelburne simply to please old Cephas Doane, naturally. I know what you've got, Jim. So does Dr. Nicholls. You'll be in the varsity to-morrow. But here's the point of what I've been trying to say; Junior Doane hasn't been very decent to you——"

"Oh, he's been all right."

"Yes, I know. But he's a funny fellow; not a bit of a snob—I don't mean that, but—but——"

"You mean he hasn't paid much attention to me." Deacon smiled grimly. "Well, that's all right. As a matter of fact, I never really have got to know him. Still, I haven't got to know many of the fellows. Too busy. You haven't paid much attention to me, either; but I like you."

Rollins, whose father was a multimillionaire with family roots going deep among the rocks of Manhattan Island, laughed.

"Bully for you! You won't mind my saying so, Jim, but I had it in my mind to ask you to be a bit inconsequential—especially when Doane was around—about your taking his place. But I guess it isn't necessary."

"No,"—Deacon's voice was short—"it isn't."

"Junior Doane, of course, will be hard hit. He'll be game. He'll try to win back his seat. And he may; I warn you."

"If he can win it back, I want him to."

"Good enough!" The captain started to walk away, then turned back with sudden interest. "By the way, Jim, I was looking through the college catalogue this morning. You and Doane both come from Philadelphia, don't you?"

"Yes."

"I asked Doane if he knew you there. Apparently not."

"No, he didn't." Deacon paused as though deliberating. Suddenly he spoke. "I knew of him, though. You see, my father works in the bank of which Mr. Doane is president."

"Oh!" Rollins blinked. "I see."

Deacon stepped forward, placing his hand upon the captain's arm.

"I don't know why I told you that. It isn't important at

all. Don't say anything to Doane, will you? Not that I care. It—it just isn't important."

"No. I get you, Jim. It isn't important." He flung an arm over the young man's shoulder. "Let's go back to dinner. That rotten time-row has given me an appetite."

There was that quiet in the Baliol dining room that evening which one might expect to find after an unsatisfactory time-trial. Nations might be falling, cities burning, important men dying; to these boys such events would be as nothing in the face of the fact that the crew of a traditional rival was to be met within the week—and that they were not proving themselves equipped for the meeting.

"If any of you fellows wish to motor down to the Groton Hotel on the Point for an hour or two, you may go," said the coach, pushing back his chair. He had begun to fear that his charges might be coming to too fine a point of condition and had decided that the relaxation of a bit of dancing might do no harm.

"Yeaa!" In an instant that subdued dining apartment was tumultuous with vocal outcry, drawing to the doorway a crowd of curious freshmen who were finishing dinner in their room.

"All right!" Dr. Nicholls grinned. "I gather all you varsity and second varsity men want to go. I'll have the big launch ready at eight. And—oh, Dick Rollins, don't forget; that boat leaves the hotel dock at ten-forty-five precisely."

"Got you sir. Come on, fellows. Look out, you freshmen." With a yell and a dive the oarsmen went through the doors.

Deacon followed at a more leisurely gait with that faint gleam of amusement in his eyes which was so characteristic. His first impulse was not to go, but upon second thought he decided that he would. Jane Bostwick was stopping at the Groton. Her father was a successful promoter and very close to Cephas Doane, Sr., whose bank stood back of most of his operations. Deacon had known her rather well in the days when her father was not a successful promoter. In fact, the two had been neighbours as boy and girl, had played together in front of a row of prim brick houses. He had not seen her in recent years until the previous afternoon, when as he was walking along the country road, she had pulled up in her roadster.

"Don't pretend you don't remember me, Jim Deacon," she had laughed as the boy had stared at the stunning young woman.

Jim remembered her, all right. They talked as though so many significant years had not elapsed. She was greatly interested, exceedingly gracious.

"Do you know," she said, "it never occurred to me that Deacon, the Baliol rowing man, was none other than Jim Deacon. Silly of me, wasn't it? But then I didn't even know you were in Baliol. I'm perfectly crazy about the crew, you know. And Mother, I think, is a worse fan than I am. You know Junior Doane, of course."

"Oh, yes—that is, I—why, yes, I know him."

"Yes." She smiled down upon him. "If you're ever down to the Groton, do drop in. Mother would love to see you. She often speaks of your mother." With a wave of her hand she had sped on her way.

Curiously, that evening he had heard Doane talking to her over the telephone, and there was a great deal in his manner of speaking that indicated something more than mere acquaintance.

But Deacon did not see Jane Bostwick at the hotel—not to speak to, at least. He was not a good dancer and held aloof when those of his fellows who were not acquainted with guests were introduced around. Finding a wicker settee among some palms at one side of the orchestra, Deacon sat drinking in the scene.

It was not until the hour set for the return had almost arrived that Deacon saw Jane Bostwick, and then his attention was directed to her by her appearance with Junior Doane in one of the open French windows at his right. Evidently the two had spent the evening in the sequestered darkness of the veranda. No pair in the room filled the eye so gratefully; the girl, tall, blonde, striking in a pale blue evening gown; the man, broad-shouldered, trim-waisted, with the handsome high-held head of a patrician.

A wave of something akin to bitterness passed over Deacon—bitterness having nothing to do with self. For the boy was ruggedly independent. He believed in himself; knew what he was going to do in the world. He was thinking of his father, and of the fathers of that young man and girl before him. His father was painstaking, honourable, considerate—a nobleman every inch of him; a man who deserved everything that the world had to give, a man who had everything save the quality of acquisition. And Doane's father? And Jane Bostwick's father?

Of the elder Doane he knew by hearsay—a proud, intolerant wholly worldly man whose passions, aside from finance, were his son and Baliol aquatics. And Jane Bostwick's father he had known as a boy—a soft-footed, sly-faced velvety sort of a man noted for converting back lots into oil-fields and ash-dumps into mines yielding precious metals. Jim Deacon was not so old that he had come to philosophy concerning the way of the world.

But so far as his immediate world was concerned, Junior Doane was going out of the varsity boat in the morning—and he, Jim Deacon, was going to sit in his place.

It came the next morning. When the oarsmen went down to the boathouse to dress for their morning row, the arrangement of the various crews posted on the bulletin-board gave Deacon the seat at stroke in the varsity boat; Junior Doane's name appeared at stroke in the second varsity list.

There had been rumours of some sort of a shift, but no one seemed to have considered the probability of Doane's losing his seat—Doane least of all. For a moment the boy stood rigid, looking up at the bulletin-board. Then suddenly he laughed.

"All right, Garry," he said, turning to the captain of the second varsity. "Come on; we'll show 'em what a rudder looks like."

But it was not to be. In three consecutive dashes of a mile each, the varsity boat moved with such speed as it had not shown all season. There was life in the boat. Deacon, rowing in perfect form, passed the stroke up forward with a kick and a bite, handling his oar with a precision that made the eye of the coach glisten. And when the nervous little coxswain called for a rousing ten strokes, the shell seemed fairly to lift out of the water.

In the last mile dash Dr. Nicholls surreptitiously took his stop-watch from his pocket and timed the sprint. When he replaced the timepiece, the lines of care which had seamed his face for the past few days vanished.

"All right, boys. Paddle in. Day after to-morrow we'll hold the final time-trial. Deacon, be careful; occasionally you clip your stroke at the finish."

But Deacon didn't mind the admonition. He knew the coach's policy of not letting a man think he was too good.

"You certainly bucked up that crew to-day, Deacon." Jim Deacon, who had been lying at full length on the turf at the top of the bluff watching the shadows creep over the purpling waters of the river, looked up to see Doane standing over him. His first emotion was one of triumph. Doane, the son of Cephas Doane, his father's employer, had definitely noticed him at last. Then the dominant emotion came—one of sympathy.

"Well, the second crew moved better too."

"Oh, I worked like a dog." Doane laughed. "Of course you know I'm going to get my place back, if I can."

"Of course." Deacon plucked a blade of grass and placed it in his mouth. There was rather a constrained silence for a moment.

"I didn't know you came from my city, Deacon. I—Jane Bostwick told me about you last night."

"I see. I used to know her." Inwardly Deacon cursed his natural inability to converse easily, partly fearing that Doane would mistake his reticence for embarrassment in his presence, or on the other hand set him down as churlish and ill bred.

For his part Doane seemed a bit ill at ease.

"I didn't know, of course, anything Jane told me. If I had, of course, I'd have looked you up more at the college."

"We're both busy there in our different ways."

Doane stood awkwardly for a moment and then walked away, not knowing that however he may have felt about the conversation, he had at least increased his stature in the mind of Jim Deacon.

Next day on the river Junior Doane's desperation at the outset brought upon his head the criticism of the coach.

"Doane! Doane! You're rushing your slide. Finish out your stroke, for heaven's sake."

Deacon, watching the oarsman's face, saw it grow rigid, saw

his mouth set. Well he knew the little tragedy through which Doane was living.

Doane did better after that. The second boat gave the varsity some sharp brushes while the coxswains barked and the coach shouted staccato objurgation and comment through his megaphone, and the rival oarsmen swung backward and forward in the expenditure of ultimate power and drive.

But Jim Deacon was the man for varsity stroke. There was not the least doubt about that. The coach could see it; the varsity could feel it; but of them all Deacon alone knew why. He knew that Doane was practically as strong an oar as he was, certainly as finished. And Doane's experience was greater. The difficulty as Deacon grasped it was that the boy had not employed all the material of his experience. The coxswain, Seagraves, was a snappy little chap, with an excellent opinion of his head. But Deacon had doubts as to his racing sense. He could shoot ginger into his men, could lash them along with a fine rhythm, but in negotiating a hard-fought race he had his shortcomings. At least so Deacon had decided in the brushes against the varsity shell when he was stroking the second varsity.

Deacon thanked no coxswain to tell him how to row a race, when to sprint, when to dog along at a steady, swinging thirty; nor did he require advice on the pacing and general condition of a rival crew. As he swung forward for the catch, his practice was to turn his head slightly to one side, chin along the shoulder, thus gaining through the tail of his eye a glimpse of any boat that happened to be abeam, slightly ahead or slightly astern. This glance told him everything he wished to know. The coach did not know the reason for this peculiarity in Deacon's style, but since it did not affect his rowing, he very wisely said nothing. To his mind the varsity boat had at last begun to arrive, and this was no time for minor points.

Two days before the Shelburne race the Baliol varsity in its final time-trial came within ten seconds of equalling the lowest downstream trial-record ever established—a record made by a Shelburne eight of the early eighties. There was no doubt in the mind of any one about the Baliol crew quarters that Deacon would be the man to set the pace for his university in the supreme test swiftly approaching.

News of Baliol's improved form began to be disseminated

in the daily press by qualified observers of rowing form who were beginning to flock to the scene of the regatta from New York, Philadelphia, and various New England cities. Dr. Nicholls was reticent, but no one could say that his demeanour was marked by gloom. Perhaps his optimism would have been more marked had the information he possessed concerning Shelburne been less disturbing. As a fact there was every indication that the rival university would be represented by one of the best crews in her history—which was to say a very great deal. In truth, Baliol rowing enthusiasts had not seen their shell cross the line ahead of a Shelburne varsity boat in three consecutive years, a depressing state of affairs which in the present season had filled every Baliol rowing man with grim determination and the graduates with alternate hope and despair.

"Jim," said the coach, drawing Deacon from the float upon which he had been standing, watching the antics of a crew of former Baliol oarsmen who had come from far and wide to row the mile race of "Gentlemen's Eights" which annually marked the afternoon preceding the classic regatta day, "Jim, you're not worried at all, are you? You're such a quiet sort of a chap, I can't seem to get you."

Deacon smiled faintly.

"No, I'm not worried—not a bit, sir. I mean I'm going to do my best, and if that's good enough, why—well, we win."

"I want you to do more than your best to-morrow, Jim. It's got to be a super-effort. You're up against a great Shelburne crew, the greatest I ever saw—that means twelve years back. I wouldn't talk to every man this way, but I think you're a stroke who can stand responsibility. I think you're a man who can work the better when he knows the size of his job. It's a big one, boy—the biggest I've ever tackled."

"Yes, sir."

The coach studied him a minute.

"How do you feel about beating Shelburne? What I mean," he went on as the oarsman regarded him, puzzled, "is, would it break your heart to lose? Is the thought of being beaten so serious that you can't—that you won't consider it?"

"No sir, I won't consider it. I don't go into anything without wanting to come out ahead. I've worked three years to get into the varsity. I realize the position you've given me will help me, make me stand out after graduation, mean almost as much as my diploma—provided we can win."

"What about Baliol? Do you think of the college, too, and what a victory will mean to her? What defeat will mean?"

"Oh," Deacon shrugged; "of course," he went on a bit carelessly, "we want to see Baliol on top as often——" He stopped, then broke into a chuckle as the stroke of the gentlemen's eight suddenly produced from the folds of his sweater a bottle from which he drank with dramatic unction while his fellow-oarsmen clamoured to share the libation and the coxswain abused them all roundly.

The eyes of the coach never left the young man's face. But he said nothing while Deacon took his fill of enjoyment of the jovial scene, apparently forgetting the sentence which he had broken in the middle.

But that evening something of the coach's meaning came to Deacon as he sat on a rustic bench watching the colours fade from one of those sunset skies which live ever in the hearts of rowing men who have ever spent a hallowed June on the heights of that broad placid stream. The Baliol graduates had lost their race against the gentlemen of Shelburne, having rowed just a bit worse than their rivals. And now the two crews were celebrating their revival of the ways of youth with a dinner provided by the defeated eight. Their laughter and their songs went out through the twilight and were lost in the recesses of the river. One song with a haunting melody caught Deacon's attention; he listened to get the words.

> Then raise the rosy goblet high,
> The senior's chalice and belie
>   The tongues that trouble and defile,
>   For we have yet a little while
> To linger, you and youth and I,
>   In college days.

A group of oarsmen down on the lawn caught up the song and sent it winging through the twilight, soberly, impressively, with ever-surging harmony. College days! For a moment a dim light burned in the back of his mind. It went out suddenly. Jim Deacon shrugged and thought of the morrow's race.

It was good to know he was going to be a part of it. He could feel the gathering of enthusiasm, exhilaration in the atmosphere—pent-up emotion which on the morrow would burst like a thunderclap. In the quaint city five miles down the river hotels were filling with the vanguard of the boat-race throng—boys fresh from the poetry of Commencement; their older brothers, their fathers, their grandfathers, living again the thrill of youth and the things thereof. And mothers and sisters and sweethearts! Deacon's nerves tingled pleasantly in response to the glamour of the hour.

"Oh, Jim Deacon!"

"Hello!" Deacon turned his face toward the building whence the voice came.

"Somebody wants to see you on the road by the bridge over the railroad."

"See me? All right."

Filled with wonder, Deacon walked leisurely out of the yard and then reaching the road, followed in the wake of an urchin of the neighbourhood who had brought the summons, and could tell Deacon only that it was some one in an automobile.

It was, in fact, Jane Bostwick.

"Jump up here in the car, won't you, Jim?" Her voice was somewhat tense. "No, I'm not going to drive," she added as Deacon hesitated. "We can talk better.

"Have you heard from your father lately?" she asked as the young man sprang into the seat at her side.

He started.

"No, not in a week. Why, is there anything the matter with him?"

"Of course not." She touched him lightly upon the arm. "You knew that Mr. Bell, cashier of the National Penn Bank, had died?"

"No. Is that so! That's too bad." Then suddenly Deacon sat erect. "By George! Father is one of the assistant cashiers there. I wonder if he'll be promoted." He turned upon the girl. "Is that what you wanted to tell me?"

She waited a bit before replying.

"No—not exactly that."

"Not exactly—— What do you mean?"

"Do you know how keen Mr. Doane, I mean Junior's father

is on rowing? Well,"—as Deacon nodded,—"have you thought how he might feel toward the father of the man who is going to sit in his son's seat in the race to-morrow? Would it make him keen to put that father in Mr. Bell's place?"

Deacon's exclamation was sharp.

"Who asked you to put that thought in my mind?"

"Ah!" Her hand went out, lying upon his arm. "I was afraid you were going to take it that way. Mother was talking this afternoon. I thought you should know. As for Junior Doane, I'm frank to admit I'm awfully keen about him. But that isn't why I came here. I remember how close you and your father used to be. I—I thought perhaps you'd thank me, if—if——"

"What you mean is that because I have beaten Doane out for stroke, his father may be sore and not promote my father at the bank."

"There's no 'may' about it. Mr. Doane will be sore. He'll be sore at Junior, of course. But he'll be sore secretly at you, and where there is a question of choice of cashier between *your* father and another man—even though the other man has not been so long in the bank—how do you think his mind will work; I mean, if you lose? Of course, if you can win, then I am sure everything will be all right. You must——"

"If I can win! What difference would that——" He stopped suddenly. "I've caught what you mean." He laughed bitterly. "Parental jealousy. All right! All right!"

"Jim, I don't want you——"

"Don't bother. I've heard all I can stand, Jane. Thank you." He lurched out of the car and hurried away.

She called him. No answer. Waiting a moment, the girl sighed, touched the self-starter and drove away.

Deacon had no idea of any lapse of time between the departure of the car and himself in his cot prepared for sleep—with, however, no idea that sleep would come. His mood was pitiable. His mind was a mass of whirling thoughts in the midst of which he could recognize pictures of his boyhood, a little boy doing many things—with a hand always tucked within the fingers of a great big man who knew everything, who could do everything, who could always explain all the mysteries of the big, strange, booming world. There were many such pictures, pictures not only relating to boyhood, but to his own struggle at Baliol, to the placid little home in Philadelphia and all that it had meant, all that it still meant, to his father, to his mother, to him, Any act of his that would bring sorrow or dismay or the burden of defeated hope to that home!

But on the other hand, the morrow was to bring him the crown of toilsome years, was to make his name one to conjure with wherever Baliol was loved or known. He knew what the varsity *cachet* would do for his prospects in the world. And after all, he had his own life to live, had he not? Would not the selfish, or rather the rigorous, settlement of this problem, be for the best in the end, since his making good would simply be making good for his father and his mother? But how about his father's chance for making good on his own account?

A comrade in the cot adjoining heard a groan.

"Eh! Are you sick, Deacon? Are you all right?"

"Sure—dreaming," came the muffled reply.

There was something unreal to Deacon about the morning. The sunlight was filled with sinister glow; the voices of the rowing men were strange; the whole environment seemed to have changed. It was difficult for Jim Deacon to look upon the bronzed faces of the fellows about the breakfast table, upon the coach with his stiff moustache and glittering eyeglasses—difficult to look upon them and realize that within a few hours his name would be anathema to them, that forever where loyal men of Baliol gather he would be an outcast, a pariah.

That was what he would be—an outcast. For he had come to his decision: Just what he would do he did not know. He did not know that he would not stroke the Baliol varsity. Out of all the welter of thought and travail had been resolved one dominant idea. His father came first: there was no evading it. With all the consequences that would follow the execution of his decision he was familiar. He had come now to know what Baliol meant to him as a place not only of education, but a place to be loved, honoured, revered. He knew what his future might be. But—his father came first. Arising from the breakfast-table, he spoke to but one man, Junior Doane.

"Doane," he said, drawing him to one side, "you will row at stroke this afternoon."

The man stared at him. "Are you crazy, Deacon?"

"No, not crazy. I'm not feeling well; that's all."

"But look here, Deacon—you want to see the coach. You're off your head or something. Wait here, just a minute." As Doane hurried away in search of Dr. Nicholls, Deacon turned blindly through the yard and so out to the main road leading to a picturesque little river city about nine miles up the stream.

June was at her loveliest in this lovable country with its walled fields, its serene uplands and glowing pastures, its lush river meadows and wayside flowers. But of all this Deacon marked nothing as with head down he tramped along with swift, dogged stride. Up the river three or four miles farther on was the little city of which he had so often heard but never seen, the little city of Norton, so like certain English river-cities according to a veteran Oxford oarsman who had visited the Baliol quarters the previous season. Deacon had an interest in strange places; he had an eye for the picturesque and the colourful. He would wander about the place, filling his mind with impressions. He had always wanted to go to Norton; it had seemed like a dream city to him.

He was in fact striding along in the middle of the road when the horn of a motorcar coming close behind startled him. As he turned, the vehicle sped up to his side and then stopped with a grinding of brakes.

Dr. Nicholls, the coach, rose to his full height in the roadster and glared down at Deacon, while Junior Doane, who had been driving, stared fixedly over the wheel. The coach's voice was merely a series of profane roars. He had ample lungs, and the things he said seemed to echo far and wide. His stentorian anger afforded so material a contrast to the placid environment that Deacon stood dazed under the vocal avalanche, hearing but a blur of objurgation.

"Eh?" He paused as Junior Doane placed an admonishing hand upon his arm.

"I beg your pardon, Doctor; but I don't think that is the right way. May I say something to Deacon?"

The coach, out of breath, nodded and gestured, sinking into his seat.

"Look here, Jim Deacon, we've come to take you back. You can't buck out the race this way, you know. It isn't done. Now, wait a minute!" he cried sharply as the boy in the road made to speak. "I know why you ran away. Jane Bostwick called me up and told me everything. She hadn't realized quite what she was doing——"

"She—she bungled everything."

"Bungled! What do you mean, Dr. Nicholls?"

"Nothing—nothing! You young idiot, don't you realize you're trying to kill yourself for life? Jump into the car."

"I'm not going to row." Deacon's eyes smoldered upon the two.

Studying him a moment, Dr. Nicholls suddenly grasped the seriousness of Deacon's mood. He leaped from the car and walked up to him, placing a hand upon his shoulder.

"Look here, my boy: You've let a false ideal run away with you. Do you realize that some twenty-five thousand people throughout this country are having their interests tossed away by you? You represent them. They didn't ask you to. You came out for the crew and worked until you won a place for yourself, a place no one but you can fill. There are men, there are families on this riverside to-day, who have traveled from San Francisco, from all parts of the country, to see Baliol at her best. There are thousands who have the right to ask us that Shelburne is not permitted to win this afternoon. Do you realize your respons——"

Deacon raised his hand.

"I've heard it said often, Dr. Nicholls, that any one who gets in Cephas Doane's way gets crushed. I'm not afraid of him, nor of any one else, on my own account; but I'm afraid of him because of my father. My father is getting to be an old man. Do you think I am going to do anyth——" Deacon's voice, which had been gathering in intensity, broke suddenly. He couldn't go on.

"Jim Deacon!" There was a note of exhilaration in Junior Doane's voice. He hastily climbed out of the car and joined the coach at Deacon's side. "I'm not going to defend my father now. No one knows him as I do; no one knows as I do the great big stuff that is in him. He and I have always been close and——"

"Then you know how he'd feel about any one who took your place in the boat. He can't hurt me. But he can break my father's heart——"

"Deacon, is that the opinion you have of my father!"

"Tell me the truth, Doane; is there the chance under the conditions that with a choice between two men in the bank he might fail to see Father? Isn't it human nature for a man as dominant and strong as he is, who has always had or got most of the things he wants, to feel that way?"

"Perhaps. But not if you can win out against Shelburne. Can't you see your chance, Deacon? Go in and beat Shelburne; Father'll be so glad he'll fall off the observation-train. You know how he hates Shelburne. Any soreness he has about my missing out at stroke will be directed at me—and it won't be soreness, merely regret. Don't you get it?"

"And if we lose——"

"If we lose, there's the chance that we're all in the soup."

"I'm not, if I keep out of this thing——"

"If we lose with *me* at stroke, do you suppose it will help you or any one related to you with my father when he learns that Baliol *would probably have won with you stroking?*

"My Lord, Jim Deacon," Doane went on as the other did not reply, "do you suppose this is any fun for me, arguing with you to swing an oar this afternoon when I would give my heart's blood to swing it in your place?"

"Why do you do it, then?"

"Why do I do it? Because I love Baliol. Because her interests stand above mine. Because more than anything I want to see her win. I didn't feel this way when you beat me out for stroke. I'll admit it. I didn't show my feelings, but I was thinking of nothing but my licking——"

"Ah!"

"Just a minute, Jim. I didn't realize the bigness of the thing, didn't appreciate that what I wanted to do didn't count for a damn. Baliol, only Baliol! It all came to me when you bucked out. Baliol is all that counts, Jim. If I can help her win by rooting from the observation-car, all right! But —don't think it's any fun for me urging you to come back and row. For I wanted to row this race, old boy. I—I——"

Doane's voice faltered. "But I can't; that's all. Baliol needs a better man—needs you. As for you, you've no right to consider anything else. You go in—and win."

"Win!" Jim Deacon stood in the road, rigid, his voice falling to a whisper. "Win!" Into his eyes came a vacant expression. For a moment the group stood in the middle of the road as though transfixed. Then the coach placed his hand upon Deacon's arm, gently.

"Come Jim," he said.

The afternoon had gone silently on. Jim Deacon sat on the veranda of the crew-quarters, his eyes fixed upon the river. Some of the crew were trying to read; others lounged about talking in low voices. Occasionally the referee's launch would appear off the float, the official exchanging some words with the coach while the oarsmen watched eagerly. Then the launch would turn and disappear.

"Too rough yet, boys. They're going to postpone another hour." Twice had the coach brought this word to the group of pent-up young men who in a manner of speaking were sharing the emotions of the condemned awaiting the executioner's summons. Would the up-river breeze never subside and give them conditions that would be satisfactory to the meticulous referee?

Deacon lurched heavily in his seat.

"What difference does it make so long as the shells won't sink?" he asked.

"We're ready," replied Dick Rollins. "It's Shelburne holding things up; she wants smooth water, of course. It suits me, though. Things will soften up by sunset."

"Sunset!" Deacon scowled at the western skies. "Well, sunset isn't so far off as it was."

Word came, as a matter of fact, shortly after five o'clock. The coach, with solemn face, came up to the cottage, bringing the summons. After that for a little while Jim Deacon passed through a series of vague impressions rather than living experience. There was the swift changing of clothes in the cavernous boathouse, the bearing of the boat high overhead to the edge of the float, the splash as it was lowered into the water. Mechanically he leaned forward to lace the stretcher-shoes, letting the handle of his oar rest against his stomach; mechanically he tried to slide, tested the oarlock.

Then some one gripped the blade of his oar, pushing gently outward. The shell floated gingerly out into the stream.

"Starboard oars, paddle." Responsive to the coxswain's sharp command Deacon plied his blade, and in the act there came to him clarity of perception. He was out here to win, to win not only for Baliol, but for himself, for his father. There could be no thought of not winning; the imminence of the supreme test had served to fill him with the consciousness of indomitable strength, to thrill his muscles with the call for tremendous action.

As the shell swept around a point of land, a volume of sound rolled across the waters. Out of the corner of his eye he caught view of the long observation-train, vibrant with animation, the rival colours commingled so that all emblem of collegiate affiliation was lost in a merger of quivering hue. A hill near the starting-line on the other side of the river was black with spectators, who indeed filled points of vantage all down the four miles of the course. The clouds above the western hills were turning crimson; the waters had deepened to purple and were still and silent.

"There, you hell-dogs!" The voice of the coxswain rasped in its combativeness. "Out there is Shelburne; ahead of us at the line. Who says it'll be the last time she'll be ahead of us?"

Along the beautiful line of brown, swinging bodies went a low growl, a more vicious rattle of the oarlocks.

Suddenly as Jim Deacon swung forward, a moored skiff swept past his blade, the starting-line.

"Weigh all." The coxswain's command was immediately followed by others designed to work the boat back to proper starting-position. Deacon could easily see the Shelburne crew now—big men all, ideal oarsmen to look at. Their faces were set and grim, their eyes straight ahead. So far as they gave indication, their shell might have been alone on the river. Now the Baliol shell had made sternway sufficient for the man in the skiff to seize the rudder. The Shelburne boat was already secured. Astern hovered the referee's boat, the official standing in the bow directing operations. Still astern was a larger craft filled with favoured representatives of the two colleges, the rival coaches, the crew-managers and the like.

"Are you all ready, Baliol?"

"Yes, sir." Deacon, leaning forward, felt his arms grow tense.

"Are you all ready, Shelburne?"

The affirmative was followed by the sharp report of a pistol. With a snap of his wrist Deacon beveled his oar, which bit cleanly into the water and pulled. There followed an interval of hectic stroking, oars in and out of the water as fast as could be done, while spray rose in clouds and the coxswain screamed the measure of the beat.

"Fine, Baliol." The coxswain's voice went past Deacon's ear like a bullet. "Both away together and now a little ahead at forty-two to the minute. But down now. Down—down—down—down! That's it—thirty-two to the minute. It's a long race, remember. Shelburne's dropping the beat, too. You listen to Papa, all of you; he'll keep you wise. Number three, for God's sake don't lift all the water in the river up on your blade at the finish. Shelburne's hitting it up a bit. Make it thirty-four."

"Not yet." Deacon scowled at the tense little coxswain. "I'll do the timing." Chick Seagraves nodded.

"Right. Thirty-two."

Swinging forward to the catch, his chin turned against his shoulder, Deacon studied the rival crew which with the half-mile flags flashing by had attained a lead of some ten feet. Their blades were biting the water hardly fifty feet from the end of his blade, the naked brown bodies moving back and forth in perfect rhythm and with undeniable power registered in the snap of the legs on the stretchers and the pull of the arms. Deacon's eyes swept the face of the Shelburne coxswain; it was composed. He glanced at the stroke. The work, apparently, was costing him nothing.

"They're up to thirty-four," cried Seagraves as the mile flags drew swiftly up.

"They're jockeying us, Chick. We'll show our fire when we get ready. Let 'em rave."

Vaguely there came to Deacon a sound from the river-bank—Shelburne enthusiasts acclaiming a lead of a neat half a length.

"Too much—too much." Deacon shook his head. Either Shelburne was setting out to row her rival down at the start, or else, as Deacon suspected, she was trying to smoke Baliol out, to learn at an early juncture just what mettle was in the rival boat. A game, stout-hearted, confident crew will always do this, it being the part of good racing policy to make a rival know fear as early as possible. And Shelburne believed in herself, beyond any question of doubt.

And whether she was faking, or since Baliol could not afford to let the bid go unanswered, a lead of a quarter of a length at the mile had to be challenged:

"Give 'em ten at thirty-six!" Deacon's voice was thick with gathering effort. "Talk it up, Chick."

From the coxswain's throat issued a machine-gun fusillade of whiplash words.

"Ten, boys! A rouser now. Ten! Come on. One—two—three—four—oh, boy! Are we walking! Five—six—are they anchored over there? Seven—oh, you big brown babies! Eight—Shelburne, good night—nine—wow!—ten!"

Deacon, driving backward and forward with fiery intensity, feeling within him the strength of some huge propulsive machine, was getting his first real thrill of conflict—the thrill not only of actual competition, but of all it meant to him, personally: his father's well-being, his own career—everything was merged in a luminous background of emotion for which that glittering oar he held was the outlet.

Shelburne had met the spurt, but the drive of the Baliol boat was not to be denied. Gradually the two prows came abreast, and then Deacon, not stopping at the call of ten, but fairly carrying the crew along with him, swung on with undiminished ferocity, while Seagraves' voice rose into a shrill crescendo of triumph as Baliol forged to the lead.

"They know a little now." Deacon's voice was a growl as gradually he reduced the beat to thirty-two, Shelburne already having diminished the stroke.

Deacon studied them. They were rowing along steadily, the eyes of their coxswain turned curiously upon the Baliol shell. He suspected the little man would like nothing better than to have Baliol break her back to the two-mile mark and thus dig a watery grave. He suspected also, that, failing Baliol's willingness to do this, the test would now be forced upon her. For Shelburne was a heavy crew with all sorts of staying power. What Deacon had to keep in mind was that his eight was not so rugged and had therefore to be nursed along, conserving energy wherever possible.

It was in the third mile that the battle of wits and judgment had to be carried to conclusion, the fourth mile lurking as a mere matter of staying power and ability to stand the gaff. Deacon's idea was that at present his crew was leading because Shelburne was not unwilling for the present that this should be. How true this was became evident after the two-mile flags had passed, when the Shelburne oarsmen began to lay to their strokes with tremendous drive, the boat creeping foot by foot upon the rival shell until the Baliol lead had been overcome and Shelburne herself swept to the fore.

Deacon raised the stroke slightly, to thirty-three, but soon dropped to thirty-two, watching Shelburne carefully lest she make a runaway then and there. Baliol was half a length astern at the two-and-a-half mile mark, passing which the Shelburne crew gave themselves up to a tremendous effort to kill off her rival then and there.

"Jim! They're doing thirty-six—walking away."

The coxswain's face was white and drawn.

But Deacon continued to pass up a thirty-two stroke while the Shelburne boat slid gradually away until at the three-mile mark there was a foot of clear water between its rudder and the prow of the Baliol shell.

Deacon glanced at the coxswain. A mile to go—one deadly mile.

"Thirty-six," he said. "Shelburne's can't have much more left."

The time had passed for study now. Gritting his teeth, Deacon bent to his work, his eyes fixed upon the swaying body of the coxswain, whose sharp staccato voice snapped out the measure; the beat of the oars in the locks came as one sound.

"Right, boys! Up we come. Bully—bully—bully! Half a length now. Do you hear? Half a length! Give me a quarter, boys. Eh, Godfrey! We've got it. Now up and at 'em, Baliol. Oh, you hell-dogs!"

As in a dream Deacon saw the Shelburne boat drift into view, saw the various oarsmen slide past until he and the rival stroke were rowing practically abeam.

"That's for you, Dad," he muttered—and smiled.

He saw the men swing with quickened rhythm, saw the spray fly like bullets from the Shelburne blades.

"Look out." There was a note of anguish in Seagraves' voice. "Shelburne's spurting again."

A malediction trembled upon Deacon's lips. So here was the joker held in reserve by the rival crew! Had Baliol anything left? Had he anything left? Grave doubt was mounting in his soul. Away swept the Shelburne boat inches at a stroke until the difference in their positions was nearly a length. Three miles and a half! Not an observer but believed that this gruelling contest had been worked out. Seagraves, his eyes running tears, believed it as he swung backward and forward exhorting his men. Half a mile more! The crews were now rowing between the anchored lines of yachts and excursion-craft. The finish boat was in sight.

And now Deacon, exalted by something nameless, uttered a cry and began to give to Baliol more than he really had. Surely, steadily, he raised his stroke while his comrades, like the lion-hearts they were, took it up and put the sanction of common authority upon it. Thirty-four! Thirty-six! Not the spurt of physical prowess, but of indomitable mentality.

"Up we come!" Seagraves' voice was shrill like a bugle. He could see expressions of stark fear in the faces of the rival oarsmen. They had given all they had to give, had given enough to win almost any race. But here in this race they had not given enough.

On came the Baliol shell with terrific impulse. Quarter of a mile; Shelburne passed, her prow hanging doggedly on to the Baliol rudder.

Victory! Deacon's head became clear. None of the physical torture he had felt in the past mile was now registered upon his consciousness. No thought but that of impending victory!

"Less than a quarter of a mile, boys. In the stretch. Now—my God!"

Following the coxswain's broken exclamation, Deacon felt an increased resistance upon his blade.

"Eh?"

"Innis has carried away his oarlock." The eyes of the coxswain strained upon Deacon's face.

Deacon gulped. Strangely a picture of his father filled his mind. His face hardened.

"All right! Tell him to throw his oar away and swing with the rest. Don't move your rudder now. Keep it straight as long as you can."

From astern the sharp eyes of the Shelburne cox had detected the accident to Baliol's Number Six. His voice was chattering stridently.

Deacon, now doing the work practically of two men, was undergoing torture which shortly would have one of two effects. Either he would collapse or his spirit would carry him beyond the claims of overtaxed physique. One stroke, two strokes, three strokes—a groan escaped his lips. Then so far as personality, personal emotions, personal feelings were concerned, Jim Deacon ceased to function. He became merely part of the mechanism of a great effort, the principal guiding part.

And of all those rowing men of Baliol only the coxswain saw the Shelburne boat creeping up slowly, inexorably—eight men against seven. For nearly a quarter of a mile the grim fight was waged.

"Ten strokes more, boys!"

The prow of the Shelburne shell was on a line with Baliol's Number Two.

"One—two—three—four——" The bow of the Shelburne boat plunged up abeam Baliol's bow oar.

"Five—six—God, boys!—seven——"

The voice of the coxswain swept upward in a shrill scream. A gun boomed; the air rocked with the screech and roar of whistles.

Slowly Deacon opened his eyes. Seagraves, the coxswain, was standing up waving his megaphone. Rollins, at Number Seven, lay prone over his oar. Innis, who had broken his oarlock, sat erect; Wallace, at Number Five, was down. So was the bow oar. Mechanically Deacon's hand sought the water, splashing the body of the man in front of him. Then suddenly a mahogany launch dashed alongside. In the bow was a large man with white moustache and florid face and burning black eyes. His lips were drawn in a broad grin which seemed an anomaly upon the face of Cephas Doane.

If so he immediately presented a still greater anomaly. He laughed aloud.

"Poor old Shelburne! I—George! The first in four years! I never saw anything quite like that. We've talked of Baliol's rowing-spirit—eh! Here, you Deacon, let me give you a hand out of the shell. We'll run you back to quarters."

Deacon, wondering, was pulled to the launch and then suddenly stepped back, his jaw falling, his eyes alight as a man advanced from the stern.

"Dad!"

"Yes," chuckled Doane. "We came up together—to celebrate."

"You mean—you mean——" Jim Deacon's voice faltered.

"Yes, I mean——" Cephas Doane stopped suddenly. "I think in justice to my daughter-in-law to be, Jane Bostwick, that some explanation is in order."

"Yes, sir." Deacon, his arm about his father's shoulder, stared at the man.

"You see, Dr. Nicholls had the idea that you needed a finer edge put on your rowing spirit. So I got Jane to cook up the story about that cashier business at the bank."

"You did!"

"Yes. Of course your father was appointed. The only trouble was that Jane, bright and clever as she is, bungled her lines."

"Bungled!" Deacon's face cleared. "That's what Dr. Nicholls said about her on the road, the day I bucked out. I remember the word somehow."

"She bungled, yes. She was to have made it very clear that by winning you would escape my alleged wrath—or rather, your father would. I knew you would row hard for Baliol, but I thought you might row superhumanly for your father."

"Well," Jim Deacon flushed, then glanced proudly at his father—"you were right, sir—I would."

PROFESSOR TODD'S USED CAR

By L. H. ROBBINS

From *Everybody's Magazine*

HE WAS a meek little man with sagging frame, dim lamps and feeble ignition. Anxiously he pressed the salesman to tell him which of us used cars in the wareroom was the slowest and safest.

The salesman laid his hand upon me and declared soberly: "You can't possibly go wrong on this one, Mr. Todd." To a red-haired boy he called, "Willie, drive Mr. Todd out for a lesson."

We ran to the park and stopped beside a lawn. "Take the wheel," said Willie.

Mr. Todd demurred. "Let me watch you awhile," he pleaded. "You see, I'm new at this sort of thing. In mechanical matters I am helpless. I might run somebody down or crash into a tree. I—I don't feel quite up to it to-day, so just let me ride around with you and get used to the—the motion, as it were."

"All you need is nerve," Willie replied. "The quickest way for you to get nerve is to grab hold here and, as it were, drive."

"Driving, they say, *does* give a man self-confidence," our passenger observed tremulously. "Quite recently I saw an illustration of it. I saw an automobilist slap his wife's face while traveling thirty miles an hour."

"They will get careless," said Willie.

Mr. Todd clasped the wheel with quivering hands and braced himself for the ordeal.

"Set her in low till her speed's up," Willie directed. "Then wiggle her into high."

It was too mechanical for Mr. Todd. Willie translated with scornful particularity. Under our pupil's diffident manipulation we began to romp through the park at the rate of one mile an hour.

Willie fretted. "Shoot her some gas," said he. "Give it to her. Don't be a-scared." He pulled down the throttle-lever himself.

My sudden roaring was mingled with frightened outcries from Todd. "Stop! Wait a minute! Whoa! Help!"

Fortunately for my radiator, the lamp-post into which he steered me was poorly rooted. He looked at the wreckage of the glass globe on the grass, and declared he had taken as much of the theory of motoring as he could absorb in one session.

"This is the only lesson I can give you free," said Willie. "You'd better keep on while the learning's cheap."

To free education and to compulsory education Mr. Todd pronounced himself opposed. Cramming was harmful to the student; the elective method was the only humane one. He put off the evil hour by engaging Willie as a private tutor for the remaining afternoons of the month.

I have met many rabbits but only one Todd. He would visit me in the barn and look at me in awe by the half-hour. Yet I liked him; I felt drawn toward him in sympathy, for he and I were fellow victims of the hauteur of Mrs. Todd.

In my travels I have never encountered a glacier. When I do run across one I shall be reminded, I am certain, of Mr. Todd's lady.

"So you are still alive?" were her cordial words as we rolled into the yard on the first afternoon.

"Yes, my dear." His tone was almost apologetic.

"Did he drive it?" she asked Willie.

"I'll say so, ma'am."

She looked me over coldly. When she finished, I had shrunk to the dimensions of a wheelbarrow. When Todd sized me up in the warehouse only an hour before, I had felt as imposing as a furniture van.

"Put it in the barn," said Mrs. Todd, "before a bird carries it off."

I began to suspect that a certain little stranger was not unanimously welcome in that household. For a moment I was reassured, but only for a moment.

"John Quincy Burton says," she observed, "that a little old used car like this is sometimes a very good thing to own."

"That is encouraging," said Todd, brightening. In his relief he explained to Willie that John Quincy Burton drove the largest car in the neighbourhood and was therefore to be regarded as an authority.

"Yes," Mrs. Todd concluded, "he says he thinks of buying one himself to carry in his tool-box."

Willie was an excellent teacher, though a severe disciplinarian.

But by way of amends for the rigours of the training, Willie would take Mr. Todd after the practice hour for a spin around the park. At those times I came to learn that the collision I had had with a trolley-car before Todd bought me had not left me with any constitutional defect. I still had power under my hood, and speed in my wheels. But what good were power and speed to me now? I doubted that Todd would ever push me beyond a crawl.

Yet I had hope, for when his relaxation from the tension of a lesson had loosened his tongue he would chatter to Willie about self-confidence.

"Some day you say, I shall be able to drive without thinking?"

"Sure! You won't have to use your bean any more'n when you walk."

At nights, when no one knew, Mr. Todd would steal into the barn and, after performing the motions of winding me up, would sit at the wheel and make believe to drive.

"I advance the spark," he would mutter, "I release the brake, I set the gear, and ever so gently I let in the clutch. Ha! We move, we are off! As we gather speed I pull the gear-lever back, then over, then forward. Now, was that right? At any rate we are going north, let us say, in Witherspoon Street. I observe a limousine approaching from the east in a course perpendicular to mine. It has the right of way, Willie says, so I slip the clutch out, at the same time checking the flow of gasoline. . . ."

Thus in imagination he would drive; get out, crank, get in again, and roll away in fancy, earnestly practising by the hour in the dark and silent barn.

"I'm getting it," he would declare. "I really believe I'm getting it!"

And he got it. In his driving examination he stalled only once, stopping dead across a trolley track in deference to a push-cart. But he was out and in and off again in ten seconds, upbraiding me like an old-timer.

Said the inspector, stepping out at last and surely offering a prayer of thanks to his patron sa nt: "You're pretty reckless yet on corners, my friend." But he scribbled his O. K.

The written examination in the City Hall Mr. Todd passed with high honours. Willie, who was with us on the fateful morning, exclaimed in admiration: "One hundred! Well, Mr. Todd, you're alive, after all—from the neck up, at least."

In gratitude for the compliment, the glowing graduate pressed a bonus of two dollars into the panegyrist's palm. "Willie," he exulted, "did you hear the inspector call me reckless?"

I can scarcely think of the Todd of the succeeding weeks as the same Todd who bought me. He changed even in looks. He would always be a second, of course, but his frame had rigidity now, his lamps sparkled, he gripped the wheel with purposeful hands and trampled the pedals in the way an engine likes. In his new assurance he reminded me strongly of a man who drove me for a too brief while in my younger days—a rare fellow, now doing time, I believe, in the penitentiary.

No longer Todd and I needed the traffic cop's "Get on out of there, you corn-sheller!" to push us past the busy intersection of Broad and Main streets. We conquered our tendency to scamper panic-stricken for the sidewalk at the raucous bark of a jitney bus. In the winding roads of the park we learned to turn corners on two wheels and rest the other pair for the reverse curve.

One remembered day we went for a run in the country. On a ten-mile piece of new macadam he gave me all the gas I craved. It was the final test, the consummation, and little old Mr. Todd was all there. I felt so good I could have blown my radiator cap off to him.

For he was a master I could trust—and all my brother used cars, whether manufactured or merely born, will understand what comfort that knowledge gives a fellow. I vowed I would do anything for that man! On that very trip, indeed, I carried him the last homeward mile on nothing in my tank but a faint odour.

II

Mrs. Todd was one of those gentle souls who get their happiness in being unhappy in the presence of their so-called loved ones. She was perpetually displeased with Todd.

His Christian name was James, but she did not speak Christian to him. When she hailed him from the house she called him "Jay-eems"—the "eems" an octave higher than the "Jay."

He would drop the grease-can or the monkey-wrench to rush to her side.

"Look at your sleeves!" she would say. "Your best shirt!" Words failing her, she would sigh and go into a silence that was worse than words. He was a great burden to her.

Humbly he entreated her one day for an obsolete toothbrush. "I want to clean spark-plugs with it," he explained.

"Next," she replied, icily, "you'll be taking your little pet to the dentist, I suppose."

From such encounters Jay-eems would creep back to the barn and seek consolation in tinkering around me.

He liked to take the lid off my transmission-box and gaze at my wondrous works. He was always tightening my axle-burrs, or dosing me with kerosene through my hot-air pipe, or toying with my timer. While he was never so smart as Willie about such things, he was intelligent and quick to learn; and this was not surprising to me after I discovered the nature of his occupation in life.

I had taken him to be a retired silk-worm fancier, a chronic juryman, or something of the sort. But shiver my windshield if he wasn't a professor in a college!

On the morning when first he dared to drive me to his work, the college must have got wind of our coming, for the students turned out in a body to cheer him as he steered in at the campus gate, and the faculty gathered on the steps to shake his hand.

A bald-headed preceptor asked him if he meant to cyanide

me and mount me on a pin for preservation in the college museum. The chancellor inquired if Todd had identified me. Todd said he had. He said I was a perfect specimen of *Automobilum cursus gaudium*, the most beautiful species of the *Golikelleæ* family. It was the nearest he ever came to profanity in my hearing. I suppose he got it from associating with Willie.

They demanded a speech, and he made one—about me. He said that my name was *Hilaritas*, signifying joy. He said, among other flattering things, that I was no common mundane contraption, though such I might seem to the untutored eye. In their studies of the Greek drama they had read of gods from the machine. I was a machine from the gods. In my cylinders I consumed nectar vapour, in my goo-cups ambrosia, in my radiator flowed the crystal waters of the Fount of Bandusia.

Three other items of his eulogium I remember: The breath of Pan inflated my tires, I could climb Olympus in high, and he, James Todd, a mere professor in a college, while sitting at my wheel, would not bare his head to Zeus himself, no, nor even to the chairman of the college board of trustees.

His nonsense appeared to be as popular in that part of town as it was unpopular in another. They gave the varsity yell with his name at the end.

The day came when Mrs. Todd risked her life in our sportive company. She made it clear to us that she went protesting. She began her pleasantries by complaining that my doors were trivial. Straightening her hat, she remarked that the John Quincy Burtons' car top never took a woman's scalp off.

"But theirs is only a one-man top," Todd hinted vaguely.

"Whatever you mean by that is too deep for me," she said, adding bitterly, "Yours is a one-boy top, I presume."

He waived the point and asked where she preferred to make her début as an automobilist.

"Back roads, by all means," she answered.

As we gained the street a pea-green Mammoth purred past, the passengers putting out their heads to look at us.

"Goodness!" she sighed. "There go the John Quincy Burtons now."

"We can soon join them," said Todd confidently.

She expostulated. "Do you think I have no pride?" Yet we went in pursuit of the John Quincy Burton dust-cloud as it moved toward the park.

"Since you have no regard for my feelings," said she, "you may let me out."

"Oh, no, Amanda, my dear. Why, I'm going to give you a spin to Mountaindale!"

"I do not care to be dragged there," she declared. "That is where the John Quincy Burtons ride."

"Aren't they nice people? It seems to me I've heard you sing hosannas to their name these last twenty years."

They were nice people indeed. That was just it, she said. Did he suspect her of yearning to throw herself in the way of nice people on the day of her abasement? If he chose to ignore her sentiments in the matter, he might at least consider his own interests. Had he forgotten that John Quincy Burton was chairman of the board of trustees of the college? Would the head of the department of classical languages acquire merit in Mr. Burton's eyes through dashing about under Mr. Burton's nose in a pitiable little last-century used car that squeaked?

Todd gripped the wheel tighter and gave me gas.

"You missed that storm sewer by an inch!" she exclaimed.

"My aim is somewhat wild yet," he admitted. "Perhaps I'll get the next one."

"Jay-eems!"

"My dear, we have a horn, remember."

"You did not see that baby carriage until we were right upon it! Don't tell me you did, sir, for I know better."

"I saw it," said Todd, "and I was sure it wouldn't run over us. As you see, it didn't. Trust a baby carriage my love."

His humour, she informed him, was on a par with his driving. Also it was in poor taste at such a moment.

In time of danger, he replied, the brave man jests.

We were now in the park. We clipped a spray of leaves off a syringa bush. On a curve we slid in loose gravel to the wrong side.

"James Todd!"

"Yes, my dear?"

"Let me out! I decline to be butchered to make a holiday for a motormaniac."

"Don't talk to the motormaniac," said Todd.

She clutched a top support and gasped for breath, appalled at his audacity, or my speed, or both. In the straight reaches I could see the Burton Mammoth a quarter of a mile ahead. When it swung into the broad avenue that leads to the mountain, we were holding our own.

"You are following them—deliberately," said Mrs. Todd.

"Yet not so deliberately, at that. Do you feel us pick up my dear, when I give her gas? Aha!" he laughed. "I agree with you, however, that the order of precedence is unsatisfactory. Why should we follow the Burtons, indeed?"

We went after them; we gave them the horn and overtook and passed them on a stiff grade, amid cheers from both cars. But all of our cheering was done by Todd.

"Now they are following us," said he. "Do you feel better, my dear?"

"Better!" she lamented. "How can I ever look them in the face again?"

"Turn around," he suggested, "and direct your gaze through the little window in the back curtain."

She bade him stop at the next corner. She would walk home. She was humiliated. Never had she felt so ashamed.

"Isn't that an odd way to feel when we have beaten the shoes off them?"

"But they will think we tried to."

"So we did," he chuckled; "and we walked right past them, in high, while Burton was fussing with his gear shift. Give our little engine a fair go at a hill, my dear——"

"I am not in the least interested in engines, sir. I am only mortified beyond words."

She had words a-plenty, however.

"Isn't it bad enough for you to drive your little rattletrap to college and get into the paper about it? No; you have to show it off in a fashionable avenue, and run races with the best people in Ashland, and scream at them like a freshman, and make an exhibition of me!"

His attention was absorbed in hopping out from under a truck coming in from a side street. A foolish driver would have slowed and crashed. I was proud of Todd. But his lady was not.

"You have no right to go like this. You don't know enough. You will break something."

He had already broken the speed law. Unknown to him, a motor-cycle cop was tagging close behind us on our blind side.

"If you think this is going, my dear," said Todd reassuringly, "wait till we strike the turnpike. Then I'll show you what little Hilaritas can really do."

"Stop at the car barns," she commanded.

We crossed the car-barn tracks at a gallop. The cop rode abreast of us now. "Cut it out, Bill," he warned.

"You see?" she crowed. "You will wind up in jail and give the papers another scandal. Why didn't you stop at the car barns?"

"Because we are going to Mountaindale," he explained cheerily; "where the nice people drive. Perhaps we shall see the John Quincy Burtons again—as we come back."

"If we ever do come back!"

"Or how would you like to have supper with them up there?"

She had gone into one of her silences.

III

We settled down for the long pull over First Mountain. Todd slowed my spark and gave me my head. Then he addressed the partner of his joy-ride in a new voice: "Amanda, my dear, you and I need to have a frank little understanding."

She agreed.

"For some years past," he began, "I have borne without complaint, even without resentment, a certain attitude that you have seen fit to adopt toward me. I have borne it patiently because I felt that to an extent I deserved it."

My floor boards creaked as she gathered her forces for the counter attack. He went on recklessly:

"In the beginning of our life together, Amanda, you were ambitious. You longed for wealth and position and that sort of thing, in which respect you were like the rest of men and women. Like most people, my dear, you have been disappointed; but unlike most of them you persist in quarrelling with the awards of fortune, just as to-day you are quarrelling with this plebeian car of ours. As you speak of Hilaritas, so you speak of me. At breakfast this morning, for example, you reminded me, for perhaps the tenth time since Sunday, that you are chained to a failure. Those were your words, my dear—chained to a failure."

"Do you call yourself a dazzling success?" she asked.

"Not dazzling, perhaps," he replied, "and yet—yes—yes, I believe I do."

"What I told you at breakfast was that Freddy Burton makes one hundred dollars a week, and he is only twenty-four—not half as old as you."

"Freddy Burton is engaged in the important occupation of selling pickles," Todd answered, "and I am only an educator of youth. Long ago I reached my maximum—three thousand dollars. From one point of view I don't blame you for looking upon me as a futility. I presume I am. Nor will I chide you for not taking the luck of life in a sportsmanlike spirit. But I do insist——"

"At last!" she broke in. "At last I understand some pencil notes that I found yesterday when I cleaned out your desk. A minute ago I thought you were out of your head. Now I see that this—this frightfulness of yours is premeditated. Premeditated, James Todd! You prepared this speech in advance!"

Between you and me, she was right. I had heard him practise it in the barn.

He took her arraignment calmly. "Hereafter," said he, "please refrain from cleaning out my desk."

I heard her catch her breath. "You have never talked to me like this before; never!" she said. "You have never dared. And that is precisely the trouble with you, James Todd. You won't talk back; you won't speak up for your rights. It is the cross of my life."

From the sound, I think she wept.

"You are the same in the outside world as you are at home. You let the college trustees pay you what they please. You slave and slave and wear yourself out for three thousand a year when we might have twenty if you went into something else. And when your building-loan stock matures and you do get a little money, you spend it for this—this underbred little sewing-machine, and lure me out in it, and lecture me, as if I—as if I were to blame. I don't know what has come over you."

I knew what had come over him. I knew the secret of the new spirit animating the frail personality of Professor Todd. And Willie knew. I recalled that boy's prophetic words: "The quickest way to get nerve is to grab hold here and drive." I worried, nevertheless. I wondered if my little man could finish what he had started.

He could. As we rolled down the mountain into the ten-mile turnpike where he and I had rediscovered our youth, he concluded his discourse without missing an explosion. I knew his peroration by heart.

"To end this painful matter, my dear, I shall ask you in future to accord me at least the civility, if not the respect, to which a hard-working man and a faithful husband is entitled. I speak in all kindliness when I say that I have decided to endure no more hazing. I hope you understand that I have made this decision for your sake as well as for mine, for the psychological effect of hazing is quite as harmful to the hazer as to the hazed. Please govern yourself accordingly."

He opened the throttle wide, and we touched thirty-five miles. I felt a wild wabble in my steering-gear. I heard Todd's sharp command—"Kindly keep your hands off the wheel while I am driving."

At the Mountain Dale Club Todd descended.

"Will you come in and have a lemonade, my dear?" he asked. There was a heartbroken little squeak in his voice.

"Thank you," she replied frigidly. "I have had all the acid I can assimilate in one pleasant day."

"May I remind you," said he, stiffening with the gentle insistence of a steel spring, "that I am not to be addressed in sarcastic tones any longer?"

The Mammoth slid up beside us. The stout John Quincy Burton at the wheel shouted jovially: "I tell you what, Todd, when our soberest university professors get the speed bug, I tremble for civilization!"

My owner grinned with pleasure.

"Mrs. Todd," said Burton, "after that trimming from

your road-burning husband, I'll stand treat. Won't you join us?"

"Yes, Mrs. Todd, do be persuaded," Mrs. Burton chimed in. "After twenty miles with your Barney Oldfield you need nourishment, I'm sure. You and I can talk about his recklessness while he and Mr. Burton have their little conference."

If Todd had an appointment for a conference there at that hour with Burton, I am positive it was news to Mrs. Todd and me. I could feel her weight growing heavier on my cushion springs.

"Thank you for the invitation," she replied, "but I am so badly shaken up, I prefer to sit out here."

To which her husband added, laughingly: "She wouldn't risk having her new car stolen for anything."

It was twilight before we started for home, the Burtons pulling out ahead of us. At the beginning of the climb over the mountain I saw the Mammoth stop. We drew alongside.

"Out of gas, confound it," growled Burton, "and five miles from a service station!"

"I'd lend you some, only I haven't much myself," said Todd. "Got a rope?"

"Yes, but——"

"Oh, we can. We can pull you and never know it. Hitch on behind. We like to travel in stylish company, Mrs. Todd and I."

So we towed them over the mountain and left them at a red pump. John Quincy Burton's gratitude was immense.

"The pleasure is all ours," Todd assured him. "But, say, old man!"

"Well?"

"You ought to buy a little old used car like this some time to carry in your tool-box."

They were still laughing when we drove away.

Not a word did Mrs. Todd utter on the homeward journey; but in the privacy of our humble barn—

"Oh!" she cried. "I could *die!* Why did you have to say that to Mr. Burton?"

"Amanda!"

She subsided, but she had not surrendered.

"You didn't tell me you had an engagement with him. What——"

Todd laughed. "I was chosen this week, my dear, as a grievance committee of one, representing the teaching staff at the college, to put a few cold facts into John Quincy Burton's ear."

"You?"

"Precisely, my dear. I was the only man in the faculty who seemed to have the—the self-confidence necessary. And I made Burton see the point. I have his promise that the college trustees will campaign the state this summer for a half-million-dollar emergency fund, a good slice of which will go toward salary increases."

"Well! I must say——"

She did not say it. Silently she left us.

He lingered a while in the barn. He opened my hood, for I was quite warm from the towing job. He examined a new cut in one of my tires and loosened my hand-brake a notch. He couldn't seem to find enough to do for me.

From the house came a hail. I am not sure that he did not hold his breath as he listened.

"James, dear!" again.

"Hello!" he answered.

"James, dear, won't you bring your automobile pliers, please, and see if you can open this jar of marmalade?"

My little man went in whistling.

THE THING THEY LOVED

By MARICE RUTLEDGE

From *The Century Magazine*

"They had vowed to live only for one another. The theme of their love was sublime enough, but the instruments were fallible. Human beings can rarely sustain a lofty note beyond the measure of a supreme moment."

WHEN she told her husband that David Cannon had arranged for her a series of recitals in South America, she looked to him for swift response. She was confident that anything touching on her professional life would kindle his eye and warm his voice. It was, in fact, that professional life as she interpreted it with the mind of an artist, the heart of a child, which had first drawn him to her; he had often admitted as much. During one year of rare comradeship he had never failed in his consideration for her work. He would know, she felt sure, that to go on a concert tour with David Cannon, to sing David Cannon's songs under such conditions, presented good fortune in more than one way. He would rejoice accordingly.

But his "Why, my dear, South America!" came flatly upon her announcement. It lacked the upward ring, and his eye did not kindle, his voice did not warm. He himself felt the fictitious inflection, for he added hastily, with happier effect: "It's a wonderful chance, dearest, isn't it?" His voice by then had gained in heartiness, and his smile, always worshipful when turned on her, contained this time something of apology. So close were they, though, in thought, spoken or unspoken, that he had sounded a tiny alarm. Her radiance perceptibly waned. A moment before she had stood, a glowing, vital creature, beside him, eyes and lips singing a duet of delight; now with questioning heart she leaned toward her loved one.

"What is it? Don't you want me to go? I thought you liked David. Can't you come, too, Oliver?"

"You know I can't, dear," she heard him say with an attempt at lightness. Then he added: "But it's a great chance for you. You'll take it, of course. It was only the thought of losing you even for a little while. What selfish brutes we men are!" He had recovered himself, had defined his passing reserve in loverlike terms, and was newly aware of unworthiness. The luxury of tender persuasion, of arguing her into a sense of sweet security, concerned him next. He could not say enough, and said too much.

They were mellow against an intimate background of yellow walls lit by fire and lamps. Myra's grand piano projected sleek and dark from a corner of warm shadow. The silver tea-set gleamed pale on a slender-legged table; a fragrance of narcissus spread dreamily. Oliver sank on the couch, drawing her down where she could become all feminine. She was that, and most adorably, her bright hair soft about lax brows, her full lips parted, her strong white hands lying in his like brooding birds. He talked on, and she played content for a while; but a moment came when with a sudden maternal gesture she drew his dark, willing head to her shoulder.

"Let's forget South America for to-night," she said.

He would not, could not, drop the subject. He had been so clumsy in not realizing what it all meant to her; but her news had come as such a surprise. She had seen David Cannon, then, that afternoon?

Yes, he was on his way down to her to settle the date of their concert and to propose this South American scheme. But she need not decide immediately.

He protested that her triumph there would crown him. If he were not a poor young architect attached to his blue prints, he would follow her. As it was, his duller duty lay at home. She caught a flatness of tone, and met it with a vigorous profession of faith in his work. His art was more useful than hers, more enduring. His music was in stone; hers was no greater than the trilling of a bird. He thought this over, moved from her embrace, sat erect, and patted his tie. Well, he summed up, each had a working life converging to a common end. Let her sing Cannon's songs to South America. Her voice would reach him. Then let her come back quickly. He could not conceive of life without her. It would seem strange to be a bachelor again, he went on, with a sigh meant to be comical. He supposed he would eat at his club when he was not invited out. He hoped her friends would take pity on him.

"You mean our friends," she corrected.

"You're the magnet, dear."

"I attracted you," she conceded happily. Then, with a start, she said: "Do you know what time it is? And we're dining with the Wickeses at seven."

"I never have you to myself any more," he objected. "If I were an old-fashioned husband, I should be jealous of every one who sees or talks to you."

"But you're not an old-fashioned husband," she reminded him.

"I try not to be." He had risen from the couch, and was making his way to the door, where he paused to look back at her. "Wear the blue brocade to-night, dear, and do your hair that new way."

"The way Martigues suggested? I thought you didn't like it."

He hesitated only a second.

"It's a bit extreme," he had to confess, "but it suits you."

She came toward him then, laughing.

"You see, you give me over to them."

"I can afford to," he said.

They were late, of course, to the dinner. Despite her effort at brightness, Oliver felt her graver mood. He watched her with a shadowy anxiety. Her smile, when her glance sought him out among the chattering guests, did not entirely reassure him. He had never loved her more than this evening when she seemed so removed from him, so easily and brilliantly a guest of honor. What hold had these strangers on her? They could only misread the superficial sparkle of her eyes, the gracious movements of her uncovered neck and arms. He decided then that the blue brocade was too conspicuous. She must not wear it in South America. And her honey-coloured hair, piled high, with a fantastic Spanish comb flaring above the topmost curls, struck him as needlessly theatrical. He blamed Martigues for that. His humour was not improved by the Basque painter's voluble compliments on the success of a coiffure he felt to be his own creation. The fellow was too familiar, thought Oliver, with increasing irritation. He darkened, grew glum and silent; and when, after dinner, Martigues approached him with a luckless tribute to Madame Shaw's superlative loveliness, he answered curtly, and turned on his heel. Myra witnessed the brief discourtesy, and later very gently taxed him with it. What had the unfortunate artist done? He faced her like a sulky boy and would not answer; but she was quick to penetrate his grievance. She laughed then, as a woman laughs who has nothing to conceal, declaring that Martigues's taste was not infallible, and that Oliver knew best what became his Myra. She soon wooed him back to his old charming self, and the incident passed. But there were others on the following days, and Myra grew thoughtful.

She and Oliver were seldom alone. Her joy of life, her vitality, her very talent, depended on a multitude of impressions, on innumerable personal contacts. She belonged to a rich, throbbing world of emotions; she gathered passion for her song from the yearnings, the anonymous aspirations, even the crudities of the human forces about her.

She was Oliver's most gloriously when most surrounded. His pride was centred on her; it was centred, however, on the brilliant returns of her actual presence—a presence which was never too far removed in flesh or spirit to deprive him of a certain naïve assumption of ownership. That she should continue all the dear, familiar fascinations beyond his sight or touch, in a far-away land, with David Cannon as a daily companion, was another matter. Not that he was jealous of David. No one man stood out as a rival. But Cannon travelling with Myra, sharing artistic triumphs with her, escorting her to entertainments given in her honour, Cannon, in fact, associated in foreign minds with the beautiful cantatrice, offended the inviolable rights of his lover's vanity. He would have her less beautiful, less gifted, not more faithful.

Exquisitely sensitive where he was concerned, Myra detected this subtle change in his attitude toward her and her work. The origins of the change, she knew, were obscurely lodged in the male egoism. He himself was not aware of them. He seemed nearer and dearer than ever, even more ardent. He wanted her constantly within range of his eyes and hands that he might in a thousand coaxing or, often, petulant ways assert a fond dominion. She yielded gladly to that sweet pressure. Strangely enough for a woman of her independent habits, to be so loved, roused elemental instincts the more powerful since she had never before given them outlet. So she allowed his illusions of mastery full play, which was dangerous, as gradually she altered the delicate balance of their relationship.

A restless month went by. It was February.

Unfortunately, Oliver's work failed to engross him. He grew moodier, more exacting. If Myra arrived home late, he wanted to know where she had been, whom she had seen. Were they dining out, he muttered unsociable objections; were people coming to the house, he complained of the lack of privacy. What a whirl they lived in! So they did, but what was the remedy? Myra herself felt helpless in a tangle of engagements. They overpowered her. She could not seem to cut her way through them. Then there were rehearsals for the concert. David Cannon came to her or she went to him nearly every day. Usually Oliver was present, putting in his opinion between each song. Did David think the South Americans would appreciate that kind of music? How did he think they would like Myra? And so on and on.

David Cannon, never patient, a rough-tongued, self-absorbed genius, resented these interruptions, and was brief in his methods of expressing as much. Even Myra, the most tactful of diplomatists, could not smooth over occasional ugly moments between the two men. She understood Oliver better than he understood himself. His unreasoning love, his apprehensive vanity, would have unsettled a less maternal spirit; but she found a kind of mystic wonder in it, he battled so blindly for possession of her. He was in her way, and she could not advance without pushing him aside. Had he come to her and blustered, "You shall not leave me for any purpose whatsoever," she would have denied him the right of dictation; but there was no such conflict of wills.

They were both involved in this love of their making—a love whose demands were treacherous. Each day brought up trivial attacks, fancied grievances, little fears unavowed; but when she sought to meet the issue squarely, it eluded her. Oliver's nightly repentance for his daily whims and suspicions drew her nightly into his arms. Enfolded there, she felt moored to his love; and, sleepless, she questioned any life apart.

Two days before the recital, David Cannon, with whom she was going over the programme for the last time, turned suddenly from the piano with an impatient shrug of his shoulders.

"Rotten!" he said brutally, peering up at her. "You're not doing yourself justice. What's the matter with you?" Beneath the strong, overhanging brow his little eyes glowered fiercely.

They happened to be alone that afternoon in his great bare studio, where no soft background or dim lights conspired to hide her dejection. She had sung badly. She knew it, but she could not answer such a brusque attack, could not defend herself against harsh questioning.

"I don't know. Perhaps I'm tired," she said.

David Cannon rose from the piano with the powerful lunging movement of a bull.

"You tired? Nonsense!" His charge sent him beyond her a pace. He wheeled and came up close. He was shorter than she, but the sheer force of the man topped her. His keen little eyes looked her over, took in her bright, drooping head, and her sloping-shouldered, slim-waisted health. "Tired!" he grunted. "That's an excuse, not a reason." He tapped his heart and forehead. "Your troubles lie here and here."

She tried to smile, with a lift of her eyebrows.

"What do you know about it?"

"I know more than you think I do," he flung at her, frowning. "You're worried about something, and when you worry, you can't sing. You're made that way, and I suppose you can't help it. Don't interrupt yet," he fairly shouted at her as she began to protest. "I've watched over and taught you for three years. I ought to know."

"I owe you a lot," she said faintly.

"You owe me nothing," he snapped. "Your debt is to ourself."

She could not fend off that merciless look, which went hrough and through her. "If my debt is to myself, I need ay only if I choose," she tried to jest.

"Don't make that mistake," he warned. "Your work is our life. I tell you that, and I know."

"I wonder," she said more to herself than to him.

He looked at her grimly.

"Just as I thought. Same old question—marriage. You're ealous, or he's jealous of God knows whom or what. And our voice goes to pieces. Which is it?" he demanded. "Is)liver misbehaving?"

"Of course not," she said indignantly.

"Humph! Well, he's faithful, you're faithful. You've oth got talent, friends, a home, a profession. What more lo you want?"

"There are other—jealousies," she said slowly, and with athering passion she went on: "I suppose I owe you some xplanation, David, though you won't understand. Oliver s the most wonderful person in the world. I never thought could love any one as I love him. And it's the same with im. But he wants me all to himself." Her hands fluttered ogether in nervous appeal. "Can't you see how it is? Since ve've been married we've never been separated a day. And now this South-American thing has come up, and he's elt—oh, I can't explain. But I'm so afraid——"

"Afraid of what?"

"It's hard to put into words," she said hopelessly. "I suppose I'm afraid of losing my happiness. Oliver's right in many ways. He never does have me to himself; I belong to so many people. It's always been my life, you know. But I thought I could combine everything when I married, and I'm beginning to see that it can't be done."

"He knew what your life was," said David.

"Does one ever know?" she said sadly. "This concert, you see, is my first important appearance since our marriage. And then my going away right after——"

David strode over to the piano and sat there silent, his head sunk on his chest, his short arms stiffly before him.

"I realize how absurd it is," she murmured; "but it isn't

just those few months. He trusts me. It's the feeling he has that this is only a beginning. I know what he means so well," she ended helplessly. David's short fingers moved over the keys. A music wild and pagan rose up, filled the room with rhythms of free dancing creatures, sank to a minor plaint, and broke off on a harsh discord as the door-bell jangled.

"There's your Oliver," he said, and went to let him in.

It was the day of the concert, and Myra wanted above all to be alone. She had never felt this way before. She dreaded the evening, dreaded facing a critical audience; she had fretted herself into a fever over it. But when she tried to explain her state of mind to Oliver that morning at breakfast, he would not hear of any prescription for nerves which did not include his company. Why should she want to be alone? If she was ill or troubled, his place was beside her. He had planned to lunch and spend the afternoon with her. Her faintly irritable "I wish you wouldn't," only wounded and shocked him. Her strength was not equal to discussion, and in the end she yielded.

For the rest of the morning he followed her about, tenderly opposing any exertion.

"I must have you at your best to-night, dear," he kept on saying. "I'm going to be proud of my Myra." He was so eager, wistful, and loving, she could not resent his care. She gave in to it with a sense of helplessness.

Soon after lunch her head started aching. She suggested a brisk walk. The air might do her good. But he persuaded her to lie down on the couch instead. The touch of his fingers on her hot forehead was soothing, too soothing. She relaxed luxuriously, closing her eyes, subdued, indifferent.

He was saying:

"What will you do, beloved, if you are taken ill in South America? No Oliver to care for you. I can't bear to think of it." Suddenly, he laid his cheek against hers. "If anything happens to you, I shall go mad."

She sat up with a swift movement that brought back an almost intolerable pain.

"Nothing will happen," she tried to say, and found herself weakly sobbing in his arms.

It was time to dress. She did her hair, to please Oliver, in a girlish way, parted and knotted low. Her gown, designed by Martigues, did not fit in with this simple coiffure. She was aware of an incongruity between the smooth, yellow bands of hair meekly confining her small head, and the daring peacock-blue draperies flowing in long, free lines from her shoulders, held lightly in at the waist by a golden cord.

"One will get the better of the other before the evening is over," she thought with a sigh, turning away from her mirror.

"My beautiful Myra!" Oliver said as if to cheer her.

"I have never looked worse," she retorted a trifle impatiently, and would not argue the point as they drove up town.

"We'll see what I really amount to now," she told herself.

She had never before so tensely faced an audience, but there was more at stake than she cared to confess, and she was not equal to it. She shone, but did not blind those thousand eyes; she sang but did not cast enchantment. And David Cannon would not help her. He sat at the piano, uncouth, impassive, deliberately detached, as if he gave her and his music over to an anonymous crowd of whose existence he was hardly aware. There was something huge and static about him, something elemental as an earth-shape, containing in and by itself mysterious rhythms. His songs were things of faun-like humours, terrible, tender, mocking, compassionate. They called for an entire abandon, for witchery, for passion swayed and swaying; but although at times Myra's voice held a Pan-like flutiness, although an occasional note true and sweet as a mate-call stirred that dark fronting mass, she failed to sustain the spell. She was too aware of Oliver leaning forward in his box, applauding louder than any one. His loyalty would force out of this fastidious audience an ovation she did not deserve. She would not look his way. "I can't sing," she thought mournfully.

Had David Cannon shown any annoyance, she might have been goaded on to a supreme effort; but he avoided her. When once she went up to him during an intermission and said timidly:

"I'm sorry, David; I'm spoiling everything," he answered indifferently:

"My songs can stand it."

She wished then that she had not begged Oliver to keep away from her until the end. She felt lonely and near to tears. As the evening wore on, lightened by spasmodic applause, she became very quiet. She even sang better, and felt rather than saw Oliver brighten. But it was too late; she had lost her audience. There were now gaps in the earlier unbroken rows; a well-known critic trod softly out; little nervous coughs and rustlings rose up.

At last it was all over. She wanted only to hide, but she was not to escape another ordeal. She and Oliver had arranged for a supper party that evening. To it they had bidden many musical personalities and several of Oliver's architect friends. She had meant to announce then the South-American recitals. The prospect of such an entertainment was now almost unendurable. She knew well what these people would say and think. Driving home with Oliver, she relaxed limp against his shoulder, her eyes closed. That haven could at least always be counted on, she reflected with passionate gratitude. His voice sounded from a distance as he talked on and on, explaining, excusing, what he could not honestly ignore. She had worked too hard. She was tired out. There was the headache, too. But she had sung wonderfully all the same.

"Please, Oliver!" she faintly interrupted.

"You made the best of it," he insisted. "David's songs, though, are beyond me."

She sat up very straight at this.

"My dear," she said in a cold voice, "I made a mess of it, and you know it. There *is* no excuse. David has every reason to be furious."

"I'd like to see him dare——"

"Please, Oliver!" she said again on a warning note of hysteria. She stared out of the window at the blur of passing lights. It was misting; the streets gleamed wet and wan beneath the lamps.

Oliver's arm went around her.

"I'm sorry, dear. Nothing matters, after all, but you and I together," he whispered.

"Nothing else does matter, does it?" she cried suddenly. "Love me a great deal, Oliver, a great, great deal. That's all I ask."

They drove on in silence for a while. She sat very quiet, her face half hidden in the high fur collar of her cloak. Now and then she glanced at Oliver, her eyes wistful.

"Oliver," she said at last, "would it make any difference to you if I never sang again?"

"Never sang again," he echoed. "I don't understand."

"I want you and my home," came from her slowly. "I've been wondering for some time how much my singing really meant to me. To-night I think I've found out. I can't seem to keep everything I started out with and be happy. I'm not big enough," she added sadly.

He was startled, incredulous.

"Myra, you don't realize what you're saying. You're tired to-night. I could not let you give up your singing. You are an artist, a big artist."

She shook her head and sighed.

"I might have been, perhaps; but no, I'm not. David could tell you that. He knows."

"It's been my fault, then, if you feel this way," he said in a melancholy voice. "I've been selfish and stupid."

The taxi slowed down before the red-brick entrance of the apartment house. She put her hand impulsively on his arm.

"Oliver, promise me something."

"Whatever you ask."

"Don't mention South America to any one. You promise?"

"But, Myra——"

"Promise."

"I won't, then. But——"

"I see Walter Mason and Martigues waiting for us," she said quickly. "Remember, not a word." She was out of the cab, hurrying forward to greet her guests. Oliver followed, his eyes mutely pleading. But she seemed her old self again, graciously animated, laughing at Martigues, who sulked because he did not like the way her hair was done.

Soon other guests arrived, and still others, all of them primed with compliments carefully prepared.

Last of all came David Cannon, who brushed away flattery with curt gestures and grunts. He sat heavily down in a corner of the room, a plate of cheese sandwiches and a frosted glass of beer before him, and turned an unsociable eye on all intruders. Myra, knowing his mood, left him alone.

"You are different to-night," Martigues whispered to her. "There is something I do not understand. You have the Madonna smile."

"I am happy," she said, and her eyes turned to Oliver, who held the look and gave it back with deeper meaning.

When later Martigues asked her to sing, she glanced again at Oliver, who nodded and smiled.

"If David will accompany me," she said then. David left sandwiches and beer but without enthusiasm. He crossed over to the piano, and peered up at her with a kind of sombre malice.

"So you will sing now," he said. "Will this do?" He played a few notes softly, and she nodded with a little smile.

It was a song about the love of a white-throated sparrow for a birch-tree of the North. All summer long the bird lived on the topmost branch and sang most beautifully. The season of southward journey came, but the white throated sparrow would not leave her tree. She stayed on alone, singing while the leaves turned gold and fell. She sang more faintly as the land grew white with the first snows and when she could sing no longer for the cold, she nestled down in a bare hollow of the white tree and let the driving flakes of the North cover her.

Oliver stood near the piano. Myra sang to and for him. She stood very tall and straight, her hair, loosened from its tight bands, soft around her face. Her voice thrilled out in the mate-call, grew fainter and sweeter as winter came on, grew poignant under the cold, quivered on the last note. As David Cannon ended with the fate theme of the tree, a genuine shiver went through the little group. There was no hesitation this time in the applause. They swept forward, surrounding her, begging her to sing again. But it was to Oliver that she turned.

"It pleased you? I'm glad."

David Cannon said nothing. He sat, his shoulders hunched, his fingers on the keys until she had refused to sing again.

"I didn't think you would," he said then, and abruptly left his post to go back to beer and sandwiches. Soon after he slipped out. Myra went with him to the hall, where they talked for a while in low voices. When she came back into the room she was smiling serenely.

She and Oliver were alone at last.

"You glorious creature!" he cried. "I'm so proud of you! Everyone was crazy about the way you sang." She walked slowly toward him.

"Oliver," she said, "I told David this evening that I wouldn't go to South America with him."

"You didn't!" His voice rose sharp and shocked.

She nodded, beaming almost mischievously.

"But I did, and nothing will make me change my mind."

"How could you be so impulsive, so foolish!" he cried.

She was looking at him now more soberly.

"Aren't you glad?"

"Myra, you mustn't! I'll telephone David at once.. I'll —you did this for me. I won't have it. You should have asked me——"

"It's no use; I'm not going," she said.

He dropped on the couch and hid his face in his hands.

"You're giving this up because of me."

She went to him.

"Oliver, look at me."

Slowly he raised his head.

"I don't see why——" he began, but she was so beautiful, so radiant, that he caught his breath and faltered.

She sat down beside him.

"Ah, but you will," she said. "It's very simple, dear. Even David understands."

"What does he think?"

"He thinks as I do," she said quickly. "He was quite relieved; honestly, dear. He didn't want any homesick woman spoiling his songs for him in South America. And then I suggested Frances Maury in my place. She has a lovely voice, and she'll jump at the chance."

"I've never heard her, but I'm sure she can't sing as well as you," he said, with returning gloom. "And it was only for two months."

She laughed as at an unreasonable child.

"It isn't the two months, dear. It's our whole life. There would be other partings, you see, other interests drawing me away. And if it became easier to leave you, then I should know that everything was wrong between us; but if it kept on being hard to divide myself between you and my work, then my work would suffer and so would you. Either way, it couldn't go on. I'm not big enough to do both," she said.

"I can't accept such a sacrifice."

"Don't you want me with you always?"

He seized her hands and passionately drew her close to him.

"Want you? I can tell you now. I've been jealous, terribly so, of everyone, everything that touched you."

"I knew it," she said. "That's one reason why I didn't sing well to-night. Now I'm free"—she threw her arms out with the gesture of flying—"I'm free to love just you. We'll start another life, Oliver, a life of our own. We'll be fireside people, dear, homely lovers content to sit and talk of an evening. You'll find me very valuable, really, as a partner," she said eagerly. "I've never been near enough to your work. And it's such wonderful work!" With an impulsive movement she went over and closed the piano. "I'll only open it when you ask me to," she said.

The process of elimination was simple enough. There was a touch of melancholy in Myra's measurement of relationships, in her consciousness of their frailty. People fell away easily, leaving her and Oliver to their chosen isolation. A dozen regrets or so to invitations, a week or two of evasions over the telephone, a few friends like Martigues turned away at the door when obviously she was at home, a refusal to sing at a charity concert and, most conclusive of all, David Cannon's advertised departure with another artist, and the thing was virtually done.

Then came a succession of long intimate evenings, she and Oliver left to their caprice, she and Oliver walking and driving together, wandering where their fancy took them in the springtime of city and country. She laughed sometimes at him, he seemed so dazed by the consciousness of utter possession. "You are sure you are not bored, darling?" he would often ask these first days. She could not reassure him enough; could not find ways enough to prove to him that when a woman like herself gave of body, mind, and spirit, it was a full giving. There was exquisite pain in that giving; it was almost a terrifying thing. She was a vital creature, and must spend that which was hers, wisely or foolishly. Her ceaseless energy had always before found an outlet in her work. Now her only expression lay in Oliver. Her mind, never at rest, seized upon his working life, made it hers. But she soon learned that he regarded her self-appointed post of partner with a tender condescension edged with intolerance. She learned with a tiny shock that although in matters musical he trusted absolutely to her judgment, he did not consider the feminine intellect as equal to his own. Music, she discovered, had always been defined by him as something feminine in its application to the arts.

She became gradually aware that he objected to her visits to his office. His glance did not brighten at her entrance. He was not amused as he had been at first, when she bent over the sketches or ran her slim fingers along the tracery of blue prints, daring to question them. Sometimes she had a feeling that she did not entirely know Oliver; that there were plans of his, thoughts of his, which she did not share. She had not missed these before when her own life was full. She had time now during their long hours together to observe reactions of the cause of which she knew nothing. He was absent-minded, off on a trail that led away from her.

There came a week when he allowed her the brunt of wooing; a new dress failed to bring forth the usual compliment; a question lay unanswered where in pride she left it. Then one morning with a new crisp note in his voice, he telephoned, telling her that he must meet a man at his club for dinner that evening. Mechanically she answered, dully heard his voice warm to a sweetness that should have comforted her.

"You know I wouldn't leave you unless it were important, dearest. I can't explain now, but I may have great news for you when I come home."

She hung up the receiver thoughtfully, and turned to an apartment which seemed suddenly dreary and empty. She had no purpose in her day. The twilight hour loomed in prospect an endless, dusky loneliness. For a moment she thought of ringing him up and proposing to meet him downtown for lunch; then restrained the impulse. Was she to turn into a nagging wife! She longed now for some friend with whom she could spend the day; but she could think of none. Since her marriage with Oliver she had not encouraged intimacies. On his account she had estranged the few women to whom she might now have turned. Oliver had never understood friendships among women.

The day dragged by. For the first time in months she found herself wishing that she was going out that evening. She thought almost guiltily of David Cannon and Frances Maury, imagining herself in Frances's place. She went to the piano, tried to sing, and realized with dismay that she was sadly out of practice. After all, what did it matter? she decided moodily. Oliver rarely asked her for music.

She took up a novel and dozed over it.

At eleven o'clock Oliver came home. She knew by the way he opened the front door that the news was good. She ran to meet him; her dullness vanished.

He took her by the hand and led her into the softly lit room which seemed suddenly warm again with his presence. Then he whirled her, facing him. Her smile was a happy reflection of his own brightness.

"You'll never guess what's happened," he began.

"Tell me quickly!" she begged.

He waited a moment, with an eye to dramatic effect.

"Well, then," he said proudly, "I've been appointed on a special committee of reconstruction in France. Malcolm Wild—you've heard me speak of him—came down from Washington to-day to propose it to me. There are six of us on the committee, and I'm the youngest."

"Oliver!" She put into the exclamation something of what he expected, for he seemed satisfied. He lifted his head with a young, triumphant gesture. "It is my chance to do a great and useful work," he said. "I needn't tell you what it means. I never hoped, I never dreamed of such an honour."

"I'm so proud of you!" she cried.

He hardly seemed to hear her.

"Think of it, just think of it—to be invited to go over there with five of the biggest architects here, American money backing us! We've been given a whole section to rebuild;

I forget how many villages. It's like a dream." He passed his hand over his eyes.

"France!" she heard herself saying. "But, Oliver, it's the work of months."

He nodded happily.

"That's what it is."

"France!" she murmured in a kind of ecstasy. "I'm just getting it." She clasped her hands together. "I've always wanted to be in France with you. My dear, when do we start?"

He gave her a swift, bewildered look.

"Why, Myra, didn't you understand? I can't take you right away with me. Later, of course, you'll join me. It won't be long; a few months at most."

"I'm not to go when you go?"

Her voice, low and strained, drove straight to his heart.

"Myra, I never thought—it's a man's trip just now, darling. I—couldn't take you with me," he stammered miserably. "Passports are almost impossible to get; and then conditions over there——"

She backed away from him, her arms stiff at her sides. "When were you—planning to go?"

He stared at her pitifully.

"Beloved, don't look at me that way!"

"When were you planning to go?" she repeated.

"Next week," he said in an altered voice. "I never thought you would take it this way. I never thought—it's a great chance."

"That's what I once told you," she said slowly, and turned away that he might not see her face. "Don't touch me!" she cried as he came nearer. "Don't! I've been nervous all day, and lonely." She tried to control herself, but as his arms went around her, she began to sob like a hurt child. "If you leave me, I shall die. I can't bear it. I know it's wicked of me." Her words reached him brokenly. "It's only because you're all I have. I've given up everything; and now——"

He stood very still, staring into space, his hold on her never loosening. She stumbled on, confessing what had lain hidden in her heart until this moment. She told him things she had never thought she could betray to any one—things she had never even dared formulate. When she had done, he said in a strange, gentle voice:

"I didn't know you depended so on me. But it's all right; I won't leave you, ever. It's all right. There, dear, I understand."

She struggled free from his hold, and dried her eyes with a sudden passionate gesture of scattering tears.

"You shall go," she said fiercely. "I hate myself for acting this way. It was only because——" She could get no further.

He did not attempt to touch her again. They stood facing one another, measuring their love.

"I might go," he said at last, as if to himself; "but in going I should spoil something very precious. You deny it now, but you would remember your own sacrifice. And then, of course, you would go back to your work. I should want you to. But it would never be the same again, never."

"I won't go back."

He shook his head.

"If you didn't, you would never forgive me. Every day you spent here alone and idle would break one of those fragile bonds that hold us so closely. If only you hadn't given up South America!"

"I was wrong," she said drearily.

At last he held out his arms.

"Myra," he said, "you mean more than anything else to me. This offer pleased me; I admit it. But I can work on just as well here. I have the Cromwell house, you know, and the Newburghs may build soon. Don't let's think of it again."

She held back a moment, afraid to yield; but there was no resisting her longing, and she ran to him with a little sigh, which he softly echoed as he took her and held her close.

They had vowed to live only for one another. The theme of their love was sublime enough, but the instruments were fallible. Human beings can rarely sustain a lofty note beyond the measure of a supreme moment. Emotional as she was in her gratitude, Myra would have kept on sounding that note through the days and nights. She would not allow Oliver to forget what he had given up for her sake.

More than ever she sought to associate herself with his work. He was forced to recognize her personality there. For when skilfully she led the talk on his plans, she hunted down elusive problems, grappled with them, and offered him the solutions of a sure instinct. She did not reckon with his vanity. She was too eager to make up for a lost opportunity, as she too often explained. He came gradually to brood over what he now consented to consider a sacrifice. In passing moments of irritation he even referred to it. He broke out occasionally in fits of nerves, certain that he would be humoured and petted back to the normal. He knew well how a frown dismayed her, how deep a word could strike, what tiny wounds he could inflict. It would seem sometimes as if one or the other deliberately created a short, violent scene over a trivial difference just to relieve routine. The domestic lowlands stretched beyond the eye. He missed the broken country, the unexpected dips and curves of the unknown. Not that his heart went adventuring. He was faithful in body and spirit, but there was discontent in the looks he turned on her.

One afternoon she read in the papers that David Cannon and Frances Maury were back from South America after a triumphant series of recitals. They were to give a concert the following month. Her indifference to the news, she thought drearily, was an indication of how far she had travelled away from her old life. She did not even want to see David Cannon.

It was Oliver who brought up the subject that evening.

"David's back. If you'd been with him, how excited I should have felt to-day!" he remarked. "Odd, isn't it?"

"You would have been in France," she reminded him.

They sat on in silence for a while.

He laid his book aside with a sudden brisk movement.

"Myra, why don't you sing again?"

"For you, to-night?"

"I mean professionally," he blurted out.

She drifted across the room to a shadowy corner.

"I don't know," she said rather flatly, bending over a bowl of white roses. "I suppose I don't feel like it any more. It's hard to take things up again."

He fingered his book; then, as if despite himself, he said:

"I'm afraid, dear, that we're letting ourselves grow old."

She swung sharply about, catching her breath.

"You mean I am?"

"Both of us." He was cautious, tender even, but she was not deceived. It was almost a relief that he had spoken.

"Tell me, dear," she said from her corner. "You're bored, aren't you? Oh, not with me"—she forestalled his protest—"but just plain bored. Isn't it so?" Her voice was deceptively quiet.

He stirred in his chair, fidgeted under the direct attack, and decided not to evade it.

"I think we've been buried long enough," he finally confessed. "I love our evenings together, of course; but a little change now and then might be agreeable. Perhaps it isn't a good thing for two people to be thrown entirely on each other's company. And I've been wondering, dear" —he hesitated, carefully picking his words—"I've been wondering if you would not be happier if you had other interests—interests of your own."

"Suppose I don't want any?" She did not give this out as a challenge, but he frowned a trifle impatiently.

"I can't believe it possible," he said. "Have you lost all touch with the world?"

She came slowly forward into the warm circle of light.

"I don't seem to care for people and things as I used to. Look at me. I'm not the same Myra."

She stared at him with a deep, searching expression, and what she saw drew her up with a sudden movement of decision. Her voice, when next she spoke, was lighter, more animated.

"You're right, dear. We're growing poky. I tell you what we'll do," she continued in a playful manner. Her lips smiled, and her eyes watched as she knelt beside him, her head tilted, her fingers straying over the rough surface of his coat. He never dressed for dinner in these days. "We'll give a party, shall we?" she said. "And then everyone will know that we're still—alive."

If she had wanted to test his state of mind, she could not have found a better way. Instantly he was all eagerness. Nothing would do but that they should plan the party at once, set the date, make out a list of friends to be invited.

She was ready with pad and pencil and her old address-book, which had lain for many days untouched in her desk.

"Shall we have Frances Maury?" she suggested. "She'll remind you of me as I was before we married."

"What a gorgeous little devil you were!" he murmured reminiscently.

She wished he had not said that. Yet how absurd it was to be jealous of oneself!

Well, they would entertain again, since it pleased him. But she had lost her social instinct. This party seemed a great enterprise. She had to pretend to an enthusiasm which she did not really feel. "Am I growing old?" she wondered more than once. She had to confess to a panic of shyness when she thought of herself as hostess. That was all she would be this time. Frances Maury held the rôle of prima donna.

There were no regrets to her invitations. They came, these old friends and acquaintances, with familiar voices and gestures. They seemed genuinely glad to see her, but they did not spare her. She had grown a little stouter, had she not? Ah, well happy people risked that. And they did not need to be told how happy she was. In quite an old-fashioned way, too. Myra domesticated—how quaint that was! Did she sing any more? No? What a pity!

Her rooms had lain quiet too long. So much noise deafened her. She was suddenly aware that she *had* grown stouter. Her new gown, made for the occasion, should have been more cleverly designed. Martigues as much as told her so. She had, also, lost the power of attraction. She could not hold people's attention as she used to. She was sensitively aware of how readily one and the other drifted away after a few words. Had she not been hostess, she would often have found herself alone.

David Cannon and Miss Maury came late. Frances was fond of dramatic entrances; she had the stage sense. Myra hurried forward, aware, as she did so, that her greeting held a maternal note; that Cannon was looking through and through her with those small, relentless eyes of his. Then Oliver came up, and from the corner of her eyes she saw Frances attach herself to him. She had known that would happen.

Frances Maury was indeed a lovely creature, vivid, electric, swift, and free of movement, mellow of voice. She was like a bell. Touch her and she chimed. Oliver on one side, Martigues on the other, she made her vivacious way through the room, and was soon surrounded. Very prettily she moved her court toward Myra, drew Myra into the circle of her warmth with a gracious friendliness.

Martigues, in raptures, explained that it was he who had designed the very modern jewel she wore, a moonstone set in silver. "Isn't she adorable!" he kept on repeating.

Oliver had bent over to look at this ornament and was fingering it, his dark head close to hers. She whispered to him, and he whispered back. They were already on the best of terms.

David Cannon trod up to Myra.

"What do you think of her?" he asked abruptly. "Her high notes are not as fine as yours were, but she is improving. If she doesn't fall in love, I shall make something of her." He frowned at Oliver.

Myra flushed.

"She seems very clever," was all she could manage.

"I'll make her sing," said Cannon, and elbowed a path to her side. She pouted a little, declared she could never resist him, and moved to the piano.

Myra drew a short breath. She herself had not intended to sing, but she had hoped that Oliver or David would give her a chance to refuse. She did not feel angry or envious of this girl, she was incapable of pettiness; but she felt old and dull and lonely. Her trained smile was her only shield. She held it while Frances Maury sang. She did not look at Oliver, but his delight reached her as if she had caused it. She felt him hovering close to the piano. She knew how he was standing, how his eyes were shining. She knew, because as the warm, rich voice rose up, as Cannon's strange rhythms filled the room with a wild pagan grace, she withdrew into her memory and found there all that went on. She herself was singing; she stood free and beautiful before them all; she met Oliver's eyes.

Frances sang again and again. Oliver led the applause, and Myra sat on, smiling, her steady gaze turned inward. When it was over, she took Frances by the hand, and it was as if she were thanking herself and bidding that self adieu.

Later in the evening David Cannon came up to her and gruffly suggested that she sing.

She shook her head.

"No, my good friend."

"Why not?" He stood over her, ugly, masterful.

Her smile softened to a sweet, sad flutter of lip.

"You know why."

"Nonsense!"

"You can't bully me any more, David," she told him gently. "That's the tragic part of it," she added under her breath. She liked David, but she wished he would go. She wished they would all go. It must be very late.

It was still later, however, before the last guest departed. That last guest was Frances Maury, escorted by a glum David. Oliver had kept her on.

"Myra and I always get to bed so early that it's a relief to stay up for once," he had said.

"Of course it's much more sensible to go to bed early." Miss Maury's voice did not sound as if sensible things appealed to her.

"Oliver has to be at his office so early in the morning," Myra put in almost as an apology.

"She sees to that," came from Oliver, with a humorous inflection.

Frances Maury playfully shuddered.

"Wives have too many duties for me. I shall never marry."

"Don't," said Oliver, and realized his blunder. He glanced quickly at Myra, and was relieved to observe that she did not seem troubled.

It was David, at last, who insisted on going home. Frances obeyed him with a laughing apology.

"You've given me such a good time. I forgot the hour. May I come again?"

"Indeed you must," Myra answered hospitably.

She would not leave, however, until they had promised to come to her concert. She would send them tickets. And they must have tea with her soon. Would they chaperon her once in a while? Oliver eagerly promised to be at her beck and call. He followed her out into the hall, unmindful of David's vile temper.

Myra turned slowly back into the room, noting with jaded eyes the empty beer-bottles, crusts of sandwiches, ashes on the rugs, chairs pulled crazily about. The place still resounded with chatter and song. It no longer seemed her home.

Presently Oliver joined her.

"Well, I enjoyed that," he said with a boyish ring. "Come, now, wasn't it jolly to see people again? Everyone had a wonderful time." He hummed as he walked lightly over to the table and helped himself to a cigarette.

She dropped on the couch.

"I'm a little tired."

He lit his cigarette, staring at her over the tiny flame of the match before he blew it out.

"Why, I never noticed. You do look all in."

She straightened with an effort, put a hand to her hair.

"I'm afraid I've lost the habit."

"You'll have to get it again," he said happily. "We're going to give lots of parties. It's good for my business, too. Walter Mason brought a man here to-night who is thinking of building a house on Long Island. Walter tells me he went away quite won over."

She was all interest at once.

"Why didn't you tell me? I might have made a special effort to be nice to him."

"Oh, he had a good time," he said carelessly. "I say, Myra, your friend Miss Maury is fascinating. Sings divinely." He moved over to the couch and sat on the edge of it, absent-mindedly toying with her hand.

"She's very lovely," Myra agreed.

"Why didn't you sing?" he suddenly asked.

"I didn't need to." The little smile was back, fastened to her lips. A certain unfamiliar embarrassment fell between them. She made no effort to dissipate it.

He yawned.

"Well, you should have. Heavens! it's late! Two o'clock. I'm off to bed." He kissed her lightly on the forehead.

"I'll be along in a moment," she said.

She heard him humming in the next room, heard him moving about, heard the bump of his shoes on the floor. She lay, her eyes closed. Presently she got up, went to the piano and let her fingers wander over the keys. Then she began to sing softly. Her fine critical faculties were awake. She listened while she sang—listened as if some one else would rise or fall on her verdict. There was a curious lack of vibrancy in her notes. They did not come from the heart.

Suddenly she stopped. Oliver was calling "Myra."

She thrilled with a swift hope that brought her to her feet, flushed and tremulous.

"Aren't you coming to bed soon? It's too late for music," drifted faintly querulous down the hall.

The light went out of her face.

"I'm coming." A leaden weariness was over her. Slowly she closed the piano.

He was already asleep when she tiptoed into the room. She stood a moment staring down at him.

"The worst of it is that I shall sleep, too," she thought.

BUTTERFLIES

By ROSE SIDNEY

From *The Pictorial Review*

THE wind rose in a sharp gust, rattling the insecure windows and sighing forlornly about the corners of the house. The door unlatched itself, swung inward hesitatingly, and hung wavering for a moment on its sagging hinges. A formless cloud of gray fog blew into the warm, steamy room. But whatever ghostly visitant had paused upon the threshold, he had evidently decided not to enter, for the catch snapped shut with a quick, passionate vigour. The echo of the slamming door rang eerily through the house.

Mart Brenner's wife laid down the ladle with which she had been stirring the contents of a pot that was simmering on the big, black stove, and, dragging her crippled foot behind her, she hobbled heavily to the door.

As she opened it a new horde of fog-wraiths blew in. The world was a gray, wet blanket. Not a light from the village below pierced the mist, and the lonely army of tall cedars on the black hill back of the house was hidden completely.

"Who's there?" Mrs. Brenner hailed. But her voice fell flat and muffled. Far off on the beach she could dimly hear the long wail of a fog-horn.

The faint throb of hope stilled in her breast. She had not really expected to find any one at the door unless perhaps it should be a stranger who had missed his way at the crossroads. There had been one earlier in the afternoon when the fog first came. But her husband had been at home then and his surly manner quickly cut short the stranger's attempts at friendliness. This ugly way of Mart's had isolated them from all village intercourse early in their life on Cedar Hill.

Like a buzzard's nest their home hung over the village on

the unfriendly sides of the bleak slope. Visitors were few and always reluctant, even strangers, for the village told weird tales of Mart Brenner and his kin. The village said that he—and all those who belonged to him as well—were marked for evil and disaster. Disaster had truly written itself throughout their history. His mother was mad, a tragic madness of bloody prophecies and dim fears; his only son a witless creature of eighteen, who, for all his height and bulk, spent his days catching butterflies in the woods on the hill, and his nights in laboriously pinning them, wings outspread, upon the bare walls of the house.

The room where the Brenner family lived its queer, taciturn life was tapestried in gold, the glowing tapestry of swarms of outspread yellow butterflies sweeping in gilded tides from the rough floors to the black rafters overhead.

Olga Brenner herself was no less tragic than her family. On her face, written in the acid of pain, was the history of the blows and cruelty that had warped her active body. Because of her crippled foot, her entire left side sagged hopelessly and her arm swung away, above it, like a branch from a decayed tree. But more saddening than her distorted body was the lonely soul that looked out of her tired, faded eyes.

She was essentially a village woman with a profound love of its intimacies and gossip, its fence-corner neighbourliness. The horror with which the village regarded her, as the wife of Mart Brenner, was an eating sore. It was greater than the tragedy of her poor, witless son, the hatred of old Mrs. Brenner, and her ever-present fear of Mart. She had never quite given up her unreasoning hope that some day some one might come to the house in one of Mart's long, unexplained absences and sit down and talk with her over a cup of tea. She put away the feeble hope again as she turned back into the dim room and closed the door behind her.

"Must have been that bit of wind," she meditated. "It plays queer tricks sometimes."

She went to the mantel and lighted the dull lamp. By the flicker she read the face of the clock.

"Tobey's late!" she exclaimed uneasily. Her mind never rested from its fear for Tobey. His childlike mentality made him always the same burden as when she had rocked him hour after hour, a scrawny mite of a baby on her breast.

"It's a fearful night for him to be out!" she muttered.

"Blood! Blood!" said a tragic voice from a dark corner by the stove. Barely visible in the ruddy half-dark of the room a pair of demoniac eyes met hers.

Mrs. Brenner threw her shrivelled and wizened mother-in-law an angry and contemptuous glance.

"Be still!" she commanded. "'Pears to me that's all you ever say—blood!"

The glittering eyes fell away from hers in a sullen obedience. But the tragic voice went on intoning stubbornly, "Blood on his hands! Red! Dripping! I see blood!"

Mrs. Brenner shuddered. "Seems like you could shut up a spell!" she complained.

The old woman's voice trailed into a broken and fitful whispering. Olga's commands were the only laws she knew, and she obeyed them. Mrs. Brenner went back to the stove. But her eyes kept returning to the clock and thence to the darkening square of window where the fog pressed heavily into the very room.

Out of the gray silence came a shattering sound that sent the ladle crashing out of Mrs. Brenner's nerveless hand and brought a moan from the dozing old woman! It was a scream, a long, piercing scream, so intense, so agonized that it went echoing about the room as though a disembodied spirit were shrieking under the rafters! It was a scream of terror, an innocent, a heart-broken scream!

"Tobey!" cried Mrs. Brenner, her face rigid.

The old woman began to pick at her ragged skirt, mumbling, "Blood! Blood on his hands! I see it."

"That was on the hill," said Mrs. Brenner slowly, steadying her voice.

She put her calloused hand against her lips and stood listening with agonized intentness. But now the heavy, foggy silence had fallen again. At intervals came the long, faint wail of the fog-horn. There was no other sound. Even the old woman in the shadowy corner had ceased her mouthing.

Mrs. Brenner stood motionless, with her hand against her trembling lips, her head bent forward for four of the dull intervals between the siren-call.

Then there came the sound of steps stumbling around the

house. Mrs. Brenner, with her painful hobble, reached the door before the steps paused there, and threw it open.

The feeble light fell on the round, vacant face of her son, his inevitable pasteboard box, grimy with much handling, clutched close to his big breast, and in it the soft beating and thudding of imprisoned wings.

Mrs. Brenner's voice was scarcely more than a whisper, "Tobey!" but it rose shrilly as she cried, "Where you been? What was that scream?"

Tobey stumbled past her headlong into the house, muttering, "I'm cold!"

She shut the door and followed him to the stove, where he stood shaking himself and beating at his damp clothes with clumsy fingers.

"What was that scream?" she asked him tensely. She knotted her rough fingers as she waited for his answer.

"I dunno," he grunted sullenly. His thick lower lip shoved itself forward, baby-fashion.

"Where you been?" she persisted.

As he did not answer she coaxed him, "Aw, come on, Tobey. Tell Ma. Where you been?"

"I been catching butterflies," he answered. "I got a big one this time," with an air of triumph.

"Where was you when you heard the scream?" she asked him cunningly.

He gave a slow shake of his head. "I dunno," he answered in his dull voice.

A big shiver shook him. His teeth chattered and he crouched down on his knees before the open oven-door.

"I'm cold," he complained. Mrs. Brenner came close to him and laid her hand on his wet, matted hair. "Tobey's a bad boy," she scolded. "You mustn't go out in the wet like this. Your hair's soaked."

She got down stiffly on her lame knees. "Sit down," she ordered, "and I'll take off your shoes. They're as wet as a dish-rag."

"They're full of water, too," Tobey grumbled as he sprawled on the floor, sticking one big, awkward foot into her lap. "The water in there makes me cold."

"You spoil all your pa's shoes that a-way," said Mrs. Brenner, her head bent over her task. "He told you not to go round in the wet with 'em any more. He'll give you a lashing if he comes in and sees your shoes. I'll have to try and get 'em dry before he comes home. Anyways," with a breath of deep relief, "I'm glad it ain't that red clay from the hill. That never comes off."

The boy paid no attention to her. He was investigating the contents of his box, poking a fat, dirty forefinger around among its fluttering contents. There was a flash of yellow wings, and with a crow of triumph the boy shut the lid.

"The big one's just more than flapping," he chuckled. "I had an awful hard time to catch him. I had to run and run. Look at him, Ma," the boy urged. She shook her head.

"I ain't got the time," she said, almost roughly. "I got to get these shoes off'n you afore your father gets home, Tobey, or you'll get a awful hiding. Like as not you'll get it anyways, if he's mad. Better get into bed."

"Naw!" Tobey protested. "I seen Pa already. I want my supper out here! I don't want to go to bed!"

Mrs. Brenner paused. "Where was Pa?" she asked.

But Tobey's stretch of coherent thinking was past. "I dunno!" he muttered.

Mrs. Brenner sighed. She pulled off the sticky shoes and rose stiffly.

"Go get in bed," she said.

"Aw, Ma, I want to stay up with my butterflies," the boy pleaded. Two big tears rolled down his fat cheeks. In his queer, clouded world he had learned one certain fact. He could almost always move his mother with tears.

But this time she was firm. "Do as I told you!" she ordered him. "Mebbe if you're in bed your father won't be thinking about you. And I'll try to dry these shoes afore he thinks about them." She took the grimy box from his resisting fingers, and, holding it in one hand, pulled him to his feet and pushed him off to his bedroom.

When she had closed the door on his wail she returned and laid the box on the shelf. Then she hurried to gather up the shoes. Something on her hand as she put it out for the sodden shoes caught her eye and she straightened, holding her hand up where the feeble light from the shelf caught it.

"I've cut myself," she said aloud. "There's blood on my hand. It must 'a' been on those lacings of Tobeys."

The old woman in the corner roused. "Blood!" she screeched. "Olga! Blood on his hands!"

Mrs. Brenner jumped. "You old screech-owl!" she cried. She wiped her hand quickly on her dirty apron and held it up again to see the cut. But there was no cut on her hand! Where had that blood come from? From Tobey's shoes?

And who was it that had screamed on the hill? She felt herself enwrapped in a mist of puzzling doubts.

She snatched up the shoes, searching them with agonized eyes. But the wet and pulpy mass had no stain. Only the wet sands and the slimy water-weeds of the beach clung to them.

Then where had the blood come from? It was at this instant that she became conscious of shouts on the hillside. She limped to the door and held it open a crack. Very faintly she could see the bobbing lights of torches. A voice carried down to her.

"Here's where I found his hat. That's why I turned off back of these trees. And right there I found his body!"

"Are you sure he's dead?" quavered another voice.

"Stone-dead!"

Olga Brenner shut the door. But she did not leave it immediately. She stood leaning against it, clutching the wet shoes, her staring eyes glazing.

Tobey was strong. He had flown into childish rages sometimes and had hurt her with his undisciplined strength. Where was Mart? Tobey had seen him. Perhaps they had fought. Her mind refused to go further. But little subtle undercurrents pressed in on her. Tobey hated and feared his father. And Mart was always enraged at the sight of his half-witted son. What *had* happened? And yet no matter what had occurred, Tobey had not been on the hill. His shoes bore mute testimony to that. And the scream had been on the slope. She frowned.

Her body more bent than ever, she hobbled slowly over to the stove and laid the shoes on the big shelf above it, spreading them out to the rising heat. She had barely arranged them when there was again the sound of approaching footsteps. These feet, however, did not stumble. They were heavy and certain. Mrs. Brenner snatched at the shoes, gathered them up, and turned to run. But one of the lacings caught on a nail on the shelf. She jerked desperately at the nail, and the jerking loosened her hold of both the shoes. With a clatter they fell at her feet.

In that moment Mart Brenner stood in the doorway. Poverty, avarice, and evil passions had minted Mart Brenner like a devil's coin. His shaggy head lowered in his powerful shoulders. His long arms, apelike, hung almost to his knees. Behind him the fog pressed in, and his rough, bristly hair was beaded with diamonds of moisture.

"Well?" he snapped. A sardonic smile twisted his face. "Caught you, didn't I?"

He strode forward. His wife shrank back, but even in her shivering terror she noticed, as one notices small details in a time of peril, that his shoes were caked with red mud and that his every step left a wet track on the rough floor.

"He didn't do 'em no harm," she babbled. "They're just wet. Please, Mart, they ain't harmed a mite. Just wet. That's all. Tobey went on the beach with 'em. It won't take but a little spell to dry 'em."

Her husband stooped and snatched up the shoes. She shrank into herself, waiting the inevitable torrent of his passion and the probable blow. Instead, as he stood up he was smiling. Bewildered, she stared at him in a dull silence.

"No harm done," he said, almost amiably. Shaking with relief, she stretched out her hand.

"I'll dry 'em," she said. "Give me your shoes and I'll get the mud off."

Her husband shook his head. He was still smiling.

"Don't need to dry 'em. I'll put 'em away," he replied, and, still tracking his wet mud, he went into Tobey's room.

Her fear flowed into another channel. She dreaded her husband in his black rages, but she feared him more now in his unusual amiability. Perhaps he would strike Tobey when he saw him. She strained her ears to listen.

A long silence followed his exit. But there was no outcry from Tobey, no muttering nor blows. After a few moments, moving quickly, her husband came out. She raised her heavy eyes to stare at him. He stopped and looked intently at his own muddy tracks.

"I'll get a rag and wipe up the mud right off."

As she started toward the nail where the rag hung, her husband put out a long arm and detained her. "Leave it be," he said. He smiled again.

She noticed, then, that he had removed his muddy shoes and wore the wet ones. He had fully laced them, and she had almost a compassionate moment as she thought how wet and cold his feet must be.

"You can put your feet in the oven, Mart, to dry 'em."

Close on her words she heard the sound of footsteps and a sharp knock followed on the sagging door. Mart Brenner sat down on a chair close to the stove and lifted one foot into the oven. "See who's there!" he ordered.

She opened the door and peered out. A group of men stood on the step, the faint light of the room picking out face after face that she recognized—Sheriff Munn; Jim Barker, who kept the grocery in the village; Cottrell Hampstead, who lived in the next house below them; young Dick Roamer, Munn's deputy; and several strangers.

"Well?" she asked ungraciously.

"We want to see Brenner!" one of them said.

She stepped back. "Come in," she told them. They came in, pulling off their caps, and stood huddled in a group in the centre of the room.

Her husband reluctantly stood up.

"Evening!" he said, with his unusual smile. "Bad out, ain't it?"

"Yep!" Munn replied. "Heavy fog. We're soaked."

Olga Brenner's pitiful instinct of hospitality rose in her breast.

"I got some hot soup on the stove. Set a spell and I'll dish you some," she urged.

The men looked at each other in some uncertainty. After a moment Munn said, "All right, if it ain't too much bother, Mrs. Brenner."

"Not a bit," she cried eagerly. She bustled about, searching her meagre stock of chinaware for uncracked bowls.

"Set down?" suggested Mart.

Munn sat down with a sign, and his companions followed his example. Mart resumed his position before the stove, lifting one foot into the capacious black maw of the oven.

"Must 'a' got your feet wet, Brenner?" the sheriff said with heavy jocularity.

Brenner nodded, "You bet I did," he replied. "Been down on the beach all afternoon."

"Didn't happen to hear any unusual noise down there, did you?" Munn spoke with his eyes on Mrs. Brenner, at her task of ladling out the thick soup. She paused as though transfixed, her ladle poised in the air.

Munn's eyes dropped from her face to the floor. There they became fixed on the tracks of red clay.

"No, nothin' but the sea. It must be rough outside to-night, for the bay was whinin' like a sick cat," said Mart calmly.

"Didn't hear a scream, or nothing like that, I suppose?" Munn persisted.

"Couldn't hear a thing but the water. Why?"

"Oh—nothing," said Munn.

Mrs. Brenner finished pouring out the soup and set the bowls on the table.

Chairs clattered, and soon the men were eating. Mart finished his soup before the others and sat back smacking his lips. As Munn finished the last spoonful in his bowl he pulled out a wicked-looking black pipe, crammed it full of tobacco and lighted it.

Blowing out a big blue breath of the pleasant smoke, he inquired, "Been any strangers around to-day?"

Mart scratched his head. "Yeah. A man come by early this afternoon. He was aiming to climb the hill. I told him he'd better wait till the sun come out. I don't know whether he did or not."

"See anybody later—say about half an hour ago?"

Mart shook his head. "No. I come up from the beach and I didn't pass nobody."

The sheriff pulled on his pipe for a moment. "That boy of yours still catching butterflies?" he asked presently.

Mart scowled. He swung out a long arm toward the walls with their floods of butterflies. But he did not answer.

"Uh-huh!" said Munn, following the gesture with his quiet eyes. He puffed several times before he spoke again.

"What time did you come in, Brenner, from the beach?"

Mrs. Brenner closed her hands tightly, the interlaced fingers locking themselves.

"Oh, about forty minutes ago, I guess it was. Wasn't it, Olga?" Mart said carelessly.

"Yes." Her voice was a breath.

"Was your boy out to-day?"

Mart looked at his wife. "I dunno."

Munn's glance came to the wife.

"Yes."

"How long ago did he come in?"

"About an hour ago." Her voice was flat and lifeless.

"And where had he been?" Munn's tone was gentle but insistent.

Her terrified glance sought Mart's face. "He'd been on the beach!" she said in a defiant tone.

Mart continued to look at her, but there was no expression in his face. He still wore his peculiar affable smile.

"Where did these tracks come from, on the floor?"

Swift horror fastened itself on Mrs. Brenner.

"What's that to you?" she flared.

She heard her husband's hypocritical and soothing tones. "Now, now, Olga! That ain't the way to talk to these gentlemen. Tell them who made these tracks."

"You did!" she cried. All about her she could feel the smoothness of a falling trap.

Mart smiled still more broadly.

"Look here, Olga, don't get so warm over it. You're nervous now. Tell the gentlemen who made those tracks."

She turned to Munn desperately. "What do you want to know for?" she asked him.

The sharpness of her voice roused old Mrs. Brenner, drowsing in her corner.

"Blood!" she cried suddenly. "Blood on his hands!"

In the silence that followed, the eyes of the men turned curiously toward the old woman and then sought each other with speculative stares. Mrs. Brenner, tortured by those long significant glances, said roughly. "That's Mart's mother. She ain't right! What are you bothering us for?"

Dick Roamer put out a hand to plead for her, and tapped

Munn on the arm. There was something touching in her frightened old face.

"A man—a stranger was killed up on the hill," Munn told her.

"What's that got to do with us?" she countered.

"Not a thing, Mrs. Brenner, probably, but I've just to make sure where every man in the village was this afternoon."

Mrs. Brenner's lids flickered. She felt the questioning intentness of Sheriff Munn's eyes on her stolid face and she felt that he did not miss the tremor in her eyes.

"Where was your son this afternoon?"

She smiled defiance. "I told you, on the beach."

"Whose room is that?" Munn's forefinger pointed to Tobey's closed door.

"That's Tobey's room," said his mother.

"The mud tracks go into that room. Did he make those tracks, Mrs. Brenner?"

"No! Oh, no! No!" she cried desperately. "Mart made those when he came in. He went into Tobey's room!"

"How about it, Brenner?"

Mart smiled with an indulgent air. "Heard what she said, didn't you?"

"Is it true?"

Mart smiled more broadly. "Olga'll take my hair off if I don't agree with her," he said.

"Let's see your shoes, Brenner?"

Without hesitation Mart lifted one heavy boot and then the other for Munn's inspection. The other silent men leaned forward to examine them.

"Nothing but pieces of seaweed," said Cottrell Hampstead,

Munn eyed them. Then he turned to look at the floor.

"Those are about the size of your tracks, Brenner. But they were made in red clay. How do you account for that?"

"Tobey wears my shoes,'" said Brenner.

Mrs. Brenner gasped. She advanced to Munn.

"What you asking all these questions for?" she pleaded.

Munn did not answer her. After a moment he asked. "Did you hear a scream this afternoon?"

"Yes," she answered.

"How long after the screaming did your son come in?"

She hesitated. What was the best answer to make? Bewildered, she tried to decide. "Ten minutes or so," she said.

"Just so," agreed Munn. "Brenner, when did you come in?"

A trace of Mart's sullenness rose in his face. "I told you that once," he said.

"I mean how long after Tobey?"

"I dunno," said Mart.

"How long, Mrs. Brenner?"

She hesitated again. She scented a trap. "Oh, 'bout ten to fifteen minutes, I guess," she said.

Suddenly she burst out passionately. "What you hounding us for? We don't know nothing about the man on the hill. You ain't after the rest of the folks in the village like you are after us. Why you doing it? We ain't done nothing."

Munn made a slight gesture to Roamer, who rose and went to the door, and opened it. He reached out into the darkness. Then he turned. He was holding something in his hand, but Mrs. Brenner could not see what it was.

"You chop your wood with a short, heavy axe, don't you, Brenner?" said Munn.

Brenner nodded.

"It's marked with your name, isn't it?"

Brenner nodded again.

"*Is this the axe?*"

Mrs. Brenner gave a short, sharp scream. Red and clotted, even the handle marked with bloody spots, the axe was theirs.

Brenner started to his feet. "God!" he yelped, "that's where that axe went! Tobey took it!" More calmly he proceeded, "This afternoon before I went down on the beach I thought I'd chop some wood on the hill. But the axe was gone. So after I'd looked sharp for it and couldn't find it, I gave it up."

"Tobey didn't do it!" Mrs. Brenner cried thinly. "He's as harmless as a baby! He didn't do it! He didn't do it!"

"How about those clay tracks, Mrs. Brenner? There is red clay on the hill where the man was killed. There is red clay on your floor." Munn spoke kindly.

"Mart tracked in that clay. He changed shoes with Tobey. I tell you that's the truth." She was past caring for any harm that might befall her.

Brenner smiled with a wide tolerance. "It's likely, ain't it, that I'd change into shoes as wet as these?"

"Those tracks are Mart's!" Olga reiterated hysterically.

"They lead into your son's room, Mrs. Brenner. And we find your axe not far from your door, just where the path starts for the hill." Munn's eyes were grave.

The old woman in the corner began to whimper, "Blood and trouble! Blood and trouble all my days! Red on his hands! Dripping! Olga! Blood!"

"But the road to the beach begins there too," Mrs. Brenner cried, above the cracked voice, "and Tobey saw his pa before he came home. He said he did. I tell you, Mart was on the hill. He put on Tobey's shoes. Before God I'm telling you the truth."

Dick Roamer spoke hesitatingly, "Mebbe the old woman's right, Munn. Mebbe those tracks are Brenner's."

Mrs. Brenner turned to him in wild gratitude.

"You believe me, don't you?" she cried. The tears dribbled down her face. She saw the balance turning on a hair. A moment more and it might swing back. She turned and hobbled swiftly to the shelf. Proof! More proof! She must bring more proof of Tobey's innocence!

She snatched up his box of butterflies and came back to Munn.

"This is what Tobey was doin' this afternoon!" she cried in triumph. "He was catchin' butterflies! That ain't murder, is it?"

"Nobody catches butterflies in a fog," said Munn.

"Well, Tobey did. Here they are," Mrs. Brenner held out the box. Munn took it from her shaking hand. He looked at it. After a moment he turned it over. His eyes narrowed. Mrs. Brenner turned sick. The room went swimming around before her in a bluish haze. She had forgotten the blood on her hand that she had wiped off before Mart came home. Suppose the blood had been on the box.

The sheriff opened the box. A bruised butterfly, big, golden, fluttered up out of it. Very quietly the sheriff closed the box, and turned to Mrs. Brenner.

"Call your son," he said.

"What do you want of him? Tobey ain't done nothing. What you tryin' to do to him?"

"There is blood on this box, Mrs. Brenner."

"Mebbe he cut himself." Mrs. Brenner was fighting. Her face was chalky white.

"In the box, Mrs. Brenner, *is a gold watch and chain.* The man who was killed, Mrs. Brenner, had a piece of gold chain to match this in his buttonhole. *The rest of it had been torn off.*"

Olga made no sound. Her burning eyes turned toward Mart. In them was all of a heart's anguish and despair.

"Tell 'em, Mart! Tell 'em he didn't do it!" she finally pleaded.

Mart's face was inscrutable.

Munn rose. The other men got to their feet.

"Will you get the boy or shall I?" the sheriff said directly to Mrs. Brenner.

With a rush Mrs. Brenner was on her knees before Munn, clutching him about the legs with twining arms. Tears of agony dripped over her seamed face.

"He didn't do it! Don't take him! He's my baby! He never harmed anybody! He's my baby!" Then with a shriek, as Munn unclasped her arms, "Oh, my God! My God!"

Munn helped her to her feet. "Now, now, Mrs. Brenner, don't take on so," he said awkwardly. "There ain't going to be no harm come to your boy. It's to keep him from getting into harm that I'm taking him. The village is a mite worked up over this murder and they might get kind of upset if they thought Tobey was still loose. Better go and get him, Mrs. Brenner."

As she stood unheeding, he went on, "Now, don't be afraid. Nothing'll happen to him. No jedge would sentence him like a regular criminal. The most that'll happen will be to put him some safe place where he can't do himself nor no one else any more harm."

But still Mrs. Brenner's set expression did not change.

After a moment she shook off his aiding arm and moved slowly to Tobey's door. She paused there a moment, resting her hand on the latch, her eyes searching the faces of the men in the room. With a gesture of dreary resignation she opened the door and entered, closing it behind her.

Tobey lay in his bed, asleep. His rumpled hair was still

damp from the fog. His mother stroked it softly while her slow tears dropped down on his face with its expression of peaceful childhood.

"Tobey!" she called. Her voice broke in her throat. The tears fell faster.

"Huh!" He sat up, blinking at her.

"Get into your clothes, now! Right away!" she said.

He stared at her tears. A dismal sort of foreboding seemed to seize upon him. His face began to pucker. But he crawled out of his bed and began to dress himself in his awkward fashion, casting wistful and wondering glances in her direction.

She watched him, her heart growing heavier and heavier. There was no one to protect Tobey. She could not make those strangers believe that Mart had changed shoes with Tobey. Neither could she account for the blood-stained box and the watch with its length of broken chain. But if Tobey had been on the beach he had not been on the hill, and if he hadn't been on the hill he couldn't have killed the man they claimed he had killed. Mart had been on the hill. Her head whirled. Some place fate, destiny, something had blundered. She wrung her knotted hands together.

Presently Tobey was dressed. She took him by the hand. Her own hand was shaking, and very cold and clammy. Her knees were weak as she led him toward the door. She could feel them trembling so that every step was an effort. And her hand on the knob had barely strength to turn it. But turn it she did and opened the door.

"Here he is!" she cried chokingly. She freed her hand and laid it on his shoulder.

"Look at him," she moaned. "He couldn't 'a' done it. He's—he's just a boy!"

Sheriff Munn rose. His men rose with him.

"I'm sorry, Mrs. Brenner," he said. "Terrible sorry. But you can see how it is. Things look pretty black for him."

He paused, looked around, hesitated for a moment. Finally he said, "Well, I guess we'd better be getting along."

Mrs. Brenner's hand closed with convulsive force on Tobey's shoulder.

"Tobey!" she screamed desperately, "where was you this afternoon? All afternoon?"

"On the beach," mumbled Tobey, shrinking into himself.

"Tobey! Tobey! Where'd you get blood on the box?"

He looked around. His cloudy eyes rested on her face helplessly.

"I dunno," he said.

Her teeth were chattering now; she laid her hand on his other shoulder.

"Try to remember, Tobey. Try to remember. Where'd you get the watch, the pretty watch that was in your box?"

He blinked at her.

"The pretty bright thing? Where did you get it?"

His eyes brightened. His lips trembled into a smile.

"I found it some place," he said. Eagerness to please her shone on his face.

"But where? What place?" The tears again made rivulets on her cheeks.

He shook his head. "I dunno."

Mrs. Brenner would not give up.

"You saw your pa this afternoon, Tobey?" she coached him softly.

He nodded.

"Where'd you see him?" she breathed.

He frowned. "I—saw pa——" he began, straining to pierce the cloud that covered him.

"Blood! Blood!" shrieked old Mrs. Brenner. She half rose, her head thrust forward on her shrivelled neck.

Tobey paused, confused. "I dunno," he said.

"Did he give you the pretty bright thing? And did he give you the axe—" she paused and repeated the word loudly— "the axe to bring home?"

Tobey caught at the word. "The axe?" he cried. "The axe! Ugh! It was all sticky!" He shuddered.

"Did pa give you the axe?"

But the cloud had settled. Tobey shook his head. "I dunno," he repeated his feeble denial.

Munn advanced. "No use, Mrs. Brenner, you see. Tobey, you'll have to come along with us."

Even to Tobey's brain some of the strain in the atmosphere must have penetrated, for he drew back. "Naw," he protested sulkily, "I don't want to."

Dick Roamer stepped to his side. He laid his hand on Tobey's arm. "Come along," he urged.

Mrs. Brenner gave a smothered gasp. Tobey woke to terror. He turned to run. In an instant the men surrounded him. Trapped, he stood still, his head lowered in his shoulders.

"Ma!" he screamed suddenly. "Ma! I don't want to go! Ma!"

He fell on his knees. Heavy childish sobs racked him. Deserted, terrified, he called upon the only friend he knew.

"Ma! Please, Ma!"

Munn lifted him up. Dick Roamer helped him, and between them they drew him to the door, his heart-broken calls and cries piercing every corner of the room.

They whisked him out of Mrs. Brenner's sight as quickly as they could. The other men piled out of the door, blocking the last vision of her son, but his bleating cries came shrilling back on the foggy air.

Mart closed the door. Mrs. Brenner stood where she had been when Tobey had first felt the closing of the trap and had started to run. She looked as though she might have been carved there. Her light breath seemed to do little more than lift her flat chest.

Mart turned from the door. His eyes glittered. He advanced upon her hungrily like a huge cat upon an enchanted mouse.

"So you thought you'd yelp on me, did you?" he snarled, licking his lips. "Thought you'd put me away, didn't you? Get me behind the bars, eh?"

"Blood!" moaned the old woman in the corner. "Blood!"

Mart strode to the table, pulling out from the bosom of his shirt a lumpy package wrapped in his handkerchief. He threw it down on the table. It fell heavily with a sharp ringing of coins.

"But I fooled you this time! Mart wasn't so dull this time, eh?" He turned toward her again.

Between them, disturbed in his resting-place on the table, the big bruised yellow butterfly raised himself on his sweeping wings.

Mart drew back a little. The butterfly flew toward Olga and brushed her face with a velvety softness.

Then Brenner lurched toward her, his face black with fury, his arm upraised. She stood still, looking at him with wide eyes in which a gleam of light showed.

"You devil!" she said, in a whispering voice. "You killed that man! You gave Tobey the watch and the axe! You changed shoes with him! You devil! You devil!"

He drew back for a blow. She did not move. Instead she mocked him, trying to smile.

"You whelp!" she taunted him. "Go on and hit me! I ain't running! And if you don't break me to bits I'm going to the sheriff and I'll tell him what you said to me just now. And he'll wonder how you got all that money in your pockets. He knows we're as poor as church mice. How you going to explain what you got?"

"I ain't going to be such a fool as to keep it on me!" Mart crowed with venomous mirth. "You nor the sheriff nor any one won't find it where I'm going to put it!"

The broken woman leaned forward, baiting him. The strange look of exaltation and sacrifice burned in her faded eyes. "I've got you, Mart!" she jeered. "You're going to swing yet! I'll even up with you for Tobey! You didn't think I could do it, did you? I'll show you! You're trapped, I tell you! And I done it!"

She watched Mart swing around to search the room and the blank window with apprehensive eyes. She sensed his eerie dread of the unseen. He couldn't see any one. He couldn't hear a sound. She saw that he was wet with the cold perspiration of fear. It would enrage him. She counted on that. He turned back to his wife in a white fury. She leaned toward him, inviting his blows as martyrs welcome the torch that will make their pile of fagots a blazing bier.

He struck her. Once. Twice. A rain of blows given in a blind passion that drove her to her knees, but she clung stubbornly, with rigid fingers to the table-edge. Although she was dazed she retained consciousness by a sharp effort of her failing will. She had not yet achieved that for which she was fighting.

The dull thud of the blows, the confusion, the sight of the blood drove the old woman in the corner suddenly upright on her tottering feet. Her rheumy eyes glared affrighted at the sight of the only friend she recognized in all her mad, black world lying there across the table. She stood swaying in a petrified terror for a moment. Then with a thin wail, "He's killing her!" she ran around them and gained the door.

With a mighty effort Olga Brenner lifted her head so that her face, swollen beyond recognition, was turned toward her mother-in-law. Her almost sightless eyes fastened themselves on the old woman.

"Run!" she cried. "Run to the village!"

The mad woman, obedient to that commanding voice, flung open the door and lurched over the threshold and disappeared in the fog. It came to Mart that the woman running through the night with the wail of terror was the greatest danger he would know. Olga Brenner saw his look of sick terror. He started to spring after the mad woman, forgetful of the half-conscious creature on her knees before him.

But as he turned, Olga, moved by the greatness of her passion, forced strength into her maimed body. With a straining leap she sprawled herself before him on the floor. He stumbled, caught for the table, and fell with a heavy crash, striking his head on a near-by chair. Olga raised herself on her shaking arms and looked at him. Minute after minute passed, and yet he lay still. A second long ten minutes ticked itself off on the clock, which Olga could barely see. Then Mart opened his eyes, sat up, and staggered to his feet.

Before full consciousness could come to him again, his wife crawled forward painfully and swiftly coiled herself about his legs. He struggled, still dizzy from his fall, bent over and tore at her twining arms, but the more he pulled the tighter she clung, fastening her misshapen fingers in the lacing of his shoes. He swore! And he became panic-stricken. He began to kick at her, to make lunges toward the distant door. Kicking and fighting, dragging her clinging body with him at every move, that body which drew him back one step for every two forward steps he took, at last he reached the wall. He clutched it, and as his hand slipped along trying to find a more secure hold he touched the cold iron of a long-handled pan hanging there.

With a snarl he snatched it down, raised it over his head, and brought it down upon his wife's back. Her hands opened spasmodically and fell flat at her sides. Her body rolled over, limp and broken. And a low whimper came from her bleeding lips.

Satisfied, Mart paused to regain his breath. He had no way of knowing how long this unequal fight had been going on.

But he was free. The way of escape was open. He laid his hand on the door.

There were voices. He cowered, cast hunted glances at the bloody figure on the floor, bit his knuckles in a frenzy.

As he looked, the eyes opened in his wife's swollen face, eyes aglow with triumph. "You'll swing for it, Mart!" she whispered faintly. "And the money's on the table! Tobey's saved!"

Rough hands were on the door. A flutter of breath like a sigh of relief crossed her lips and her lids dropped as the door burst open to a tide of men.

The big yellow butterfly swung low on his golden wings and came to rest on her narrow, sunken breast.

NO FLOWERS

By GORDON ARTHUR SMITH

From *Harper's Monthly Magazine*

STEVE DEMPSEY was a conspicuously ingenious chief machinist's mate—one of the most ingenious in the Naval Aviation Forces, Foreign Service, and he was ingenious not only with his hands, but with his tongue. That is why I cannot guarantee the veracity of what follows; I can but guarantee that he guaranteed it.

Steve had had a varied and highly coloured career, and I think that the war, or so much of it as he was permitted to see, seemed to him a comparatively tame affair—something all in the year's work. When he was fifteen years old he was conducting his father's public garage in a town not far from Denver; at that age he knew as much about motors as the men who built them, and he had, moreover, the invaluable knack of putting his finger immediately on a piece of erring mechanism and, with the aid of a bit of wire and a pair of pliers, setting it to rights. Given enough wire and a pair of pliers, I believe that he could have built the Eiffel Tower.

Becoming restless in the garage, he determined to make his fortune quickly, and accordingly went out prospecting in the vicinity of the Little Annie mine. He bought himself a small patch of promising ground and he and another fellow shovelled away until they had no money left. So then he took up aviation.

He was one of the pioneers of the flying-men in this country. He used to fly at country fairs in an old ramshackle bus of the Wright model—a thing of sticks and canvas and wires precariously hung together. But he flew it. And he rehabilitated his finances.

When war was declared he enlisted as a gob and was sent on sea duty. He knew, of course, nothing of sea duty, but lack of knowledge of a subject had never daunted him, for he had the faculty of learning things quickly by himself and for himself. His mechanical ability asserting itself, he was made a machinist's mate, second class, and transferred over to the Aviation. When I knew him he had proved so valuable at the various air stations that he had been advanced to chief machinist's mate and was an assistant in the Technical Division at Paris headquarters.

He was a very friendly soul, always respectful enough, even when outspoken, and no more in fear of an admiral than of —well, he would have said than of a marine. During his year of service, you see, he had absorbed most of the navy traditions. He spoke the navy speech like an old-timer, and undoubtedly amplified the regular navy vocabulary with picturesque expressions of his own. Of course he was very profane. . . .

Sunday morning at headquarters was apt to be a slack morning, with not much work to do; but in intervals of idleness one could always be certain of finding something of interest to see or hear in Steve's office. Usually he would be in front of his drafting-board working on a new design for a muffler or a machine-gun turret or a self-starter, or figuring out the possibility of flying *through* the Arc de Triomphe, which he claimed could be done with six feet to spare at each wing-tip. This, and climbing the Eiffel Tower on its girders, were two of his pet projects.

On a Sunday in August of 1918 there were assembled around his drafting-board an interested and receptive audience of four—Peters, an ensign attached to the "lighter-than-air" section; Madden, a pilot on his way up from Italy to the Northern Bombing Group; Erskine, a lieutenant in the Operations Division; and Matthews, a chief yeoman.

"Yes," Dempsey was saying, "I'm *beaucoup* sorry for these here frawgs. They're just bein' massacred—that's all it is—*massacred*. And there don't anybody take much notice, either. Say, somebody was tellin' me the other day just how many the French has lost since the beginnin' of the war. Just about one million. I wouldn't believe it, but it's straight. It was a French colonel that was tellin' me out to the Hispano factory day before yesterday, and he'd oughta know because he was through the battle of the Marne and the Soam, and everything."

"Did he tell you in French?" inquired Ensign Peters, meaningly, for Dempsey's French was admittedly limited.

"Pardon?" said Dempsey, and then, grasping the innuendo: "No, sir, he did *not*. Why, he talks English as good as you and me. That's another thing about these frawgs—they can all *parlez-vous* any language. I never yet seen a Frenchie I couldn't talk to yet."

"Did you ever see anybody you couldn't talk to yet, Steve?" suggested the chief yeoman.

"Here, you, how d'ya get that way? Who was it I seen th' other night out walking in the Boy de Bullone with a skirt? And I guess you wasn't talkin'—why, you was talkin' so fast you had to help out with your hands, just like a frawg. . . . No, as I say, I feel sorry for these French in more ways than one."

"Just how do you display that sorrow?" asked Ensign Madden.

Dempsey hesitated an instant, scratched his head, and very carefully drew a line on the tracing-paper in front of him.

"Well, sir," he said, finally, "I displayed it last Sunday."

Then he relapsed into silence, and resumed work on the drawing. But as he worked he grinned quietly—a provocative grin which inspired curiosity.

"What did you do last Sunday?" prodded Peters.

The grin widened as Steve glanced up from the board. He laid aside his instruments, tilted back in his chair, and said: "Well, it wasn't very regular, what I done last Sunday, but I'll tell you if you don't have me up before a court. . . . You remember last Sunday was a swell day? Spring in the air, I guess, and everything, and everybody was out walking like Matthews, here, with a Jane. I 'ain't got a Jane, of course——"

"What!" roared Matthews.

"I 'ain't got a Jane, of course, so I decides to take a little look around all by myself. Well, I goes down the Chomps-Eleezy feelin' pretty good and sorta peppy and lookin' for trouble. I see all them army heroes—the vets and the dentists and the S O S—each with a skirt, and I passes Matthews, here, with *his* skirt clingin' to him like a cootie."

"Cut it out, you big stiff," interposed Matthews.

"Like a cootie," continued Steve, "and I got sorta depressed. So I sez, me for the quiet, unfrequented streets over acrost the river. Well, sir, I was just passin' the Loover—that big museum, or whatever it is—when I see a hearse comin' in the opposite direction. It was a pretty sick-lookin' hearse, too. It had a coupla animals hitched to it that was probably called horses when they was young, and that didn't have a steak minoot left on 'em. But they was all covered with mangy black plumes and tassels and things—you know, the way they rig 'em up when the corpse is takin' his last drive. And there was an old bird sittin' up on the box-seat with a hat like Napoleon One.

"Well, at first it looked to me like it was just the regular frawg funeral, and I didn't pay no special attention, only I give it the salute when I got opposite. Then I see that there weren't no flowers nor tin wreaths on the coffin—except there was one little buncha pinks, and they was a pretty sad-lookin' buncha pinks, too, sir. Then I see that there weren't no procession walkin' along behind—except there was one little old woman all in black and lookin' sorta sick and scared. Yes, sir, there she was walkin' all by herself and lookin' lonelier 'n hell.

"So I sez to myself: 'It's all wrong, Steve, it's all wrong. Here's a poor dead frawg, the only son of his mother and her a widow'—that's Bible stuff, sir—'goin' out to be planted with none of the gang around. It's tough,' I sez. 'I'll say it is.' Well, I told you I didn't have nothin' much to do, so I sez, 'Laffyette, cheeri-o,' and steps up beside the old lady. That makes two mourners, anyhow.

"Well, the old lady give me the once over and seen Mr. Daniels's uniform and the rooster on my sleeve, and I guess decides that I'm eligible to the club. Anyway, she sorta nodded at me and pretty soon begun to snuffle and look for her handkerchief. It wasn't no use, though, for she didn't have any.

"Meanwhile we was crossin' one of them bridges—just crawlin' along like one of the motors had quit and the other was hittin' only on three. If we'd been in the air we'd stalled sure and gone into a tail-spin. All the time I was thinkin' how to say 'Cheer up' to the old dame in French, but all I could think of at first was 'Bravo' and '*Vous-ate tray jolee!*' Still it was sorta stupid walkin' along and no conversation, so

I guess I musta had an inspiration or something, and I sez, pointing ahead at the coffin, '*Mort avec mon Dieu.*' The old lady lost her step at that, because I suppose she was surprised by a Yank speakin' good French, most of 'em relyin', like Matthews here, on the sign language, although I'll say that Matthews gets plenty far enough with that. Why, they're four girls and a widow at home that if they knew how far Matthews was gettin' with the sign language they'd be gray-headed to-day. . . . Aw, well, Matthews, quit spoilin' this drawin'. Do you wanta get me and Admiral Sims into trouble with the department?"

"Go ahead with your funeral, Steve," said Lieutenant Erskine—"unless your power of invention has failed you."

Dempsey looked up with a hurt and innocent expression on his face.

"Oh, lootenant," he exclaimed, "what I'm tellin' is gospel. It's as true—it's as true as the communikays."

"All right," said Erskine, "issue another, then."

"Well," Steve continued, "where was I? Oh yes, we was on the bridge and I'd just told the old lady that the dead soldier was in heaven by now."

"Soldier?" repeated Erskine. "What made you believe he was a soldier?"

"Why, ain't every frawg a soldier now, sir."

"How did you know, even, that it was a male frog?"

"I'm comin' to that, sir," replied Steve. "That comes next. You see, once the old lady knew I could *parlez-vous* with the best of 'em, she continued the conversation and sez, '*Mon pover fees.*' Get that? '*Mon pover fees.*' Well, that means, translated, 'My poor son.'"

At this revelation of startling linguistic ability Steve paused to receive felicitations. When they were forthcoming he proceeded.

"So, of course, I know then that the corpse is a dead soldier, and I decides to see him through until he's made a safe landing somewhere. Well, just as we was acrost the bridge, the two ex-horses doin' fine on the down grade, I seen a marine standin' on the corner tellin' a buncha girls all about Château-Teery. Well, I thought that maybe it 'ud be a good thing if he joined the funeral, because, anyway, the girls could hear all about Château-Teery the next marine they saw. So I yell out at him: 'Hey, you! Come and join the navy and see the world!'

"Well, he looks around, and, although I guess he didn't much wanta leave them girls, he decides that he'll come and see what the big game is. So he salutes the corpse and steps in beside me and whispers, 'Say, chief, what's the idea?'

"'Whadd'ya think, you poor cheese?' I sez. 'D'ya think it's a weddin'? Get in step. We're goin' to bury a French *poiloo*.'

"'Is that so?' he sez.

"'Yes, that's so,' I sez. 'Get over acrost on the other side of the widowed mother and say somethin' cheerful to her in French—if you know any.'

"'If I know any!' sez he. 'Wasn't I at Château-Teery?'

"'Well,' I sez, 'don't tell her about that. Tell her somethin' she ain't heard already.'

"'You go to blazes!' he sez, and crosses over like I told him. And pretty soon I seen him gettin' all red and I knew he was goin' to shoot some French at the old lady, and, sure enough, out he come with, '*Madame je swee enchantay*.'

"Well, sir, I like to 've died tryin' to keep from laughin' at that, because what it means translated is, 'Madam, I'm deelighted.' Trust them marines to say the right thing at the wrong time—I'll say they do.

"By the time I get under control we're opposite the French Aviation Headquarters—you know, the Service Technique on the Bullyvard Saint-Germain. Well, there was a lot of doughboys hangin' around there wastin' time, and I see one on a motor-cycle with a sergeant sittin' in the side-car. So I step out of the ranks and sez to the sergeant, 'What ya doin'?' And he sez, 'Waitin'—but there's nobody home at all, at all.' So I sez: "Well, you and your side-car is commandeered for this funeral. We're buryin' a frawg and we need some more mourners. The old lady is his widowed mother, and the corpse, he's her only son and her a widow.' He sez: 'Shure, Oi'll come, an' Oi'll be afther gettin' some o' thim other divvles to jine. Me name is Roilly.' 'Right-o, old dear,' I sez. 'I didn't think it was Moses and Straus.'

"Well, sir, Reilly was a good scout, and inside of a minute he had six doughboys lined up behind the hearse and him bringin' up the rear in the side-car. The side-car kept back-firin', and it sounded like we was firin' salutes to the dead all the way to the park.

"I wanta tell ya, that old lady was tickled. Why, there we was already ten strong, with more to come, because I drafted three gobs at the Bullyvard Raspail. They wasn't quite sober, but I kep' my eye on 'em and they behaved fine. I sez to them: 'You drunken bums, you! You join this funeral or I'll see you're put in the brig to-night.' But to make sure they'd not disgrace Mr. Daniels's uniform I put 'em right behind the widow and the marine and me.

"Well, it appears that one of 'em talks French good—real good, I mean, sir—like a frawg waiter or a coacher."

"Or a what?" interjected Erskine.

"Or a coacher," repeated Steve, with dignity. "The fact is, he talked it so good that—well, never mind that yet. He's a smart fellow, though, Mr. Erskine, by the name of Rathbone. Well, never mind—only he's a good fellow and 'ud be pretty useful here, with his French and everything.

"Well, anyway, I begun to wonder after a while where that fellow driving the hearse was takin' us to. We'd gone out the old Bullyvard Raspail a deuce of a way, and Napoleon One showed no signs of stoppin' them horses, and I didn't see no cemetery.

"I sez to the marine, 'I guess we're not goin' to stop till we get to Château-Teery,' and he sez, 'You go to hell and stop *there*.' So I sez, 'I hope the poor old lady don't understand your English.'

"The old dame, I could see, was beginnin' to get weak in the knees and was walkin' about as unsteady as the three gobs behind us. So me and the marine each grabbed an arm and she sez, '*Mercy*,' and tried to start a smile. I guess it was pretty hard goin', because the smile didn't get far.

"Well, anyway, we kep' right on and passed that stone lion out there and went right through the gates, the boys all marchin' strong and the motor-bike makin' one hell of a noise aft. When we get through the gates I fall back and I sez to the gob, 'Rathbone,' I sez, 'ask the lady where we're headed and if she trusts the driver.' So Rathbone moves up and has quite a *parlez-vous* with her.

"'Well,' I sez, 'what's she say?'

"'She sez,' sez Rathbone, 'that we're goin' to bury him in a field out here, and that there ain't no priest will bury him and there ain't no cemetery she can bury him in.'

"'That's funny,' I sez—'too poor, I guess. Well, anyway, it's a shame—I'll say it is—it's a shame.'

"'Yes,' sez Rathbone, slowly, as if he was thinkin'—'yes, it's a damn shame!'

"And the other two gobs who wasn't as sober as Rathbone, they sez, too, 'Yes, it's a damn shame.'

"'That makes the navy unanimous,' I sez, and then I begin to work my bean. I was still workin' it and it was respondin' about as well as one of them black Kabyles that are pretendin' to help build our station at Lacanau—I was still workin' it, when the old hearse swings to the right through a gate in a stone wall and brings up short in a field. There was grass in the field and daisies and things, and a lotta tin crosses stuck on mounds that I guessed was graves. It woulda been a pretty cheerful old field, I guess, if they'd let it alone, but them tin crosses looked pretty sick and the paint was peelin' off the tin flowers that people had stuck on the graves, and I guess the head gardener wasn't much of a hand at weedin'.

"Well, anyway, we all line up in a sorta circle and every one looks pretty downhearted and the three gobs gets perfectly sober, which was a relief. Then Napoleon One climbs down from his box and says somethin' in French to the old widow and points to two birds who're diggin' a hole half-way acrost the field. Rathbone sez that he sez that that is the grave and that the two birds is the grave-diggers and pall-bearers combined.

"'They are, are they?' I sez. 'This is a military funeral, ain't it? A military funeral conducted by the navy with the army for pall-bearers. And I call on Sergeant Reilly to back me up.'

"'Shure,' sez Reilly, 'but who'll be providin' the priest?'

"Well, when he sez that my old bean give a sort of throb, and I sez: 'Don't bother your nut about the priest. He'll be forthcomin' when and if needed.'

"So, while Reilly was explainin' to his six doughboys and Rathbone was bringin' Napoleon One up to date, me and the widow and the marine goes over to superintend the two birds diggin' the grave. They was two funny-lookin' old birds, too —I'll say they was. They was about a hundred years old apiece and had long white whiskers like St. Peter, and, say, they talked a whole lot more than they dug. I guess they musta been workin' on that grave for a coupla weeks—you know, ten minutes *parlez-vous* and then one shovela dirt. Me and the marine had to grab their shovels and finish the job or there wouldn't 'a' been no funeral *that* day.

"When we get back the six doughboys is all ready to give first aid to the coffin, and Rathbone is talkin' to Napoleon One like they was brothers. So I go up to them and I sez to Rathbone:

"'Looka here, Rathbone. I'm the priest at this party. See?'

"'What's that?' sez Rathbone. 'Come again.'

"'I say I'm the priest. This dead *poiloo* ain't gotta priest nor nothin' and there's his poor mother and her a widow. So I'm that missin' priest, and I'm not too proud to perform free and gratis. Get that?'

"'Hold on, chief,' sez Rathbone. 'You ain't got nothin' to wear.'

"'Nothin' to wear!' I sez. 'You poor cheese, I'm a navy chaplain.'

"'You look more like a Charlie Chaplin,' sez Rathbone.

"I guess that bird wasn't sober yet, after all, because he thought he was funny.

"'Can the comedy,' I sez, 'and you go tell the widow that Father Dempsey, the head chaplain of the U. S. Navy, has consented to perform this afternoon. Now, get it straight, and for Gawd's sake don't go and laugh or I'll put you in the brig.'

"Well, Rathbone looks at me like I was goin' to my death.

"'Good-by, chief,' he sez. 'Wait till the admiral hears of this.'

"'Haw,' I sez—'if he does I'll get decorated.'

"Well, I give Reilly the high sign and out comes the coffin on the doughboys' shoulders. Napoleon One leads the way, and Rathbone and the widow step in after the coffin, and I see that they is talkin' together *beaucoup* earnestly.

"When we get to the grave the doughboys set down the coffin beside it and all forms in a circle with me and the widow facin' each other. And then there's an anxious silence. I'll say right here that I was the most anxious, and I was sweatin' more than I guess any chaplain oughta sweat. But, by luck, I happen to think that I have my old logarithm-book in my pocket—you know, the one that's bound in black patent-leather. Looks sorta as if it might be a prayer-book or somethin' like that. Anyway, the widow, bein' a frawg widow, I figgered how she'd think maybe it was a Yank Bible issued special to the A. E. F. and condensed like malted milk or somethin'.

"So I draw the old logarithm-book outa my coat and ease up gently to the edge of the grave. The doughboys and the gobs, all except Rathbone, who is wise, acourse, begin to nudge each other and snicker. I oughta warned 'em what was comin', but I didn't have no time, it come to me so quick. So I pretended to read from the book, and sez, in a low voice and very solemn, like I was openin' the funeral, 'If any you birds here starts laughin' I'll see him after the show and I'll knock the daylight outa him.'

"'Amen,' sez Rathbone, very piously.

"'We've come here to-day,' I sez, always like I was readin' from the book—'we've come here to-day to plant a frawg soldier who's the only son of his mother and her a widow. And she's so broke that there ain't no regular priest or no regular cemetery that 'll offer their services. So I'm the priest, and it's goin' to make a lotta difference to that poor widow's feelin's when she thinks her son's got a swell U. S. Navy priest administering the rites. Now, get that straight and don't start whinnyin' like a buncha horses and gum the game.'

"Well, I stop there for breath, and Rathbone, who's right on the job, comes across with another 'Amen,' and Reilly, who's a good Catholic, sez, '*Pax vobiscum.*'

"So that's all right, and I give her the gun and go ahead.

"'This here *poiloo*,' I sez, 'I don't know much about him, but he was a regular fellow and a good old bird and treated his mother swell and everything, and I guess if we was wise to everything he'd done we'd be proud to be here and we'd 'a' brung a lotta flowers and things. He most likely was at the battle of the Marne and the Soam and Verdun, and maybe he was at Château-Teery. Anyway, he was a grand fighter, and done his bit all the time and kep' the Huns from passin'.

And I wanta tell you that we gotta hand it to these French, because they may be little guys, but they carry the longest bayonets I ever see in any man's army.'

"'Amen,' sez all the doughboys and the gobs, except one that yells, 'Alleluia!' He musta been from the South or somewheres.

"'And so,' I sez, 'we're proud to give this frawg a good send-off, and even if we ain't got a real chaplain and the guns to fire a salute with, we're doin' the poor widow a lotta good, and that's somethin'—I'll say it is.'

"'Amen,' sez the audience.

"Then I sez, 'Glory be,' and cross myself and signal the doughboys to lower away on the coffin, and I flung a handfula dirt in on top like I see 'em do always.

"Well, the poor old widow near collapsed and Rathbone and the marine had to hold hard to keep her on her pins. But Reilly created a diversion by startin' up the motor-bike, and it back-fired like a buncha rookies tryin' to fire a volley. If we'd hadda bugle we coulda sounded taps, and the musical accompaniment woulda been complete.

"Napoleon One come up and shake hands with me like I'd won the Medeye Militaire, and, before I could side-step, the widow had her arms round my neck and was kissin' me on both cheeks. Napoleon sez it was a '*Beau geste*' which I thought meant a fine joke, and I was afraid the bird was wise, but Rathbone sez no, that it meant a swell action; and the widow sez, over and over again, '*Ces braves Americains—ces braves Americains!*' The cordial entente was pretty cordial on the whole! I'll say it was."

At this point Steve Dempsey paused and glanced about as who should say, "Are there any comments or questions?" For a while there was none forthcoming, but finally Lieutenant Erskine ventured a remark.

"This occurred last Sunday?" he inquired, mildly.

"Yes, sir," said Steve—"last Sunday."

"Um," said Erskine, and without further remarks left the office.

On his return he bore a copy of *Le Matin* in his hand. He sat down and leisurely and silently unfolded the sheet. Steve had resumed his work, but I noticed that he kept an eye on Erskine.

"I wonder," said Erskine, smoothing out the newspaper on his knees—"I wonder, Steve, if you happened to see this very interesting article."

"No, sir," said Steve. "I don't read French like I speak it."

"Well," said Erskine, "I'll translate. This paper is dated last Monday, and on page two occurs the following announcement:

"American soldiers, sailors, and marines attend funeral of notorious apache. Jean the Rat, convicted murderer and suicide, and denied the offices of the Catholic Church, is buried by stalwart Americans. Department of Foreign Affairs reluctant to file protest at present time. Strange demonstration believed to be unofficial and without U. S. government sanction, although U. S. Navy chaplain delivers eloquent oration in English."

Erskine put aside the paper in silence, and we all turned to watch Steve. He was very red, even to his ears.

"Gawd!" he spluttered. "Does it really say that, sir? Honest?"

Erskine nodded. "Yes," he said. "We'll be lucky if we avoid international complications."

"An apache murderer," Steve groaned—"and me thinkin' it was a frawg hero. Will I get a court martial for it, sir?"

"I doubt it," said Erskine, "but I don't think you'll get the Congressional Medal or the Legion of Honour, either. Maybe, though, the President, in recognition of your services toward cementing the entente, will appoint you the next ambassador to France."

"Well, anyway," said Steve, still violently red about the face and ears—"well, anyway, I don't care. Even if it weren't a first-class corpse, it was a first-class funeral."

FOOTFALLS

By WILBUR DANIEL STEELE

From *The Pictorial Review*

THIS is not an easy story; not a road for tender or for casual feet. Better the meadows. Let me warn you, it is as hard as that old man's soul and as sunless as his eyes. It has its inception in catastrophe, and its end in an act of almost incredible violence; between them it tells barely how one long blind can become also deaf and dumb.

He lived in one of those old Puritan sea towns where the strain has come down austere and moribund, so that his act would not be quite unbelievable. Except that the town is no longer Puritan and Yankee. It has been betrayed; it has become an outpost of the Portuguese islands.

This man, this blind cobbler himself, was a Portuguese from St. Michael, in the Western Islands, and his name was Boaz Negro.

He was happy. An unquenchable exuberance lived in him. When he arose in the morning he made vast, as it were uncontrollable, gestures with his stout arms. He came into his shop singing. His voice, strong and deep as the chest from which it emanated, rolled out through the doorway and along the street, and the fishermen, done with their morning work and lounging and smoking along the wharfs, said, "Boaz is to work already." Then they came up to sit in the shop.

In that town a cobbler's shop is a club. One sees the interior always dimly thronged. They sit on the benches watching the artizan at his work for hours, and they talk about everything in the world. A cobbler is known by the company he keeps.

Boaz Negro kept young company. He would have nothing to do with the old. On his own head the gray hairs set thickly.

He had a grown son. But the benches in his shop were for the lusty and valiant young, men who could spend the night drinking, and then at three o'clock in the morning turn out in the rain and dark to pull at the weirs, sing songs, buffet one another among the slippery fish in the boat's bottom, and make loud jokes about the fundamental things, love and birth and death. Harkening to their boasts and strong prophecies his breast heaved and his heart beat faster. He was a large, full-blooded fellow, fashioned for exploits; the flame in his darkness burned higher even to hear of them.

It is scarcely conceivable how Boaz Negro could have come through this much of his life still possessed of that unquenchable and priceless exuberance; how he would sing in the dawn; how, simply listening to the recital of deeds in gale or brawl, he could easily forget himself a blind man, tied to a shop and a last; easily make of himself a lusty young fellow breasting the sunlit and adventurous tide of life.

He had had a wife, whom he had loved. Fate, which had scourged him with the initial scourge of blindness, had seen fit to take his Angelina away. He had had four sons. Three, one after another, had been removed, leaving only Manuel, the youngest. Recovering slowly, with agony, from each of these recurrent blows, his unquenchable exuberance had lived. And there was another thing quite as extraordinary. He had never done anything but work, and that sort of thing may kill the flame where an abrupt catastrophe fails. Work in the dark. Work, work, work! And accompanied by privation; an almost miserly scale of personal economy. Yes, indeed, he had "skinned his fingers," especially in the earlier years. When it tells most.

How he had worked! Not alone in the daytime, but also sometimes, when orders were heavy, far into the night. It was strange for one, passing along that deserted street at midnight, to hear issuing from the black shop of Boaz Negro the rhythmical tap-tap-tap of hammer on wooden peg.

Nor was that sound all: no man in town could get far past that shop in his nocturnal wandering unobserved. No more than a dozen footfalls, and from the darkness Boaz's voice rolled forth, fraternal, stentorian, "Good night, Antone!" "Good night to you, Caleb Snow!"

To Boaz Negro it was still broad day.

Now, because of this, he was what might be called a substantial man. He owned his place, his shop, opening on the sidewalk, and behind it the dwelling-house with trellised galleries upstairs and down.

And there was always something for his son, a "piece for the pocket," a dollar-, five-, even a ten-dollar bill if he had "got to have it." Manuel was "a good boy." Boaz not only said this; he felt that he was assured of it in his understanding, to the infinite peace of his heart.

It was curious that he should be ignorant only of the one nearest to him. Not because he was physically blind. Be certain he knew more of other men and of other men's sons than they or their neighbours did. More, that is to say, of their hearts, their understandings, their idiosyncrasies, and their ultimate weight in the balance-pan of eternity.

His simple explanation of Manuel was that Manuel "wasn't too stout." To others he said this, and to himself. Manuel was not indeed too robust. How should he be vigorous when he never did anything to make him so? He never worked. Why should he work, when existence was provided for, and when there was always that "piece for the pocket"? Even a ten-dollar bill on a Saturday night! No, Manuel "wasn't too stout."

In the shop they let it go at that. The missteps and frailties of every one else in the world were canvassed there with the most shameless publicity. But Boaz Negro was a blind man, and in a sense their host. Those reckless, strong young fellows respected and loved him. It was allowed to stand at that. Manuel was "a good boy." Which did not prevent them, by the way, from joining later in the general condemnation of that father's laxity—"the ruination of the boy!"

"He should have put him to work, that's what."

"He should have said to Manuel, 'Look here, if you want a dollar, go earn it first.'"

As a matter of fact, only one man ever gave Boaz the advice direct. That was Campbell Wood. And Wood never sat in that shop.

In every small town there is one young man who is spoken of as "rising." As often as not he is not a native, but "from away."

In this town Campbell Wood was that man. He had come from another part of the state to take a place in the bank. He lived in the upper story of Boaz Negro's house, the ground floor now doing for Boaz and the meagre remnant of his family. The old woman who came in to tidy up for the cobbler looked after Wood's rooms as well.

Dealing with Wood, one had first of all the sense of his incorruptibility. A little ruthless perhaps, as if one could imagine him, in defence of his integrity, cutting off his friend, cutting off his own hand, cutting off the very stream flowing out from the wellsprings of human kindness. An exaggeration, perhaps.

He was by long odds the most eligible young man in town; good looking in a spare, ruddy, sandy-haired Scottish fashion; important, incorruptible, "rising." But he took good care of his heart. Precisely that; like a sharp-eyed duenna to his own heart. One felt that here was the man, if ever was the man, who held his destiny in his own hand. Failing, of course, some quite gratuitous and unforeseeable catastrophe.

Not that he was not human, or even incapable of laughter or passion. He was, in a way, immensely accessible. He never clapped one on the shoulder; on the other hand, he never failed to speak. Not even to Boaz.

Returning from the bank in the afternoon, he had always a word for the cobbler. Passing out again to supper at his boarding-place, he had another, about the weather, the prospects of rain. And if Boaz were at work in the dark when he returned from an evening at the Board of Trade, there was a "Good night, Mr. Negro!"

On Boaz's part, his attitude toward his lodger was curious and paradoxical. He did not pretend to anything less than reverence for the young man's position; precisely on account of that position he was conscious toward Wood of a vague distrust. This was because he was an uneducated fellow.

To the uneducated the idea of large finance is as uncomfortable as the idea of the law. It must be said for Boaz that, responsive to Wood's unfailing civility, he fought against this sensation of dim and somehow shameful distrust.

Nevertheless his whole parental soul was in arms that evening, when, returning from the bank and finding the shop empty of loungers, Wood paused a moment to propose the bit of advice already referred to.

"Haven't you ever thought of having Manuel learn the trade?"

A suspicion, a kind of premonition, lighted the fires of defence.

"Shoemaking," said Boaz, "is good enough for a blind man."

"Oh, I don't know. At least it's better than doing nothing at all."

Boaz's hammer was still. He sat silent, monumental. Outwardly. For once his unfailing response had failed him, "Manuel ain't too stout, you know." Perhaps it had become suddenly inadequate.

He hated Wood; he despised Wood; more than ever before, a hundredfold more, quite abruptly, he distrusted Wood.

How could a man say such things as Wood had said? And where Manuel himself might hear!

Where Manuel *had* heard! Boaz's other emotions—hatred and contempt and distrust—were overshadowed. Sitting in darkness, no sound had come to his ears, no footfall, no infinitesimal creaking of a floor-plank. Yet by some sixth uncanny sense of the blind he was aware that Manuel was standing in the dusk of the entry joining the shop to the house.

Boaz made a Herculean effort. The voice came out of his throat, harsh, bitter, and loud enough to have carried ten times the distance to his son's ears.

"Manuel is a good boy!"

"Yes—h'm—yes—I suppose so."

Wood shifted his weight. He seemed uncomfortable.

"Well. I'll be running along, I——ugh! Heavens!"

Something was happening. Boaz heard exclamations, breathings, the rustle of sleeve-cloth in large, frantic, and futile graspings—all without understanding. Immediately there was an impact on the floor, and with it the unmistakable clink of metal. Boaz even heard that the metal was minted, and that the coins were gold. He understood. A coin-sack, gripped not quite carefully enough for a moment under the other's overcoat, had shifted, slipped, escaped, and fallen.

And Manuel had heard!

It was a dreadful moment for Boaz, dreadful in its native sense, as full of dread. Why? It was a moment of horrid revelation, ruthless clarification. His son, his link with the departed Angelina, that "good boy"—Manuel, standing in the shadow of the entry, visible alone to the blind, had heard the clink of falling gold, and—*and Boaz wished that he had not!*

There, amazing, disconcerting, destroying, stood the sudden fact.

Sitting as impassive and monumental as ever, his strong, bleached hands at rest on his work, round drops of sweat came out on Boaz's forehead. He scarcely took the sense of what Wood was saying. Only fragments.

"Government money, understand—for the breakwater workings—huge—too many people know here, everywhere —don't trust the safe—tin safe—'Noah's Ark'—give you my word—Heavens, no!"

It boiled down to this—the money, more money than was good for that antiquated "Noah's Ark" at the bank—and whose contemplated sojourn there overnight was public to too many minds—in short, Wood was not only incorruptible, he was canny. To what one of those minds, now, would it occur that he should take away that money bodily, under casual cover of his coat, to his own lodgings behind the cobbler-shop of Boaz Negro? For this one, this important night!

He was sorry the coin-sack had slipped, because he did not like to have the responsibility of secret sharer cast upon any one, even upon Boaz, even by accident. On the other hand, how tremendously fortunate that it had been Boaz and not another. So far as that went, Wood had no more anxiety now than before. One incorruptible knows another.

"I'd trust you, Mr. Negro" (that was one of the fragments which came and stuck in the cobbler's brain), "as far as I would myself. As long as it's only you. I'm just going up here and throw it under the bed. Oh, yes, certainly."

Boaz ate no supper. For the first time in his life food was dry in his gullet. Even under those other successive crushing blows of Fate the full and generous habit of his functionings had carried on unabated; he had always eaten what was set before him. To-night, over his untouched plate, he watched Manuel with his sightless eyes, keeping track of his every mouthful, word, intonation, breath. What profit he expected to extract from this catlike surveillance it is impossible to say.

When they arose from the supper-table Boaz made another Herculean effort. "Manuel, you're a good boy!"

The formula had a quality of appeal, of despair, and of command.

"Manuel, you should be short of money, maybe. Look, what's this? A tenner? Well, there's a piece for the pocket; go and enjoy yourself."

He would have been frightened had Manuel, upsetting tradition, declined the offering. With the morbid contrariness of the human imagination, the boy's avid grasping gave him no comfort.

He went out into the shop, where it was already dark, drew to him his last, his tools, mallets, cutters, pegs, leather. And having prepared to work, he remained idle. He found himself listening.

It has been observed that the large phenomena of sunlight and darkness were nothing to Boaz Negro. A busy night was broad day. Yet there was a difference; he knew it with the blind man's eyes, the ears.

Day was a vast confusion, or rather a wide fabric, of sounds; great and little sounds all woven together, voices, footfalls, wheels, far-off whistles and foghorns, flies buzzing in the sun. Night was another thing. Still there were voices and footfalls, but rarer, emerging from the large, pure body of silence as definite, surprising, and yet familiar entities.

To-night there was an easterly wind, coming off the water and carrying the sound of waves. So far as other fugitive sounds were concerned it was the same as silence. The wind made little difference to the ears. It nullified, from one direction at least, the other two visual processes of the blind, the sense of touch and the sense of smell. It blew away from the shop, toward the living-house.

As has been said, Boaz found himself listening, scrutinizing with an extraordinary attention, this immense background of sound. He heard footfalls. The story of that night was written, for him, in footfalls.

He heard them moving about the house, the lower floor, prowling here, there, halting for long spaces, advancing, retreating softly on the planks. About this aimless, interminable perambulation there was something to twist the nerves, something led and at the same time driven like a succession of frail and indecisive charges.

Boaz lifted himself from his chair. All his impulse called him to make a stir, join battle, cast in the breach the reenforcement of his presence, authority, good will. He sank back again; his hands fell down. The curious impotence of the spectator held him.

He heard footfalls, too, on the upper floor, a little fainter, borne to the inner rather than the outer ear, along the solid causeway of partitions and floor, the legs of his chair, the bony framework of his body. Very faint indeed. Sinking back easily into the background of the wind. They, too, came and went, this room, that, to the passage, the stair-head, and away. About them too there was the same quality of being led and at the same time of being driven.

Time went by. In his darkness it seemed to Boaz that hours must have passed. He heard voices. Together with the footfalls, that abrupt, brief, and (in view of Wood's position) astounding interchange of sentences made up his history of the night. Wood must have opened the door at the head of the stair; by the sound of his voice he would be standing there, peering below perhaps; perhaps listening.

"What's wrong down there?" he called. "Why don't you go to bed?"

After a moment, came Manuel's voice, "Ain't sleepy."

"Neither am I. Look here, do you like to play cards?"

"What kind? Euchre! I like euchre all right. Or pitch."

"Well, what would you say to coming up and having a game of euchre then, Manuel? If you can't sleep?"

"That'd be all right."

The lower footfalls ascended to join the footfalls on the upper floor. There was the sound of a door closing.

Boaz sat still. In the gloom he might have been taken for a piece of furniture, of machinery, an extraordinary lay figure, perhaps, for the trying on of the boots he made. He seemed scarcely to breathe, only the sweat starting from his brow giving him an aspect of life.

He ought to have run, and leaped up that inner stair and pounded with his fists on that door. He seemed unable to move. At rare intervals feet passed on the sidewalk outside, just at his elbow, so to say, and yet somehow, to-night, immeasurably far away. Beyond the orbit of the moon. He heard Rugg, the policeman, noting the silence of the shop, muttering, "Boaz is to bed to-night," as he passed.

The wind increased. It poured against the shop with its deep, continuous sound of a river. Submerged in its body, Boaz caught the note of the town bell striking midnight.

Once more, after a long time, he heard footfalls. He heard them coming around the corner of the shop from the house, footfalls half swallowed by the wind, passing discreetly, without haste, retreating, merging step by step with the huge, incessant background of the wind.

Boaz's muscles tightened all over him. He had the impulse to start up, to fling open the door, shout into the night, "What are you doing? Stop there! Say! What are you doing and where are you going?"

And as before, the curious impotence of the spectator held him motionless. He had not stirred in his chair. And those footfalls, upon which hinged, as it were, that momentous decade of his life, were gone.

There was nothing to listen for now. Yet he continued to listen. Once or twice, half arousing himself, he drew toward him his unfinished work. And then relapsed into immobility.

As has been said, the wind, making little difference to the ears, made all the difference in the world with the sense of feeling and the sense of smell. From the one important direction of the house. That is how it could come about that Boaz Negro could sit, waiting and listening to nothing in the shop and remain ignorant of disaster until the alarm had gone away and come back again, pounding, shouting, clanging.

"*Fire!*" he heard them bawling in the street. "*Fire! Fire!*"

Only slowly did he understand that the fire was in his own house.

There is nothing stiller in the world than the skeleton of a house in the dawn after a fire. It is as if everything living, positive, violent, had been completely drained in the one flaming act of violence, leaving nothing but negation till the end of time. It is worse than a tomb. A monstrous stillness! Even the footfalls of the searchers can not disturb it, for they are separate and superficial. In its presence they are almost frivolous.

Half an hour after dawn the searchers found the body, if what was left from that consuming ordeal might be called a body. The discovery came as a shock. It seemed incredible that the occupant of that house, no cripple or invalid but an able man in the prime of youth, should not have awakened and made good his escape. It was the upper floor which had caught; the stairs had stood to the last. It was beyond calculation. Even if he had been asleep!

And he had not been asleep. This second and infinitely more appalling discovery began to be known. Slowly. By a hint, a breath of rumour here; there an allusion, half taken back. The man, whose incinerated body still lay curled in its bed of cinders, had been dressed at the moment of disaster; even to the watch, the cuff-buttons, the studs, the very scarf-pin. Fully clothed to the last detail, precisely as those who had dealings at the bank might have seen Campbell Wood any week-day morning for the past eight months. A man does not sleep with his clothes on. The skull of the man had been broken, as if with a blunt instrument of iron. On the charred lacework of the floor lay the leg of an old andiron with which Boaz Negro and his Angelina had set up housekeeping in that new house.

It needed only Mr. Asa Whitelaw, coming up the street from that gaping "Noah's Ark" at the bank, to round out the scandalous circle of circumstance.

"Where is Manuel?"

Boaz Negro still sat in his shop, impassive, monumental, his thick, hairy arms resting on the arms of his chair. The tools and materials of his work remained scattered about him, as his irresolute gathering of the night before had left them. Into his eyes no change could come. He had lost his house, the visible monument of all those years of "skinning his fingers." It would seem that he had lost his son. And he had lost something incalculably precious—that hitherto unquenchable exuberance of the man.

"Where is Manuel?"

When he spoke his voice was unaccented and stale, like the voice of a man already dead.

"Yes, where is Manuel?"

He had answered them with their own question.

"When did you last see him?"

Neither he nor they seemed to take note of that profound irony.

"At supper."

"Tell us, Boaz; you knew about this money?"

The cobbler nodded his head.

"And did Manuel?"

He might have taken sanctuary in a legal doubt. How did he know what Manuel knew? Precisely! As before, he nodded his head.

"After supper, Boaz, you were in the shop? But you heard something?"

He went on to tell them what he had heard: the footfalls, below and above, the extraordinary conversation which had broken for a moment the silence of the inner hall. The account was bare, the phrases monosyllabic. He reported only what had been registered on the sensitive tympanums of his ears, to the last whisper of footfalls stealing past the dark wall of the shop. Of all the formless tangle of thoughts, suspicions, interpretations, and the special and personal knowledge given to the blind which moved in his brain, he said nothing.

He shut his lips there. He felt himself on the defensive. Just as he distrusted the higher ramifications of finance (his house had gone down uninsured), so before the rites and processes of that inscrutable creature, the Law, he felt himself menaced by the invisible and the unknown, helpless, oppressed; in an abject sense, skeptical.

"Keep clear of the Law!" they had told him in his youth. The monster his imagination had summoned up then still stood beside him in his age.

Having exhausted his monosyllabic and superficial evidence, they could move him no farther. He became deaf and dumb. He sat before them, an image cast in some immensely heavy stuff, inanimate. His lack of visible emotion impressed them. Remembering his exuberance, it was only the stranger to see him unmoving and unmoved. Only once did they catch sight of something beyond. As they were preparing to leave he opened his mouth. What he said was like a swan-song to the years of his exuberant happiness. Even now there was no colour of expression in his words, which sounded mechanical.

"Now I have lost everything. My house. My last son. Even my honour. You would not think I would like to live. But I go to live. I go to work. That *cachorra*, one day he shall come back again, in the dark night, to have a look. I shall go to show you all. That *cachorra!*"

(And from that time on, it was noted, he never referred to the fugitive by any other name than *cachorra*, which is a kind of dog. "That *cachorra!*" As if he had forfeited the relationship not only of the family, but of the very genus, the very race! "That *cachorra!*")

He pronounced this resolution without passion. When they assured him that the culprit would come back again indeed, much sooner than he expected, "with a rope around his neck," he shook his head slowly.

"No, you shall not catch that *cachorra* now. But one day——"

There was something about its very colourlessness which made it sound oracular. It was at least prophetic. They searched, laid their traps, proceeded with all their placards, descriptions, rewards, clues, trails. But on Manuel Negro they never laid their hands.

Months passed and became years. Boaz Negro did not rebuild his house. He might have done so, out of his earnings, for upon himself he spent scarcely anything, reverting to his old habit of an almost miserly economy. Yet perhaps it would have been harder after all. For his earnings were less and less. In that town a cobbler who sits in an empty shop is apt to want for trade. Folk take their boots to mend where they take their bodies to rest and their minds to be edified.

No longer did the walls of Boaz's shop resound to the boastful recollections of young men. Boaz had changed. He had become not only different, but opposite. A metaphor will do best. The spirit of Boaz Negro had been a meadowed hillside giving upon the open sea, the sun, the warm, wild winds from beyond the blue horizon. And covered with flowers, always hungry and thirsty for the sun and the fabulous wind and bright showers of rain. It had become an entrenched camp, lying silent, sullen, verdureless, under a gray sky. He stood solitary against the world. His approaches were closed. He was blind, and he was also deaf and dumb.

Against that what can young fellows do who wish for nothing but to rest themselves and talk about their friends and enemies? They had come and they had tried. They had raised their voices even higher than before. Their boasts had grown louder, more presumptuous, more preposterous, until, before the cold separation of that unmoving and as if contemptuous presence in the cobbler's chair, they burst of their own air, like toy balloons. And they went and left Boaz alone.

There was another thing which served, if not to keep them away, at least not to entice them back. That was the aspect of the place. It was not cheerful. It invited no one. In its way that fire-bitten ruin grew to be almost as great a scandal as the act itself had been. It was plainly an eyesore. A valuable property, on the town's main thoroughfare—and an eyesore! The neighbouring owners protested.

Their protestations might as well have gone against a stone wall. That man was deaf and dumb. He had become, in a way, a kind of vegetable, for the quality of a vegetable is that, while it is endowed with life, it remains fixed in one spot. For years Boaz was scarcely seen to move foot out of that shop that was left him, a small square, blistered promontory on the shores of ruin.

He must indeed have carried out some rudimentary sort of domestic programme under the débris at the rear (he certainly did not sleep or eat in the shop). One or two lower rooms were left fairly intact. The outward aspect of the place was formless; it grew to be no more than a mound in time; the charred timbers, one or two still standing, lean and naked against the sky, lost their blackness and faded to a silvery gray. It would have seemed strange, had they not grown accustomed to the thought, to imagine that blind man, like a mole, or some slow slug, turning himself mysteriously in the bowels of that gray mound—that time-silvered "eye-sore."

When they saw him, however, he was in the shop. They opened the door to take in their work (when other cobblers turned them off), and they saw him seated in his chair in the half darkness, his whole person, legs, torso, neck, head, as motionless as the vegetable of which we have spoken—only his hands and his bare arms endowed with visible life. The gloom had bleached the skin to the colour of damp ivory, and against the background of his immobility they moved with a certain amazing monstrousness, interminably. No, they were never still. One wondered what they could be at. Surely he could not have had enough work now to keep those insatiable hands so monstrously in motion. Even far into the night. Tap-tap-tap! Blows continuous and powerful. On what? On nothing? On the bare iron last? And for what purpose? To what conceivable end?

Well, one could imagine those arms, growing paler, also growing thicker and more formidable with that unceasing labour; the muscles feeding themselves omnivorously on their own waste, the cords toughening, the bone-tissues re-vitalizing themselves without end. One could imagine the whole aspiration of that mute and motionless man pouring itself out into those pallid arms, and the arms taking it up with a kind of blind greed. Storing it up. Against a day!

"That *cachorra!* One day——"

What were the thoughts of the man? What moved within that motionless cranium covered with long hair? Who can say? Behind everything, of course, stood that bitterness against the world—the blind world—blinder than he would ever be. And against "that *cachorra*." But this was no longer a thought; it was the man.

Just as all muscular aspiration flowed into his arms, so all the energies of his senses turned to his ears. The man had become, you might say, two arms and two ears. Can you imagine a man listening, intently, through the waking hours of nine years?

Listening to footfalls. Marking with a special emphasis of concentration the beginning, rise, full passage, falling away, and dying of all the footfalls. By day, by night, winter and summer and winter again. Unravelling the skein of footfalls passing up and down the street!

For three years he wondered when they would come. For the next three years he wondered if they would ever come. It was during the last three that a doubt began to trouble him. It gnawed at his huge moral strength. Like a hidden seepage of water, it undermined (in anticipation) his terrible resolution. It was a sign perhaps of age, a slipping away of the reckless infallibility of youth.

Supposing, after all, that his ears should fail him. Supposing they were capable of being tricked, without his being able to know it. Supposing that that *cachorra* should come and go, and he, Boaz, living in some vast delusion, some unrealized distortion of memory, should let him pass unknown. Supposing precisely this thing had already happened!

Or the other way around. What if he should hear the footfalls coming, even into the very shop itself? What if he should be as sure of them as of his own soul? What, then, if he should strike? And what then, if it were not that *cachorra* after all? How many tens and hundreds of millions of people were there in the world? Was it possible for them all to have footfalls distinct and different?

Then they would take him and hang him. And that *cachorra* might then come and go at his own will, undisturbed.

As he sat there sometimes the sweat rolled down his nose, cold as rain.

Supposing!

Sometimes, quite suddenly, in broad day, in the booming silence of the night, he would start. Not outwardly. But beneath the pale integument of his skin all his muscles tightened and his nerves sang. His breathing stopped. It seemed almost as if his heart stopped.

Was that it? Were those the feet, there, emerging faintly from the distance? Yes, there was something about them. Yes! Memory was in travail. Yes, yes, yes! No! How could he be sure? Ice ran down into his empty eyes. The footfalls were already passing. They were gone, swallowed up already by time and space. Had that been that *cachorra?*

Nothing in his life had been so hard to meet as this insidious drain of distrust in his own powers; this sense of a traitor within the walls. His iron-gray hair had turned white. It was always this now, from the beginning of the day to the end of the night: how was he to know? How was he to be inevitably, unshakably, sure?

Curiously, after all this purgatory of doubts, he did know them. For a moment at least, when he had heard them, he was unshakably sure.

It was on an evening of the winter holidays, the Portuguese festival of *Menin' Jesus*. Christ was born again in a hundred mangers on a hundred tiny altars; there was cake and wine; songs went shouting by to the accompaniment of mandolins and tramping feet. The wind blew cold under a clear sky. In all the houses there were lights; even in Boaz Negro's shop a lamp was lit just now, for a man had been in for a pair of boots which Boaz had patched. The man had gone out again. Boaz was thinking of blowing out the light. It meant nothing to him.

He leaned forward, judging the position of the lamp-chimney by the heat on his face, and puffed out his cheeks to blow. Then his cheeks collapsed suddenly, and he sat back again.

It was not odd that he had failed to hear the footfalls until they were actually within the door. A crowd of merry-makers was passing just then; their songs and tramping almost shook the shop.

Boaz sat back. Beneath his passive exterior his nerves thrummed; his muscles had grown as hard as wood. Yes! Yes! But no! He had heard nothing; no more than a single step, a single foot-pressure on the planks within the door. Dear God! He could not tell!

Going through the pain of an enormous effort, he opened his lips.

"What can I do for you?"

"Well, I—I don't know. To tell the truth——"

The voice was unfamiliar, but it might be assumed. Boaz held himself. His face remained blank, interrogating, slightly helpless.

"I am a little deaf," he said. "Come nearer."

The footfalls came half way across the intervening floor, and there appeared to hesitate. The voice, too, had a note of uncertainty.

"I was just looking around. I have a pair of—well, you mend shoes?"

Boaz nodded his head. It was not in response to the words, for they meant nothing. What he had heard was the footfalls on the floor.

Now he was sure. As has been said, for a moment at least after he had heard them he was unshakably sure. The congestion of his muscles had passed. He was at peace.

The voice became audible once more. Before the massive preoccupation of the blind man it became still less certain of itself.

"Well, I haven't got the shoes with me. I was—just looking around."

It was amazing to Boaz, this miraculous sensation of peace.

"Wait!" Then, bending his head as if listening to the winter wind, "It's cold to-night. You've left the door open. But wait!" Leaning down, his hand fell on a rope's end hanging by the chair. The gesture was one continuous, undeviating movement of the hand. No hesitation. No groping. How many hundreds, how many thousands of times, had his hand schooled itself in that gesture!

A single strong pull. With a little *bang* the front door had swung to and latched itself. Not only the front door. The other door, leading to the rear, had closed too and latched itself with a little *bang*. And leaning forward from his chair, Boaz blew out the light.

There was not a sound in the shop. Outside, feet continued to go by, ringing on the frozen road; voices were lifted; the wind hustled about the corners of the wooden shell with a continuous, shrill note of whistling. All of this outside, as on another planet. Within the blackness of the shop the complete silence persisted,

Boaz listened. Sitting on the edge of his chair, half-crouching, his head, with its long, unkempt, white hair, bent slightly to one side, he concentrated upon this chambered silence the full powers of his senses. He hardly breathed.

The other person in that room could not be breathing at all, it seemed.

No, there was not a breath, not the stirring of a sole on wood, not the infinitesimal rustle of any fabric. It was as if in this utter stoppage of sound, even the blood had ceased to flow in the veins and arteries of that man, who was like a rat caught in a trap.

It was appalling even to Boaz; even to the cat. Listening became more than a labour. He began to have to fight against a growing impulse to shout out loud, to leap, sprawl forward without aim in that unstirred darkness—do something. Sweat rolled down from behind his ears, into his shirt-collar. He gripped the chair-arms. To keep quiet he sank his teeth into his lower lip. He would not! He would not!

And of a sudden he heard before him, in the centre of the room, an outburst of breath, an outrush from lungs in the extremity of pain, thick, laborious, fearful. A coughing up of dammed air.

Pushing himself from the arms of the chair, Boaz leaped.

His fingers, passing swiftly through the air, closed on something. It was a sheaf of hair, bristly and thick. It was a man's beard.

On the road outside, up and down the street for a hundred yards, merry-making people turned to look at one another. With an abrupt cessation of laughter, of speech. Inquiringly. Even with an unconscious dilation of the pupils of their eyes.

"What was that?"

There had been a scream. There could be no doubt of that. A single, long-drawn note. Immensely high-pitched. Not as if it were human.

"God's sake! What was that? Where'd it come from?"

Those nearest said it came from the cobbler-shop of Boaz Negro.

They went and tried the door. It was closed; even locked, as if for the night. There was no light behind the window-shade. But Boaz would not have a light. They beat on the door. No answer.

But from where, then, had that prolonged, as if animal, note come?

They ran about, penetrating into the side lanes, interrogating, prying. Coming back at last, inevitably, to the neighbourhood of Boaz Negro's shop.

The body lay on the floor at Boaz's feet, where it had tumbled down slowly after a moment from the spasmodic embrace of his arms; those ivory-coloured arms which had beaten so long upon the bare iron surface of a last. Blows continuous and powerful. It seemed incredible. They were so weak now. They could not have lifted the hammer now.

But that beard! That bristly, thick, square beard of a stranger!

His hands remembered it. Standing with his shoulders fallen forward and his weak arms hanging down, Boaz began to shiver. The whole thing was incredible. What was on the floor there, upheld in the vast gulf of darkness, he could not see. Neither could he hear it; smell it. Nor (if he did not move his foot) could he feel it. What he did not hear, smell, or touch did not exist. It was not there. Incredible!

But that beard! All the accumulated doubtings of those years fell down upon him. After all, the thing he had been so fearful of in his weak imaginings had happened. He had killed a stranger. He, Boaz Negro, had murdered an innocent man!

And all on account of that beard. His deep panic made him light-headed. He began to confuse cause and effect. If it were not for that beard, it would have been that *cachorra.*

On this basis he began to reason with a crazy directness. And to act He went and pried open the door into the entry. From a shelf he took down his razor. A big, heavy-heeled strop. His hands began to hurry. And the mug, half full of soap. And water. It would have to be cold water. But after all, he thought (light-headedly), at this time of night——

Outside, they were at the shop again. The crowd's habit is to forget a thing quickly, once it is out of sight and hearing. But there had been something about that solitary cry which continued to bother them, even in memory. Where had it been? Where had it come from? And those who had stood nearest the cobbler-shop were heard again. They were certain now, dead certain. They could swear!

In the end they broke down the door.

If Boaz heard them he gave no sign. An absorption as complete as it was monstrous wrapped him. Kneeling in the glare of the lantern they had brought, as impervious as his own shadow sprawling behind him, he continued to shave the dead man on the floor.

No one touched him. Their minds and imaginations were arrested by the gigantic proportions of the act. The unfathomable presumption of the act. As throwing murder in their faces to the tune of a jig in a barber-shop. It is a fact that none of them so much as thought of touching him. No less than all of them, together with all other men, shorn of their imaginations—that is to say, the expressionless and imperturbable creature of the Law—would be sufficient to touch that ghastly man.

On the other hand, they could not leave him alone. They could not go away. They watched. They saw the damp, lather-soaked beard of that victimized stranger falling away, stroke by stroke of the flashing, heavy razor. The dead denuded by the blind!

It was seen that Boaz was about to speak. It was something important he was about to utter; something, one would say, fatal. The words would not come all at once. They swelled his cheeks out. His razor was arrested. Lifting his face, he encircled the watchers with a gaze at once of imploration and of command. As if he could see them. As if he could read his answer in the expressions of their faces.

"Tell me one thing now. Is it that *cachorra?*"

For the first time those men in the room made sounds. They shuffled their feet. It was as if an uncontrollable impulse to ejaculation, laughter, derision, forbidden by the presence of death, had gone down into their boot-soles.

"Manuel?" one of them said. "You mean *Manuel?*"

Boaz laid the razor down on the floor beside its work. He got up from his knees slowly, as if his joints hurt. He sat down in his chair, rested his hands on the arms, and once more encircled the company with his sightless gaze.

"Not Manuel. Manuel was a good boy. But tell me now, is it that *cachorra?*"

Here was something out of their calculations; something for them, mentally, to chew on. Mystification is a good thing sometimes. It gives the brain a fillip, stirs memory, puts the gears of imagination in mesh. One man, an old, tobacco-chewing fellow, began to stare harder at the face on the floor. Something moved in his intellect.

"No, but look here now, by God——"

He had even stopped chewing. But he was forestalled by another.

"Say now, if it don't look like that fellow Wood, himself. The bank fellow—that was burned—remember? Himself."

"That *cachorra* was not burned. Not that Wood. You darned fool!"

Boaz spoke from his chair. They hardly knew his voice, emerging from its long silence; it was so didactic and arid.

"That *cachorra* was not burned. It was my boy that was burned. It was that *cachorra* called my boy upstairs. That *cachorra* killed my boy. That *cachorra* put his clothes on my boy, and he set my house on fire. I knew that all the time. Because when I heard those feet come out of my house and go away, I knew they were the feet of that *cachorra* from the bank. I did not know where he was going to. Something said to me—you better ask him where he is going to. But then I said, you are foolish. He had the money from the bank. I did not know. And then my house was on fire. No, it was not my boy that went away; it was that *cachorra* all the time. You darned fools! Did you think I was waiting for my own boy?

"Now I show you all," he said at the end. "And now I can get hanged."

No one ever touched Boaz Negro for that murder. For murder it was in the eye and letter of the Law. The Law in a small town is sometimes a curious creature; it is sometimes blind only in one eye.

Their minds and imaginations in that town were arrested by the romantic proportions of the act. Simply, no one took it up. I believe the man, Wood, was understood to have died of heart-failure.

When they asked Boaz why he had not told what he knew as to the identity of that fugitive in the night, he seemed to find it hard to say exactly. How could a man of no education define for them his own but half-denied misgivings about the

Law, his sense of oppression, constraint and awe, of being on the defensive, even, in an abject way, his skepticism? About his wanting, come what might, to "keep clear of the Law"?

He did say this, "You would have laughed at me."

And this, "If I told folk it was Wood went away, then I say he would not dare come back again."

That was the last. Very shortly he began to refuse to talk about the thing at all. The act was completed. Like the creature of fable, it had consumed itself. Out of that old man's consciousness it had departed. Amazingly. Like a dream dreamed out.

Slowly at first, in a makeshift, piece-at-a-time, poor man's way, Boaz commenced to rebuild his house. That "eye-sore" vanished.

And slowly at first, like the miracle of a green shoot pressing out from the dead earth, that priceless and unquenchable exuberance of the man was seen returning. Unquenchable, after all.

THE LAST ROOM OF ALL

By STEPHEN FRENCH WHITMAN

From *Harper's Monthly Magazine*

IN THOSE days all Italy was in turmoil and Lombardy lay covered with blood and fire. The emperor, the second Frederick of Swabia, was out to conquer once for all. His man Salinguerra held the town of Ferrara. The Marquis Azzo, being driven forth, could slake his rage only on such outlying castles as favoured the imperial cause.

Of these castles the Marquis Azzo himself sacked and burned many. But against the castle of Grangioia, remote in the hills, he sent his captain, Lapo Cercamorte.

This Lapo Cercamorte was nearly forty years old, a warrior from boyhood, uncouth, barbaric, ferocious. One could think of no current danger that he had not encountered, no horror that he had not witnessed. His gaunt face was dull red, as if baked by the heat of blazing towns. His coarse black hair had been thinned by the friction of his helmet. His nose was broken, his arms and legs were covered with scars, and under his chin ran a seam made by a woman who had tried to cut off his head while he lay asleep. From this wound Lapo Cercamorte's voice was husky and uncertain.

With a hundred men at his back he rode by night to Grangioia Castle. As day was breaking, by a clever bit of stratagem he rushed the gate.

Then in that towering, thick-walled fortress, which had suddenly become a trap, sounded the screaming of women, the boom of yielding doors, the clang of steel on black staircases, the battlecries, wild songs, and laughter of Lapo Cercamorte's soldiers.

He found the family at bay in their hall, the father and his three sons naked except for the shirts of mail that they had hastily slipped on. Behind these four huddled the Grangioia women and children, for the most part pallid from fury rather than from fear, silently awaiting the end.

However, Cercamorte's purpose was not to destroy this clan, but to force it into submission to his marquis. So, when he had persuaded them to throw down their swords, he put off his flat-topped helmet and seated himself with the Grangioia men.

A bargain ensued; he gave them their lives in exchange for their allegiance. And it would have ended there had not the sun, reaching in through a casement toward the group of silent women, touched the face of old Grangioia's youngest daughter, Madonna Gemma.

From the crown of her head, whence her hair fell in bright ripples like a gush of gold from the ladle of a goldsmith, to her white feet, bare on the pavement, Madonna Gemma was one fragile piece of beauty. In this hall heavy with torch smoke, and the sweat of many soldiers, in this ring of blood-stained weapons and smouldering eyes, she appeared like a delicate dreamer enveloped by a nightmare. Yet even the long stare of Lapo Cercamorte she answered with a look of defiance.

The conqueror rose, went jingling to her, thumbed a strand of her bright hair, touched her soft cheek with his fingers, which smelled of leather and horses. Grasping her by the elbow, he led her forward.

"Is this your daughter, Grangioia? Good. I will take her as a pledge of your loyalty."

With a gesture old Grangioia commanded his sons to sit still. After glowering round him at the wall of mail, he let his head sink down, and faltered:

"Do you marry her, Cercamorte?"

"Why not?" croaked Lapo. "Having just made a peace shall I give offence so soon? No, in this case I will do everything according to honour."

That morning Lapo Cercamorte espoused Madonna Gemma Grangioia. Then, setting her behind his saddle on a cushion, he took her away to his own castle. This possession, too, he had won for himself with his sword. It was called the Vespaione, the Big Hornets' Nest. Rude and strong, it crowned a rocky hilltop in a lonely region. At the base of the hill clustered a few huts; beyond lay some little fields; then the woods spread their tangles afar.

Madonna Gemma, finding herself in this prison, did not weep or utter a sound for many days.

Here Lapo Cercamorte, pouncing upon such a treasure as had never come within his reach before, met his first defeat. His fire proved unable to melt that ice. His coarse mind was benumbed by the exquisiteness of his antagonist. Now, instead of terror and self-abasement, he met scorn—the cold contempt of a being rarefied, and raised above him by centuries of gentler thought and living. When he laid his paws on her shoulders he felt that he held there a pale, soft shell empty of her incomprehensible spirit, which at his touch had vanished into space.

So he stood baffled, with a new longing that groped blindly through the veils of flesh and blood, like a brute tormented by the dawning of some insatiable aspiration.

It occurred to him that the delicate creature might be pleased if her surroundings were less soldierly. So oiled linen was stretched across her windows, and a carpet laid for her feet at table in the hall. The board was spread with a white cloth on which she might wipe her lips, and in spring the pavement of her bower was strewn with scented herbs. Also he saw to it that her meat was seasoned with quinces, that her wine was spiced on feast-days.

He got her a little greyhound, but it sickened and died. Remembering that a comrade-in-arms possessed a Turkish dwarf with an abnormally large head, he cast about to procure some such monstrosity for her amusement. He sent her jewellery—necklaces torn by his soldiers from the breasts of ladies in surrendered towns, rings wrested from fingers raised in supplication.

She wore none of these trinkets. Indeed, she seemed oblivious of all his efforts to change her.

He left her alone.

Finally, whenever Lapo Cercamorte met her in the hall his face turned dark and bitter. Throughout the meal there was no sound except the growling of dogs among the bones beneath the table, the hushed voices of the soldiers eating in the body of the hall. Old one-eyed Baldo, Cercamorte's lieutenant, voiced the general sentiment when he muttered into his cup:

"This house has become a tomb, and I have a feeling that presently there may be corpses in it."

"She has the evil eye," another assented.

Furtively making horns with their fingers, they looked up askance toward the dais, at her pale young beauty glimmering through rays of dusty sunshine.

"Should there come an alarm our shield-straps would burst and our weapons crack like glass. If only, when we took Grangioia Castle, a sword had accidentally cut off her nose!"

"God give us our next fighting in the open, far away from this *jettatrice!*"

It presently seemed as if that wish were to be granted. All the Guelph party were then preparing to take the field together. In Cercamorte's castle, dice-throwing and drinking gave place to drinking and plotting. Strange messengers appeared. In an upper chamber a shabby priest from the nearest town—the stronghold of Count Nicolotto Muti—neatly wrote down, at Lapo's dictation, the tally of available men, horses, and arms. Then one morning Cercamorte said to Baldo, his lieutenant:

"I am off for a talk with Nicolotto Muti. The house is in your care."

And glumly Lapo rode down from his castle, without a glance toward the casements of Madonna Gemma's bower.

She watched him depart alone, his helmet dangling from his saddle-bow. Then she saw, below her on the hillside, also watching him, the horse-boy, Foresto, his graceful figure hinting at an origin superior to his station, his dark, peaked face seeming to mask some avid and sinister dream. Was she wrong in suspecting that Foresto hated Lapo Cercamorte? Might he not become an ally against her husband?

Her gaze travelled on to the houses at the foot of the hill, to the hut where, under Lapo's protection, dwelt a renegade Arabian, reputed to be a sorcerer. No doubt the Arabian knew of subtle poisons, charms that withered men's bodies, enchantments that wrecked the will and reduced the mind to chaos.

But soon these thoughts were scattered by the touch of the

spring breeze. She sank into a vague wonder at life, which had so cruelly requited the fervours of her girlhood.

On the third day of Cercamorte's absence, while Madonna Gemma was leaning on the parapet of the keep, there appeared at the edge of the woods a young man in light-blue tunic and hood, a small gilded harp under his arm.

Because he was the young brother of Nicolotto Muti they admitted him into the castle.

His countenance was effeminate, fervent, and artful. The elegance of his manner was nearly Oriental. The rough soldiers grinned in amusement, or frowned in disgust. Madonna Gemma, confronted by his strangeness and complexity, neither frowned nor smiled, but looked more wan than ever.

Perfumed with sandalwood, in a white, gold-stitched robe, its bodice tight, its skirts voluminous, she welcomed him in the hall. The reception over, old Baldo spoke with the crone who served Madonna Gemma as maid:

"I do not know what this pretty little fellow has in mind. While I watch him for spying, do you watch him for love-making. If we discover him at either, perhaps he has caught that new green-sickness from the north, and thinks himself a singing-bird."

A singing-bird was what Raffaele Muti proved to be.

In the Mediterranean lands a new idea was beginning to alter the conduct of society. Woman, so long regarded as a soulless animal, born only to drag men down, was being transfigured into an immaculate goddess, an angel in human shape, whose business was man's reformation, whose right was man's worship.

That cult of Woman had been invented by the lute-playing nobles of Provence. But quickly it had begun to spread from court to court, from one land to another. So now, in Italy, as in southern France, sometimes in wild hill castles as well as in the city palaces, a hymn of adoration rose to the new divinity.

This was the song that Raffaele Muti, plucking at his twelve harp strings, raised in the hall of the Big Hornets' Nest at twilight.

He sat by the fireplace on the guests' settee, beside Madonna Gemma. The torches, dripping fire in the wall-rings, cast their light over the faces of the wondering servants. The harp twanged its plaintive interlude; then the song continued, quavering, soaring, athrob with this new pathos and reverence, that had crept like the counterfeit of a celestial dawn upon a world long obscured by a brutish dusk.

Raffaele Muti sang of a woman exalted far above him by her womanhood, which rivalled Godhood in containing all the virtues requisite for his redemption. Man could no longer sin when once she had thought pityingly of him. Every deed must be noble if rooted in love of her. All that one asked was to worship her ineffable superiority. How grievously should one affront her virtue if ever one dreamed of kisses! But should one dream of them, pray God she might never stoop that far in mercy! No, passion must never mar this shrine at which Raffaele knelt.

In the ensuing silence, which quivered from that cry, there stole into the heart of Madonna Gemma an emotion more precious, just then, than the peace that follows absolution—a new-born sense of feminine dignity, a glorious blossoming of pride, commingled with the tenderness of an immeasurable gratitude.

About to part for the night, they exchanged a look of tremulous solemnity.

Her beauty was no longer bleak, but rich—all at once too warm, perhaps, for a divinity whose only office was the guidance of a troubadour toward asceticism. His frail comeliness was radiant from his poetical ecstasy—of a sudden too flushed, one would think, for a youth whose aspirations were all toward the intangible. Then each emerged with a start from that delicious spell, to remember the staring servants.

They said good-night. Madonna Gemma ascended to her chamber.

It was the horse-boy Foresto who, with a curious solicitude and satisfaction, lighted Raffaele Muti up to bed.

But old Baldo, strolling thoughtfully in the courtyard, caught a young cricket chirping in the grass between two paving-stones. On the cricket's back, with a straw and white paint, he traced the Muti device—a tree transfixed by an arrow. Then he put the cricket into a little iron box together with a rose, and gave the box to a man-at-arms, saying:

"Ride to Lapo Cercamorte and deliver this into his hands."

Next day, on the sunny tower, high above the hillside covered with spring flowers, Raffaele resumed his song. He sat at the feet of Madonna Gemma, who wore a grass-green gown embroidered with unicorns, emblems of purity. The crone was there also, pretending to doze in the shadows; and so was Foresto the horse-boy, whose dark, still face seemed now and again to mirror Raffaele's look of exultation—a look that came only when Madonna Gemma gazed away from him.

But for the most part she gazed down at Raffaele's singing lips, on which she discerned no guile.

Tireless, he sang to her of a world fairer even than that of her maidenhood. It was a region where for women all feeling of abasement ceased, because there the troubadour, by his homage, raised one's soul high above the tyranny of uncomprehending husbands.

She learned—for so it had been decided in Provence—that high sentiment was impossible in wedlock at its best; that between husband and wife there was no room for love. Thus, according to the Regula Amoris, it was not only proper, but also imperative, to seek outside the married life some lofty love-alliance.

The day wore on thus. The sun had distilled from many blossoms the whole intoxicating fragrance of the springtime. A golden haze was changing Madonna Gemma's prison into a paradise.

Her vision was dimmed by a glittering film of tears. Her fingers helplessly unfolded on her lap. She believed that at last she had learned love's meaning. And Raffaele, for all his youth no novice at this game, believed that this dove, too, was fluttering into his cage.

By sunset their cheeks were flaming. At twilight their hands turned cold.

Then they heard the bang of the gate and the croaking voice of Lapo Cercamorte.

He entered the hall as he had so often entered the houses

of terror-stricken enemies, clashing at each ponderous, swift step, his mail dusty, his hair wet and dishevelled, his dull-red face resembling a mask of heated iron. That atmosphere just now swimming in languor, was instantly permeated by a wave of force, issuing from this herculean body and barbaric brain. When he halted before those two they seemed to feel the heat that seethed in his steel-bound breast.

His disfigured face still insolvable, Lapo Cercamorte plunged his stare into Madonna Gemma's eyes, then looked into the eyes of Raffaele. His hoarse voice broke the hush; he said to the young man:

"So you are the sister of my friend Count Nicolloto?"

Raffaele, having licked his lips, managed to answer:

"You mean his brother, sir."

Lapo Cercamorte laughed loud; but his laugh was the bark of a hyena, and his eyes were balls of fire.

"No! with these legs and ringlets? Come here, Baldo. Here is a girl who says she is a man. What do you say, to speak only of this pretty skin of hers?"

And with his big hand suddenly he ripped open Raffaele's tunic half way to the waist, exposing the fair white flesh. The troubadour, though quivering with shame and rage, remained motionless, staring at the great sword that hung in its scarlet sheath from Lapo's harness.

Old one-eyed Baldo, plucking his master by the elbow, whispered: "Take care, Cercamorte. His brother Nicolotto is your ally. Since after all, nothing much has happened, do not carry the offence too far."

"Are you in your dotage?" Lapo retorted, still glaring with a dreadful interest at Raffaele's flesh. "Do you speak of giving offence, when all I desire is to be as courteous as my uneducated nature will allow? She must pardon me that slip of the hand; I meant only to stroke her cheek in compliment but instead I tore her dress. Yet I will be a proper courtier to her still. Since she is now set on going home, I myself, alone, will escort her clear to the forest, in order to set her upon the safe road."

And presently Madonna Gemma, peering from her chamber window, saw her husband, with a ghastly pretense of care, lead young Raffaele Muti down the hill into the darkness from which there came never a sound.

It was midnight when Lapo Cercamorte rëentered the castle, and called for food and drink.

Now the shadow over the Big Hornets' Nest obscured even the glare of the summer sun. No winsome illusion of nature's could brighten this little world that had at last turned quite sinister. In the air that Madonna Gemma breathed was always a chill of horror. At night the thick walls seemed to sweat with it, and the silence was like a great hand pressed across a mouth struggling to give vent to a scream.

At dinner in the hall she ate nothing, but drank her wine as though burning with a fever. Sometimes, when the stillness had become portentous, Lapo rolled up his sleeves, inspected his scarred, swarthy arms, and mumbled, with the grin of a man stretched on the rack:

"Ah, Father and Son! if only one had a skin as soft, white, and delicate as a girl's!"

At this Madonna Gemma left the table.

Once more her brow became bleaker than a winter mountain; her eyes were haggard from nightmares; she trembled at every sound. Pacing her bower, interminably she asked herself one question. And at last, when Lapo would have passed her on the stairs, she hurled into his face:

"What did you do to Raffaele Muti?"

He started, so little did he expect to hear her voice. His battered countenance turned redder, as he noted that for the sake of the other she was like an overstretched bow, almost breaking. Then a pang stabbed him treacherously. Fearing that she might discern his misery, he turned back, leaving her limp against the wall.

He took to walking the runway of the ramparts, gnawing his fingers and muttering to himself, shaking his tousled hair. With a sigh, as if some thoughts were too heavy a burden for that iron frame, he sat down on an archer's ledge, to stare toward the hut of the renegade Arabian. Often at night he sat thus, hour after hour, a coarse creature made romantic by a flood of moonlight. And as he bowed his head the sentinel heard him fetch a groan such as one utters whose life escapes through a sword-wound.

One-eyed Baldo also groaned at these goings-on, and swallowed many angry speeches. But Foresto the horse-boy began to hum at his work.

This Foresto had attached himself to Lapo's force in the Ferrarese campaign. His habits were solitary. Often when his work was done he wandered into the woods to return with a capful of berries or a squirrel that he had snared. Because he was silent, deft, and daintier than a horse-boy ought to be, Lapo finally bade him serve Madonna Gemma.

Watching his dark, blank face as he strewed fresh herbs on her pavement, she wondered:

"Does he know the truth?"

Their glances met; he seemed to send her a veiled look of comprehension and promise. But whenever he appeared the crone was there.

One morning however, Foresto had time to whisper:

"The Arabian."

What did that mean? Was the Arab magician, recluse in his wretched hut below the castle, prepared to serve her? Was it through him and Foresto that she might hope to escape or at least to manage some revenge? Thereafter she often watched the renegade's window, from which, no matter how late the hour, shone a glimmering of lamplight. Was he busy at his magic? Could those spells be enlisted on her side?

Then, under an ashen sky of autumn, as night was creeping in, she saw the Arabian ascending the hill to the castle. His tall figure, as fleshless as a mummy's, was swathed in a white robe like a winding sheet; his beaked face and hollow eyesockets were like a vision of Death. Without taking her eyes from him, Madonna Gemma crossed herself.

Baldo came to the gate. The ghostly Arabian uttered.:

"Peace be with you. I have here, under my robe, a packet for your master."

"Good! Pass it over to me, unless it will turn my nose into a carrot, or add a tail to my spine."

The foreigner, shaking his skull-like head, responded:

"I must give this packet into no hands but his."

So Baldo led the sorcerer to Cercamorte, and for a long while those two talked together in private.

Next day Madonna Gemma noted that Lapo had on a new,

short, sleeveless surcoat, or vest, of whitish leather, trimmed on its edges with vair, and laced down the sides with tinsel. In this festive garment, so different from his usual attire, the grim tyrant was ill at ease, secretly anxious, almost timid. Avoiding her eye, he assumed an elaborate carelessness, like that of a boy who had been up to some deviltry. Madonna Gemma soon found herself connecting this change in him with the fancy white-leather vest.

In the hall, while passing a platter of figs, Foresto praised the new garment obsequiously. He murmured:

"And what a fine skin it is made of! So soft, so delicate, so lustrous in its finish! Is it pigskin, master? Ah, no; it is finer than that. Kidskin? But a kid could not furnish a skin as large as this one. No doubt it is made from some queer foreign animal, perhaps from a beast of Greece or Arabia?"

While speaking these words, Foresto flashed one look, mournful and eloquent, at Madonna Gemma, then softly withdrew from the hall.

She sat motionless, wave after wave of cold flowing in through her limbs to her heart. She stared, as though at a basilisk, at Lapo's new vest, in which she seemed to find the answer so long denied her. The hall grew dusky; she heard a far-off cry, and when she meant to flee, she fainted in her chair.

For a week Madonna Gemma did not rise from her bed. When finally she did rise she refused to leave her room.

But suddenly Lapo Cercamorte was gayer than he had been since the fall of Grangioia Castle. Every morning, when he had inquired after Madonna Gemma's health, and had sent her all kinds of tidbits, he went down to sit among his men, to play morra, to test swordblades, to crack salty jokes, to let loose his husky guffaw. At times, cocking his eye toward certain upper casements, he patted his fine vest furtively, with a gleeful and mischievous grin. To Baldo, after some mysterious nods and winks, he confided:

"Everything will be different when she is well again."

"No doubt," snarled old Baldo, scrubbing at his mail shirt viciously. "Though I am not in your confidence, I agree that a nice day is coming, a beautiful day—like a pig. Look you, Cercamorte, shake off this strange spell of folly. Prepare for early trouble. Just as a Venetian sailor can feel a storm of water brewing, so can I feel, gathering far off, a storm of arrows. Do you notice that the crows hereabouts have never been so thick? Perhaps, too, I have seen a face peeping out of the woods, about the time that Foresto goes down to pick berries."

"You chatter like an old woman at a fountain," said Lapo, still caressing his vest with his palms. "I shall be quite happy soon—yes, even before the Lombard league takes the field."

Baldo raised his shoulders, pressed his withered eyelids together, and answered, in disgust:

"God pity you, Cercamorte! You are certainly changed these days. Evidently your Arabian has given you a charm that turns men's brains into goose-eggs."

Lapo stamped away angrily, yet he was soon smiling again.

And now his coarse locks were not unkempt, but cut square across brow and neck. Every week he trimmed his finger-nails; every day or so, with a flush and a hangdog look, he drenched himself with perfume. Even while wearing that garment—at thought of which Madonna Gemma, isolate in her chamber, still shivered and moaned—Cercamorte resembled one who prepares himself for a wedding, or gallant rendezvous, that may take place any moment.

Sometimes, reeking with civet-oil, he crept to her door, eavesdropped, pondered the quality of her sighs, stood hesitant, then stealthily withdrew, grinding his teeth and wheezing:

"Not yet. Sweet saints in heaven, what a time it takes!"

He loathed his bed, because of the long hours of sleeplessness. He no longer slept naked. At night, too, his body was encased in the vest of whitish soft skin.

One morning a horseman in green and yellow scallops appeared before the castle. It was Count Nicolotto Muti, elder brother of the troubadour Raffaele.

Lapo, having arranged his features, came down to meet the count. They kissed, and entered the keep with their arms round each other's shoulders. Foresto brought in the guest-cup.

Nicolotto Muti was a thin, calm politician, elegant in his

manners and speech, his lips always wearing a sympathetic smile. By the fireplace, after chatting of this and that, he remarked, with his hand affectionately on Cercamorte's knee:

"I am trying to find trace of my little Raffaele, who has vanished like a mist. It is said that he was last seen in this neighbourhood. Can you tell me anything?"

Lapo, his face expressionless, took thought, then carefully answered:

"Muti, because we are friends as well as allies I will answer you honestly. Returning from my visit with you, I found him in this hall, plucking a harp and singing love-songs to my wife. I say frankly that if he had not been your brother I should have cut off his hands and his tongue. Instead, I escorted him to the forest, and set him on the home road. I admit that before I parted from him I preached him a sermon on the duties of boys toward the friends of their families. Nay, fearing that he might not relate his adventure to you, in that discourse I somewhat pounded the pulpit. Well, yes, I confess that I gave him a little spanking."

Count Nicolotto, without showing any surprise, or losing his fixed smile, declared:

"Dear comrade, it was a young man, not a child, whom you chastised in that way. In another instance, as of course you know, such an action would have been a grievous insult to all his relatives. Besides, I am sure that he meant no more than homage to your lady—a compliment common enough in these modern times, and honourably reflected upon the husband. However, I can understand the feelings of one who has been too much in the field to learn those innocent new gallantries. Indeed, I presume that I should thank you for what you believed to be a generous forbearance. But all this does not find me my brother."

And with a sad, gentle smile Count Nicolotto closed his frosty eyes.

Cercamorte, despite all this cooing, received an impression of enmity. As always when danger threatened, he became still and wary, much more resourceful than ordinarily, as if perils were needed to render him complete. Smoothing his vest with his fingers that were flattened from so much sword-work, Lapo said:

"I feel now that I may have been wrong to put such shame upon him. On account of it, no doubt, he has sought retirement. Or maybe he has journeyed abroad, say to Provence, a land free from such out-of-date bunglers as I."

Nicolotto Muti made a deprecatory gesture, then rose with a rustle of his green and yellow scallops, from which was shaken a fragrance of attar.

"My good friend, let us hope so."

It was Foresto who, in the courtyard held Muti's stirrup, and secretly pressed into the visitor's hand a pellet of parchment. For Foresto could write excellent Latin.

No sooner had Count Nicolotto regained his strong town than a shocking rumour spread round—Lapo Cercamorte had made Raffaele Muti's skin into a vest, with which to drive his wife mad.

In those petty Guelph courts, wherever the tender lore of Provence had sanctified the love of troubadour for great lady, the noblemen cried out in fury; the noblewomen, transformed into tigresses, demanded Lapo's death. Old Grangioia and his three sons arrived at the Muti fortress raving for sudden vengeance. There they were joined by others, rich troubadours, backed by many lances, whose rage could not have been hotter had Lapo, that "wild beast in human form," defaced the Holy Sepulchre. At last the Marquis Azzo was forced to reflect:

"Cercamorte has served me well, but if I keep them from him our league may be torn asunder. Let them have him. But he will die hard."

Round the Big Hornets' Nest the crows were thicker than ever.

One cold, foggy evening Lapo Cercamorte at last pushed open his wife's chamber door. Madonna Gemma was alone, wrapped in a fur-lined mantle, warming her hands over an earthen pot full of embers. Standing awkwardly before her, Lapo perceived that her beauty was fading away in this unhappy solitude. On her countenance was no trace of that which he had hoped to see. He swore softly, cast down from feverish expectancy into bewilderment.

"No," he said, at length, his voice huskier than usual, "this cannot continue. You are a flower transplanted into a dungeon, and dying on the stalk. One cannot refashion the past. The future remains. Perhaps you would flourish again if I sent you back to your father?"

He went to the casement with a heavy step, and stared through a rent in the oiled linen at the mist, which clung round the castle like a pall.

"Madonna," he continued, more harshly than ever, in order that she might not rejoice at his pain, "I ask pardon for the poorness of my house. Even had my sword made me wealthy I should not have known how to provide appointments pleasing to a delicate woman. My manners also, as I have learned since our meeting, are unsuitable. The camps were my school and few ladies came into them. It was not strange that when Raffaele Muti presented himself you should have found him more to your taste. But if on my sudden return I did what I did, and thus prevented him from boasting up and down Lombardy of another conquest, it was because I had regard not only for my honour, but for yours. So I am not asking your pardon on that score."

Lowering her face toward the red embers, she whispered: "A beast believes all men to be beasts."

"Kiss of Judas! Are women really trapped, then, by that gibberish? Madonna, these miaowing troubadours have concocted a world that they themselves will not live in. Have I not sat swigging in tents with great nobles, and heard all the truth about it? Those fellows always have, besides the lady that they pretend to worship as inviolate, a dozen others with whom the harp-twanging stage is stale."

"All false, every word," Madonna Gemma answered.

"Because ladies choose to think so the game goes on. Well, Madonna, remember this. From the moment when I first saw you I, at least, did you no dishonour, but married you promptly, and sought your satisfaction by the means that I possessed. I was not unaware that few wives come to their husbands with affection. Certainly I did not expect affection from you at the first, but hoped that it might ensue. So even Lapo Cercamorte became a flabby fool, when he met one in comparison with whom all other women seemed mawkish. Since it was such a fit of drivelling, let us put an end to it. At sunrise the horses will be ready. Good night."

Leaving her beside the dying embers, he went out upon the

ramparts. The fog was impenetrable; one could not even see the light in the sorcerer's window.

"Damned Arabian!" growled Lapo, brandishing his fist. He sat down beside the gate-tower, and rested his chin on his hands.

"How cold it is," he thought, "how lonely and dismal! Warfare is what I need. Dear Lord, let me soon be killing men briskly, and warming myself in the burning streets of Ferrara. That is what I was begotten for. I have been lost in a maze."

Dawn approached, and Lapo was still dozing beside the gate-tower.

With the first hint of light the sentinel challenged; voices answered outside the gate. It was old Grangioia and his sons, calling up that they had come to visit their daughter.

"Well arrived," Lapo grunted, his brain and body sluggish from the chill. He ordered the gate swung open.

Too late, as they rode into the courtyard, he saw that there were nearly a score of them, all with their helmets on. Then in the fog he heard a noise like an avalanche of ice—the clatter of countless steel-clad men scrambling up the hillside.

While running along the wall, Lapo Cercamorte noted that the horsemen were hanging back, content to hold the gate till reinforced. On each side of the courtyard his soldiers were tumbling out of their barracks and fleeing toward the keep, that inner stronghold which was now their only haven. Dropping at last from the ramparts, he joined this retreat. But on gaining the keep he found with him only some thirty of his men; the rest had been caught in their beds.

Old Baldo gave him a coat of mail. Young Foresto brought him his sword and shield. Climbing the keep-wall, Cercamorte squinted down into the murky courtyard. That whole place now swarmed with his foes.

Arrows began to fly. A round object sailed through the air and landed in the keep; it was the head of the Arabian.

"Who are these people?" asked Baldo, while rapidly shooting at them with a bow. "There seem to be many knights; half the shields carry devices. Ai! they have fired the barracks. Now we shall make them out."

The flames leaped up in great sheets, producing the effect of an infernal noon. The masses in the courtyard, inhuman-looking in their ponderous, barrel-shaped helmets, surged forward at the keep with a thunderous outcry:

"Grangioia! Grangioia! Havoc on Cercamorte!"

"Muti! Muti! Havoc on Cercamorte!"

"God and the Monfalcone!"

"Strike for Zaladino! Havoc on Cercamorte!"

Lapo bared his teeth at them. "By the Five Wounds! half of Lombardy seems to be here. Well, my Baldo, before they make an end of us shall we show them some little tricks?"

"You have said it, Cercamorte. One more good scuffle, with a parade of all our talent."

The assailants tried beams against the keep gate; the defenders shot them down or hurled rocks upon their heads. But on the wall of the keep Cercamorte's half-clad men fell sprawling, abristle with feathered shafts. A beam reached the gate and shook it on its hinges. Lapo, one ear shot away, drew his surviving soldiers back into the hall.

He ordered torches stuck into all the wall-rings, and ranged his men on the dais. Behind them, in the doorway leading to the upper chambers and the high tower, he saw his wife, wild-looking, and whiter than her robe.

"Go back, Madonna. It is only your family calling with some of their friends. I entered Grangioia Castle abruptly; now it is tit for tat."

The crone brought two helmets, which Lapo and Baldo put on. Then, drawing their long swords, they awaited the onset.

The keep gate yielded, and into the hall came rushing a wave of peaked and painted shields. But before the dais the wave paused, since in it were those who could not forego the joy of taunting Lapo Cercamorte before killing him. So suddenly, all his antagonists contemplated him in silence, as he crouched above them with his sword and shield half raised, his very armour seeming to emanate force, cunning, and peril.

"Foul monster!" a muffled voice shouted. "Now you come to your death!"

"Now we will give your carcass to the wild beasts. your brothers!"

"Let my daughter pass through," bawled old Grangioia; then, receiving no response, struck clumsily at Lapo.

With a twist of his sword Lapo disarmed the old man, calling out:

"Keep off, kinsman! I will not shed Grangioia blood unless you force me to it. Let Muti come forward. Or yonder gentleman dressed up in the white eagles of Este, which should hide their heads with their wings, so long and faithfully have I served them."

But none was ignorant of Cercamorte's prowess; so, after a moment of seething, they all came at him together.

The swordblades rose and fell so swiftly that they seemed to be arcs of light; the deafening clangour was pierced by the howls of the dying. The dais turned red—men slipped on it; Cercamorte's sword caught them; they did not rise. He seemed indeed to wield more swords than one, so terrible was his fighting. At his back stood Baldo, his helmet caved in, his mail shirt in ribbons, his abdomen slashed open. Both at once they saw that all their men were down. Hewing to right and left they broke through, gained the tower staircase, and locked the door behind them.

On the dark stairway they leaned against the wall, their helmets off, gasping for breath, while the enemy hammered the door.

"How is it with you?" puffed Lapo, putting his arm round Baldo's neck.

"They have wrecked my belly for me. I am finished."

Lapo Cercamorte hung his head and sobbed, "My old Baldo, my comrade, it is my folly that has killed you."

"No, no. It was only that I had survived too many tussles; then all at once our Lord recalled my case to his mind. But we have had some high times together, eh?"

Lapo, weeping aloud from remorse, patted Baldo's shoulder and kissed his withered cheek. Lamplight flooded the staircase; it was Foresto softly descending. The rays illuminated Madonna Gemma, who all the while had been standing close beside them.

"Lady," said Baldo, feebly, "can you spare me a bit of your veil? Before the door falls I must climb these steps, and that would be easier if I could first bind in my entrails."

They led him upstairs, Lapo on one side, Madonna Gemma on the other, and Foresto lighting the way. They came to the topmost chamber in the high tower—the last room of all.

Here Cercamorte kept his treasures—his scraps of looted finery, the weapons taken from fallen knights, the garrison's surplus of arms. When he had locked the door and with Foresto's slow help braced some pike-shafts against it, he tried to make Baldo lie down.

The old man vowed profanely that he would die on his feet. Shambling to the casement niche, he gaped forth at the dawn. Below him a frosty world was emerging from the mist. He saw the ring of the ramparts, and in the courtyard the barrack ruins smouldering. Beyond, the hillside also smoked, with shredding vapours; and at the foot of the hill he observed a strange sight—the small figure of a man in tunic and hood, feylike amid the mist, that danced and made gestures of joy. Baldo, clinging to the casement-sill on bending legs, summoned Cercamorte to look at the dancing figure.

"What is it, Lapo? A devil?"

"One of our guests, no doubt," said Cercamorte, dashing the tears from his eyes. "Hark! the door at the foot of the staircase has fallen. Now we come to our parting, old friend."

"Give me a bow and an arrow," cried Baldo, with a rattle in his throat. "Whoever that zany is, he shall not dance at our funeral. Just one more shot, my Lapo. You shall see that I still have it in me."

Cercamorte could not deny him this last whim. He found and strung a bow, and chose a Ghibelline war-arrow. Behind them, young Foresto drew in his breath with a hiss, laid his hand on his dagger, and turned the colour of clay. Old Baldo raised the bow, put all his remaining strength into the draw, and uttered a cracking shout of bliss. The mannikin no longer danced; but toward him, from the hillside, some men in steel were running. Baldo, sinking back into Cercamorte's arms, at last allowed himself to be laid down.

Through the door filtered the rising tumult of the enemy. Lapo Cercamorte's blood-smeared visage turned businesslike. Before grasping his sword, he bent to rub his palms on the grit of the pavement. While he was stooping, young Foresto unsheathed his dagger, made a catlike step, and stabbed at his master's neck. But quicker than Foresto was Madonna Gemma, who, with a deer's leap, imprisoned his arms from behind. Cercamorte discovered them thus, struggling fiercely in silence.

"Stand aside," he said to her, and, when he had struck Foresto down, "Thank you for that, Madonna. With such spirit to help me, I might have had worthy sons. Well, here they come, and this door is a flimsy thing. Get yourself into the casement niche, away from the swing of my blade."

A red trickle was running down his legs; he was standing in a red pool.

It began again, the splitting of panels, the cracking of hinges. The door was giving; now only the pike-shafts held it. Then came a pause. From far down the staircase a murmur of amazement swept upward; a babble of talk ensued. Silence fell. Cercamorte let out a harsh laugh.

"What new device is this? Does it need so much chicanery to finish one man?"

Time passed, and there was no sound except a long clattering from the courtyard. Of a sudden a new voice called through the broken door:

"Open, Cercamorte. I am one man alone."

"Come in without ceremony. Here am I, waiting to embrace you."

"I am Ercole Azzanera, the Marquis Azzo's cousin, and your true friend. I swear on my honour that I stand here alone with sheathed sword."

Lapo kicked the pike-shafts away, and, as the door fell inward, jumped back on guard. At the threshold, unhelmeted, stood the knight whose long surcoat was covered with the white eagles of Este. He spoke as follows:

"Cercamorte, this array came up against you because it was published that you had killed and flayed Raffaele Muti, and, out of jealous malignancy, were wearing his skin as a vest. But just now a marvellous thing has happened, for at the foot of the hill Raffaele Muti has been found, freshly slain by a wandered arrow. Save for that wound his skin is without flaw. Moreover, he lived and breathed but a moment ago. So the whole tale was false, and this war against you outrageous. All the gentlemen who came here have gone away in great amazement and shame, leaving me to ask pardon for what they have done. Forgive them, Cercamorte, in the name of Christ, for they believed themselves to be performing a proper deed."

And when Lapo found no reply in his head, Ercole Azzanera,

with a humble bow, descended from the high tower and followed the others away.

Lapo Cercamorte sat down on a stool. "All my good men," he murmured, "and my dear gossip, Baldo! My castle rushed by so shabby a ruse; my name a laughing-stock! And the Marquis Azzo gave them my house as one gives a child a leaden gimcrack to stamp on. All because of this damned vest, this silly talisman which was to gain me her love. 'In the name of Christ,' says my friend, Ercole Azzanera. By the Same! If I live I will go away to the heathen, for there is no more pleasure in Christendom."

So he sat for a while, maundering dismally, then stood up and made for the door. He reeled. He sank down with a clash. Madonna Gemma, stealing out from the casement niche, knelt beside him, peered into his face, and ran like the wind down the staircase. In the hall, with lifted robe she sped over the corpses of Cercamorte's soldiers, seeking wine and water. These obtained, she flew back to Lapo. There the crone found her. Between them those two dragged him down to Madonna Gemma's chamber, stripped him, tended his wounds, and hoisted him into the bed.

Flat on his back, Cercamorte fought over all his battles. He quarrelled with Baldo. Again he pondered anxiously outside of Madonna Gemma's door. He instructed the Arabian to fashion him a charm that would overspread his ugly face with comeliness, change his uncouthness into geniality. He insisted on wearing the vest, the under side of which was scribbled with magical signs.

Madonna Gemma sat by the bed all day, and lay beside him at night. On rising, she attired herself in a vermilion gown over which she drew a white jacket of Eastern silk embroidered with nightingales. Into her golden tresses she braided the necklaces that he had offered her. Her tapering milky fingers sparkled with rings. Her former beauty had not returned—another, greater beauty had taken its place.

A day came when he recognized her face. Leaning down like a flower of paradise, she kissed his lips.

THE END